One Hand Waving Free

by Ellen Hofmann

Copyright © 2011 by Ellen Hofmann

Cover design by Danielle J. Alexander

Dedicated to Charles DeFanti,

who always told me to "just keep writing"

Table of Contents

Prologue: Down the Shore

Chapter One: The Johnny Pump and the Last Gate

Chapter Two: Hey, Mr. Spaceman

Chapter Three: "Arthur Treachers, May I Help You?"

Chapter Four: Midtown

Chapter Five: New York's Finest

Chapter Six: The Creative Department

Chapter Seven: Babylust

Chapter Eight: It Was Only a Kiss

Chapter Nine: "Mam-ma"

Chapter Ten: Life in the Spirit

Chapter Eleven: "I Am a Jealous God"

Chapter Twelve: The Upper Hand

Chapter Thirteen: "Let's Be Careful Out There"

Chapter Fourteen: A Kiss from a Rose

Epilogue: Altocumulus Stratiformis

"One Hand Waving Free"   Hofmann

Prologue

To go forward, Marie must first go back. She is aware that this is not a particularly profound or noteworthy statement. Isn't it a key component in psychiatric theory the world over? No one ever gets to walk into the doc's office, state his name and issue, and take it from there, no. There must be a chiseling, an unraveling, a digging, to find the real moment the "issue" began to form. It's like retracing your steps to find your lost car keys. You can't just say, well, let me check every nook and cranny in the house all willy-nilly. You have to put some semblance of order to your search. You have to *think*, which isn't always a comfortable thing.

Of course, the point of all this "going back" in therapyland, Marie believes, is to pinpoint the exact place and time you became, well, you. It is to find the second, the moment, the incident, when you had the chance to be someone else, someone better, perhaps. For some reason, people feel compelled to find that "spot," because, as they sit here today in their own misery, they have to know that there was an exact place it all went wrong. Or maybe Marie is being narrow-minded, only speaking for the miserable people. Maybe the happy people have no need whatsoever to go back, except to occasionally congratulate themselves.

That's therapy, though. She doesn't really believe in therapy. She wants to go back, yes, but she isn't trying to find a certain place, or change the past. She only wants to tell the story. That's all.

Not that she hasn't told it. She just hasn't made a conscious effort to put it together from beginning to whatever the end may be. Up until now, all she's done is spew her story in bits and pieces to a very select few listeners, although she really threw it out there as if no one was listening at all. She created a listener just to have the chance to speak, to justify saying what she longed to say. She chose a listener just so she wasn't the person who speaks to herself on the elevator, or walking down a busy Manhattan street.

"One Hand Waving Free"   Hofmann

Well, that is not completely honest. She does indeed wonder when she went wrong. She wonders when, for instance, she had a chance to be, say, Irene Forgioni, who knew in 7th grade that she wanted to be a lawyer. Irene was perky and smart, and wore glasses, and maybe there is the clue: she *wore* her glasses, and Marie was *supposed* to wear her glasses, but kept them tucked vainly away and faced a blurry world with a clear face. Glasses in the 70's were functional and not chic, and allowed all to see exactly what was important to the wearer or non-wearer. Irene was pretty, the kind of pretty that fairy-tale movies cover up with a pair of hideous glasses, making the audience not even suspect, then later remove to unveil a beauty potential – and happiness – reached at last.

Irene, Marie has heard through the sour grapevine, is not only beautiful today but she is indeed a lawyer, and Marie thinks she wears contact lenses. When or if Irene looks back, she does not see the things Marie sees, short nasty scenes in quick bursts before her eyes, explaining it all – her uncle slipping his hands down her shirt at 14, or Ray DeCoursey turning her over at age 16, doing things that she had not yet learned were even possible to do – no! And yet these scenes explain nothing at all, because they are from the already-too-late time. At 14, Marie was already the quivering, naked-eyed girl that these things could be done to. She was already so clearly not Irene.

Marie knew she wanted to be a writer since 4th or 5th grade, but she had just as much certainty as Irene that she would never be one. She already knew that she was just not that kind, even though her teachers had already begun to rave about her work. When this absolute sureness of failure came to live inside her gut, she did not know. And so she must go back further still.

This story is not about Irene, but she and Marie are from the same neighborhood. Ridgewood, Queens, NY. A street neighborhood. Indeed, Marie is sure that if any resident, past or present, tried to command one image of his or her childhood there, they would instantly see asphalt clearly, while all other images came slowly into focus. Or, at least, asphalt in their early years, and then a gradual switch to black tar, when they were at last allowed to play in the coveted "gutter," where chalk wrote far more smoothly. Marie's world was comprised then of simple parameters: the Johnny pump and the "last gate." It was between these two landmarks that she was allowed to play.

These restrictions were so her mother could find her when she wanted her back. Marie could still see her mother, well; *half* of her through the open window, but even half was a force to be reckoned with. High above, silhouetted by the late day sun, her voice boomed all the way down the edge of the last gate:

"Maaaaarrrrrriiiieeee!"

She always pretended, for just one split second, that she didn't hear. It wasn't that she was embarrassed that her flesh and blood was hanging out a window in a housedress, yelling in a more resonant voice than a drill sergeant, no. Half the moms on Bleecker Street could do *that*. She pretended because for that shred of time, she was in control of her life. After all, Marie didn't really want to come outside in the first place. Nine times out of ten, she was dumped out here, she and her sisters, on the pretense of getting "fresh air." Marie knew that her mother's real motive was to keep the house clean.

The house, of course, was only an apartment, large by New York standards, but small for one accommodating five children, although it was four for a while. In Queens, an apartment is not referred to as a "1-bedroom" or a "studio." A hopeful landlord listing the apartment just lists the number of rooms, including the kitchen, and sometimes even the bathroom. Just rooms. Whatever the hell you did with them was your own business. Marie's family of seven lived in six rooms, rooms set up all in a row like boxcars, which is what the "RR" stood for in the Ridgewood Times ad: railroad. Right now, playing in the street, she was separated from her mother's now louder football coach voice by a front stoop and two long flights of stairs.

"Whaaaaattttt????"

"Time for supper."

"What are we having?" she yells back absentmindedly.

Her mother is gone, the window closed. Marie gathers up her sister, climbs the three flights to her castle, passing, on the way, the different smells of other dinners, usually Italian dinners, and then...SLAP!

She does not know what hit her, but she is crying and there is her mother, standing over her. "Never, ever ask what we are having for supper. It's nobody's business but ours."

Therein lies a clue; Marie is sure, to how she started to become who she was. How could she know, at age 6, that her Wednesday night menu was classified information, so sensitive that her mother feels compelled to leave pots bubbling on the stove, and wait in semi-darkness to strike the offender who dared to ask? How could her mother's housecoat, and the time of their evening meal, be spilled out freely from the top of a three-story building, but the actual bill of fare be a source of shame and secrecy?

It will be a long time before Marie understands her mother, or sees her as just a 50's housewife, insecure and stressed and denied any opportunity greater than finding just the right curtains for her rented kitchen. What Marie sees now is a large powerful woman who has never second-guessed herself, a woman who has never been really young, a woman born with children and refusing Dr. Spock's help, but thanks anyway. It is useless to question her, but Marie always does:

"Why, mom? Why can't I ask what's for supper?"

"Because I said so."

Marie does not want to be slapped again, but she burns inside with indignation! Why *can't* she *just* have an answer? Perhaps she might even understand! "Well, honey, we cannot divulge our culinary choices because, you see, Mr. Walter across the way might be green with envy that we are having potato pancakes, while he, poor man, is having spaghetti for the third night this week," or "If Mrs. Viola, our landlord, knows we can afford London Broil, she will raise our rent." Marie is certain that the explanation must be very simple, and having suffered corporal punishment for her misdemeanor, she feels she is entitled.

Usually, and thankfully, Marie has no time to work out these key details of her past. Life now is blessedly busy, and stress is the catchword of anyone who attempts to exist in these times. 'Exist' isn't even the right word; it is nearly a mark of success to be more bogged down, out of breath, in debt, and pressed for time as the next weary traveler. Marie parents four, teaches 24, and has little doubt that she has "made it," based on the current criteria. She winces as she recalls that once, she made it her mission to pile more on her plate – art classes, piano lessons, traveling soccer – just to be able to roll her eyes with the best of them and say the words, "I'm sooo stressed out."

Now, though, she is "down the shore," a New Jersey phrase that has only replaced her "at the beach" in the last decade or so. Here, she need only reapply sun block to ward off yet another round of wrinkles, and be on time, in position, by the bay at sunset. She has taken to rating the sunsets, on a scale of one to ten, but there hasn't been a ten in years. The sun only graces the sky with the right combination of miraculous hues and color-catching clouds when Marie is out of film or has forgotten her camera altogether. She remembers the last time she stood helplessly awestruck at God's handiwork, empty camera in hand, realizing how precious a moment is. The Acme store was only one short beach block away, but she knew the show would be over before she got through the express checkout with Kodachrome in hand.

Now Marie keeps her eyes on the sky, and searches for that lost sunset. She knows it involves a certain type of cloud – cumulus? – but she has long forgotten her cloud names, even though she had to know them relatively recently for her Praxis test. At the same time, she wonders if she is living one of those O.Henry, "last leaf" situations: that if she ever captures a flawless, top ten sunset, she will surely die right there on the bench by the bay.

On a truly ambitious day, she tries to listen attentively to the voices inside her head, and searches for more than lost sunsets. She wonders if it is too dramatic a metaphor to believe that her camera was too often empty, missing the best of times, unprepared and unseeing when she really should have been looking. Perhaps that explains why her lover is long gone and her husband longs to leave.

Chapter One: The Johnny Pump and the Last Gate

Cookie Caccia is the unofficial boss of Bleecker Street, at least the female division. Marie cannot place nor dispute her authority. Sitting on the ground inside little Joanna's gate, Marie reaches to stroke a coveted Barbie fashion in Joanna's pink plastic case.

"Leave go of it," Cookie says, with a touch on Marie's offending arm.

Marie attempts what she knows will be useless defiance. "I…just want to…look at it a minute," she says feebly.

The pressure on her arm increases. "Leave go of it, I said," and Marie looks directly into Cookie's face, trying to fathom what she sees there, or more importantly, trying to decipher what Cookie does not see in her own face.

Defeated, Marie "leaves go," knowing it doesn't matter a bit that this is not fair. The item in question is Joanna's possession, not Cookie's, and Joanna is younger than Marie, and more than happy to invite Marie's jealous admiration of her things. Cookie is older than both of them, 10 or so, that double-digit age in which Barbie is left to sleep in a dusty case with Ken forever. Giving up Barbie is a sacred milestone, and the savvy Cookie is sure to have crossed it, but there are enough true Barbie believers about for her to get a quick fix every now and then.

Joanna's mother calls her for dinner, and the case closes, both literally and figuratively, as the miniature negligee disappears and the metal clasp clicks shut. Marie stands, brushing her knees where the concrete has left little pebbly marks, and looks quickly around for her sister. Lisa is sitting near the curb, legs criss-crossed, with enough gap in her short pants leg to show her cotton flowered drawers. Lisa's face shows none of the humiliation and frustration that crossed Marie's seconds before, because Lisa is blissfully young and not yet aware of her shortcomings.

"Whatcha doin'?" Marie asks, even though she is not interested and anyway, she can see for herself that Lisa is watching ants move about in a crack in the sidewalk.

"Nuthin'," Lisa answers without looking up. "It's time to go in?"

Marie scans the third floor windows of the brick building, searching for her own call to freedom from the authority up high. Today her mother's body will appear from her grandmother's building, which is why she and her sister are playing on Cookie's side of the street in the first place. The rules are different here; the Johnny pumps in different spots, and there is no real "last" gate.

Even outside Marie's play parameters, her world is small. She lives on one side of the street, her grandmother on the other. One of her mother's friends, Mary, lives just past the dreaded large tree, centered in the middle of the block, from which caterpillars fall into children's hair as they whisk by. Her Aunt Ellen lives two blocks down on St. Nicholas Avenue, and two doors down, her mother's friend and shopping companion, Irma, resides with her two daughters, one of which is Marie's best friend. Marie does not have any friends that aren't children of her mother's friends, and not a single one of the people in her small world owns the house they live in.

Marie takes in stride that there is a postcard-shaped backyard attached to her house that she will never play in, and that she will never own a dog. Backyards and dogs are for landlords, who, in spite of their good fortune, are never happy. Owning property serves only to make them guarded and watchful, ever suspicious of imprudent tenants' brats swinging on the gate or spilling bubbles on the stoop.

While Marie is looking up, her mother is walking toward her, sparing her voice just this once and fetching her daughters in person. Minus the housedress, her mother is quite classy, wearing bright red lipstick and high heels just to walk the fifty paces to her own mother's home. She never wears pants. She is not a small woman, but Marie has never thought of her as fat, probably because children do not use many adjectives when identifying their parents. Her mother looks like her mother. That's all.

Helene is a woman who loves her children more than life, but right now she operates on the instinct of a mother duck and the business-like manner of a top-notch exec. It's suppertime, and it's up to her to get the right people in their places.

Her efficient eyes find two girls in one sweep, then move on to find her son, an asphalt graduate who spends all day, every day, playing stick ball or skully in the street. Or at least, that is what the girls think he is doing. They don't exactly know, because they pay very little attention. The boys play with the boys, the boys play beyond their own borders, and even if they spot Robert in the course of their outdoor sentence, they will barely acknowledge each other. They do know that he is allowed past the last gate but not off the block, and occasionally put him to use if they have reason to be "crossed" to that foreign land known as the other side of the street. It is rare for Marie and Lisa to require their brother's precious crossing hands, but this does not stop Robert from looking extremely put upon when one of them stands helplessly curbside, calling his name.

Marie also knows that the rules are different for Robert, for he is the only son, the prince, a boy surrounded by three and then four sisters. First of all, to Marie's amazed speculation, Robert *wants* to be out. He spends his inside time preparing for his outside time, repairing his bat with electrical tape or melting old crayons into bottle caps. He leaps up with his last mouthful of lunch, or supper, the four words forming as one before he has swallowed, "C'I-g'out?" He will be the only family member who actually gets away with just tossing his plate into the kitchen sink without lifting a sponge or a towel, and his sisters will not start resenting this until years later.

Marie and Lisa have already latched on like magnets to their mother's right and left hand, anticipating food and dolls and television, all those comforts now locked away behind black iron and cream-colored brick. They eye their green painted front door, however, and anticipate the wait, because even their 'no one dares to defy me" mom will not get Robert on the first try.

"Rooobbberrrt!" She does not get to spare her voice after all.

Heads will turn, ears will perk, and sometimes, people will help. "He's on Peter's stoop, Mrs. Meyers," "He's in Richie's hallway," "He's down Carl's cellar," "I'll get him, what should I tell him?" The hunt will last exactly as long as her mother's patience, she will be on the verge of locating him herself, first giving a freezing "stay right here" look to her daughters that will have them checking the precise location of their feet within the concrete slab. Just as they are measuring the distance of their rubber-toed shoe to the nearest crack, Robert will turn up and say, "What, Ma?"

'He doesn't even look scared,' Marie thinks, but dwells not long on the subject, for she is only relieved that their unit is now complete, after a few groans and "do I have to's" and "can I stay out longer's," they will begin their ascent to the place called home. There are only two members still outstanding – her father and older sister – but they will find their way to the dinner table on their own, the first coming from work, the other abiding the time on her watch, for she is allowed to play in that exotic land known as "around the block."

Her father's arrival is marked by the dumping of change, from his long pockets to his dresser, in his bedroom, third boxcar in. He will say hello to his children, askew on living room sofas, chairs, the floor, and the strength of their response will be proportional to the popularity of the television show that is mirrored and glowing in their eyes. He is unhurt by this; having driven an 18-wheeled truck all day, Fred Meyers is simply happy to be home. Whatever stories he has to tell about his day are for his wife's ears, and shortly after the clatter of coins comes the sounds of muffled grown-up talk.

Anne's arrival will be marked by nothing, just a flash of color as she whizzes by, the eldest in the family and the only one with a room to herself. Bob Dylan's voice, or Joe Cocker's, or maybe the Beatles, will then signify that Marie's household is now complete: stereos and television, supper smells and clattering dishes, laughter and bickering.

"Kids…come set the table," her mother will yell through three rooms.

And then they were assembled at dinner, five assigned seats and later a high chair, when her mother delighted Marie with a change-of-life baby. Marie does not remember when her seat became her seat. She is inexplicably placed at the head of the table, opposite her father, and so her dinner view is always himself, and the windows behind him that look out at washlines and telephone poles, and brick structures in various earth tones across the way.

Conversation is permitted at dinner, with few rules. A mouth may be full, subject matter is not censored, but there is a certain pecking order. Her mother is telling all of today's shopping trip.

"So I'm on Myrtle Avenue," she says, only Marie hears it as "Murt Lavenue, "and I stop in the Five and Dime…"

Marie arranges her food on the plate, four separate things, three of them usually an auburn color -- breaded chicken cutlets, French Fries, applesauce – and one a brighter hue, green beans or beets. She alternates between listening and daydreaming; she was not only with her mother on this excursion, she has heard this story already told to one person on the phone, and knew she would hear it several more times before it was archived.

"Those are on sale, I told the girl, but she goes right on ringing, like she doesn't even hear," her mother enjoys spinning a tale and she does it well. "I said, honey, get me your boss, I have a bone to pick with him."

"You didn't say that, mom," Marie interjects, her plate temporarily forgotten. "You said, 'Can I please talk to your manager.' I heard you."

Her mother stops, blinks, turns slowly, and then fastens her eyes on Marie as if she is attempting to weld their gazes together. "*I* am telling a story, Marie. I *know* what I said."

"But mom, that is *not* what you said. I heard you."

"I have the last word in this house, Marie. Not you. Me." Helene turned back to her father as if that settled it, and a hush descends over the table as morsels of food became temporarily inert between molars, forks in mid-air, eyes cast down or moving tentatively from side to side.

Her father gave her a brief passing look of sympathy before turning his attention back to her mother, but her siblings just figure it was Marie's turn. Does she imagine it, or it is too often her turn? Ann is the oldest, Robert the only boy, Lisa is the baby of the family for a while. Marie is the true "middle child," telling her father one day, "I am never first, and I am never last," and genuinely bewildered as to why he finds this so funny.

Soon supper will be over and the sun will reflect orange in the windows on Bleecker Street, the city sounds will fade, from children playing to adults smoking and talking on front stoops, perhaps a late night dog walker, and finally, nothing at all. Another day will have passed, and no one will have known if it was a better day somewhere else in the world. Least of all Marie.

*****

Later, there will be very few days that really stand out in the endless stretch of sidewalk sunlight hours. Oh, there would be a few "incidents," for sure, like the humid day the Hispanic woman across the street went into the spray of the Johnny pump. There were a few things that made this incident noteworthy. The first was that, even though Marie's friendly neighborhood fire department came around with sprinkler caps for the fire hydrants, so as to enable young city slickers to beat the heat, Marie and her sister were not allowed to partake of this pleasure. "That is something ghetto children do," Helene proclaimed, while never exactly saying what ghetto children were and why Marie was not one of them. When a dictionary later enlightened Marie that the actual meaning of the offensive word is "neighborhood," she is truly befuddled.

The offense of the Hispanic woman, besides possibly being Hispanic in a German-Italian neighborhood, is that following her outdoor shower, it is possible to see right through her shirt. Well, Marie can't see anything, but from three stories up, her mother can.

"Disgusting," Helene says, as she and Marie hang side-by-side from the window, surveying the land like king and queen.

"What?" Marie asks, with a typical child's enthusiasm for the nasty, foul or grotesque.

"Two brown circles, popping right through," her mother answers, pointing to Anita Gonzalez. "Why doesn't she just sit there naked?"

Marie's eyes locate the wrongdoer, but she misses her mother's point. She is taken completely with the sight of Mrs. Gonzalez's 4-month-old baby girl on her lap. There is nothing distasteful about a woman with a baby.

"Oh mommy, look at her baby," Marie croons. "I held her today. She was sleeping and I…"

"It's a wonder she doesn't just nurse her baby right through her shirt," Helene cuts in. Marie has no idea what her mother is talking about. She does not see brown spots, she does not know what nursing is, but she knows her mother is agitated, and she takes her hand. In this moment, she knows her mother would *never* do whatever bad thing Mrs. Gonzalez is doing, and for this, she is pleased.

And so, there were incidents. The day Juanita Perez threatened to beat Marie up, and then Juanita's aunt came out, and then Marie's mother ended up coming out and arguing with the aunt, and then the aunt said the word "fuck" right there in the street, and her mother said that she had a mouth like a truck driver, another idiom lost on Marie since her dad *was* a truck driver and never to her knowledge said the "f" word. It was just a chalk-written word Marie learned to read in the streets, soon after first grade.

Marie never doubted for a second the power of being able to read. She knew early there was magic in printed words, and viewed starting school as being let in on a wondrous secret, that being the ability to break the code that existed in the squiggles in storybooks. And so, she devoured John, Jean and Judy, their dog Spot and cat Puff, and the other children in her basal reader, in spite of the fact that their lives did not resemble hers in the slightest. They had a house, one that did not share a wall on each side with adjacent houses. They had a yard, and a picket fence, and they had Spot and Puff. This did not deter Marie from greedily absorbing their lives, as soon as her knowledge of vowels and consonants made it possible.

******

So that was it. Just incidents and images to break up what seemed like endless stretches of hazy sidewalk. Short days outside during the school year, longer days in the summer. There are really only a few things that stood out. One was the birth of her baby sister, Louise, 10 years her junior. Marie did not know the term, "change-of-life baby," but she did find it unusual to have another family member long after she thought of them as complete. The pregnancy was short and easy for Marie, one day her father and mother were smiling, his hands on her shoulders, then her mother grew larger, then she disappeared for a few days, and returned with a tiny, red-haired human that surpassed any doll that Marie had ever owned. Like anything else that Marie found blissful, Louise could only be had in limited quantities. Helene did not believe in spoiling babies, and so Marie's requests to hold her sister were usually denied.

Another significant event was the day Marie fell in love with the New York City Police Department. She had always feared cops, because the impression she got was that they were out to get her family.

While driving to Glenhead or Commack or any distance that inevitably led to small children getting on each other's nerves, Marie was sure to hear these words:

"Calm down back there! Keep it up and your father will get a ticket. I see the police right behind us."

Police were also very concerned with how children behaved in restaurants, it seemed. When they assembled around white tablecloths aching for spills, sugar packets screaming to be opened, and clear water glasses filled with ice begging to be rattled, Marie's mother kept her children in line with law enforcement: "Do I have to go get a policeman to get you kids to behave?"

And then, one day they were "robbed."

They were all – Marie, Robert, Lisa and their mom – across the street at grandma's house. Another third floor apartment, it offered no more entertainment than their own home, except the unconditional, spoiling love only grandparents can bestow. Grandpa was a jokester and a storyteller, and his rhetoric could ward off television for a time, while grandma amused them with food, specifically 'sourballs,' which she kept in abundance in a glass crystal bowl on the dining room table.

When it was time to leave, the flock was gathered, and the journey across began. Marie chattered in her mother's ear as they walked – indeed, Marie rarely shut up and once, her mother told her that she was vaccinated with a phonograph needle.

They clattered up the stairs, past Mr. Viola's door, then past the Iorio family's door and finally, up to their own.

"Mom!! Our door is already opened!" Lisa yelled down to her mother, still puffing as she dragged her own weight up the last flight.

"Lisa, *stop*," her mother said sternly, and something in her mother's voice made every child stop on whatever step they were on. They waited as her mother squeezed by them, and walked into the apartment first.

It was a mess. If Marie had any conception of what burglary was, she imagined it to be a few methodical, fastidious people gently and carefully taking whatever items they wished to own, as if doing a little shopping trip in someone's else's home. She never imagined that they rummaged and tossed and broke things as they searched for anything of value.

Her mother gave a soft moan, 'ohhh,' and for a moment, Marie thought it was only the mess that troubled her. Some mean and malicious people had come like demons and hit Helene Meyers where it hurt the most: they made a mess of her carefully Pledged, Windexed, vacuumed and dust-mopped home.

Her siblings looked around with wide eyes, and Marie wondered if they were as caught up in the drama as she was. Nothing like this had ever happened to them before.

"Fred, we've been robbed," she heard her mother sobbing on the phone. 'Robbed' was the word she used, over and over, to everyone she told, and 'robbed' was the word Marie would use much later when she wrote a story about it. 'Robbed' was the word Helene used when she called the police.

Soon, two officers were in her small home, towering over her, and the dining room table, made bulkier by all their apparatus and noisier by the radio that kept talking even though their owners paid little attention. Marie was quiet, behaving, so as not to earn her parents the dreaded ticket.

As it turned out, theirs was the only apartment in the building that had been burglarized. The officers, while not detectives, solved this case for them quite easily: their building neighbors both owned dogs. Fierce, barking, frightening dogs that had Marie racing up the stairs if a door had been inadvertently left open. No one, not even 'robbers,' messed with Venus and Prince.

"Mam, I'm tellin' ya, get a dog," the tall officer said to her mother, and Marie stood stock still, looking first at the officer, then at her mother. What was this? The *law* was ordering her *mom* to get a dog? Could her mother ignore this edict?

After the police were gone, Irma and Aunt Ellen came over to help clean up the mess. That night, there was much muffled grownup talk in the kitchen, and in the dining room after Marie was supposed to be sleeping.

The robbers made off with their television set, a bit of jewelry, and not much else. The television was replaced quickly, and within a month, they had a something else: a puppy named Koko.

Someday, Marie would relay this story to a police officer while lying in his arms, and she will say, playfully, that this was the day she began loving cops. It was her destiny. After all, they had made her mother get a dog.

****

If Marie and her sisters were sitting around, as adults, discussing their childhood, they would compare notes on what they considered the best of times, and the worst of times. For the latter, Lisa might mention the time she was in the bathtub getting her hair washed, so scared of getting soap in her eyes that she slipped and slithered through her mother's hands, raising Helene's level of frustration to fury, and ultimately causing her mother to slap her repeatedly on her wet back. Lisa had red eyes and hand-shaped welts on her back for days, and, not surprisingly, did not get over her fear of the bath for quite some time.

Marie, too, had her share of beatings, most often with a wooden spoon, which she supposed wasn't readily available that day in the tub. And yet, she would not consider these the most grievous abuse of her childhood. For that, Marie might focus more on the times she was simply misunderstood, or unjustly treated, for no physical pain ever equaled her mother's statutes that she, and only she, "got the last word."

"But why, mom, why do I have to wear leotards to school when no one else does?"

"Because I am not everyone else's mother."

Mostly, times were not good or bad, they were just times, replayed in misty flashes with the same few backdrops: School. The Living Room. The Dining Room Table. And, of course, The Street. The Street prevailed as the primary vista; one a set director would take extra time and care with, telling his crew, "Listen, this mom didn't even have a driver's license. We're talking about kids who pounded the pavement, five steps to her one stride, to get to school, to the doctor, to the butcher...everywhere. Make sure you have enough gray paint."

The luminous shades would be reserved for the times that forever stood out as the scenes from a happy childhood. The sparkling lights of their Christmases, for instance, would make the canvas, for all five of them were sinfully overindulged, waking up year after year to piles of presents that seemed to leap straight from the pages of the Sears Wish Book. Was it only the gifts that made these times so special, or was it the notion that love was a generous thing, unconditional and unrestrained, bestowed sans tiresome, senseless rules?

    The other splash of color was blue with shimmering gold, their yearly vacation to Lake George in the Adirondack Mountains. Marie was just six when they began a long annual tradition of driving a snugly packed, dragging station wagon over the Tappan Zee Bridge and up the New York Thruway, an hour past Albany to Bolton Landing.

    Here, street lamps did not diffuse the glow of the night sky, and earthy paths replaced concrete. Like Fresh Air Fund children, the Meyers brood embraced country air, stepping out a screen door each morning blissfully barefoot, the smell of cedar in their noses. For two weeks they lived in swimsuits that dried in the sun, using the rainy days to search for salamanders in tall wet grass, feeling mud squish between their toes. They became familiar with terms like, "road to the lake," or "the foot of the mountain," and forgot boundaries like the last gate.

    So far removed was this from fire hydrants and blacktop that, when the fourteen days were up, they gathered round the station wagon with dragging feet. Even Robert, "the boy," had his nose pressed to the window pane as the laden car crunched back up the gravelly path, and the girls cried hard until they fell asleep, waking only as the oppressive heat told them they had crossed the line into the five boroughs.

    Marie would later look back at Lake George as a significant pivot in her life, a moment that changed all that followed. She would someday believe strongly that life is a series of pivotal moments, and small subcategories of pivotal moments. She thought, should anyone sit down to make their own timeline, it would not be straight, but rather very specific turns at unclear intersections that determine the course of one's life. She did not believe that Robert Frost stopped in the woods only on a snowy evening, or came to a fork in the road only once, but rather, six or seven crucial times. In fact, she believes that on any drunken honest evening, anyone could sum up his or her entire life in six pivots.

    The trick, always, is finding the pivot. Sometimes we are sure a turn was in one place, when in fact we turned blocks and blocks before. Sometimes we direct our lives, and other times we stand still while others secure our fate.

    The year Marie's mother gave birth to baby Louise, her parents decided to skip the annual pilgrimage to the Adirondacks. Perhaps it was fiscally unfeasible, or perhaps two-month-old babies in pre-carseat times did not appreciate five-hour drives. Whatever the reason, they decided not to go. Point A. Then, they decided to go later in the summer. Point B. Because of these two simple points, Marie met her future husband.

Chapter Two : Hey, Mr. Spaceman

Marie sat poolside in her new bathing suit; the first one that actually had cups in the top to support her budding chest. At age 11, Marie stared at her breasts three and four times a day, willing them to grow just a little bit faster, to make the protrusion in her top less material and more flesh.

"Marie! Look here," her father called, and 'click, hum' went his latest camera. It was the kind that took snapshots that were perfectly square, and Marie knows this because the photo would someday become her possession, and she would look intently at the young girl in it, her clear skin and long auburn hair, and wonder if she was ever really pure of heart.

Her father set the camera down and began to chase Lisa around the pool, threatening to toss her in. He picked her up, none too gently, and swung her to and fro as she squealed. Marie looked on, already hoping that she looked too old to participate in such antics. Fred Meyers was a difficult man to ignore. He had red hair and a red face, tattooed arms that obviously spent long hours hanging out truck windows, and a loud, ready laugh. He knew what vacation was for. While Marie's mother simply relocated her childcare and cleaning responsibilities to a more rustic home, her father shook off the highway completely and drank well the rewards of the working life. He ran, he chased, he did cannonballs off the diving board – "Watch me empty all the water from this pool, kids!"

The only trappings from home Fred Meyers brought along were freebies from Hiram Walker, the company he drove for. These were in the form of displays intended for liquor stores, and so right now Marie looked on as her siblings played in the pool with large blow-up Scotch bottles, and a Styrofoam surfboard bearing the name of a whiskey. She was not embarrassed, not even when the surfboard somewhat disintegrated, scattering particles of pink Styrofoam around the pool. Her dad's toys were cool.

Across the pool, another family looked on silently. They, too, had a number of children, and Marie picked up quickly that one girl looked about her age. In the everlasting way that women check each other out, Marie jealously took in the girl's long golden sea of hair, and then let her eyes measure the girl's chest. The girl's one-piece swimsuit was more unsophisticated than Marie's own, so it was difficult to get an accurate gauge on her size. Still, she was lovely, making Marie absolutely certain that she would never want to be Marie's friend, even a temporary vacation friend.

The girl, apparently, was not burdened with such insecurities, for she was walking around the pool.

"I'm 11," she said, "How old are you?"

"I'm 11, too," Marie answered, not finding it remotely peculiar that the more vital part of introduction was their ages. If these didn't mesh, names were not necessary.

"I'm Tara." And that began their friendship that would last, unencumbered and uncomplicated, until Tara became her sister-in-law.

They played all that week, in which time Marie discovered that Tara, too, was one of five children, although she was more endowed with brothers, having three, one of which was just a year older than herself. She discovered that Tara's family was quieter than her own, keeping to themselves, speaking softly, escaping notice as much as possible. Her mother had a lilting Irish voice, and never called Tara from the cabin porch as Helene did, announcing supper to each and every resort dweller, as if it feeding a family was something all should applaud. No, Mrs. Kavanagh actually waited until her children were a foot or two away, well within earshot, to let them in on the secret of their upcoming meal.

The rules were different for those children too. Once, while splashing about in the lake, Marie heard Tara refer to her brother as a 'brat.'

"Tara!" her father called. His accent was Scottish, but Marie didn't know the difference then. "Come over here," he said, and Tara did.

Mr. Kavanagh brought his daughter close, but Marie strained her ears, because she couldn't imagine what Tara's sin could be.

In a low growl, Mr. Kavanagh said, "Tara. None of my children are brats."

Marie stared on in wonder as Tara sat miserably on the dock, denied the privilege, temporarily, of swimming, and she felt punished as well since she was denied a playmate. She went over in her head all the things she called her brother and sisters: "Idiot," "Jerk," sometimes preceded by the word, "Stupid," and she couldn't help thinking that her parents would be grateful to hear as playful a word as "brat." Imagine being grounded for such an innocent word.

The Kavanaghs were different. They saw no particular reason to befriend the Meyers family, even though their children were playing together, or perhaps they saw a reason and wished they didn't. When Marie's mother was at the pool or the lake, she attempted the "look at us, we are both mothers, look what we deal with" mode of sociability, and Mrs. Kavanagh gave an obligatory smile, but her heart didn't seem to be in it.

Marie was enthralled with them, their quiet manners and soft voices, but she was especially captivated by Tara's 12-year-old brother Brendan, who reminded her of her only love interest up to this point, the pop star Donny Osmond. Dark full hair, parted on the side, and a round full face. But Brendan was real, and here, and he liked her, too. It was easy to tell. He splashed her, he dunked her, he teased her, and he made fun of her. They played games in the water that allowed them to touch. For two weeks she tried to be where he was, sorely let down if her plans were thwarted. Brendan was far more evasive, finding it less imperative to find her, or maybe he was just more subtle. Was that the first red flag in their relationship, her greater need of him than he of her? If it was, it was the first of many.

"Hey, I thought you were at the lake," he said, coming up behind her, laughing. "That's why I came to the pool."

Marie laughed but felt her first of many hurts, her first of many times wondering if he was serious or joking, if he found her interesting or ridiculous. She'd wonder later if there were ever a moment, frozen, when they were equals, when he wasn't better than her. Her father took a group shot of all the kids before they left that year, and the photo became another square of time for scrutiny.

****

Soon after, Marie met her best friend. On that day, Marie was walking the dog, wearing hot pink polyester shorts and a v-neck sleeveless pale pink polyester top. She will remember this because it was the last day she would ever think that this was a cool outfit. Her mother, of course, had picked it out, since Marie had no say whatsoever in what she wore, but the truth was, she loved it. It accentuated the little she had, and she watched herself in passing car windows as she walked the dog.

"Walking the dog" had become a euphemism for "hunting for boys." It was futile to hunt for them on Bleecker Street, since they were all her brother's friends, and so saw her forever as a pain. She adored one, but Cookie Caccia had claimed him, much as she had claimed the Barbie outfit years before. The best of everything on Bleecker Street belonged to Cookie. She walked down the street in platform shoes, chinos and a tube top, with purpose and privilege emanating in every step.

Marie just walked. Koko pulled. She got to the end of Bleecker and turned on to St. Nicholas Avenue, heading away from school and the route she knew too well. She let the dog wrench her arm towards Linden, hoping this was the day something different happened.

At the end of the street, she heard music. Somewhere, someone was blasting a boom box, and the song, "The Lion Sleeps Tonight" filled the air. Marie followed the sounds to an abandoned building across the street, where two girls were laughing, one still and one swaying.

"Hey, nice dog," said one, and Marie took that as an invitation to cross the street.

"What are you *wearing*?" said the other, and Marie noted fast the uniform of the two girls: sweatshirt and denim.

"Don't you even know us?" the first one said, "We're in your fuckin' grade."

Marie did know them, sort of, but she was at a loss for words. They *were* in her grade. Laura and Terry. But how could it be that they looked so much older than her, so much cooler than her? Both had large chests, one enhanced by a Mickey Mouse shirt that allowed the mouse's ears to rest on each breast. Laura caught her looking.

"I know, right? Right on my tits. The boys are always saying it, 'Hey Laura, can I touch your Mickey Mouse ears?"

"Yeah and you let them," Terry said. Her own chest was buried under cotton and denim, a blue zip-up sweatshirt with a dungaree jacket on top. She turned to Marie. "She is so fucking boy crazy. When are you going to turn this stupid song off?"

"I gotta go, anyway," Laura said, "My grandmother made supper." She picked up the boom box, "You gonna be out later?"

"Maybe. Call for me." And then Marie and Terry were alone.

"Do you always dress like that?" Terry asked, "You look like a piece of Bazooka."

"Umm...naw..." Marie answered, picking up the lingo quickly, "I have to go out to this stupid dinner with my family. I had to look 'nice,' my mom said. You know how it is." Marie was mentally saying goodbye to the pink ensemble she treasured just moments before, and mourning its loss. She was also wondering if she even owned Levi's.

Marie looked curiously at Terry, and felt sure she was prettier than her friend; but Terry held far more fascination for the boys at school and even the men that passed by in the street. She was short but not dainty, with a square build and strong legs, and gave the impression she could love hard but fight harder. She hid a tanned, oblong face behind long thin hair and tinted glasses, but there was no hiding the full chest that lurked under her ever-present dungaree jacket. Marie tried to see past the denim to the hint of feminine color beneath.

"I get my shirts from this cool store on Woodward and Grove," Terry said, "It's all, like, irregular shit, but you can hardly tell. It's cheap so my mother doesn't care. I can bring you there."

That was how it began. The store was actually once a corner deli, but an old couple started selling factory rejects out of cardboard boxes and a few clothing racks. It had a makeshift sign out front covering the old deli name but not completely, but to Terry, the name of the store was "Woodward and Grove."

"Mom, can I have money for Woodward and Grove? I want to buy clothes."

"What's wrong with the clothes I buy you," Helene asked, just as Marie knew she would.

Eventually, Helene approved of the store, because the shirts were decent and cost between fifty cents and three dollars. A really nice one was five dollars. What Helene did not really approve of was Terry. She looked like trouble to Helene, which only served to heighten Marie's devotion to her. Little by little, Terry taught Marie the proper way to dress, and their friendship grew, from their preteens into their teenage years.

Terry also solved Marie's boy problem. She hung out in front of a corner Laundromat on Bleecker and Seneca Avenue, with a real crowd and a complete other world for Marie. She sat on Terry's stoop watching the girls link arms with the boys, dancing to blasting boom boxes, passing drinks in paper bags, and talking. They were always talking, their voices cutting through the night, audible from a half a block in either direction. They were older than Terry, but let her in to their circle since she lived on the block. Marie was not given this honor.

"They don't really know you," Terry explained, "I only really get to hang with them when I'm alone."

Marie watched them with an ache like day old hunger. They were part of something. She was not. They had a "hang-out" — critical for any chance of social success. A street corner, a set of church steps; it didn't matter. It only mattered that your people showed up each night.

    Marie had Terry and she had hope. On days together, they walked past the Laundromat on the pretense of needing something from the deli on the other side. They were permitted only one walk-by per day, so as not to be obvious, and Marie soaked in as much as she could for the split second she was in close proximity. She tried to decipher the secret to acceptance. She watched how they moved. How they laughed. She memorized snippets of conversation. She watched how the girls acted silly and flirty, while the boys strummed invisible guitars to Led Zeppelin songs. Actually, Terry had to tell her that they were Led Zeppelin songs. True, Marie had given up the Osmonds, but no one had really told her what rock stars to like instead. This burden, too, rested on Terry. In truth, Marie hated Led Zeppelin, and Jimi Hendrix, and The Doors, but Terry assured her that this wasn't something she should admit. It was a matter of self-preservation.

******

    And then, one day in the middle of another futile summer, when Marie was 14 years old, there was a block party on her street. Perhaps the tackiest of Queens events, the block party was a chance for residents, especially yard-less residents, to shed their nearly non-existent inhibitions and have a huge party in the middle of the street. The neighborhood police cooperated by providing big orange cones and blue wooden horses to block off the street to traffic, and for once even the primary grades frolicked in the gutter. To complete the tawdry scene, food and alcohol were consumed inside gates and on front stoops, while a hired group of musicians played songs like, "We're an American Band," with heavy Italian accents: "We comma to you town, we gonna potty it down, we an Ame'ican band."

    The entire street buzzed with thick Queens accents and unrestrained, intoxicated laughter, their neighbor Beatie punctuating each hearty guffaw with, "Ya son of a bitch!" that resonated at least as far as Simanski's gate. With no threat of cars, watchful parent eyes became lazy, knowing the kids were around here someplace, and both generations reveled in the freedom.

Marie was bored. She didn't get it. Up the stairs and down the stairs, carrying, carrying, carrying, her mother yelling their names over and over. "Marie, take down the sausage and pepper...and *don't* drop it." "Robert, carry the soda." "Lisa, here is a package of plastic utensils. *Now*, Lisa." Her mother ate it up – it was another chance to act overworked and unappreciated, the quintessential mother of five, Jesus feeding the flock – but it all seemed much hoopla for something that amounted to eating outside instead of in, with basically the same people you saw every day. Marie yearned to leave, find Terry up the street, but this counted as a "family" event, and it took a lot of alcohol to make Helene's eyes relax their hold.

And then she saw them. All of them. They had left their Laundromat, and come to hang out on her side of Bleecker Street, forbidden though it was. Terry was with them, and she strode right up to Marie with a short blonde boy.

"We crashed your party," she said, "Another reason for your ma to hate me."

"She doesn't hate you," Marie began, "She..."

"Yeah, yeah, okay," Terry cut off whatever feeble defense she was putting together, then gestured towards the boy next to her. "This is Bobby," Terry said, "He wanted to meet you."

Bobby never became a pivot in Marie's life. He became the first of many in a long straight line. He was the first suitor in Marie's coming out ball, a launch pad for wayward trips that would each rob her of something she wouldn't know was missing until it was too late to get it back. Like the way a bus pulls away with your purse on the seat, and you don't realize until you don't have keys to your house. By then, retrieving what you lost would be an arduous process, and you'd wonder how you could be so careless with something you needed so much.

Bobby called for her, hunted for her, every day after the block party. Marie's family teased her.

"He's outside right now, Marie, just waiting for you to walk by."

"Doesn't that boy ever give up?" That was her mother, sounding suspicious, a tone Marie should have just made up her mind to get used to right then and there. Helene was wary of any male ardor directed at her daughters.

Marie's father, on the other hand, loved it, hurrying her out the door when Bobby came to call, excusing her from dishes, forgiving her a few tardy moments returning home. Was it because Bobby informed him of his desire to join the navy? Hard to say, but this was another pattern forming, that of her father offering her up like Lot in the Bible, to any amiable stranger who showed a little interest.

"God, he worships the ground you fuckin' walk on," Terry said one day, and Marie glowed with pride. There was only one problem, one she hadn't yet disclosed to anyone, not even her best friend. She didn't like Bobby. She didn't like his short body and large arms, his gruff voice or the way he tilted his head to talk to her. She tried to find charm in these things, but the truth was, she felt cheated. Here was someone who adored her, in spite of the fact that the first time he attempted to make out with her, she didn't even know enough to open her mouth. After kissing her front teeth, he leaned back and said, "hmmm, that was good," and Marie was grateful and annoyed at the same time. Why couldn't she just like him? Why did she take a different route when she saw his pathetic form, semi-kneeling and reading the newspaper on her corner?

And then, one day, he invited her to a party. With them. All of them. It was at a kid named Carl's house, a tall, beautiful boy with long blonde hair. He was 16 years old, one of the younger ones like Bobby, and Marie wished he were the one that stalked her daily. But who cares, for now, she had Bobby and Bobby gotten her *in*. In. She was about to infiltrate the group, to become one of *them*.

She spent all day picking out her clothes, in that ironic way that teenagers take special care to handpick outfits that will make them look like everyone else. Chinos had replaced the customary jeans, but it was always the top that mattered more. It was pale blue and soft, with a row of small buttons that defined the valley between her breasts. Her mother looked on, suspiciously, half-surprised that she had given permission for this and reserving the right to veto this decision at the first hint of impropriety.

"One more button needs to close on that shirt," she said intrusively, adding, "I'm not thrilled about this party, you know."

Marie buttoned the button, knowing full well she could undo it the minute she was out the door and not understanding why her mother didn't realize that as well. She was not going to mess with this chance, this gift, this opportunity to join the ranks of the accepted, and she would have put on a Peter Pan collar if it got her out the door.

"Bye, mom, I'm going," she yelled when Terry, not Bobby, came to get her, to check her out, give her approval, prep her on the way.

"Phew, you look alright," she said, clearly relieved. "I thought you would have to change at my house and I'm not sure I had anything that would fit you."

"I know," Marie replied, "My mother was giving me so much shit." She fumbled on the word 'shit' slightly, still not quite used to the mandatory act of cursing, written in stone in the teen code of conduct.

Bobby intercepted them at the corner, cutting in like a dance partner, or perhaps a groom confiscating his bride for the final steps to the altar. Terry relinquished her with a final checkout, her eyes warning her that this was it and don't blow it.

"You look nice," Bobby said with the head tilt.

They climbed the two flights to the apartment above, and Marie noted that the hallway was more dingy than her own, the stairs bare, and the smells from other tenants' recent meals more unpleasant. For a second, Marie wondered if perhaps we just got used to our own building odors, the same way we never noticed the warm musk of our family members; the same way we think that our own skin has no scent at all, except in the obvious dark corners. She shook the thought and walked faster, trailing Bobby, with Terry a few steps behind.

And then she was in. It was packed; a street corner's worth of bodies crammed into a box that Marie supposed was a living room. It was impossible to see everyone at once, since they traipsed in and out of the main room from doors to other boxes. Bobby led Terry and her through to a room piled high with coats, with a bed somewhere beneath.

"You can leave your jackets in here," he said, and then noticed that Marie wasn't wearing any outerwear, risking the chill for exhibition purposes, and Terry was only wearing the dungaree jacket that was part of her person.

"Want something to drink?" he asked, and Marie nodded, and squeezed past him, her eyes darting around the room, wondering how she could lose him in so small a space? She only had this one evening to make them like her, so that tomorrow she and Terry could walk lazily up to the Laundromat corner and say, "hey, what's up?" and stay there. But how could she do it, with the music so loud and the bottles clinking and the continuous bustle making her invisible?

Carl and a few others, she learned, were out on the fire escape. This sounded like a good place to practice her charms, so she headed that way, with Bobby tailgating.

"Bob-bbby! S'up?!" Suddenly, there was this guy in front of her, tall, with a beard.

"Hey Jason," Bobby said, and turned to her, "Marie, this is my cousin Jason."

"Hi," she said, and forgot about the fire escape.

Bobby interrupted. "Watch her for a second, Jay, while I go find some beer."

Later, Marie would only remember how their conversation started, and how it ended, and only tidbits in between. Jason said, "So, you're going out with my cousin?" and Marie tripped over herself to deny it. "No, no, we're just friends, that's all." She found out he was 18, four years older than herself. She noticed that his eyes were very blue.

It ended in the room with all the coats. In between there was a bit of shifting from foot to foot, some giggling, and a bit of arm touching. Marie spoke in a voice she didn't not recognize, sing-song-y and almost babyish, but when she made out with Jason on the stack of coats, she knew she did it right. All tongue and no teeth.

The party ended for her then and there, and so did all chance for acceptance. Bobby walked her home without speaking, and she didn't know the extent of the damage until Terry called her the next day.

****

"What…the fuck…were you thinking?"

"I just…liked him…and…"

"Marie. They are *all* talking about you. You made Bobby look like a fucking fool. You made out with his fucking *cousin*, for God's sake! In front of fucking *everyone*. I mean, I know you don't like the guy, but…God."

"Alright," Terry kept talking since Marie was speechless with misery, "damage control. We'll say you were wasted."

"But…Bobby…he knows…he was getting me beer," Marie wished hard to have the moment back. "Terry, I hadn't had a thing to drink yet."

"You were wasted, Marie," Terry said firmly. "We were drinking earlier, before the party. It's the only way."

They went with the story, but it didn't help. She apologized to Bobby; feebly mentioning the earlier binge drinking, and he mentioned that he knew alcohol was evil, since his father was an alcoholic who had left them years before. He forgave her, but never again waited on her street corner, and she never again walked past the Laundromat to get to the deli. She continued to meet Jason, but even he could not gain her the rite of passage into the group. This was lost to her forever, and she grieved deeply for it.

****

Her father hated Jason, referring to him as "the bearded bastard," and her mother said he wanted "one thing," and that it would be "statutory rape" because of his age. The surprising thing was Jason genuinely liked her, which pretty much guaranteed his eventual demise, in spite of how much fun it was to have a high school graduate pick her up from 8th grade.

Marie spent the next year picking up guys in the street, making out on cars and in cars, against walls in back alleys, portraying herself to all as a wild thing, a free spirit, a girl far too untamed to hang out with one group in one place. Eventually she gave her virginity to a 22-year-old guitar player named Ray, in a sweaty apartment on Woodbine Street, an event so confusing, she went home wondering what else she had lost. Still, Marie was convinced she was in love with him, and she was on her way to see him, bouncing down the avenue, scantily clad, checking herself out in passing windows, and glorifying in the hungry looks of all the newsstand guys under the el as she strutted by, when a sign on an empty storefront stopped her: "Coming soon, Arthur Treachers Fish and Chips. Taking applications now."

Against the colored glass, she studied her image, a source of sinful pride just seconds before, now falling tenderly short. She may have left a trail of men and boys behind her that yearned to grope her, to pant into her ear that she was beautiful, but instinct whispered harder words into her soul. Marie was 16, and already so ruined that she questioned her ability to serve the captain's fish fillets on cardboard plates.

She shook her image and yanked on limited fabric in a hopeless attempt at modesty. Switching to autopilot, she opened the door, and forever bent the course her life would take. It was just a teenager's first job, but Marie would remember the door, the street, the sign, the sound of her heart beating against the noise of the M train going by overhead for the rest of her life. She would always wonder what might have happened had she deemed herself unfit and walked on.

There was only one person inside. It took Marie a minute to find him, and she felt her legs beg to change direction.

"Yes?" he said, a pockmarked face with eyes that fixed upon her and did not leave. He had to know why she came in, but he still waited for her to say it.

"I'm here…about…the sign," she faltered, wondering if his eyes were filled with mockery, scorn? There seemed to be a hint of a smile in his thin lips, not lecherous, but not warm, either. And he kept on watching, as if something on her was exposed and he was daring her to fix it.

Without a word, he handed her an application, and watched as she filled it out. It didn't take long; she had very little to say. She handed it back, mumbled thanks, turned and tried to walk steadily to the door.

"I'm Hans," he said just before she reached the door. "I'll let you know."

She was hired that day, and given a uniform checked in autumn colors, with a matching scarf to wrap around her head. It was several weeks before the store opened, and during that time, she diligently memorized the menu.

Marie was right about one thing. She was somewhat unfit to serve the secret recipe. From her first day, she was too slow. She was too careful. Someone else would grab the order while she was still trying to decipher what "cc" meant on the ticket. Hans berated her constantly. "Let's go, malaka, there's two fillets in an "original," watch me, ONE, TWO, see? Can you count to two?" She heard the word "malaka" many times before she realized it was a Greek for fool, or something like that. The store was owned by Greeks, mafia types who stopped in daily, presumably to count their money. Hans was the manager.

Already, Hans was everyone's hero, and no wonder. He was in his mid-thirties and worked in a fast food joint. The yellow paper cups he drank from all day were filled with straight vodka. He had a filthy mouth, and was particularly graphic with females. And he rarely went home to his young wife at closing time, preferring to hang out with his teenaged employees, who some day might understand that he was a loser. But not today.

Marie soon found that going to work was her favorite thing to do. Gradually, "Treachers" became her street corner, her Laundromat, her abandoned building, her hangout. Amidst the clatter of trays was the banter she recognized from Terry's crowd, the easy jokes and jargon, sexual innuendos, and the feeling of ownership of this moment. Marie savored the sound of every syllable out of each mouth, including her own.

"I just cleaned this toaster, and no one is allowed to order another chicken sandwich tonight," Jane proclaimed near closing time.

"Yeah, that's what you think," Marie gestured to the door, "The movie just let out."

"Oh shit! We are never going to get out of here!" That was Donna, forlornly staring at the crowd that just entered.

"Where are we going, anyway?" Natalie added.

"I think Hans said we were going down to Kelly's," Libby said from behind, lifting a metal crate out of the deep fryer, "Chicken's up."

"Would you fucking people stop talking and just work?" Hans' voice came from the back, and they all stopped to see if the customers heard, holding back laughter but not really.

"Sorry. He's crazy. Can I help you?" Marie asked, and they all cracked up again.

And so it went. Night after night, from 5 to closing, and beyond. On Marie's days off, she went straight there, as did most of them on their days off, pretending to be stopping on their way to somewhere else, but never really getting there. They accused each other of having no life, as they sat for hours in the booth nearest the front, sucking down sodas until Hans said, "All right, losers, time to go," which meant that the owner was on his way to check in.

Marie did have a life but it hadn't improved much outside of this sanctuary. If anything, it grew sleazier, as Treachers gave her a whole new line up of careless boys to tease. Not her fellow workers, no, never them. They were her comrades. Rather, she chose from the local customers, boys who came in on their breaks from the newsstand, or McDonalds or Carvel across the street, the bakery or Bohacks. And of course, her favorite local business: the police department.

"Can I help you, Officer Calderone?" Marie was always sure to read their nametags, causing a quick flicker of surprise and a ready smile.

"Yeah, I want a shrimp boat, and I want to give you a ride in a police car."

Hans watched each exchange from the back, as did the others, and as soon as she put the last napkin on the tray, they swooped.

"I said the cops get a discount, Marie, not your pussy," Hans declared, more to the others than to her, waiting for their approving guffaws, which came, but only after a stunned and uneasy silence.

Pete whispered, "Are you crazy? That guy is too old for you."

"How many guys *are* you seeing?" Richie asked.

Marie still saw Ray, still loved Ray, but love was hard. When he got around to it, he took her to the nicest places, like Benihana's in the city, and during those times she tried to dazzle him with conversation that would make him forget that he was six years older. But what could she talk about? Algebra class? The school play? He, in turn, preferred a light mix of meaningless chatter and jokes, until she gave up and admitted that they were just biding their time until they made their way to an empty bed.

"Why don't we ever talk about anything serious?" she asked him one night, and his answer was quick and smiling, "I seriously want to take off your clothes."

Afterwards, he sat at the edge of the bed and played his guitar, and Marie listened, half sleepy, half sick from what her body had just done. This was the moment she told her friends about: "We make love, and then he sings to me." The truth was, his favorite song was "Mr. Spaceman" by the Byrds. Not even to herself would Marie admit that there was no romance in this.

To drive home the point, he would not call the next day, or any day. He would wait until she wandered into his workplace, Carvel, and begin the cycle once again. She waited, her young faith still naïve and strong. They had been naked together. How could two people have such a different take on what that meant?

Defeated, she finally just asked him: "Why don't you ever call after we've been...together?"

"Well, you know, your father doesn't really like me," he said in a voice completely void of hurt at this offense, "and anyway, you got plenty of boyfriends."

    She stared at him, awash in her love and want of him, and dismantled by his careless treatment of this gift. He refused to believe that he had been her first. He said it was because she hadn't bled. In fact, she had broken her hymen at the age of nine, jumping from the closet in the hall bedroom, and landing straight on the pointed edge of a broken doll carriage, but Marie knew Ray would not believe her, and this knowledge bled away another drop of her self-worth. She could feel it trickle away without a clue where the leak was, or how to stop it.

    "I am not seeing that many guys," she told Richie, after Officer Calderone and his shrimp boat were gone. "I love only one person. He plays guitar for me after we do it." She launched into her star-crossed tale, playing on her father's venomous hatred for her true love to justify his very noticeable absence in her life.

    "Love sucks," Richie sympathized, "Shrimp's up. Hans, when can I take my break?"

    "When you suck that guy's dick," Hans responded, referring to the pungent homeless man who had just entered the store. "I'll go get him for you." He went to the front of the store, really to ask the man to leave, and then they were laughing again, and Marie's life was no longer up for group analysis.

    Two weeks later, Marie sat sobbing in the bedroom she shared with her sister.

    A room was a place filled with posters and knickknacks, stuffed animals and a stereo, a desk and a drawer where a diary could hide. It was a novel thing, having a room, since her parents had purchased their first house a year before, with her grandparents and something called a "GI bill." Even though she shared it with Lisa, the room was a retreat, a haven, and today; it was a place to blast Springsteen and cry in peace.

    The door burst open, and there was her mother. Marie nearly hit the ceiling, instinctively scanning the room to see if any part of her private existence was out for her mother to pounce on. Closed doors meant nothing to Helene. It would no more dawn on her to knock than it would the dog. Helene was commander-in-chief of her household. All doors belonged to her. "Marie, I need you to run to the drugst…what's the matter?" Helene was a bloodhound, and merciless, and a tear-streaked face was like prey in a hole; she would plant herself in front of it until it something came out.

Marie summoned her most irritated voice and said, "Nothing, ma."

Unacceptable. All thoughts belonged to Helene as well.

"Nothing? Nothing? Well, it can't be nothing. You're crying," Helene stated the obvious, her voice rising. She did not yet sound concerned for her daughter's welfare, just miffed to be left out of the secret to her misery.

"I'm telling you, mom, it's nothing."

"Would you turn that goddamn music down so we can talk? God, that man's voice is terrible."

"Mom, he is only the latest poet of rock and roll."

"Well, if he is a poet, he should write. He shouldn't sing. Now, what's wrong?" Helene's large frame sealed off all exits, and her face became a searchlight.

For a brief moment, Marie wondered what it would be like to have a television mom, like Carol Brady, for instance who always lightly tapped on Marsha, Jan and Cindy's bedroom, then waited, hand still slightly poised, mid-air, a thoughtful expression on her tilted face. 'What if Jan wasn't ready to talk just yet?' she was thinking. 'Perhaps I should come back later?'

"Welllll???" Helene's voice liquefied the vision of Mrs. Brady. She was growing impatient, and if she could have reached out and extracted information from Marie physically, she would have begun squeezing by now. "I'm in the middle of laundry. I'm waiting."

"Mom, I am just in a bad mood. I don't know what's wrong. Nothing."

"Okay, Marie," she sighed, gearing up for a thick laying on of guilt, "keep it to yourself, then. Only if you insist on not telling me, then don't walk around with a long puss on your face. I don't want to see it if I'm not good enough to know the reason."

Marie could have pointed out that she was not "walking around" with her "long puss," that it was safe behind a deliberately closed door, but her mother was getting ready to leave, and to speak now was to delay the process.

"And don't turn that stereo up so loud," she said before she slammed the door, and then Marie was safe.

She gravitated instantly to the stereo, careful not to turn the volume "so loud," but yearning to hear it again. Springsteen was her hero, the only person on earth that really understood. He sung of love the way she knew it, fast and raunchy love, love in alleys and the back seat of cars, desperate and lonely.

The truth was, Marie couldn't have told her mother what was wrong if she tried. This was far out of her mother's league, and she knew it.

It happened two nights ago. She and Ray were going through their usual ritualistic courting dance, and they were up to the part where she put her clothes back on and went home with that familiar sinking feeling.

Suddenly, he touched her, pushed her back down. "Not yet," he said, softly enough for her to anticipate an outpouring of, until now, unrealized love for her.

"Turn over," he said, and she did, even though she was tired of acquiescing so gracefully to his whims.

She was mildly curious. They rarely did it twice, and never tried other positions, although she knew there were various possibilities.

"Lift up a little," he said, and now she was on all fours and filling slowly with apprehension. Did she know how to do it this way? Would it be another awkward muddle of movement, accompanied by sweaty slapping sounds and over in seconds?

Suddenly, a searing pain went through her, and she nearly buckled but he held on fast to her waist. She struggled to understand quickly: *What* hurt? She gritted her teeth and gripped the sheets, then tried to locate the source of the pain. It had never hurt before.

Slowly, with each thrust, realization came to her. He *was* inside her, but not where he should be. Disbelief shook her body, but it was no match for the piercing rhythmic pain she felt even in her earlobes. She squeezed her eyes shut; grateful that Ray could not see her contorted face, and waited for it to stop.

After some indefinite blur of time, he abruptly collapsed on her, causing her to fold beneath his weight.

"How was that?" he whispered playfully in her ear, and her mind continued to race. *How was that? How was that?* What did that mean? That he knew or that he didn't?

"Good," she mumbled, half into the sheets. Did he know? Or didn't he? Was it an accident? Was it what he intended?

Despite the lingering pain and the bleeding, it took Marie two days to start crying over the event, because forty-eight hours were required to comprehend that he wasn't going to call this time, either. The typical time lapse convinced her that he couldn't possibly know that their last encounter had been atypical. Surely he would have *something* to say if he knew.

Marie had come to identify a voice inside of her, the whisper of her enemy, and that enemy was herself. The voice came to taunt and mock her, and point out the obvious: she was nothing. With steadfast dedication, the voice missed no opportunities to prove its point, and never ran out of examples of people who would never do what she did. Sometimes it was low and snickering, and other times it reverberated in her brain: "Of course he knew. He used you. He knew he could. He won't call now. Why should he? He got what he wanted."

She needed someone to talk to. She thought of Terry, briefly, but their friendship had faded after she began working at Treachers. Her new best friend, Jane, was a coworker, and Marie adored her; but she was too, well, *normal*. There was no evidence of a tortuous, shaming voice in *her* head. Jane was not particularly pretty, but sailed around the store with a blind self-assurance that Marie would have given every paycheck to purchase if she saw it for sale in a Myrtle Avenue shop window. Jane had an easy rapport with Hans, and he kept his most degrading jokes from her. She jogged in the morning, she played the drums, and she played on a softball team. Of course, she tried to act fashionably fucked up – they all did, it an unwritten rule – but everyone knew that she had it pretty together. And so, Marie spent half her time being Jane's friend, and the other half worrying that she would somehow lose that friendship.

In either case, she couldn't tell her about what happened with Ray. She knew Jane wasn't a virgin, either, but she wistfully spoke of a boy named Paul who loved her and moved away. Marie obsessed about that boy at times, how genuine he must have been, and sensitive, how he didn't care if Jane was beautiful because to him, she was. She pictured his eyes looking into Jane's, telling her that he would never hurt her. He would be eternally grateful that he got to be "the one." And, of course, sensibly, Paul was the same age as Jane.

Fast-forward to Ray's words – "how was that?" – and Marie shivered. When Jane recanted her tale of lost love, Marie rejoined with the bed and the guitar playing, each word falling out of her mouth with the exactness that could only be the product of a practiced lie.

Chapter Three: Arthur Treachers, May I Help You?

The following week, Marie was lost in thought walking to Arthur Treachers, with her head down, and so missed the usual chances to flirt with everyone she passed. Indeed, she passed the newsstand without even noticing, until a whistle made up look up. "You don't say hello, anymore?" asked Seth, probably the prettiest boy she had ever seen. She had gone out with him a few times, until his girlfriend told her to "lay off," and then she went out with him more.

"Sorry," she said, taking only one step back, "I'll stop by on my break," she started to say, but then the train came screeching by and she turned and kept going.

She walked past the bakery, which carried no fresh-baked goods whatsoever, and today didn't notice the life that existed on this five-way street intersection. It was a dingy place, where sun streamed in only in the patches allowed by the steel beams of the elevated tracks. Conversation here followed the same pattern; stopping every 8-10 minutes, so if you were in the middle of a deep debate, you had better learn how to hold your thoughts or shout. Funny, if you were waiting for the M train above or the LL below, they never came fast enough, but if you were in the midst of the most meaningful exchange of ideas of your life, they came with impeccable efficiency. You could bet on at least ten interruptions in an hour's time.

The dialogue in Marie's head, however, always roared on, an express making no stops. She was often pensive these days, carrying on a constant debate through all her routines, not even relenting when she was actually speaking to a flesh-and-blood human being. Marie could not stop analyzing her life long enough to live it; not a word passed her lips that she did not later evaluate.

Treachers was empty when she arrived, the lunch rush over and the dinner rush not yet underway. Donna was working the entire front alone.

Donna was another one who commanded the respect that Marie ached for, a maddening irony since she was a high school dropout.

"Where is everyone?" Marie asked from across the counter.

"Back. And everyone is only Hans and this new guy," Donna said, lazily wiping down the counter, "Been dead as a doornail in here all day. That's good, though, I was wrecked from last night."

"Where were you last night?" Marie absently asked, but she was being polite. She suspected that Donna only put up with her.

"Rick's," was her one word answer. She had moved on to wiping down the soda machine.

"Ohhh, and what were you doing at Rick's that made you so wrecked, hmmmm?" Marie asked, sounding ridiculous even to herself.

"Ummm…doing Rick. Geez, Marie, get a grip."

Marie gave up and walked to the back. She was early, and Hans didn't allow anyone to punch in before time. She might as well change and grab a soda.

In her locker, she discovered an open bottle of Smirnoff's, and was about to pick it up, then stopped. If Hans had to quickly smuggle his booze, it could only mean one thing: owners.

"Good evening," a voice from behind said, and she slammed the locker shut and heard the bottle inside fall over. "How are you?"

All of the Greek owners had lecherous looks about them. They said 'good evening' in halting English, and then stood as if waiting for you to strip. This one was Jim; a dumpy tired looking man who obviously wasn't first in line for the family fortune.

"Fine, Jim, and you?" Marie stood still, blocking the door, and silently vowed to kill Hans. If you said hello to Jim and didn't step away immediately, you were basically saying, 'Fine, Jim, would you like to feel me up?' Already he had one hand on her arm.

Marie shifted from foot to foot, squirmed a lot, but that would never save her. The vodka was trickling down the front of the lockers, the scent of it distinct, but Jim appeared not to notice, because now his hand was wandering.

"Adonia," he said, or something like that, which was either Greek for something or he didn't know her name. His hand was now on one breast, and he was beginning a slow grind against her pelvis, which pushed her tight against the locker. She felt the dripping spirits soak into the seat of her pants. Just as she was beginning to fear that she would soon know what a Greek tongue tasted like, Hans appeared out of nowhere.

"Hey, malaka, you're late," and Jim fell off her. She looked at the time clock and saw that she was, indeed, a minute late, and wondered how she would rescue her work clothes now. And then she noticed the man with Hans.

"Marie, this is the new assistant manager, Manny. Manny, this is Marie."

And just like that, her life took a definite and abrupt twist, though she didn't feel a thing. No lights and sirens, no bolts of lightening, no flutters of her heart: just a panting Greek, a dripping bottle of vodka, and a time clock that kept docking her pay, minute by minute. And yet, someday, this scene from her life would get more replay time than any other before.

Manny nodded his head and didn't smile or speak, just stared and waited, as if someone had said, "This is the pope" and she neglected to kiss his ring. Marie's first thought, "Wow, this guy is going to be a real asshole to work for," was quickly replaced by, "oh God, he thinks I'm fucking Jim." Hans was savvier, however, or maybe just his nose was. An alcoholic surely can identify the smell of that which sustains him, and so he moved to get everyone out of the immediate area.

"C'mon, Manny, I'll show you the office. Jim, I have the night drop," and all feet began to shuffle. Before leaving, Hans leaned down and whispered, "You'd better clean all this up, malaka," and then she was alone.

"One Hand Waving Free"   Hofmann

*****

She didn't see much of Manny that evening. Donna screamed at her to get her ass out there so she could go home, Marie said thanks a lot for telling her Jim was around; then Jane arrived, the evening rush started, and Manny basically followed Hans around.

As hard as Marie would later wrack her brains over it, she wouldn't recall having a single feeling about Manny at all the entire night. Perhaps she and Jane exchanged a few random comments about having a new boss, and would this one last any amount of time, but then it was back to business. They noted that Hans was being a real dick, but that is how he always was when training a new person. It wasn't really about how to work the fryer or balance the register. He was territorial. He liked to show how cool he was. He liked to set the tone.

"Marie likes to put out for all the customers. Napkins, I mean. She likes to put out extra napkins. Right, malaka?" he said, patting her ass. He did not do this with Jane, Marie noted, and for once, she felt anger instead of self-pity.

"Cut it out, Hans, just cut it out. I'm not in the mood."

Manny smiled politely at Hans' jabs at her, but it was clear he was just finding his way. All the assistant managers eventually became Hans' puppets, laughing hardily at every word out of his mouth, insulting the crew, and attempting to match him 8-ounce cup for 8-ounce cup on the vodka. Marie did not expect Manny to stand on some moral higher ground.

She also knew why she discounted him so readily. He wasn't much to look at, so he did not awaken any desires in her, but more than that, he was Puerto Rican, for god's sake! Marie was indoctrinated from near infancy by parents who started sentences with, "I'm not prejudiced, but…" that Puerto Ricans were out of the question. She accepted this as matter-of-factly as she accepted that her family would never own a cat, or visit Europe. That's just the way it was. Well she remembered the day Rafael Reyes walked her home from school in 7th grade. Her grandfather happened to be outside, and his look could have frozen lava. Certainly it froze anything inside Marie that would be inclined in that direction ever again.

Her grandpa took her aside that day and gently listed all of the reasons that Marie was simply "too good" for "that kind." Perhaps the well-intentioned, grandfatherly tone stilled her rebellious nature, because for once, she didn't challenge the notion. She stored the information neatly away – "I am too good for Puerto Rican guys" – and henceforth made do with the many other nationalities available to her.

And so the day Marie met Manny passed without incident, save the fact that she worked with a damp uniform and the aroma of evaporating vodka. The school year had just started when Manny appeared, and it was Marie's last in high school. In fact, she had enough credits to graduate early, in January, and it didn't occur to her that she was better off taking a few extra meaningless credits and savoring what was left of her freedom. At least she might have considered having one more summer.

She lived for the summer; lived for the beach. She figured out that she could bike the 10 miles to Rockaway in one hour exactly, and so gave up on the trains. It made her feel like a free spirit, shoving a towel in the rungs of her bike, packing only a book and a water bottle, and taking off alone for the ocean.

Sometimes, she eyed the tiny bungalows near the Cross Bay Bridge, and imagined that she lived there; actually, she embellished the fantasy by imagining herself living there, alone, with Ray's baby. She would care for the baby, and support herself by working in the snack stand on the boardwalk on 116th Street, keeping the infant napping nearby in a stroller. Someday, she would tell Ray he had a daughter – it was always a girl in her dreams – and he would be sorry for the way he had treated her, maybe even cry when he saw himself in his daughter's eyes.

What Marie could not handle was the future her mother had already laid out for her. Upon graduation, Helene expected her to leave Treachers behind and get a "real job," as a secretary, of course, as she wasn't qualified to do much more. In fact, she wasn't really even qualified for secretarial work; her typing was slow and her sten was slower.

Still, Helene saw Marie doing exactly what her big sister Anne had done; secure a position at some plush midtown office. Anne had also married at the age of 20, and Marie guessed that Helene expected her eldest to work only until she had a baby.

Sometimes, Marie timidly mentioned that her teachers thought she had real potential as a writer, and that she should seriously consider attending college.

"College?" her mother would practically spit the word out. Really, Marie would cringe as if the word had wet her cheek. "College?" Helene would repeat, "Who has money for *college*? Not me. You? Have you been saving?"

Marie felt an instant rage boil inside her at this. She no longer contained these rages, having noted long ago that the most her mother could do was slap her:

"*Maybe*, ma," she began, her heart pumping hard, "Maybe I could have saved *something*, not enough, but *something,* if you hadn't made me pay *you* so much *money*." Helene required all her children to give her "living expenses" as soon as they started pulling in a minimum wage. For Marie, this was twenty dollars a week, out of a paycheck that was never larger than sixty dollars, and often smaller.

Helene reacted swiftly, the tears of a practiced guilt inflictor coming to her eyes: "I can't believe how ungrateful you are. Your father and I give everything we have to you children. And now that you're working, you don't think you owe us *anything*?"

"No one I know has to pay their parents," Marie sputtered, "No one! Wait, not no one. There is one person. Jane. She does. Know why, ma? Because they put it aside for her for *college*, ma. *College.*"

"Why do you need college, anyway, Marie?" her mother continued to sniffle, but her voice never wavered, "I didn't go to college."

"Well, mom, I want to have a future," Marie began, with the frustration of one who knows her best argument will get her nowhere.

"Are you saying I had no future?" Helene seized on Marie's words like a starving man to lunch, paying little attention to the content, and growing stronger with each bite. "You think I didn't do something important with my life? That what I did wasn't good enough? I raised you, didn't I?"

Helene waited for an answer, but Marie had none except, "I have to go to work," as she picked up her uniform, "and by the way, Robert doesn't pay you anything."

"He has car insurance to pay," Helene shouted at her back, but Marie was gone.

It troubled Marie, later, that she was too self-absorbed then to notice Manny until he was a solid part of her world. It was only a matter of weeks, really, but those missing weeks became puzzling once he became vital to her. It was like finding herself leaning up against a brick wall, when all along she thought she was standing on her own. She wondered where that wall was a moment ago, and when, exactly, did the tension in her back begin to ease?

Manny bonded with the boys first. He worked alongside them, and there seemed to be an instant camaraderie that was void of the lewd framework that kept them loyal to Hans. They laughed, true, but they didn't snicker. Manny was a cool boss, but he didn't force them out of their comfort zone. True to prophecy, however, Manny did begin hitting the bars with his own boss at closing time, and often in the middle of the day. It was inevitable; no one expected anything less.

That was the extent of what she noticed. She couldn't recall, for instance, what she and Manny talked about before they started really talking. Was there even one scrap of dialogue that wasn't related to fish fillets? She thought she might recall a polite question or two, or were those directed at Jane?

It was the day Officer Calderone came in that changed everything. That she knew. She had been seeing him for the last month, "seeing him" meaning that she made out with him in his car two or three times a week, now that Ray stopped calling altogether. He was 27 years old, and already divorced, telling her, in that macho cop drawl, that his wife just couldn't "take the job." He showed Marie a small fading wedding photo he still kept in his wallet, with so many crinkles zigzagging across it, she could barely make out the face of the bride and groom. She barely cared anyway; she wanted him to forget about that woman and concentrate on *her*. Never mind that he never took her anywhere except Forest Park Drive, where, in the words of Springsteen, "desperate lovers park." Never mind that he never asked her to dinner or even a movie. Never mind that he spent most of their precious kissing time talking about his ex-wife. She was seeing a police officer ten years older than her, and he was the perfect person to fall in love with her.

There was another thing, though: he would not go beyond the making out part, no matter how hard she tempted, even looking away once when she peeled her shirt off in the dark parking lot. Officer Calderone was well aware of the law he upheld, and he was not touching her until she reached the legal age of consent.

It was just the end of a movie rush when he stopped in, and a few people were lingering at the counter, waiting for orders that were still in the fryer. She was doing the thing Hans abhorred – chatting with him while waiting for the food to appear – but Hans was off tonight. Jane was out front, collecting ketchup bottles for refilling, one of the other girls was in the back, and Manny had sent the guys out on break.

"I've got this," he said, lifting greasy cuisine out of the vat to check on it, adding to Marie, "What are you waiting for?"

"Umm, two chicken fillets, three fish fillets, and seven shrimp," she replied, checking tickets and setting empty boat-shaped paper plates single file in front of the heat lamps. One by one, she filled and removed them, as Manny produced the food – "shrimps up, chicken's up, fish is up" – and one by one, the customers took their trays and sat, until only Calderone remained at the counter.

"And what's he waiting on?" Manny asked her, gesturing towards the police officer.

"Him? Noth…" she started to say, and then slowly a smile spread across her face. She turned to Manny, and whispered, "Actually, Manny, he is waiting on my 18th birthday."

He seemed to smile, frown, and raise his eyebrows, all at the same time, but all he said was: "I'll be in the back. Call me if you need me." Then he filled up a soda that was just soda, and headed back.

"Need you for what?" Marie asked, "Food or protection?"

He turned and looked at her. This would be an eternal imprint, the way Manny looked at her. His eyes were a rich cornucopia, a deep dark basket of gifts, each one precious and every one bestowed on her in a way that pleaded for her to take them.

"Whichever one you need, Marie," he said, and looked at her one more second before he left.

And that was it. She felt the wall behind her, and she leaned against it gratefully.

******

They talked constantly after that. All right, she talked. He mostly listened. And commented. She spilled all, about Ray, the real version of Ray, how she had given herself to him and he didn't believe it, and then he had hurt her. She told Manny that he had been the only one, and how *no one* believed that, because she ran off with every boy that came along and let them do everything but. *And she didn't even know why*, why she acted so free and so wild when all she really wanted was someone to love her, the way she imagined that love should be, intense and unshakable, driven and sublime. She told him how she yearned to make something of her life, something that would earn the respect of others, so that boys would not unzip their pants in cars while fumbling for the back of her neck, assuming without asking.

She expounded on her latest dilemma; how from the 6th grade teachers wrote across her papers, "You are going to be a great author someday," or "You show true talent. Don't waste it," and how it appeared she was going to do just that. Her mother seemed to think that all it took to be a great writer was paper and pencil, and maybe that was true for Virginia Wolfe, but Marie needed more guidance. She didn't know how to translate writing into a working career that would allow her to still contribute to Helene's "living expenses."

    She told him how she and Jane talked about moving out, getting an apartment, and how her mother had flipped out when she mentioned it. Not because it was impractical or that she was worried that Marie couldn't make it on her own; no, it was more that Helene really didn't *want* Marie to make it on her own. Helene seemed to think that her daughter's successful independence somehow discredited her own existence, and she was determined not to see it happen.

    All of this overflowed from her, in between rushes or after hours or on her breaks, and Manny understood. She could tell he understood by the way he responded or sometimes didn't, sometimes just sighed or touched her hair. She felt he took the trouble to take temporary residence inside her soul, that he would not let one of her emotions slip by him without trying it on.

    She talked too much to listen, but she did learn that he was 22 – the same age as Ray – and that he had gone to college for accounting and dropped out in his senior year. He was vague about why, and Marie didn't really ask, probably because they were both content to let her do most of the divulging. From the start there was something uneven about their friendship, as if he were a toy she had opened on Christmas morning from some benevolent Santa, who expected nothing at all in return, not even good behavior. Whether she deserved him or not, Manny was hers, always hers, and she knew instinctively that she would not lose him.

    The thing they shared equally was laughter. They cracked up over everything from five to closing, and when it was busy, he scribbled notes that only she would understand on the register tape, so that when she checked an order, she broke into giggles. Once, when her pal Calderone came strolling in, Manny rushed to the register, and after ringing him up, wrote, "Are you ripe yet?" across his ticket. Marie spotted it just as she was about to lay it on his tray, and quickly pulled it back, gasping that she needed to go to the ladies' room and falling into hysterics in the back.

Jane hated working with both of them, and no wonder. They talked over her, around her, and sometimes even through her.

"Would you two shut the hell up for two minutes," Jane asked, irritated, and that just set them laughing again. For the next hour, however, they tried to be mindful of her feelings, making every effort to include her in their merrymaking, but it was no use. It was as if they were two magnets, striving to keep a piece of wood between them. The piece would inevitably slip, and they would go back to clinging fast.

Sometimes, Jane or even Hans would catch Manny refilling the ketchup bottles, or cleaning the toaster, and say, "That's not your job, what the hell are you doing that for?" and Manny would mumble something about it being dead tonight, or finishing up the books early.

"Marie," Hans would say, "what the fuck is Manny doing your job for? Can you tell me why he is doing your job? Are your fucking fingers broken?"

"I don't know, Hans," Marie would say, her glee barely contained, "Hey Manny, what the fuck are you doing my job for?"

"No way...this is *your* job?" And then they laughed again.

The truth was, he did anything for her, anything. It started with ketchup bottles and it never stopped. He listened to her speak as if every word offered a new clue to making her happy, like a piano tuner with his ear to every key to insure perfect tone. If she came to work with a slight cold, he ran out to the drugstore; if she was late returning from break, he punched her time card for her. He left countless little gifts in her locker for her to find upon her arrival, often based on things he had heard her say, and sometimes he left a ten or twenty dollar bill, if he knew she was having difficulty with her "living expenses."

Marie might have found all of this somewhat excessive; might have even surmised that one or both of them was falling in love, but she didn't. She thought of Manny as a friend. She knew it was odd for a friend to give so much and ask so little, but she closed her eyes and soaked it up like sunshine at Rockaway, the kind that warms with no hint of

51

humidity. When something is good and freely given, it is much easier to take than to question. In those days, Marie walked to and from work smiling to herself.

The friend balloon lost some air when Marie started seeing Matt, a fairly new employee. He was cute, blonde and safe, because, ironically, he was a year younger than she was; in fact, he was the youngest boy she had ever been with. He was not particularly enamored with her – in fact, he was far more passionate about the Doors, claiming that Jim Morrison was still alive and in hiding – but they managed, especially since, coincidentally, Jane had just begun breaking the work/date rule by seeing Mike. Together, they did normal teenage things, like seeing a movie, or taking the LIRR out to Nassau Coliseum to see Aerosmith, or just hanging out in each other's houses.

Manny was appalled by Ray's behavior, but he was far more put out by Matt. Marie said very little about him – there wasn't much to say, really – and so offered Manny no opportunities to push her hair out of her eyes, lift her chin and tell her that she was too extraordinary to let anyone treat her badly. If Marie was less naïve, she might have detected the hint of smug satisfaction mixed in with her friend's ready compassion when she sobbed Ray's latest transgression. It was Manny's chance to prove himself the better man, but these chances weren't readily available with Matt. And so he searched for them.

"So what are you doin' tonight?" Manny asked her casually, while counting the drawer, "Wanna go grab a cup of tea at the diner?"

She smiled. He knew not to say coffee or soda. "Can't," she said, "me and Jane and Matt and Mike are headed out for Speaks, that is, if we can get in." Speaks was a rock club out on Long Island.

"Oh, that's right, Matt's under-aged, isn't he?" Manny was now studying the rolls of nickels and pennies.

"Manny, *I'm* under-aged, too. Or did you forget?" She smiled again; she knew he wouldn't. "At least for another three months. Only Jane is 18. She's driving, so…"

He interrupted, something he never did. "Won't it be kind of weird when you're 18 and Matt isn't? Kind of like taking your baby brother out… 'I'll take a screwdriver and get a soda pop for my boyfriend here,'" he broke off in a laugh.

"I dunno. I guess. But I did the older guy thing and that didn't get me anywhere, either, now, did it?" Last week she had seen Ray walking his dog with another woman, one that looked older, well, probably his age. She was pretty, with short dark hair; unlike her long tresses that once Ray claimed to love. Marie thought of how Ray's first line to her was about the hair that hung to her waist; about the reddish highlights that reminded him of his Irish Setter. "Want to see him?" Ray had asked, and seeing the dog had been their first date.

What did he like about this woman, whose dark eyes contrasted Marie's green ones, and tall lanky figure rivaled her shorter, fuller frame? Marie studied her, and caught Ray's eye, but they said nothing. Matt or not, Marie was devastated; they had never officially broken up.

Manny was talking, but Marie was still fixated on that scene. She knew things were better now, hanging out with Jane, going actual places instead of living between damp sheets. She and Matt hadn't even slept together yet, truth is, she doubted Matt had ever slept with anyone. They were still at that fumbling kissy-feely stage, and it definitely gnawed at her that she knew so much more than he. She mulled over how to help him along without letting on that she done it, done it front and back, actually.

"I just think you're too good for him," Manny went on, "You're way more mature than he is. The other day I saw him goofing around in the back like…"

"Manny," she interrupted, "*you* think I'm better than everyone." And she wondered for a brief moment what the hell was wrong with that?

The day next she strolled to work, the same feeling of anticipation guiding her steps as always since Manny's arrival. She was anxious to tell him about her night; the band, the conversation, her mother's reaction was she arrived home over an hour late. She forgot to ask Matt if he was working today and she hoped not; she and Manny talked a lot better in his absence.

She missed the irony of that last thought: she hoped her *boyfriend* – cause that is what Matt was, right? – was not around because she wanted to be with her *friend*. This would be the first of many solid empirical truths that would escape Marie entirely in regards to Manny, and would someday cost her dearly. It calmly stood in front of her like an indisputable mathematical proof: Manny was the constant in her life, the invariable; it was he that replenished her soul when it was spent.

When she arrived, Matt was, unfortunately, working, and he looked miserable.

"That friend of yours is an asshole," he said by way of a greeting, and she continued to the back.

"What are you doing to Matt?" she asked Manny before he could speak, and she guiltily noted that her voice was playful, not indignant.

"Nothing," he replied, his eyes nearly twinkling, and she raised her eyebrows.

"Hey, he just hates to be out on deck cleaning tables, that's all. And he hates taking out the trash all the time. But he doesn't have to be a baby about it. Oh wait, he is kind of young, I keep forgetting – is he like that with you? Does he whine when you don't hold his hand crossing the street? Does he hide his head in your chest at scary movies? Does he..."

"You're terrible," Marie cut in, laughing, "and completely off-base. I'll have you know that Matt has been crossing the street alone for two weeks now."

Matt appeared just as they burst into giggles, and he shook his head and walked back out. She followed him, quick to make amends, but she knew it was going to be a very long night.

****

In fact, it was a long couple of months. Manny was too good a person to outright torture Matt, but he pounced on any occasion to make him look foolish. If Matt so much as mispronounced a word, Manny was on it. Eventually, she asked Hans to stop putting her on the schedule with Matt, claiming that he distracted her, and Hans stared at her like she had three breasts, but complied. And so it was she and Manny once again, talking through the night.

"You know, Marie," Jane said one night, "Matt really likes you. He may not show it, but he does."

"Aww, c'mon, Jane," Marie scoffed, "I'm just something to do for a while. He never looks the least bit excited to see me, never so much as tells me I look good, nothing."

"He's just intimidated by you, that's all," Jane went on. "You have your life so together, it worries him."

"*I* have my life so together? *Me*? Well, there's a switch." Marie was incredulous.

"You do. You're graduating from high school early, you'll be off working in the city soon. Matt just figures you'll leave him behind."

Because I will, Marie thought to herself. Strange, this business of being always too good for one person, not good enough for another. She was not good enough for Ray, even though what was he? The child of a line-up of foster parents, he and his sister basically dumped by alcoholic parents, and out on his own since he was 17. Matt's father, also, abandoned his mother and brother, but somehow she was too good for *him*. And she was too good for Puerto Ricans, even a respectable, hard-working one; the kind her mother would say "isn't a typical spic."

Manny had walked her home from work a few times, and her mother invited him in, and offered him something to drink. She seemed to genuinely like him, perhaps because he did the thing that Helene adored: he sat and chatted with *her*, instead of trying to disappear somewhere with Marie. Still, Marie saw something that Manny didn't; that her parents liked him within a hidden context, and certainly not the "this man would make an amazing husband for my daughter" context, that's for sure. It was more like the way people who had one black friend referred to that person as "my black friend Susan," or "I was with Susan the other day; you know her, right? The black one?" If Manny had been black, she doubted if he would have made it as far as her kitchen, but he was light enough to be "my daughter's Puerto Rican friend."

One night, some type of karma had her working with Manny, without Matt or Jane or Hans; just a bunch of new girls hired to handle the Christmas shoppers that kept the front door swinging, letting in a gust of cold air every time. With the appearance of new females, the guys were in their element, lifting their metal baskets in strut-like fashion, announcing the completion of fried fish in voices a few octaves deeper than usual. Of particular interest was a tiny Puerto Rican girl named Lucy. She had a sweet voice and a stunning face, and Marie found herself continually watching Manny, to see if he was drawn to her.

Marie was only working 5-8; a time slot coveted by all because you made your money but didn't have to clean up anything. You could walk out expounding on how great it was to have your night, even if you did come skulking back three hours later to see what everyone else was up to. A few of them walked out and didn't return – Donna never spent a second more than she had to at what she called her "place of employment" – but most of them showed up around closing time in various stages of inebriated.

Marie had plans to meet up with Matt and them later but she was entirely unenthused, even grouchy, about the prospect. She didn't want to go home, either. The truth was, she wanted to stay right where she was, because the idea of Manny closing up with Lucy was driving her mad. It not only aggravated her; it aggravated her more because she should not have cared.

They were in the middle of one of their deep, truth-seeking talks that night, the kind she loved most, when they expressed their romantic ideals, and clutched each other's hands in passionate agreement. It was suspended over and over by the influx of more customers, and each time Marie held on hard to her last thought, so as to pick up where they left off. The patrons were an irritation to her, and she impatiently threw their fish at them and raced back to Manny's side for another five or ten minute spell. They both agreed that Hans would have been aghast at their lack of professionalism.

What did they talk about? Everything. It was one of those talks you wished you could record and play back over and over. It started because Manny had asked her what she wanted for Christmas.

"I want…peace. And not on Earth, either. In my head. I want to rest. I'm seventeen and I'm so tired."

She told him how her brother was in love, with her childhood friend of all people. She told him how she could cry seeing Robert carefully pick out a Christmas gift for Trish, how they had gone to the mall together and he picked up silky blouses or hair ornaments and kept saying, "Trish would look great in this. Wouldn't Trish look great in this?"

"Know what I'm getting Matt?" she went on, "A black light poster. That's it. A freaking black light poster."

"Well, what's he getting you?" There was no Matt-bashing tonight. Manny knew it wasn't necessary.

"I have no idea. But I'm guessing he isn't giving me peace." She looked into Manny's eyes, and something almost dawned on her.

"You and I are idealists, Marie. We have an image of how we think things should be. We hate settling for less than that image." Manny spoke wistfully, shaking his head slightly as if shaking off a less than perfect version of life.

Marie punched out at 8, and then stayed another hour to sit in the office while Manny pretended to do the books. They were high on how naturally they connected, giddy with the intoxicating blend of their thoughts. She surely must have been drunk, because she had trouble standing up. Twice she tried, saying almost inaudibly, "I've got to meet Matt," and twice sitting right back down again, until someone up front yelled for Manny, and Marie finally left.

She walked home in a stupor, snippets of conversation repeating in her head, and when she reached her front door, she sailed past her mother and father watching TV and headed straight for the telephone.

"Arthur Treachers Fish and Chips, thank you for calling, may I help you?" Hans was the one who insisted that they all say the whole thing, even though it came out rushed and indistinct.

"Manny," she began, hesitated and kept going, "Manny, what is going on with us?"

"I love you," he answered. "I love you. That is what is going on with us."

She hung up, dazed, then picked up the phone to cancel her plans with Matt. Three hours later, she went back to Arthur Treachers, telling her mother she forgot something, and walked past Lucy cleaning the toaster oven and straight to the back.

"Hey," he said, with an attempt at lightheartedness, "I thought you were going out. Why did you come back?"

"Because you love me," she told him. "I came back because you love me. Do you want to go to the diner?" And then she started crying.

******

There may have been a few days after where Marie actually considered having a real relationship with Manny. She kept his words a secret, kept them like gems in a tiny treasure chest, opening it to gaze upon them in awe. The jewels served no real purpose, since Marie did not return Manny's love, but they were precious nonetheless, and she glorified in just owning them. They were her security, her hidden kitty, something to smile about in the middle of her worst day. She remembers last summer, going over to her older sister's house on the most brutal of hot days because Ann and her husband had a pool. Once she arrived, though, she would never actually go in the water. She and Ann would just lie in lounge chairs next to it, because just knowing it was there was enough. Manny's love was like that. It was enough to just know it was there. Once a day Marie whispered it to herself – "he loves me" – and for a moment, felt the peace she longed for.

Now she and he had new things to talk about. She wanted to know how and when he knew how he felt, and he told her that it was instant, that the minute he saw her guarding the trickling vodka, he knew. And then they began backtracking, conjuring different scenes from the past three months, asking, "What were you really thinking when I did such and such?" and "Oh my god, remember the day I touched your hand and..." and "I almost told you when..." and of course, "I was crushed when you slept with Matt."

Still, it didn't trouble Manny that she didn't say, "I love you, too." He didn't offer his feelings as something she was obligated to pay for. He was content enough to love her and have her know it and accept it. He lavished gifts upon her now without an ounce of restraint, and when Christmas came he presented her with a necklace that held a gold locket, on the back of which he had engraved three words: "Peace. Love, Manny."

Marie didn't give him a Christmas gift. She hadn't a clue what to give him. Well, she chipped in with the rest of the crew to give him two tickets to a Broadway play, but when he asked her to go with him, she promptly refused. Flustered and confused, she feebly mumbled that Matt would be pissed off, but what sense did that make? Did Matt ever say he loved her?

And that was another sticky situation. Now that Manny had confessed, should she still share with him the graphic details of her ridiculous sex life? Surely he had been imagining such things all along, but she didn't *know* he was, and that made her feel suddenly shy.

Still, those were mere details, as insignificant as worrying about paying taxes on a billion dollar lottery win. Marie won, and she glowed with Christmas spirit that year, even though her mother told her that she would be using the occasion to get Marie much needed "interview clothes." Manny's love was a basis for belief in herself, and with belief, came hope.

She would always remember the Christmas party at Treacher's that year. Happiness, Marie had found, was a photo op, a thing that startles like the flash on her father's instamatic. You're in the moment, tingling to your toes but somehow unaware, when there is a bright light and a second of clarity: 'Oh, I know what this is! This is happiness.' Is it any wonder people take photo after photo of joyful occasions, to study in their darker times?

Coincidentally, Marie had her father's camera that night, and she caught her friends unawares with it, her *friends*. It was difficult not to feel sentimental about them; even the ones who made her feel stupid, like Donna. Tonight Marie compulsively touched their sleeves when she talked, her cheeks flushed with alcohol and exhilaration. And all the while she felt Manny's eyes cherishing her; she could look away and know he never did. It emboldened her to match Hans, insult for insult, making the others say, "Whoooa...she got you there!" and watching them laugh with tears streaming down their faces. All this, she caught on film, and even though there was no photo of her in the envelope she picked up later from the drugstore, she could feel herself in every frame.

Matt got completely wasted, and so Jane, the only one amongst them who possessed a car, offered to drive him home. The stars began to align, and Manny pulled his eyes off her to diligently rip the label off a beer bottle. They stayed on task until Matt was safely gone, then rose slowly, and Marie nearly dropped hers before they made contact.

"So, I guess I'll walk you home, then?" he sort of asked.

"I guess," she answered.

Hans had probably sucked down two bottles of straight vodka, but he was instantly alert.

"Yeah, Manny, what don't you walk Marie home?" he gushed, but without a slur. "You really should. It's not like you have anywhere else to go. Right, Manny? You just have your *empty* house to go home to. Take your time, Manuel. It's not like someone's *waiting* for you."

"What was that about?" Marie asked, when they were outside. They could see their breath, but enjoyed the false warmth of liquid spirits.

"That? Oh, you know...Hans." He walked close but didn't touch her. He was quiet, but that was okay. They both could feel the night in that extra-sensory way, smelling the ink and tobacco from the closed newsstand, hearing the metallic clink of cheap Christmas bells, feeling the rumble of a distant train.

"Cold tonight," he said, but that was just a space he needed to fill.

"Manny, I…" she began, but she was not used to drinking, and so a long line of profound and insightful phrases were swirling and bumping into each other behind her eyes, "I…really have to pee."

"Well, you're out of luck there," he said with a grin, and they stopped in the middle of the street, their bodies pivoting to take in closed doorways all around, "Nothing's open. Come on, it's not much further."

For an answer, Marie settled herself comfortably in the recessed doorframe of some pizza place, and he instinctively moved against her. Marie recognized this setup; the one where a boy trapped her up against something, and conveniently forgot that she had put herself there first. She wondered dizzily if these countless alcoves on Ridgewood streets were created for just this purpose, for boys to dominate and girls to plead innocent.

She remembered hearing that good Catholic girls never opened their mouths or lifted their hips willingly; they were obligated to put up some sort of fight, so as to stare God shamelessly in the face when the fight was lost. Marie had more or less followed this philosophy primarily because it was remarkable for heightening male ardor, although there were consequences if you ever decided the fight was real. There were words for girls like that.

This wasn't a boy, though; this was Manny. Her mouth fell open as if tired and her eyes fell shut as if in agreement, and he kissed her slowly and tentatively, as if waiting for her to realize who was doing it.

She would have liked to say that it was earth shattering, love's true kiss, sure to awaken her from some deep and lonely sleep. It wasn't. Indeed, the most noteworthy thing about kissing Manny was the lack of urgency, the kissing part being the entire event, not a precursor to better things. One of Manny's hands was cupping her chin, the other supporting himself against the peeling paint of the doorway, and neither moved on to more appealing areas, which may have been hard to find under her coat anyway. When they pulled apart for a second, it wasn't to look from right to left to summon up where to possibly find a suitable horizontal surface. It was apparently just to breathe, and they did, and then kissed one more time.

Marie didn't know exactly how long this went on, but she knew why it ended. She became increasingly aware of his weight against her full bladder, and she gently pushed him off. For him it signified that she had possibly come to her senses, and so he whispered, "I love you," sadly before standing straight and turning away.

They walked the rest of the way quietly, an arms length apart, until they turned on to her block. Then he stopped, and she went on a few paces until she realized it, and turned to face him.

"I love you," he said again, as if he felt a great need to redeem himself for some irrepressible action on his part.

Marie looked down and said the words she would say a thousand times in their lifetime, until the day the right ones came to her.

"I know." She looked up and found his eyes, and said it again: "I know." Then she turned and they continued walking to her door.

******

Of course Helene was awake when she got home. She was doing a crossword puzzle at the kitchen table, but quickly pushed it aside.

"Well, it's about time you showed up" she began immediately, "Everyone else is already home, and I'm dying to go to bed."

It was like someone had just stripped away warm blankets on a frosty cold morning. Marie was still mentally trying to yank them back, to get to that place where she was before, but she was groggy and Helene held tight.

"Ma, I told you, you don't have to wait up for me…" but Helene stopped her cold.

"Why are your cheeks so red?" she asked.

"It's cold outside, Ma." She had so wanted to make it to the safety of her room, to slip herself between real blankets and savor her evening, pulling out each part for delicious scrutiny, especially the end. No such luck.

"Not that cold," came the rebuttal. "If it were that cold, your lips would be blue. Your lips are red, too, swollen…like someone's been kissing you. Who's been kissing you?" Helene moved in for a closer look, as if a clue to her violator's identity may still rest on her mouth.

"Yeah, right, ma, my lips look like someone's been kissing me." Marie was only able to pull off a derisive tone because she truly didn't know lips could swell from locking with another pair. She thought her mother was making it up.

"Who walked you home?" Helene continued, looking through Marie to see if someone still lurked there. "You didn't walk home alone."

Ahh, now there was a Catch 22. Either answer served to incriminate her. One invited a barrage of further questions, the other a lecture on how unsafe the streets were at night.

"Manny walked me home." She gave him up, and waited.

"Manny? *Manny* walked you home?" It wasn't the answer Helene was expecting, but it was workable. "What does Manny want with you, anyway?"

"He's just a friend, ma. He doesn't want anything."

"I don't think so, Marie. He hangs around you entirely too much."

"Ma, he's a friend. I have to pee," she added, remembering, finally, that she had a valid excuse for cutting the conversation short.

"Let me tell you something, Marie," Helene had a habit of speaking to Marie's departing form often these days, "I've lived way longer than you, so depend on the wisdom of my years. Listen to me. Men and women cannot *be* 'just friends'. It isn't possible. Someone always wants more."

"Well, then, I guess he wants more," Marie said, already two steps up.

******

Marie didn't see Manny for a few days after that, and she always considered that lapse as something akin to a lengthy scene change in a play, a time when things went on behind the curtains that were soon to be revealed. When the players returned, they had a fresh purpose, something they had plotted in the semi-darkness. The setting, too, had changed, although upon closer inspection, a shrewd audience could see it was simply a new arrangement of the same things.

There was no real plot, however, the "players" simply revealed what had been there all along, shaming the spectators for not noticing sooner. Upon checking her schedule, Marie found that for the first time, she was working on Manny's day off. That was a Sunday. Monday found her jittery and inattentive in school, her anticipation of her first "post-kiss" conversation with Manny sapping her to the point of exhaustion. Her hand wandered repeatedly to clutch the locket around her neck, as if it would still her.

Upon arrival at Treachers, however, she found to her dismay and disbelief that he had taken the evening off. She was thirty minutes early, and strode to the back with the purpose of an addict about to score a fix. Hans sat in the office.

"Hey, Marie." He knew. She knew he knew that she was perturbed. It showed in how few words he used, how he used her name instead of some derogatory term of endearment. They both knew what question was suspended between them, and she wouldn't ask where Manny was because he still might appear. She tried to keep her eyes from straying, from searching for him like some lost puppy.

"You're early," Hans said, still enjoying the moment. "Trying to catch up on tidying your locker?"

"Nah, just had nowhere to go," she said casually. Pride would not allow her to ask Hans about Manny. Still Marie felt forsaken, reminiscent of weeks of waiting for the phone to ring after a night with Ray. Shouldn't the kiss have affected Manny deeply? Shouldn't *he* have been the one who could not wait another day for the chance of picking up where they left off? Suddenly, no excuse for his absence seemed good enough; if he loved her, he should be there tonight. They should be sharing impassioned glances under the heat lamps, where right now only a forlorn row of fish fillets kept warm.

Perhaps Marie's last vestige of hope came from her trust in the look Manny gave her when he pulled away from her lips and stated his feelings. Could anyone fake so tender an expression? The tiniest seed of her womanly wisdom began to sprout in that instant, as she scanned her memory for a time when she had been duped by a look such as that. It had never happened. This was real, she resolved, and it quieted her opposing inner voices, if not forever, at least long enough to get to closing time.

She was listlessly wiping down the counters when Hans came through to lock the front doors. He was singing.

"I wanna kiss you all over...and over again," he drawled.

"Matt picking you up tonight?" Hans asked, vaguely looking around.

"No," she faltered, "He's...busy."

"Well, I'll walk you home," Hans said, and in the absence of a good excuse, Marie accepted his offer. For the second time in less than a week, she found herself walking home in silence with one of her bosses. This night was much colder, and the quiet more uncomfortable, so she kept the pace.

"So, you and Manny are real *pals*, huh?" he sneered.

"I mean," Hans went on, "the guy is such a pussy around you."

"We're friends," she said. Marie's 'friend' homily was starting to sound as practiced as her old 'guitar on the bed' one, but Hans stopped it cold with a deliberate snicker.

"Yes, I *know*, Marie, you're *friends*," he dragged out the word. "That's his story, too, ya know. Of course, he spent $125 on that pretty locket around your neck, but I guess that's just what *good* friends do."

Marie's hand rose as if to defend the locket, but it was well protected by layers of down and nylon. She kept waiting for Hans' point. *Was* he jealous? Because if he sought to make her miserable by telling her a man spent a chunk of money on her, he was definitely taking the wrong approach.

"I'm sure his wife understood that you were just friends when she found the receipt in his pocket."

She stopped, partly because of what he said, and partly because they were passing the pizza place, which was forever holy ground for her. Remembering what had transpired there fueled her, and she boldly looked up at Hans and smiled.

"Manny *isn't* married," she said with conviction, and turned to keep going.

"Really?" he said, with the voice of a talk show host, "That's interesting."

"He *isn't*," she went on, and then asked triumphantly, "Then what is his *wife's* name?" as if the inability to produce a suitable name discredited the entire supposition.

"Madeline." Hans answered quickly. "She's ugly and fat. I asked Manny how a little guy like him manages to do *her*. Does he have to balance on top of her or something?" The image apparently delighted Hans, because he was now laughing to himself.

They were now upon her block, and the spot where Manny said 'I love you' again those few nights ago. She repeated to Hans, "I know Manny isn't married. We talk about everything. He would tell me if he was married."

Even as she said this, she realized something. *They* didn't talk about everything. *She* talked about everything. *He* listened. He *responded.* He confirmed and comforted. He expressed ideas and ideals but not actual facts. In all their conversations about love, he had never mentioned being in that state, or having his heart broken, or any other point of reference. She provided all the tangible material for their intangible topics, and she was too narcissistic to notice.

Marie knew Manny would have some explanation. She wanted to race into her house and call him, and it killed her now that she couldn't. When they reached her front gate, she turned to Hans and said forcefully, "Well, it does *not* matter *if* Manny has a wife. We are *just* friends."

"Sure, sure, if you say so," Hans said.

****

If Monday was a nail-biting extravaganza for Marie, Tuesday was nothing short of mental hell. She considered not going to school at all, just lying in bed and counting the hours until she could confront Manny. To extend the pattern of cruel ironies, tonight Manny was working and she was off, but that would not deter her; she would stop by as soon as she could escape her house. Helene's new thing was "family time," an edict that became effective as each child acquired more and more independence.

"This is not a fast food joint," she'd say over the dinner table, "You cannot eat and take off. I would like to see you once in a while, too."

Helene's latest matriarchal ruling may have been a reaction to a remark by her own father, who jokingly mentioned that their house was starting to resemble a kennel full of female dogs in heat: "Every male in the neighborhood seems to come sniffing around." Helene was sensitive to comments like these from her father, and her knee-jerk reaction was to draw her flock closer.

Not tonight. Marie ate, washed, dried, put away dishes, all to the beat of her pounding heart, and then she mustered all the authority that she could to say she was going out for one hour.

"One hour," Helene confirmed and Marie was out the door, racing past all the doorways that might have contained other lovers on other nights.

She burst through the tinted front door, and found him out front, wiping down the tables. She didn't allow him to say "hello" or "what's up?" or anything, she just strode breathlessly to his side and let out her question like an overfilled balloon spurts air upon blessed release.

"Manny, are you married?"

He stopped, put down his rag. He dropped his hands at his sides like one surrendering, and answered her.

"Yes," he said. "Yes I am," and waited for some response from her. When none came, he went on.

"I got married 8, no, 9 months ago," he began, picking the washrag up so as to maintain the façade of working, "on March 11. I don't know why I didn't tell you."

He continued on to the next table, and Marie followed, watching him sweep away the unsightly remains of another's food. For a moment they both studied congealed tartar sauce as if scraping it off was a mutual problem of considerable proportion. Then he continued cleaning, and speaking.

"It was a mistake right from the first," he said, "I knew almost within an hour of saying the words 'I do.' Maybe I knew it beforehand, too, but I didn't know what to do about it. Like being on a train you can't stop."

She smiled; she and Manny both resorted easily into metaphors. They reached for images to give fuller clarity to their heartfelt expressions, only he said she did it better than he did. Perhaps he just gave her more opportunity.

"Anyway…Madeline," he had a tough time releasing her name, making her official, "insisted on the wedding. That's not an excuse. She just threatened…different things if we didn't do it."

For the next hour, Marie followed Manny as he swept, scraped, wiped and talked. She learned that Madeline was his college girlfriend, at Baruch in the city, and felt her first pang of jealousy. Marie could not even name a college, but Madeline, *she* was educated. Time would disprove this theory, but it didn't help at the moment. Right now it just hurt.

"In our senior year," he went on, ever moving, "she had this idea. She said we should drop out of school, and get married instead. I don't know why I even considered it. I was in school for accounting, did I tell you that?" Marie nodded, remembering that he said he dropped out of school, and chastising herself for an unforgivable lack of curiosity as to why.

"I was a great student," he mumbled, "and my education meant a lot to my parents. At first I said no to Madeline, but she cried so much. She said we could always go back and finish later. She screamed...said I didn't love her...she even said she would kill herself. So registration came and went, I didn't register, and I told my mom and dad."

The next table was clean, so he sat and dropped the rag, physically demonstrating his defeat. Marie sat across from him, facing the door to be on watch for visiting owners. She was intent on not interrupting, and so waited as he sat shaking his head for a few minutes.

"The next part is the hardest," he went on. "Soon after registration ended, she called me. She said her parents freaked out when she told them she was dropping out, and that they *made* her register. *Made* her," he repeated, looking briefly at Marie.

"I guess there were things I could have done. I could have gotten back in, somehow. I sound like such a faggot, to use Hans' words. She begged me to marry her anyway, said don't worry, I would finish school. And we got married," he finished, picking up the rag again and looking around the deck.

The tables were clean, but they continued walking in a circle around the store, as if waiting to catch crumbs as they fell.

"I helped her graduate, do you believe that? I helped her cram for exams, and I wrote her papers for her," he said, shaking his head again, "But it didn't matter in the end. I took a job at Jack-in-the-Box so we could live, and she works in a department store. I switched to Treachers because there were too many hold-ups at Jack-in-the-Box. Did I ever tell you I was held up at gunpoint?" he asked, smiling.

"You can still graduate," Marie whispered fervently. She wanted to take his hands as she spoke, but they were still in motion, pausing here and there to add emphasis to a phrase, and walking on.

"Manny," she went on, "You can go back to school. You can go part-time." She really had no idea what she was talking about, but it sounded viable; everything seemed possible for people other than herself. She reached out, and touched his shoulder, stopping him for a second.

"Manny," she repeated, "You can get divorced." She said it triumphantly, as if she had just solved a math equation that thus far had escaped brilliant minds.

He turned, faced her, and put both hands on her shoulders. "Marie," he said gently, as if addressing a child, "Spanish people do not get divorced." And that was when Katos entered the store, and Manny went on to the next spotless table, scrubbing as if trying to remove the color. She turned to walk away, towards the kitchen, slowly as if she had just arrived and needed to check her schedule.

"Wait," he said softly, and she did, aching for as many words out of his mouth as he could utter before Katos reached his side.

"I said I didn't know why I didn't tell you. But I do. I wanted what was happening with us to be real."

"I just wish I didn't have to hear it from Hans," she replied, and turned, forgetting she was bound for the kitchen. Instead she headed for the door, muttering an absent, "Hey, Katos," as she passed him, and stepping out into the frigid night air. These was cruel, these short intervals of conversation that left her dizzy with new information. Crueler still were the few blocks she had to process it all, before arriving home.

"That wasn't an hour," Helene's omnipresent voice came from somewhere, and Marie settled in for a long night of 'family time.'

****

Of course Marie forgave Manny, but there was no more kissing in doorframes. There was no decision to stop; it just did not happen anymore. Instead, they devoted their affection to a more balanced exchange of friendship. They spoke of everything except that single kiss, and if Manny felt a loss, he didn't show it.

If Marie had to describe their relationship to anyone, she might say, "We are just friends except he loves me," as if this were a happy glitch. She might more honestly admit that they were friends *because* he loved her, but she would never say, "We are friends because I love him." She saw no connection between friendship and love. Love was passion, and she could not see it in the way they savored words from each other mouths, or laughed with simultaneous pleasure, or fell silent when overcome with the strength of their bond. She did not analyze why she could not wait for the next time their minds would mesh. Love was passion, but he was peace.

A few things transpired in the weeks that followed. First, Manny's wife visited the store, whether to confirm her own existence or confirm the existence of the locket around Marie's neck, no one knew. Marie found her instantly distasteful, and decided irrefutably that her opinion was unbiased. Madeline was large and loud, quelling all Marie's fears of an attractive, educated woman. Marie was surprised to see she was not Puerto Rican, although Manny said she was half Spanish, and did her best to hide it.

She stayed about an hour, and there was never a moment that she wasn't obvious, asking Manny questions about dinner and shopping and curtains and anything else that proved they shared a life. She was sure to mention insignificant personal details from far across the counter, her nasally voice filling the store, although Marie guessed whose ears they were intended for. Naïve about men, perhaps, but Marie knew exactly what women did to one another. Some were subtle when staking their claim, but Madeline was pathetically transparent. Marie looked once at Manny and made a silent date to discuss it later.

"God, Manny, she is awful. What were you *thinking*?" Marie was gleeful; there was no contest here.

"I don't know," Manny said quietly, and Marie straightened her face and remembered she was supposed to be a friend.

"Well, I mean, what *were* you thinking?" She modified her tone, not the question. "Did you love her?"

"I don't know," he said again, "She was the first real girlfriend I ever had. And things were fun in our college days. I stood under her window and threw rocks, and climbed up and snuck in her bed." Manny was talking mostly to himself. "I think maybe she was just my first steady source of sex."

"So you *married* her?" Marie quipped, in the voice of a radio helpline host, concerned for the caller but maintaining disdain for the benefit of the others that were tuned in for entertainment. "For *sex*?"

"I didn't marry her for sex, Marie," he answered, and the weary wisdom in his tone stilled her, "but when you are young, you confuse lust with love. You love doing it so much, you think you love the person you're doing it with."

Marie did not appreciate the image of Manny loving anything but her, however misguided that love was. She strove to get their conversation back on track, the soothing repetition of Madeline jibes.

"Yeah, but how could even the sex be good with *her*?" Once again, Marie forgot to question the fervor in her protest.

"Sex is always good until you know it can be better," he replied, looking at her meaningfully, and erasing her demons. "I love you, by the way."

"I know," Marie answered. And she did. "Manny," she added, "You need to get away from that woman. You need a divorce."

"Okay," he smiled, "Want to tell her together tomorrow? I'd be careful, though, she is bigger than both of us." That ended the conversation, but Marie wondered, in her teenage innocence, what was so hard about getting divorced.

The next incident gave Manny cause for glee. There was a party at Pete's house, and Marie couldn't go, a result of one of Helene's arbitrary decisions: "Just stay home tonight, for once." Somewhere in between the first keg and the second, Matt made out with the new girl, Lucy, in the back seat of Jane's Toyota.

She knew immediately that something was up the next day at work. Everyone tiptoed around her, looking at her sympathetically, until finally she got the information out of Pete by pretending she already knew. Marie could hardly believe that Matt, so unworthy of her, could betray her, but when Manny walked in with a spring in his step and his eyes fairly dancing, she knew it was true.

"You're happy about this?" she accused him.

"I wouldn't say *happy*, exactly. Just…" he stopped when her eyes brimmed with tears, "Oh, c'mon. He isn't worth it. I'm just…I thought this would help you realize it."

It didn't. Matt's misbehavior only increased Marie's resolve to keep him, and that is what she did, right up until the day that Brendan re-entered her life.

Chapter Four: Midtown

Marie graduated from high school in January, in a lonely ceremony shared mostly with students who were graduating late. She was still two weeks away from turning 18, and she felt that her life was over.

She soon began her long days of schlepping into the city for job interviews. Dressed in long skirts and high boots, chosen by Helene, she prayed that somehow being clad by her mother would guarantee some measure of success.

Job-hunting, Marie found, was the ultimate form of humiliation. Instead of warding off life's demeaning moments, she was now actively seeking them, walking from plush office to plush office to openly display her inadequacies. For a moment or two, some prospective employers might be fooled by the package she presented, but once past Helene's embellishments, they would inevitably issue a typing test, and their eyebrows would rise at the results.

Marie got used to sitting on lush leather sofas, under the disdainful eye of elderly secretaries, fidgeting in new pantyhose while waiting to be rejected. It was during those times that Manny carried her; she sat, staring at the black tips of her wasted boots, and clung to her mantra: "I can't type, I can't take dictation, but Manny loves me. I can't be that bad." It was the earliest rendition of the background music of her life, a hymn of hope and self-preservation.

Headhunters sighed when she returned, offer-less, and shuffled papers on their desks, mumbling, "Whatever will we *do* with you?" and then, "What about this one? It doesn't pay much, but with your skills…" and sent her out again to less luxurious places with fewer names gilded on squeaky clean glass doors.

After a particularly grueling day of rejections, Marie burst into Treachers, scanning for Manny, and thought she would die if he had taken the night off.

"Is Manny in the back?" she asked her sister, who had recently begun working there.

"Yup," she answered, "He isn't alone, though. He's surrounded by Greeks."

Marie walked to her locker, straining at the office door to hear what was going on. She got a soda, and paced, tried to talk with Lisa, and paced again.

"Happy birthday, by the way," Lisa said, "Legal at last. Finally you can drink."

At last, Katos and Jim opened the office door, and Marie suffered through their lame pleasantries before they walked out the front door.

She ran to the back to tell Manny about her day, but for once, he went first.

"Guess what, Marie? I'm leaving this store. Katos said I'm needed in the Flushing store. Next week is my last week." And now, they both looked miserable.

They had a little going away thing for Manny, and Marie gently stored away the moments that would close one of her chapters. She was pretty sure she would not hear from Manny again, that those perfunctory words, "Keep in touch," really meant nothing at all. 'We don't even possess each other's home telephone numbers, for chrissake,' she thought, their entire lives having only been lived within the confines of a fast-food restaurant.

Marie stayed on at Treachers, but it lost its luster, and now, she was finally getting some ideas about her future.

****

Periods of change were usually blurry to Marie, transitional tornados that scattered familiar things aside, and landed her with a bang in a whole new place. She related to the tiny breathless "oh" that popped out of Dorothy's mouth, when the twister released her house and the ground rushed to meet it, and she realized the swirling had stopped. Marie had an identical jolt just a few weeks after Manny's farewell bash. She looked up one afternoon, and found herself sitting at her desk in the media department of Compton Advertising.

She was typing on her IBM Selectric, at her own careful pace, in front of the

Assistant Media Director's office, her boss, Joe Hayeck. Marie felt a sudden tingle that made her pause over the keys, a moment of contentment announcing itself with a soft touch. She looked down the long hallway lined with other clattering secretaries, and her eyes rested on her brother Robert's girlfriend, Trish. She was the reason Marie had gotten the job, putting in a good word with Ann Maguire, the personnel director. Miss Maguire was kind, and Marie typed a bit better than usual on her test; and suddenly, here she was.

Marie *wanted* this. She wanted it badly. Compton didn't have the prestige of a J. Walter Thompson or an Ogilvy and Mather, but it was swanky enough for Marie, occupying six floors of a Madison Avenue office building, with real *departments*, like executive, media and creative, the latter of which was Marie's eventual goal.

"Media department, may I help you?" The phone broke Marie's reverie. She loved answering it, loved the professional sound of her voice, and sometimes she substituted, 'Marie Meyers speaking' instead of 'May I help you?' just to feel it roll off her tongue. When her boss' line rang, she had to say; "Joe Hayeck's office," and even that carried great magnitude for her, being so entrusted to care for another.

Joe was a droll man in his 50's, tall, fit and balding. He was vague and lightly sarcastic, and it was difficult to tell when he was serious. At the interview, he asked Marie what she 'could do.'

"Well, I can type, and take some shorthand," she said helplessly, torn between sense and sensibility: the need to get the job and the obligation to be honest about her skills.

"Typing's good," he said, nodding, "As you can see, we have typewriters here."

"Well, want to see my resume?" she entreated, looking for anything that would keep her from further spoken words, "It's in my bag."

"A resume? How can you have a resume? You haven't done anything yet," he said, but not unkindly.

"Well, I worked, and I went to school," Marie's jaw rose, and her mantra sung softly in her ears.

"Well, I thought you might have gone to school," he said, "No need to prove it. Ms. Maguire sent you up here so I guess that means you are all right. She has no real reason to harm me. Do you have any questions?"

Marie had heard that intelligent questions – ones that reflected some knowledge of the company – are imperative on an interview, but she could think of none. The thoughts that kept popping into her subconscious weren't questions at all—they were pleas: Please let me stay here. Please give me this job. Please don't fire me in a week.

Finally, she sputtered, "Can I still have a week off in summer? I have a vacation planned."

"Well, I guess so," Joe replied, standing, "although I don't know how we will get on without you for a week. 'We' means the people you will be working for. Let's go meet them."

And that is how she got here, she happily concluded, and went back to typing. Marie worked for Joe and a media planner named Mary Ann, and a media planner in training named Sharon, a secretary whose promotion opened the spot for Marie. Her annual salary was $7, 876, and she had no idea if it was good or bad. She only knew what she felt: that life had begun in some recognizable fashion, and now her voices were frenetic whispers, urging her to find her way. Helene's pressure, Ann Maguire's pity, and even Manny's love were not going to take her where she wanted to be.

****

Her romance with Matt was fizzling; they were just going through the motions without much enthusiasm, doubling with Mike and Jane, and hitting the same old haunts. There is no place like Manhattan to instill a touch of newfound superiority in a person, perhaps even snobbery, and Marie felt much more than a river's width away from Queens when she walked the city's spirited streets. When the four of them went to see the Kinks at "the Garden," Marie felt that she had led them to *her* city; she now knew 34th Street as part of a metropolis, and not just a train stop. She walked up to Central Park on sunny days, sitting in Grand Army Plaza under the green general on his green horse with red testicles, wondering if it was a shortage of paint or lack of weathering that caused the stark color disparity. She ate her first croissant, telling her boss Mary Ann that she had just eaten this "delicious flaky thing with ham and cheese inside," and blushing when Mary Ann told her the name as if it were less than revolutionary. She grew woozy on incense in a store called Azuma on Lexington and 54th, she relished the size of bookstores, and she rubbernecked her way through Bloomingdale's and Saks Fifth Avenue, marveling at all the sparkle and the conspicuous lack of price tags.

Joe never ate out. He was far too frugal for that. Marie adored Joe, although she was often taken aback by his humor. Once, when his wife called, she delivered the message as he was walking back to his office.

"Would that be my first wife that called?" he asked.

"I...don't know," Marie stammered. She hated making mistakes.

"Well, did she give her *name*?" he continued.

"No, she just said your wife. I just assumed you would...I'm sorry."

"That would be Teri," Joe said, nodding his head, "my first wife. She never gives her name when she calls."

Marie felt redeemed, then thought of something. "Well, what is your second wife's name, so I know, in case she called."

"Oh, I don't have a second wife," Joe told her, stone-faced, "just the one wife."

"But you called her your first wife! I'm confused."

"Well, she is my first wife, isn't she? She is the first woman I ever married. Hopefully, she'll be my last." And he turned and walked into his office.

When she got off the train at night, she was chock full of her latest "Joe stories," and entertained her mother with them. Like the time he put two invitations on her desk with a note on top that simply had the number "2" and a picture of a nose. Or the time he asked for a paper fastener by playing charades, lifting both arms straight up, then spreading them horizontally across. Or the time she heard him say, "help" in a low voice from behind her, and walked in to find him on the floor, having leaned back too far in his swivel chair.

Helene was glad to see Marie so content, and "I told you so" was often beneath the surface of her statements. To her mother, a secretarial position for the second in command in the media department was success enough, and she had no idea of the aspirations that burned in her daughter. She was sure they put the college issue aside forever, and raised Marie's "living expenses" to better reflect her current salary.

They had a bitter argument soon after Marie got her driver's license. Helene wasted no time telling her that now she would be expected to pay something towards car insurance.

"Ma, I don't even drive the car! No one ever lets me!" Marie's words were choked with frustration that bordered on rage, and she clenched her hands together and held tight on to her tears.

"Well, you might," Helene said, "Even if you borrow it once, you need to be put on our car insurance. What if you got into an accident?"

Marie thought of her humble paycheck, beaten and starved by too many insatiable hands. The irony of working in a prosperous city was that it cost money – money just to get there, money to eat there, and money to look like you belonged there. At 18, Marie already had credit card debt, having obtained a Lerners account and used it to further enhance her wardrobe. Helene's contribution stopped at interview outfits, except for the dreaded days she arrived home with bags and said to Marie, "I bought you a jacket (or a skirt, or a blouse). You owe me $40.00." Marie may have indeed needed the featured article of clothing, but she needed to establish her own pace for purchases, and to learn which needs were immediate, and which would have to wait.

Marie put on her most patient, loving voice, and hoped for the best. She still had faith in words, maintaining that misunderstanding came from putting them in erroneous order, or with offensive intonation. "Mom," she said, "I cannot afford car insurance. I can't afford the clothes you keep bringing home. I know you mean well, but I'm trying…" she bit her lip and braced herself, "to save for college."

"You don't need college, Marie," Helene returned, equally patient, "You already have a job. You need clothes. And I need car insurance money."

The next day, Marie walked to a pawnshop on Metropolitan Avenue, and hocked her high school ring, and a gold bracelet from some long ago Christmas. She paid her mother one hundred dollars, and Helene never asked how she found the money after all. Marie couldn't part with Manny's locket, however. She still kept it safe around her neck, as a hopeful prayer for the peace it represented.

In June, Marie slipped into Joe's office and asked if he had a minute.

"Just a minute? I think so. I wonder why they say, "If a task is once begun, never leave it til it's done?" That isn't true. See all these projects on my table? One thing you should know is that you should never finish one project and start another, no. You start them all. That way if, say, Procter and Gamble calls and says, 'what's the status of my primetime buys?', you don't say, 'well, I don't know, I've been doing taking care of Austin Nichols this week.' Get it?" He took one last loving look at his plans, and then focused on her, "Okay, I have a minute now."

"I need to leave early today. But don't tell anyone. I have to go to my prom."

"Prom? Like a high school prom?"

"Yes. You see, I graduated, but my boyfriend…didn't yet. So I'm kind of going to his prom, I guess. Don't tell anyone!" she said again.

"My lips are sealed," he said, "Don't you go telling anyone by mistake, now. Anything else?"

"Yes. Remember when I first started here, you said I could still take a week off in summer?" Marie was still shy around her boss.

"I said *that*? Wow, I must have really wanted you on board. Well, yes, if you say I said it, I suppose you wouldn't lie. Where are you going?"

"Lake George," Marie answered, "the second week of July. If that's okay."

"Well, I hope you aren't going with the prom king," Joe scolded, then added, "Never mind! Don't tell me if you are. I don't want to know."

Marie giggled. "I'm going with my friend...my *girl*friend. I used to go there every year as a kid, and we thought we'd go together."

"As a *kid*, you say? My goodness, what are you *now*?"

I have no idea, Marie thought, but rose slowly from her chair. "I'm going to the Xerox room for MaryAnn," she said, "Need anything?"

When she returned from Xeroxing, there was a note on pink, 'While you were out' paper. It said, "Vacation approved. And by the way, the prom king called."

****

Summer began, Marie's first without freedom. Each morning, she dutifully rode the stifling subway, sharing the same oppressive air with other watery sufferers, stooping towards an unseen ocean as if it were the city of Mecca. In truth she was okay with it, having to become a weekend dweller at the beach and spending the other five days in central air conditioning, but she would never display this acceptance in front of her mother. She wanted some sympathy for the loss of her precious summer days, but there were certainly easier things to be found.

Advertising agencies obviously considered their people to be the most delicate of inspired minds, requiring careful nurturing, because Compton employees only had to work a half-day on Fridays in summer. The catch was that they had to arrive a half hour earlier each day, but the catch in that was that no one really did it. Like the two-hour lunch, it was an insider joke, and the most anyone did was show up 15 minutes early and spend that time getting coffee at the canteen. A half-day on Friday was mental preparation for the weekend, and no one could begrudge an ad exec such a minor perk.

The shortened week pacified Marie, as did her upcoming getaway. She and Jane had talked about going somewhere, and Marie knew her older sister had taken off for Puerto

Rico with friends at age 18, so what could Helene say? Why they hadn't chosen a more exotic location than Bolton Landing, Lake George, Marie couldn't say. It was a childhood spot for both of them, and they went with what they both knew.

They took the Greyhound bus early Saturday morning, after Jane's father gave them a lift to the Port Authority so they could bring their bikes. Marie wanted them to do this completely on their own, it being their first time trying such a thing, but she recognized their limitations.

Jane was far more matter-of-fact, having not been subjected to as much overprotection as Marie over the years, and viewing this trip as another earned rite of passage. Marie tried to match her casual stance, the way she drifted off to sleep in between happy bus banter, but she used the time to fill her head with romantic scenarios of what lay ahead. She always anticipated coming upon, at any turn, the thing that would change her life, the way an actress or musician waits for that one big break.

Five hours later, they arrived at the bus stop, and even Jane began to show signs of enthusiasm. For the last thirty minutes of the bouncy ride, they both looked out the window, recalling landmarks, comparing youthful memories, and determining what had changed. Then the winding road at last offered up their first unobstructed view of the glistening lake, backed by the Adirondacks, and they both stilled in silent respect, as if God had just politely requested their attention. 'Funny,' Marie thought as she mentally inhaled the vista before her, 'I didn't know that lake was beautiful when I was little. I only knew it was fun to swim in. And I'm not sure I ever really saw those mountains before.' She knew she would never again take this scene for granted.

"Actually, those aren't even mountains," Jane said, as if compelled to break the spell, "Well, they sort of are. They are the tail end of the Appalachians. But I think technically, they are only plateaus."

"Well, it's going to be fun getting our luggage over these plateaus by bike," Marie challenged, slightly disheartened by Jane's dismissal of such panoramic mastery, "but at least it isn't that far."

They had agreed to stay at Kellem Acres Resort; the site of Marie's two-week family escapes so long ago, mainly because it had fallen into just enough disrepair to make the price just right. Jane was slightly taken aback when she saw it, claiming it was more "rustic" than she had imagined, but they quickly settled into one of the "housekeeping cottages," and officially began their vacation.

Marie remembered that the grownup way of starting any respite from the mundane – aka Helene's way – was to head straight for the grocery store to stock up on all the temporary necessities. Three hundred miles away from home; she rebelled against this ludicrous mandate. Well she remembered arriving at Kellem as a child – bursting forth from the station wagon, free from the collective hot breath of her relations, and beholding the breezy paradise that was now hers for the taking – only to find herself right back in that same wagon, heading for Grand Union in town, to get the groceries they needed for the week.

"We're going straight to the pool," Marie commanded Jane, as soon as they unpacked.

"Don't we need stuff to eat?" she asked, and Marie stopped her cold.

"Later. We have time. I'm hot from everything, biking, unpacking," Marie knew she sounded like a big baby, "I need to swim before we do anything else."

"Okay," Jane said, and went to get her suit, "but not too long. We need food."

And that became the first second of the first step of the series of events that pivoted her future. Because, there, sitting at the pool as they arrived, Marie noting to Jane that there hadn't always been a fence enclosing the chlorine body of water, was her old friend, Tara Kavanagh.

Marie stopped still outside the gate, to confirm what she already knew. There was no denying the long, straight, golden hair she coveted so many years ago. Once again, Marie's eyes moved straight down Tara's body, to see if there was anything else she coveted. By then, Tara had looked up from her book, and her return recognition was instantaneous.

"Well, if it isn't my old friend, Marie Meyers," she said, "Don't just stand there, come on in. Rory, look whose here."

Marie's heart instantly thumped, with one thought: *Brendan is here.* She fought to keep her eyes on Tara's face, and not to do an obvious search for him. It never occurred to her that the Kavanaghs, or anyone from her family's time, still came here. Didn't everyone eventually decide that it was too far to drive, too insipid for teenagers, too frivolous an allocation of funds?

Marie tried to remember the last time she got a letter from Tara. They had written back and forth for a few years, Marie's letters copious and thick, Tara's scant both in frequency and actual word count. Once again, Marie deemed another's existence more valuable than her own, assuming that short letters exemplified a more engaging life, which naturally denied one time to put pen to paper. Eventually, her own gushing scribes embarrassed her, and she edited with a discerning hand. She did always ask, 'how is your family doing?' however, hoping Tara would read between the lines and know she meant, 'how is Brendan?' She never did, and soon their word exchange dissolved completely.

"I didn't know you were coming here," Tara was still going on, "You never write to me anymore! You used to write the best letters. Are you still going out with that older guy?"

Marie flushed, and looked quickly at Jane, as if caught in a lie. She was not even sure which 'older guy' Tara referred to, or how much she had embellished the details in a long ago missive. Jane fortuitously came to her rescue.

"I'm Jane," she said, holding out her hand, "Marie's friend. Nice to meet you."

"Tara," she answered, "Did you come up with Marie's family?"

"No, it's just us," Marie interjected, pride seeping through just a bit, before she rushed on to ask, "Where's the rest of your family?"

"Well, actually, it's just me and my mom and my younger brother Rory this time," Tara answered, without a hint of suspicion, "Everyone else is working."

Marie remolded her crestfallen face quickly, feeling each muscle strain to pull back to a look of nonchalance. *He isn't here.* She was sorely disappointed, forgetting that she was here to enjoy her friend and her independence.

"We're here for two weeks," Tara was saying, "Oh look, here comes my mom. She'll be happy to see you."

Marie did have a wonderful time those six days. She and Jane behaved like brand new tourists, biking ten miles to Lake George Village to visit the wax museum, looking at the shops, and mini-golfing. They went horseback riding, and even took their first ride on the Ticonderoga, a cruise boat that put them both to sleep for most of the three-hour tour.

After each activity, they would return to Kellem, and hang out at the pool or lake, or cook their own dinner at their cabin and talk well into the night. Tara often joined them. She got on well with Jane, because she knew how to ask the kind of questions that people love to answer, diverting attention away from herself and conveying real interest in her companion. Marie would learn that this was a Kavanagh gift. Tara was also cautious not to step on the timeworn toes of established friendships, so no one was threatened by her presence.

Tara's mother, who Marie would later think of as Brendan's mother, was also good to them, picking up items at Grand Union when she went, and providing cooking and other advice where needed. Mostly, Mrs. Kavanagh just seemed to like Marie, sitting around the pool and chatting with her about her family, asking her about her job with the motherly warmth that Marie craved. Marie would soon use this week as a basis for comparison, when the context of her relationship to the Kavanagh family changed, and so did the climate of the maternal response to her.

The week ended, and all were sad, all said their thanks and hugged goodbye. Tara's last words stayed in her head for the whole bus ride home:

"You work in the city now. We can get together anytime. I'll be back in a week. Call me!"

Tara would be back in a week. Brendan was home now. And that was why, back at her desk first thing Monday morning; Marie dialed the Kavanaghs' number.

****

He answered on the first ring, and she wondered how she recognized his voice when that wasn't possible. She hadn't heard it in seven years.

"Is Tara there?" she asked, dragging each word out of her mouth like pieces of long sweet taffy. This was her plan, to pretend she was looking for Tara. Brendan would not realize that she knew his sister wasn't there.

"Noooo," he said, matching her singsong tone.

"Who is this?" Marie asked. She thought it best to verify that she was flirting with the right person, before going on.

"Brendan," he said, and he sounded as if they were playing some sort of game, so she playfully asked, "Do you know who this iiiissss?"

"Susie?" Brendan asked, and Marie's thin confidence rapidly fled down her throat. Who was Susie?

Too late. She had started this and must see it through. "Noooo," she kept up her mischievous tone, but she could hear the cracks, "It's Marie…Meyers…do you remember me?"

He laughed, and it was a sweet sound. "You sound just like Susie, the little girl my sister baby-sits. She's 5."

There was a silence as Marie's breath rested between relief and indignation. On the one side, Susie was not competition. On the other, Brendan thought Marie sounded like a 5-year-old.

She cleared her throat and lost the syrupy sweetness, but there wasn't much she could do to deepen her voice. It was only husky when she had a cold.

"Well, how are you, anyway?" she asked, and they were off and running.

They talked about his day, which had included buying bedding for his fraternity room at NYU – "I got these weird sheets with spaceships on it, and a matching comforter. They were cheaper" – and how he was moving in a few weeks. They talked about her job in "midtown," a word she had hardly used before since it was the only town she really knew in New York. She told him how it took her years to realize that Queens and Manhattan were not far apart, that she could have visited Tara long before this. Somehow that led to a discussion of the subway, and then he told her how once he dropped his glasses in a Port Authority toilet.

Joe paced by her desk, not once but twice, and she knew her resentment was unfair. Yes, this was work; yes, she had just returned from vacation, but she was relishing this discourse the way one loves a warm bubble bath, immersed in fizzy iridescent exuberance, and she didn't want to get out until the banter went cold. She had the sense, even then, that capturing Brendan in an unguarded moment was a rare and precious thing.

'Five more minutes,' she thought, hoping Joe would simply go away, and at least allow her to gracefully wait until the next pause.

She needn't have worried. Suddenly, Brendan said more than asked, "Hey, aren't you at *work*?" And whoosh, the plug was pulled.

They said all the 'well' lines, "Well, I'll let you go," "Well, I'll tell Tara you called," "Well, good luck at NYU," "Well, congrats on your job," but not, "Well, we should get together." Marie hung up feeling elated and cheated at the same time.

"How was your vacation," Joe asked from right above her, making her jump out of seat, "Or are you still on it?"

She smiled, and began feeding paper into her typewriter. "It was great," she said, absently, as if too busy to talk, "Lots to catch up on, though."

"With who? The prom king?" Joe asked, and then, thankfully, went back into his office.

Her fingers found the home keys, a sensation that was oddly satisfying to her, as was the solid sound of the metal embossed ball firming thwacking the paper through an inky ribbon. The raised word, "Compton," boldly stared at her, but the black letters appearing bit by bit below the letterhead spoke nothing of media buys or upcoming presentations. At her beckoning, the mechanism was calling up the prose that would make Brendan call her back just three days later.

"For information on where to buy the best sheets in Manhattan, or how to get the smell of Port Authority toilet off your glasses, or if you just need to talk, call Compton Advertising at (212) 654-1100, extension 301, and talk to the girl who says, 'Media, may I help you?' in a 5-year-old's voice."

And so it began. "You know," he said after she answered the phone, "when I first starting reading, I thought, 'What a coincidence, I just bought sheets,' and then I thought, 'Who the heck knew I dropped my glasses in the Port Authority toilet?' but by the time I got to the part about the 5-year-old, I figured it out."

They agreed to meet the next day, Friday, a half day, and Marie thanked the gods that there would be no maddening hours to count and project with, or opportunities for him to cancel, because she knew she would not. 'One night,' she thought, was all she had to sleep, 'and then a few hours.'

There was one glitch, just one, which niggled at her like a run in pantyhose: tomorrow night she was going to the Cars concert in Central Park, with Mike and Jean, and…Matt. Essentially, she had two "dates" in one day, six hours apart, although she had long stopped thinking of Matt as a date. A wiser woman might have postponed the rendezvous with Brendan, but she was hungry for it, and shook the interfering demons that vied for position in rational thought. Marie *wanted* this; therefore, it *would* work out. And so she boarded the train Friday morning with a hobo's sack to contend with the day.

How she got through the morning, she didn't know. Of course time dragged, and so did her typing, alternating moments of deliberate speed with motionless pauses in which only her thoughts raced. *What would he be like now? Would he like her? Could he love her?* Lost in thought, her fingers rested heavily on the keys until one or two yelped under the pressure and smacked her page in protest with a typo. Then, like one daydreaming at a traffic light, Marie broke the spell and accelerated.

"Marie," Joe came out of his office, holding a sheet of paper and scratching his balding head, "Mistakes are an acceptable part of life. Lack of proofreading, well, that's just deplorable. Look up deplorable after you fix this letter."

He watched as she took the page and searched quickly for the offending word. She couldn't find it. In vain, she re-read the letter, hoping to redeem herself, but most of his correspondence to Procter and Gamble made little sense to her, anyway.

"I don't see," she began, but she knew it was no use. If he said it was there, it was.

"Look in the address," he said, teacher-like, mildly scolding.

And there it was. "Procter and Bamble," plain as day.

"Looks more like a bumble to me," he said, and she suspected he had rehearsed that line and patiently waited to deliver it. He walked offstage and back to his office before she could reply.

She went back to 'unbambling' her letter, and painstakingly kept her focus until the receptionist called and said she had a visitor at the front desk.

The corridor seemed longer as she headed for reception, like an infinity mirror, desk beyond desk seemingly leading to nowhere. At the end of the line, there was a turn leading to reception, and Marie was reminded of the moment in the Dating Game when the bachelor of choice was revealed. These were her last moments of wondering how Brendan looked now; in a moment, she would know.

She was instantly disappointed. He was so…thin. This wasn't a problem in itself, but in that suddenly she felt gawky and large, already a mismatch for him. In her shallow mind, people who belonged together were supposed to look the part.

On his face were the aforementioned glasses, and even these she had imagined incorrectly. She had pictured something John Lennonish, but these were definitely more along the lines of Clark Kent. Behind them, though, his eyes were a warm brown, and she resisted the urge to pull off the offending spectacles for a closer look.

"You made it," she said, forgiving herself for the feeble comment; all new things began with weak, awkward commentary.

"Yes," he said, adding to her statement of the obvious. He had a nice smile.

"Well, I'll show you around, and then I'll change my clothes, and then we can go out to lunch," she managed to get out without once stopping for air.

"I'm here because of a letter," he said, grinning, "I thought we were going to buy sheets and disinfect my glasses."

'This is never going to work,' she thought, walking him past the now deserted desks towards her own. She had no precise reason why not. It could not be as simple as his body mass and choice of glasses, and yet, those things kept returning to her as she changed out of her work attire in the ladies' room. She pulled on the outfit she had chosen last night, shorts and a thin tank top designed to expose her premium parts, but now she wished she could keep them under cover. Something about Brendan made her feel garish.

When she returned to her desk, he was writing on her "While you were out" pad, quickly ripping off a page and folding it up.

"I took a message for you," he said, "but you can't read it until later."

Marie experienced a moment of panic – 'did Matt call?' – and moved to take the paper from his hand, but he held fast. "The caller was very adamant," he said, "You definitely must not peek until later."

"Okay," she replied, feigning disinterest, "Ready to go?"

What did she notice most about that day? That he talked, but she chattered.

Only she deemed it necessary to fill every nook of air space with an onslaught of verbiage, as if words were oxygen in short supply. That he was funny, quick-witted and teasing, making her laugh again and again. And that he was different, different from all the others, but also different from her as well.

They went to Nathan's on 58th Street for lunch, whether by culinary choice or fiscal necessity, she couldn't say. They just ended up there.

She did recognize the moment he began edging into her heart. Reaching across to grab a french fry, he knocked a cup of soda off the table, futilely trying to catch it before it hit the floor. As the lid popped off and the beverage began to bleed across the tiles, he looked up at her and said, "The good thing about this place is, if you don't like something they serve, you can just throw it on the floor." And then, "Someone will be here in a second. I'll just tell him I didn't like it," as a Nathan's employee arrived with a mop.

Afterwards, they strolled through Central Park, stopping to sit on a rock or a bench, and talking about Lake George and the past – "You used to follow me everywhere, as I recall" – and keeping it light, not like her talks with Manny, not like they were immediately trying to solve each other's mysteries. Marie wanted him to touch her, and was not used to prompting such an advance.

"Let's keep walking," he said, popping up in the midst of a silence made for tongues to meet, and she reluctantly stood and started walking. The winding path led to the zoo entrance, where a sign announced that admission was ten cents.

"Tell ya what, I'll treat," he said, reaching into his pocket.

They strolled past mammals of all varieties, all glumly incarcerated in black wrought iron, trying their best to forget the life they left behind. Soon, they were standing in front of the polar bear cage, where the prisoner was pacing, back and forth, as if waiting to hear the verdict on his murder trial.

"Why does he do that?" Marie asked, as Brendan gripped the bars with both hands, and her eyes caught his unbuttoned sleeves hanging down.

"He's restless, I guess," Brendan continued watching, but Marie had seen her opportunity. She squeezed herself under one hand and leaned against the cage, imprisoning herself between his arms. Coyly, she buttoned one sleeve, then the other, like a loving mother concerned about a sudden chill. But there was nothing maternal about the way she looked at him when she finished, nor in the way her hands inched up his chest to his shoulders, locking their bodies tighter still.

Of course he kissed her then. She left him with no other options. Marie felt the moment in an extra-sensory way, and an everlasting way; the sultry August day, the heady unexplored scent of him mixed with the musky aroma of God's creatures, the soft padding of heavy feet behind her, the bars between her shoulder blades. This was the kiss, *their* kiss, and a permanent part of their story. This was the moment they began, right there, while the polar bear watched.

The barrier broken, they now had a new agenda, that of acquainting their mouths more thoroughly. They continued to walk, but stopped more; they continued to sit, but talked less. Even talk itself changed focus, centering only on the uncomplicated joy of kissing, occasionally intermixed with some exchange of information. But not much.

They continued this way until, in a city of rushing faces, a most unlikely thing happened. They were interrupted.

"Hey, Brendan," a voice said, in what Marie would soon dub 'collegiate drawl,' though she would find it difficult to describe. It was a bored but privileged sound, pretentious, or maybe Marie was just sensitive. "I thought that was you," the voice went on.

Brendan stood, distancing himself from her in a way that was subtle but not unnoticed. His demeanor changed, the way it does when males address males, but Marie was sensitive about that, too.

"Hey, Maurice. Are you headed up to the concert already?"

"Yeah. General admission, you know?" Maurice gave her a brief look, and then asked, "Should I save some seats?"

"No," Brendan responded quickly, looking back at Marie, "I'll…we'll…get up there."

They talked for a few seconds more, something about classes, a name here and there, while Marie processed two galling truths. The first was that apparently she was not going to be introduced to Maurice. The second was that it was unlikely that there were two concerts in Central Park that evening, so she and Brendan would soon be at the same one.

There was a third truth as well. She didn't want to leave him. Already, she saw the two folding chairs that Maurice would save, and how she and Brendan would occupy them mainly by standing in front of them as the music sliced the air; already, she saw her hand resting possessively on one of his newly buttoned sleeves, relying on body language when the amplifiers ridiculed any attempt at conversation. She envisioned the faces of other Maurices, and saw a new place for herself amongst them, beside Brendan. Plus, there were a hundred more kisses to be had between now and then, and only these could ease the wait.

"What time is it?" Brendan asked, and she saw Maurice was gone.

"I never wear a watch," Marie answered. 'It is something you will know about me,' her mind continued, 'You will say, 'my girlfriend never wears a watch' with a secret smile, 'she doesn't like the feel of it on her wrist'…sit down, Brendan,' her mind pleaded, 'and let's keep knowing.'

"My friends and I have tickets to the Cars tonight," he explained, "I said I'd meet them at the entrance since I knew I'd be up this way anyway."

Suddenly, Marie knew why the polar bear paced. He wasn't restless; he was reenacting. He was thinking, 'I was walking, just walking, and then I ended up here. How the hell did I end up here? How do I get back to where I was before?'

"Actually, I'm meeting friends, too," Marie conceded, "to go to the concert. I have to meet them back at my office."

"Oh good," Brendan said in a "so that settles it," voice that almost hurt, causing one of her hands to rise in defense.

"Wait," she said, willing herself not to plead, "Just one more minute."

He settled down on the bench, and she tried to regain the moment, smiling and walking her fingers up his shirt, making their way behind his neck and coaxing his face to hers, when, remarkably, they were once again stopped.

"Brendan! Were you looking for us?" Then, "Obviously not!"

"Do you know everyone in this park?" Marie said, teasingly, against his lips, and savored their final merge of breath before he broke away.

"I have to go," he said, and she strained to hear regret in his voice. He straightened, smoothed his shirt, and even adjusted his Clark Kent glasses before giving her a quick kiss goodbye. "I'll see you there!" he said, and she watched him link up with his friends.

The rain started as she ran back down 58th Street to her office building. She knew Jane, Mike and Matt would be waiting out front, but suddenly, she remembered something, and entered her building through Schaeffer's, the restaurant on the side. She took the elevator up, and ran through the semi-darkness to her desk. There it was, the pink message Brendan had taken while she was changing.

"I'm glad I stopped by," it said, in chicken scrawl that would soon become dearly familiar. She touched it once, tenderly, before folding it gently and putting it in her bag; then raced back to the elevators.

"How the hell are you late when we're the ones who came in from Queens?" Matt asked, irritably, and without a word, Marie packed him away in a place she was leaving behind.

The rain allowed her to take cover under Jane's umbrella throughout the concert; thankfully, most of the audience was obscured by cumbersome rows of wet hexagons. She searched for Brendan and Maurice with her eyes, but with the intent of keeping herself hidden. She had spent the latter part of the afternoon locking lips with one guy; it would not do to be seen with another.

If the concert was awesome, it was wasted on Marie. She spent half of it lamenting at the cruel irony that placed her in the wrong row of folding chairs, beside the wrong guy, neglecting to recall that Brendan hadn't exactly invited her to be with his crowd, anyway.

She spent the other half planning, to the beat of her racing heart, a way to see him again.

****

For Marie, everything was urgent, requiring fast and furious attention, and nothing was permitted the pleasure of running its course. She placed no faith in happenstance; when she wanted something, even something simple, she wanted it passionately, and it made her breathless, consuming her until it was safely tucked away in her grasp. It would always be this way, and some would admire her determination; they would say, "That Marie, when she wants something, she stops at nothing to get it." But it would be disdained by others, Brendan for sure, and herself most of all. Ideas gave her no rest, coming on like feverish storms in her chest; she felt their arrival the way one feels the first flush of illness, but there was no antidote. She relied on conquest to ease the pain, and dreaded the force of her own desires.

Right now, she desired Brendan, and perhaps he wanted her, too, but she had no trust in that. And so, when she arrived home late that night, she wrote him yet another letter.

11:05 PM August 24th.

Dear Brendan,

I started writing this letter (in my head) as soon as I left you outside Central Park. – I was on my 8th or 9th page when the Cars did 'Candy-O' and I really was anxious to get home and put it down on paper. Actually, I must be nuts to write to you tonight because I'm so tired – everyone went to the bar after the concert and I didn't make it. Hey listen, Kavanagh, after I left you, I went back to my office, just to check out the message you left me. Now I'm going to ask you how you could've known you were 'glad you stopped by' if you wrote that before you spent the day with me? ESP? Wishful thinking? Either way, that tiny message was extremely heartwarming, because I was glad you stopped by and I hoped you were, also. It was really nice being with you and not once did I regret bulldozing you into it (tee *hee).*

And so it went, for five loose-leaf pages, front and back, continued through Saturday and late Sunday, when he called her. He was at work, at the patient information desk of Cabrini Medical Center, and he put her on hold several times.

"You should be honored," his voice was soft and low, "I'm making nuns wait in order to talk to you."

"I *am* honored," she said.

"You know, I looked all over for you at that concert," he said, "Hold on," and then, "I have to go. Want to meet on Monday?"

She did. She cradled the phone for a moment after he was gone. He had called. They were real. They had begun.

******

"So, how's it going with the Irishman?" her father asked, a few days later. No doubt, Fred Meyers was intrigued. He remembered the Kavanaghs well, those elusive Lake George poolsiders who spared the Meyers little notice. He seemed almost proud that his daughter was able to nab the attention of one.

Naturally, Helene had a different take. "You know," she said, in a voice that almost begged for a podium beneath it, "that Mrs. Kavanagh was supposed to go to Aida's with me…the beauty parlor in Bolton…one week. Remember that, Freddy? I'd always invite her and she would always say, sure, she'd love to go. She never went," Helene finished, making her lips a straight line as if it were a damn shame. "I've always thought they were snobs, those Kavanaghs. It's like their shit didn't stink."

Marie cringed at her mother's words; words she now considered to be "Queens-like" now that she knew the refinement of Manhattan, and especially Brendan's Manhattan. She had always considered the city a place where people worked, or visited during the holidays, a place where no one could live or park a car. Brendan grew up there, and unlike every Queens teenager, never even had the desire to own a car.

"They aren't snobs, mom," Marie said, and now they were even, for Marie's new intonation probably irked Helene, "They're just kind of shy."

It would be the first of many Brendan-related defenses, all of which would carry some slight thread of falsehood. Marie had only two evenings before had her first visit to the Kavanagh home, and she couldn't exactly say she felt at ease.

First, they seemed to want to overlook the fact that she had come with Brendan. More than once, it was stated "how nice it was" that Marie had finally come to visit Tara, especially since she was leaving for the University of Hartford in a week. Tara's friend, Anna, was also there, and she too was leaving for college. And so it became a little bon voyage party for academia, and a non-issue that she walked in with Brendan.

Gone was the Mrs. Kavanagh of a few weeks prior, who attended affably to her needs in Lake George. She was replaced by a woman whose melodic brogue took on a higher pitch, and who, upon answering the door, took a look at her short shorts and said, "Marie, where are the rest of your trousers?"

The next day, when she called him, his brother answered.

"Is Brendan there, Dennis?" she asked, but he didn't try to engage her in conversation. Instead, she heard Dennis call his brother by saying, "Brendan, someone's on the phone for you. Sounds like Minnie Mouse."

She did have one moment of glory, but it came from Tara's friend, Anna. Taking her aside before dinner, she whispered, "How did you get Brendan Kavanagh to go out with you? Half of Tara's friends have tried for years, including me. I didn't even think he liked *girls*. What is your secret?" And so Marie got to tell someone of her conniving phone call and the events that followed.

The unenthusiastic reception bewildered Marie, but no matter. Little could detract from her excitement of these days, and questions like her father's 'How's it going with the Irishman?' filled her with delicious anticipation. She loved just talking about Brendan, and so she redirected her attention to her dad.

"He's moving to the fraternity in just a few days," Marie announced, "in the Village. He goes to NYU."

"No kidding," her father could not be more captivated, "Bet he gets a lot of action down in that frat house."

And that was another thing. Soon, she would be directing her affection to a guy who did not live with his parents. Her letters and cards would receive no scrutiny; her phone calls handed over sans commentary. In early conversations, when Brendan mentioned going back to college, she was deflated; they had just begun and already their time was up. She later did not admit that she didn't realize that New York University was in New York *city*, and that the lower section of that city was attached to the one she knew.

Only one thing tinted the brightness of those days, and it was this: her dad's tone of wonderment had become the new voice inside her head, accompanying an uneasy feeling that she had landed a prize that was not meant to be hers, and one that she did not deserve. She perceived purity in Brendan that made her feel soiled, just as his stature on that first day made her feel graceless.

Marie was almost sure Brendan was a virgin, and his being one suddenly made even sex a plaything of the impure. She had no proof, but there was something about the hesitance of his touch that suggested more than just decorum. Where once she might have brazenly assisted the fumbling of male hands, now she muted her lust with a layer of shame. She hated knowing better than he how to touch her; hated knowing how many had touched her before.

The next time she saw him, using the apathetic streets of New York as a confessional, she blurted it out, "I've been with a lot of guys, you know."

They had just eaten lunch in the park and were sauntering down Fifth Avenue, having only used half of her misnamed lunch "hour." Whatever they had been talking about, it was certainly not their prior sexual escapades, and so Brendan looked justifiably confused. She felt a slight hiccup in his walk, as if he were about to stop in his tracks, and then his step regained its rhythm. Whatever thought stilled him for that millisecond, fled with the return of motion, and Brendan seemed determined to make light of it.

"Been where? To the movies? Concerts? Where have you been?" he asked, smiling, but she couldn't let it go.

"Stop. I mean, well, have you been with a lot of girls? Have you been with anyone?" she asked, but she didn't know what answer she wanted. How could any of his exploits redeem her?

"I've been with girls," he said, still gently ribbing, "and I used to hear from Tara about all these old guys you were going out with."

"I just thought you should know that I'm not a virgin." There, she said them, words that she could not conceive of saying to anyone else as a form of apology, not in the 70's, not at the age of 18. Already she had placed Brendan just one step higher than herself, and she would keep him climbing until the distance between them was terrible to breach.

*****

The brochures from Bernard Baruch College came in the mail that same day. Marie had called to request them, and her hands trembled on the phone as if the faceless drone on the other side of the wires would need a reason that she qualified for even so insignificant an investment of time and postage.

Marie pored over them when they arrived. She was both daunted and energized by their presence; she fondled them, allowing nothing to crinkle the glossy catalogue cover decorated with smiling intellectuals. Possessing these meant she had taken a step, and any increment was validation, proof that she wasn't just who she was, but also who she intended to be.

It took her three days to fill out the application, even though it was hardly intricate. She had no way of knowing that Baruch was not Yale or Harvard, or even NYU, for that matter, and their acceptance policy was less than stringent. With careful marks she printed her information, as if she would be judged on penmanship, then reduced the page to envelope size in a perfectly proportioned tri-fold.

"I just applied to college," she announced, returning to her house from a walk to the mailbox. She amused herself with visions of her family gathering together, hugging her, telling her they were proud, that she was the first in the family to become a scholar, but for once, the reality did not depress her. She went, instead, to the living room, and called Manny.

"Arthur Treachers, Flushing, can I help you?" His voice was harried, and she glanced at the clock and noted that it was rush hour.

"I just applied to college," she said, and waited, like one fishing on the banks of a sunlit bay, certain the catch would come and relishing the silence.

"Oh Marie, you did it," he said tenderly, and his voice confirmed that she had done far more than simply lick an envelope.

They talked for a few minutes more, but she heard the clatter of trays and humming of register tape and knew he was working the front.

"I'll let you go," she said reluctantly.

"I'll call you Monday. Maybe we can do lunch. By the way, I have news for you, too. I'm coming back to the Ridgewood store."

"Really?" she asked, and already she was contemplating. Would it be the same? She only worked there one night a week. Would they work together? She had Brendan now; would she still turn to Manny for reassurance? An outsider with a clearer vantage point might note that Brendan was not the first recipient of her college application news.

Marie hung up and immediately walked over to Treachers, ever possessive of Manny news, to tell them of his anticipated return. She hung out for about an hour, sitting in a booth with Hans, who already knew about Manny. There was no one else in the store that would even care; the turnover at Treachers was nearly complete.

"So, your hero returns," Hans said, but he had new flesh in the store to taunt, and she was no longer a target.

"Yup," she said, matching his nonchalant tone, and ignoring the tiny flutter inside her chest.

"What's going on with you and Matt?" Hans asked, and the flutter stopped.

"Nothing," she said. There was no way to elaborate on that statement, so she fell silent.

"Does *he* know that nothing is going on?" Hans laughed, and rose to return to the kitchen.

The truth was that she never officially broke up with Matt, just as she had never officially broken up with Ray, or anyone for that matter. There was never any airport scene or returning of jewelry or tear-stained cheeks to mark the end of Marie's relationships. They just sort of faded away.

The next day was Friday, and since Brendan worked at Cabrini on Saturday and Sunday nights, Friday night was the only weekend afforded to them. She had asked him to come and meet her parents; or, rather, reacquaint himself with them. Her half days were finished, so they agreed to meet "downtown" for dinner, and take the train to Queens afterwards. It was their two-week anniversary.

Marie was enthralled with it all; the meeting of her boyfriend in the city at night, the hopping on trains to dash from 59th Street to 14th, the burgers and fries at places called "Jimmy Days" or "Shakespeare's", sitting outside on the sidewalk, watching people savor the last of summer.

Brendan made her laugh. He had what she would later call "an Irish sense of humor," subtle and mischievous, and she kept her eyes glowing upon his face all through dinner. When the check came, he reached into his wallet, pulled out a plastic card and whispered, "I'll get this." Then he slapped down his NYU student ID and added; "I'll just tell them to put it on my book bill."

She could hardly wait to bring him home. She could hardly wait for a lot of things.

On the way to the train station, she backed him on to a Toyota with Jersey plates, and kissed him with blatant invitation, maneuvering her body to enable access for wherever his hands chose to roam. They stayed on her waist, and the kiss ended.

"Did you know that the drinking age in New Jersey is 19?" he asked, pushing her gently off the car, "See all the license plates? They come through the tunnel just to drink here."

Marie filed the tidbit for future use, and the night hid her flush of humiliation. She had done it again, played the part of the slut, thrown her body at him and suffered his apparent ability to resist. How did she keep on getting this wrong?

They took the LL in silence, both unwilling to raise their voices above the decibels of metal on metal. When they reached Myrtle, they switched for the M train upstairs, and on the elevated platform, resumed conversation.

"I used to get off here to get home," she said, "and walk just a few blocks. Now we are in Glendale. It's a better neighborhood. I still come down here 'cause I work one night a week in Arthur Treachers."

Brendan nodded his head and so she kept talking. "One of these days you will have to meet the 'Treacher Creatures.' They're my friends. Well, I hang out in a lot of different places, but mostly with them."

"The ones from the Cars concert?" he asked.

"Mmmhmmm," she replied, "Yeah, that was a few of them. They are probably in Kelly's tonight. That's a bar closer to my house." She looked down the tracks to search for the distant light, "Damn, the M train seems like it comes every five seconds when I'm in Treachers," she mused.

"You can see it from there?" he asked politely.

"I can hear it," she clarified, "Even from behind the counter. Oh, here it comes."

They got on the M train and got off just two stops later, on Fresh Pond Road. "We still have a bit of walk," she apologized, "This is *not* the city."

They ambled along Fresh Pond, stopping here and there to talk or make out on cars with New York plates, mostly at her initiative. She almost wanted to prove that she could kiss him and leave it at that, reclaiming a few ounces of her self-respect. She also wanted to pick up the pace, to get him to her house and display him as a prize to her family.

They were just disengaging from such a kiss when they heard the sounds of hooting and laughing, and she looked up to see Matt and Mike and a few others passing by. She knew they saw her, but they said nothing, and she turned to Brendan and said, "Let's go."

"Who was that?" he asked.

"That was sort of, I guess, my ex-boyfriend," she said shyly.

"Oh," he said, and she should have left it at that. She should not have felt compelled to offer further explanation, but how could she know? Her next words would become engraved somewhere in Brendan's mind, as solid as an inscription in stone; a stone he would repeatedly beat her with. She was 18, an age when most of what one says is foolish and forgettable, but she would not be granted this luxury.

"Well, he kind of still has rights to me," she said lightly, unthinkingly, "I never actually broke up with him."

They reached her house soon after, and for Marie, the night was magic. The unrequited fumbling on the Jersey car was forgotten, as was the Matt incident. Brendan charmed her family, and Marie glowed with pride. Helene asked about his family, saying, "You know, me and your mother used to always make plans to go the beauty parlor in Bolton. But we just never had the time." Her father showed him the Irish blessing they had hanging in the kitchen.

She showed him her room, her life, her dog, her world, the phone she used when she called him late at night. She timidly showed him the Baruch catalog with the application torn out.

"Oh, Baruch," he said, "UCLA. Know what that means?"

"No, what?" she asked eagerly.

"University on the corner of Lexington Avenue," he said, laughing and brushing her hair out of her eyes.

At the end of the evening, he rose to go, and she walked downstairs with him. Her father was still up, and she knew it was deliberate.

"C'mon, I'll run you to the station," he said, and began a new tradition.

12:15pm September 7

Dear Brendan,

You've been gone thirty minutes and I'm lying in bed thinking about you.

This is just to say thanks for everything – thanks for taking me home, for stopping along the way, for holding me tight, for being so sweet in my house, and most of all, for being in my life.

Love, Marie

She walked on clouds the entire weekend, irritating her mother profusely, and on Monday, she walked into work, eager to meet Manny for lunch and tell him that she was in love.

****

He called in the morning, and in a hushed, mysterious voice, cancelled their plans.

"What's wrong?" she asked, still elated with her news, "Madeline sitting on you or something? Hey, you can tell me all about it on Thursday! Don't you start this week at Treachers...*my* Treachers?"

"Marie," he said steadily, in measured words that quieted her, "Marie. I'm not coming back to the store. I'm not coming back to Treachers at all." There was a pause, and then he said her name for the third time, "Marie. I've been called up by the NYPD. I just found out Friday night. I'm going to be a cop."

Chapter Five: New York's Finest

Everyone likes to say they "know a cop." More than any other occupation, law enforcement is one that common folk like to cozy up to. They start conversations with, "My friend, the cop, he says…" or proudly whip out mini-versions of a loved ones shield and say, "My son is with the NYPD." They flaunt PBA cards on dashboards, and nod to them when pulled over for doing 80 on the parkway. Glancing at the card for redemption, they lean closer to the detaining officer and say, in their best cop lingo, "Sorry, sir. My good friend is 'on the job.'"

Marie was no different, but the timing was wrong. She knew she was about to become "*really* good friends with a cop," and the thought pleased her in a pretentious way that had little to do with Manny himself. It was a conversation piece; a tiny jewel to add to a stash that once was bare. She had larger, shinier jewels in that collection now.

She listened as he told his story, but like so many of Manny's rare monologues, she would swear later that he had "never told her this." Like so many words, these would only later become her own.

"I was standing on line for a movie with Madeline when I heard," he rushed on, as if knowing his spotlight time was limited. Manny's voice was a mixture of Hispanic and everything a Puerto Rican of his time does to cover that sin. The result was cottony and indistinct, and some day, painfully endearing.

"I had my transistor with me, and I was listening for the names," he went on, "and I heard it. I got a perfect score on the test. And know what Madeline said when she heard? You'll never believe it."

Marie had no idea how you found out you were a cop from a radio broadcast, but she had no inclination to ask. She did not stop to wonder why she didn't even know that

Manny had taken the aforementioned test. At Madeline's name, however, her ears perked, and she shifted in her seat as if moving closer for a juicy punch line.

"What did Madeline say?" she asked.

"I just found out, and I was smiling and she turned to me and said, in this pissed off voice, she says, 'I just knew you would go and get a hundred on that test.' That was it. Not another word. We went to the movie and it was like nothing happened."

She and Manny would forever seize moments like these, chances to be the better person, the more compassionate mate, the outraged friend. They would both be given ample opportunities, but it was Marie's turn now.

"Damn, Manny, I can't believe that," she said in her 'I would never say such a thing' voice, "Does she want you to be a Treacher's manager all your life?"

"She wanted me to be an accountant," he said, and suddenly remembered his role in her life, "So, what's new with you anyway? Did you get into Baruch?"

She did; but still savoring her altruistic stand, Marie offered him little about her own life. They talked about how he would be entering the Police Academy immediately, and about how they were not to be reunited at Treachers after all. "But the Academy is on 19th and Third," he said, "so I'll be in the city, too." After a few more congratulations – "You, too," he said, "about school. You are on your way" – and a few more disparaging Madeline remarks – "I just can't believe she wasn't happy for you" – they hung up.

Marie smiled contentedly as she placed the phone gently in its cradle. She had that rare sense that life was good, *that* she was good; she replayed hers and Manny's conversation and took note of how quick and colorful she sounded.

The truth was, Marie was enamored with her life right now. She had indeed gotten into Baruch, and had mulled through the registration process like something to be conquered with great and exacting care. She found the 'Advertising Copywriting' course, then backtracked through the repeated word, "prerequisite" to find the course she could take right now. It was called, "Advertising Fundamentals" and she printed the course number carefully in the white boxes, then waited 90 minutes in the registrar's office to plop the paper in front of a woman who clearly did not share her enthusiasm.

"You can't take this," the bored voice said after tapping a few keys on a computer.

Marie felt it fast, the panic, the need to beg, and the urge to shake some feeling into the dull eyes before her. "Why not," she nearly wheezed from the weight that had seized her lungs.

"Junior status required," the voice droned, "It says so right here."

"But I need this course now," Marie's voice got smaller with each word. The android had finally looked up, not at Marie, but through her to the long line of registration hopefuls, and clearly her dream of completing her workday took precedence over Marie's dreams of the future.

Her dejection must have struck some chord in the hard heart, because as Marie slowly lifted her paper up, the voice said, "You can probably take it as a non-matric."

"Okay," Marie breathed, exhaling relief, and let the paper fall back down, but the woman's heart instantly hardened, and she pushed the paper back again.

"Non-matrics register next week. The course might be full by then," and then she was done with Marie. "Next," she said pointedly, more to hasten one human out of her sight than to draw another closer.

Marie was left to learn what a "non-matric" was, then to become one, and finally, to wait the tortuous few days to bring her still unwrinkled, revered paper back to the place of her prior rejection. This time, there was no wait, and a different woman tapped computer keys, one that Marie imagined had a more compassionate face. Within seconds, she got her course, and just like that, she was a college student.

This status became essential when she attended her first NYU fraternity party. Here, Marie learned quickly that the prerequisite for the line, "What do you do?" in the business world is the line, "Where do you go?" in the scholastic arena, and thankfully, she had an answer. She had to mask the awe in her voice when she responded, and also to suffer the retort she now suspected was an insult, "Oh, UCLA. University on the corner of Lexington Avenue," but nothing quelled the gratitude that washed over her for the simple ability to say, "I go to Baruch."

Eyes glazed over if she launched into further detail, and she found she had to shout over the band anyway. Fraternity parties had little to do with intellectual talk and everything to do with loud music and Jack Daniels, and maybe dancing and definitely sex. Couples disappeared and returned, the floor became stickier, and people passed out on worn sofas. The party ended when there was no one left standing, but Marie had to be on the LL train long before that.

She did get another thing she wanted on the night of that first party. It happened right after she finished helping Brendan sell tickets at the front door. They weren't touching at all, but this time she knew there would be no crossed signals. The space between them was tangible and thin, like a bubble they were not permitted to pop until a certain time. He was nervous, fumbling when he ripped off a ticket, and compulsively playing with them when there was a lull. She watched him and waited with her heart pounding, until someone came to take over, and then they both tore up the stairs to his room.

It was better than she thought it would be; he knew more than she thought he would know, but it was also Brendan, and love covers a multitude of blunders in the dark. What didn't last quite long enough was easily repeated, and it was hours before they returned to the party.

He took her home on the train that night, and walked to her door, then turned around and took the train back to his home. She began another letter as soon as he left, and dotingly addressed it to 85 W. Third Street, his new address, a place she could not wait to return to. She lay awake then until dawn, replaying the night, the people she had met, imagining them to be better than the ones she had known thus far. She delighted in how the girls had looked at her, suspiciously, like she had secured a prize through some illegal method. Last, she envisioned their tangled moments in his room, feeling his hair through her fingers, soft like his voice, and she tenderly touched the spot where he had left a puddle on her midsection.

2am September 10
Dear Brendan,
    More and more often, I am amazed at how sweet a person you are. I love that you are shy, and I love that you are quiet, I love what I can see, but I love even more the things I have to stop and wonder about you…I love what we shared tonight.

This was her life now. She often saw herself outside of it, meeting Brendan in Loeb Student Center, or strolling with him through Washington Square Park where guitarists played for coins and the smell of marijuana was heady. She met him outside a building on Mercer Street where he took karate classes, and they rushed back to his room to reenact and perfect what she now called making love. Then they ate at one of "their" places, Triumph or Chocerero's or Sandolinos, where the floor was covered in sawdust. Food is a joyous experience for the amorous, a delicious way to wait until their apparatus was refueled.

She was in love. She went to college. She worked in Manhattan. Her best friend was almost a cop. With these tallies on her belt, she felt lucky, and luck gave her the urge to push on. One Monday morning, she took the elevator upstairs, and visited the Creative Department.

****

The Creative Department was markedly different from the media department. Most outsiders would imagine only this atmosphere when imagining an ad agency. They would picture people dressed in jeans and eccentric ties, or long hippie skirts, with curious hairstyles and inexplicable ways. In some ways, they would be right. By virtue of its name, this was where it happened. The people here had a right to feel that they were somewhat above decorum.

For Marie, it was like suddenly coming upon the Emerald City, hearing the little voices singing that she was "out of the woods, out of the dark, out of the night." She only visited now because she could finally see her shining destination, even if she couldn't yet reach it. She was going to school, and school was her yellow brick road.

She didn't stay long; she felt too conspicuous, as if soon someone would say she had no right to be there. She took in the glossy ads upon the bright orange walls – Cunard, Seagrams, Duncan Hines – and read names upon cubicles. There were far more cubicles here than in media, as if open space allowed creativity to breathe better.

"Soon," she whispered to herself, "Soon," and alarm for once did not smash cymbals in her chest, responding instead to her self-soothing voice. She would get here.

If there was ever a time that Marie hardly knew what was going on beyond the borders of her own world, it was now. If complacency could be blended at medium speed with benevolence, the end mixture embodied Marie; content to the point of kindness and smugness alike. She could smile at strangers on the elevator and never notice them at all.

Robert became a firefighter during this self-absorbed time, and framed FDNY photos of him soon filled the walls of their home. This, too, became just another special possession that Marie tucked away; for now she knew a fireman and a cop.

She breezed through her front door at end of the day, sometimes straight from work and other times much later, after class or seeing Brendan. Instead of immediately fleeing to her room, however, she graced her mother with stories from her day, first boiling the teakettle and providing them each with a cup.

"The Kavanaghs would die if they saw how we make tea," she began, "just tossing one bag in a cup. They always make a pot, and the kettle has to still be whistling when the water gets poured in."

"Well, I've been making tea for years and no one has complained," Helene said, looking at her as if trying to make a diagnosis.

"Oh, I know," Marie said good-naturedly, "I'm just saying. Know what happened the other day? Brendan was making a sandwich here, and he reached into the bag of bread but there were only the two ends left, and I grabbed them out of his hand and threw them in the trash. I said, "You don't have to eat those, we have another loaf." Turns out, the ends are his favorite. He thought he was lucky to get both."

"He is so funny," she went on, "He tells me about his trip to Ireland last year. And it was hilarious. I gotta tell you this…"

And on she went. Sometimes, her mother did laugh at Marie's stories, but not without reservation. The truth was, Helene was disappointed in Brendan. He was polite but reticent, gracious but not familiar. She saw no trace of the boy Marie described, and it miffed her to know that he existed.

"I'm taking off a day this week to go to Asbury Park," Marie went on, "I asked Brendan to go with me so we can see where Bruce started out."

"Bruce who? I thought you've been to Asbury Park?" Helene almost accused, "Didn't you take the bus down during the summer?"

"Bruce Springsteen…and yes, I went there, but…I mean, I wanted to show it to Brendan," she explained, "It is one of my special places. I want him to see it. I was so glad he said yes."

"Well, why wouldn't he?" Helene asked, and Marie sipped her tea.

Each night, Marie called Brendan from the phone in her bedroom, while Lisa tossed and turned beside her.

"I can't stand it," Lisa sat up in bed when she hung up, "All I hear is 'okay, okay, me too, I can't wait' in these little whispers. God, it's sickening."

"Sorry," Marie said, getting under the covers.

Earlier that evening, Lisa had nearly walked in on her and Brendan, under the pool table in the basement room adjoining theirs. Marie had stunned Brendan by pushing him down as they passed the table and sucking him off fast and hard, swallowing and zipping him back up just as the top step received the first tap of feet. They quickly turned on the tv and looked engrossed, Marie holding Brendan's hand to revel in its quivering.

Lisa, she knew, had a boyfriend, but what did she know of this? She was seeing one of the Treacher kids, and this was part of a fading life for Marie now. She did bring Brendan around to meet them, but both she and he both seemed to prefer his friends to hers, and certainly his venue over hers as well. Marie only tried to maintain a solid bond with Jane, but she had to admit it was suffering.

Love in its most perfect form is not permitted to last very long, which is why cynical psychologists like Scott Peck prefer to call it other things. It is easier to brush off this heightened state of emotion as mere "infatuation" than it is to admit that you let it slip right through your open hands.

Marie did not say, "I love you" to Brendan first. Oh, she dropped the word plenty, but it was always cushioned: "I love your eyes." "I love the way you touch me." "I love being with you." Instinct cautioned her against spewing the ultimate confession; for always in Brendan she sensed something fragile and costly, and she was hesitant to handle it.

And so it was with great astonishment that she heard him spew the forbidden words first. They were walking through Central Park on a day that the first suggestion of autumn tickled the air. Marie was talking about her mother.

"I just don't know how I can keep paying her," she said, "especially since I just started paying for college." She liked the way that sounded. "But she won't give me a break, not the tiniest break."

"Well, isn't she just saving the money for you?" Brendan asked, earnestly.

"Saving it? For me?" She looked at him like he had two heads. "No way," she said, almost laughing, "For what? So I can go to college? Ha, little late for that one."

"I don't know, your future," Brendan replied, "I never heard of parents who didn't save for their child's future."

"Well, welcome to my world," she said, then looked at him, "Why are you with me anyway? I am always a wreck. Have you figured it out yet?" She tried to make the last part sound light and teasing, but it squeaked false at the end. She really wanted to know.

"You forced me," he said, "Remember?" But when she continued to wait, his eyes dropped to his hands. "Actually," he said softly, "I think that I might love you."

Marie would never understand the words that left her mouth at that moment, and would forever wish she could recant them. Upon hearing her beloved bare his soul before her, she reached over, picked up his hand, and in her most comforting voice, said:

"No you aren't. Don't worry. You think you are, but you aren't. I know. It will pass." She kissed his hand in a way that could only been seen as patronizing, and then gently released it.

He looked at her, bewildered and she probably looked stricken herself. She would spend the next few weeks trying to get him to say it again, and when the words did come, the evidence to support them would have started to fade.

Marie would someday question why she so readily believed a declaration of love from Manny's lips, but was immediately dubious of one from Brendan. She would someday see her life as a diagram or a map; with red pushpins in certain danger zones, warning flags juxtaposed against shades of soft tranquil blue. The red represented incidents in which she failed Brendan, the blue the backdrop of acceptance that Manny provided.

Loving Brendan, and being loved in returned, Marie learned, carried with a certain set of conventions. It wasn't that Marie wasn't eager to comply with her beloved's decrees; on the contrary, she was more than willing to mold herself to his likeness. It was that each new rule caught her off guard, each situation a pop quiz in the midst of a lazy week, or one of her mother's bewildering sudden slaps when she was a child. At one moment, life was good, and Marie was savoring it; at the next, she was trying to regain a piece of lost ground, and get back to where she stood firmly just seconds before.

She stumbled in the most innocuous of moments. Like the time he went off skiing in Vermont with a few of his friends. After a weekend on the slopes, he returned, limping, with an ace bandage wrapped around his ankle.

"Oh my gosh, what happened?" she asked, eager to hear, eager – too eager – to help, to soothe.

"Nothing," he said, and she felt it, though slight, the pulling away. Her hands fell by her sides and she willed them to stay there. In truth, she wanted to grab hold of him and squeeze hard; he had sacrificed one of their precious weekends for this ski trip, and she at least wanted signs that he had missed her. She felt it, the tingling in her hands, screaming for the chance to extract something she hoped lay under his skin; a sweeter juice yet untapped.

"Nothing happened but you're limping? Oka-ay…" she drifted, pretending, always pretending, not to care.

"Hey, don't be like that," he half laughed, and his voice was excruciating in its assurance, "I just mean there was no ski accident, nothing dramatic. We stopped at a rest stop on the way home, and I twisted my ankle getting out of the van."

They both had a good laugh over it, and made love deftly, Marie taking care to inflict only pleasure and no further pain, and she lay in his arms afterwards on top of her universe. A few days later, she told her family about her adorable Brendan, who skied for 48 hours on the killer trails but twisted his ankle stepping two feet out of a van. And that was where she stumbled.

"You *told* them???" he asked, incredulous, hurt. "Marie, I told *you* that. Not your family. It was private." He shook his head.

"Well, yeah," she sputtered, her chest constricted, "It was funny. Remember, we laughed about it. We *both* laughed," she finished, replaying the moment to check her memory. He *had* laughed, hadn't he?

"Yes, Marie, *we* laughed. That doesn't mean you should tell your family about it."

"Well, I mean, what is the big deal? It's not like you *fell* out of the van. It's not like you were wasted. I'm sorry," she said, and she was: sorry for herself, sorry to get it wrong.

"I guess if something is secret, you should tell me," she added, and auto-added this latest rule to her database.

They got over that, of course, but her database continued to fill. Once she continued a conversation they were having on an elevator. It was G-rated, and she was savoring their rapport, unwilling to miss a beat, but his face stilled her, and he made a little shushing sound with his lips, and so she knew that talking in public was not acceptable. Nor was kissing, of course, their first days together having been an exception she would someday need explained.

Karate, too, was a mystical thing, far above sharing with the commoners, least of all loudmouth Queens peasantry. Brendan went four nights a week, and taught it a few afternoons at NYU, and yet it was probably easier to get Clark Kent to reveal his secret doings than it was Brendan.

Marie had told her family that Brendan "practiced karate" a few weeks after she herself found out that "going to practice" did not mean he was on a softball team, and a few weeks before she had learned "the rule" about subjects permissible for disclosure. Too late, she realized that this would intrigue her father, and "how was karate?" would soon be part of his greeting when they arrived at her house conspicuously late. She literally had to ask her parents to stop mentioning it, and of course, this set off the guard dogs inside Helene's head, opening up a whole other can of worms.

"We can't *mention* it??" Helene asked, and she was smiling, smiling in the way that surely a cat must grin when a mouse has suddenly lost all methods of escape and can only wait in misery. Helene had found a chink in Brendan's armor, something she had longed to find for months.

"Well, Brendan is a very private person," Marie said defiantly, her instinct for defending him newly born and flourishing. Helene wasn't having it.

"Private? Over karate classes? That seems like more than private, seems a bit obsessive. Should we refer to him as "grasshopper?" Helene looked to her husband for approval, and got it; for the next several weeks her father would stop when he saw Marie and say, "if you can snatch this pebble from my hand…" even though this was a reference from a TV show called, "Kung Fu."

And then there was the day with the cheesecake, another day that Marie would remember always, another red flag, and another time that pure contentment and good cheer were sapped by some stealthy pickpocket she never saw coming.

They had been seeing each other six or seven months by this night, and were solidly incorporated in each other's worlds. In fact, they were out at McZak's, the pub where her brother was a busboy on Friday nights, partly to supplement his income, and partly because he actually enjoyed being that close to beer. "They" was her sister Anne and her husband, and Trish, her brother's girlfriend, people Marie had begun to enjoy now that she had found someone suitable to share them with.

Marie still felt new to this club, this status of secure coupling, in which you feigned a bit of disdain for the familiarity you had with your mate, lovingly complaining about his annoying habits with the voice of understanding. Trish was best at it, lowering her voice in a conspirator's whisper and moving close before she gushed, "Know what Robbie did last week?" causing Marie and Anne to hear about a side of their brother they had never known. Indeed, they would never think to call him, "Robbie."

The greatest sign of Anne's endorsement of Marie's relationship was the fact that she, a married woman, allowed Marie and Brendan to share a bed – or, rather, the pull-out sofa – when they slept at her house. Helene believed that the barely legal-aged couple slept there so as to spare her "waiting up" for them when they had too much to drink, or stayed out way too late, and trusted her firstborn implicitly to keep them honest and on separate sofas.

The blunder Marie made that night in McZak's was in assuming that it was okay to acknowledge something that everyone knew, anyway. They had finished their burgers – delectable greasy things that only a bar restaurant can produce – and she, Anne and Trish decided to split a piece of cheesecake. When it was presented with three forks, they dug in lazily, gently scraping off creamy bits between the prongs, then licking blissfully and slowly, and yes, almost sensuously. And then Marie said it.

"You have to admit, cheesecake is even better than sex."

There were no shocked silences, no suspension of movement, no gasps. Anne agreed and went on licking; Trish said something to the effect of "speak for yourself," and amidst giggles and saliva, the moment was over. But not for Brendan. She saw the muscle twitch in his face, and it was a muscle she would come to despise, breathing evidence of Brendan's displeasure, a lecture brewing behind his cheekbones.

He waited until, ironically, they were nearly naked on the thin mattress of Anne's Castro Convertible, and about to quietly indulge in the act Marie favored second to cheesecake, when Brendan said, "You really shouldn't have said that, you know."

She stopped, her hands poised on his "Yes" belt buckle, recently undone and seconds from releasing him, and wondered if she kept on going, pretending not to have heard, could she stop him from saying another word? Could she, with her mouth, still the disparaging words about to spill from his?

Too late, she hovered too long. He moved slightly and kept going, unbelievably; at 19 years of age, he drew satisfaction more from justice than foreplay. Incredibly, he thought he could have one and then the other, without missing a stroke.

"You know, that line about the cheesecake…being better than sex," he delivered each word like a light slap, not like Helene's, no, far more subtle and precise. "That's kind of private, don't you think?"

"Not really," Marie answered, unable to do now what she would someday learn how to do: stare at him incredulously, entertaining the possibility *he*, and not she, had a screw loose somewhere, "I mean, I've eaten cheesecake in front of my family plenty of times."

The joke served only to deepen the furrows in his forehead, and his belt buckle nearly refastened itself. "This isn't funny, Marie," he said, "Do you realize that by saying that, you are admitting to everyone that you've had sex?"

She should have laughed; should have crumpled back upon the pillows and rocked the bed with spasms of hilarity, and kept going until he felt discomfited and sheepish. But that was not who she was, not then. Instead, she reattempted her attack on his sheltered lower half, but this time her intent was different.

"I'm sorry," she said, "I didn't know it would hurt you." And she proceeded to make it up to him in the only way she knew how.

******

These were the things that she did not share with Manny when she saw him, noting that the stark truth, as they knew it, had fallen a bit by the wayside. It also confounded her to some degree that Manny appeared to be less in need of sob stories of failed love, his own or hers, having found glory in his imminent title of Officer Torres. His stories that used to start with, "Know what Madeline did?" receded, replaced with ones that usually began with, "Me and the guys at the academy," which only steeled Marie's will to keep her own stories nothing short of rapturous.

"I slept at the fraternity last night," she said dreamily across the table at lunch, "There was a dance, and oh my god, it was so much fun. There is this guy in the band, Gary..." she rushed on, unwilling to be generous, to share their time with equal portions of hyped happiness.

"What do I see in your bag?" he asked, remarkably not even listening to her, caught by the paperback sticking out of the top of her oversized tote. She carried her life with her, even to lunch.

"It's a book I'm reading…Brendan told me it was good, about…"

"*Trinity?*" he almost snickered, "You're reading Trinity? Is this a requirement for sleeping with an Irish guy, reading Trinity? What next, Marie? Maybe monogrammed shamrocks on your panties?"

This, too, was new: Manny making fun of her, and not completely void of disdain. Like her mother, he maintained that she had sold out, become a suck-up, fallen deep into the deplorable sin of idolatry.

"Jesus, Manny, it's a *book*. A book." She might have said 'a goddamned book' but she eliminated that kind of talk since Brendan. "How does reading a *book* make me lose my precious identity?" 'Trinity' was a well-known book about the Irish Republican Army.

"Never mind," he said, and they continued to talk and not talk, her extolling the joys of fraternity parties and bedroom scenes to follow, and him describing the painstaking process through which one becomes an officer of the law. At last they seemed equals.

****

It was when Manny graduated from the academy that he finally managed to dazzle Marie; that he, in fact, took her breath away, giving her an everlasting page in her unspoken memoirs. It was a humdrum workday, and she was typing like everyone else when he marched through Compton's reception area and presented himself to her in full uniform. She heard him before she saw him, of course; heard the schizophrenic crackle of his radio, the element of surprise lost to the clatter of inarticulate urgent voices tuning in and out. It was a sound she would grow to know, those choppy unidentified utterances punctuating their own whispers in the darkness, with only one word reverberating consistently like an omen: over. Over. Over.

It wasn't the radio, however, that stilled her typing fingers, but the hush that met it, as other fingers were frozen mid-stroke at the delightful possibility of some afternoon scandal. There was, after all, a police officer in the building, making his way down the runway of desks with steadfast purpose. Speculation bloomed like wildflowers as all waited to see who had transgressed, and how dramatic their apprehension would be.

Marie watched, too. She watched because she didn't immediately recognize him. He wore his hat low on his forehead, ridiculously low, another potential source of great endearment. She couldn't see his eyes at all, and the shadow from the brim hid the next third of his countenance as well. And so, she was startled when his stride slowed in front of her desk, causing her to look directly up at him. Just as recognition ebbed across her face, he reached down, grabbed her arm, and said in a voice intentionally loud:

"Excuse me, m'am. You will have to come with me."

And that was it. In some small way Manny reclaimed her in that moment. Marie glanced up at the clock, saw it was nearly lunchtime, stood up and allowed him to escort her out, knowing they were both loving it; the wide eyes that followed them out, and the tongues aching to wag upon their disappearance.

"Oh my god, Manny," she began as soon as the elevator doors closed, but she realized she wasn't ready to joke just yet. He was too…beautiful was the word that kept coming to her mind. Blue and shiny and steely, and beautiful. Her heart brimmed with something blissfully sweet, and she called it pride for now.

"Wow," she almost whispered, and touched his shoulder tentatively, as if somehow now her civilian's caress was a minor infraction. "Wow," she repeated, "Manny, you did it." This was all she said out loud, but she heard other, more telling words slip silently from her mind, echoing loudly off the elevator walls for only her to hear: *"and you're mine. You did it, and you are mine. You will always be mine."*

"I love you," he replied to her thoughts, "and I think there are some days that I'm allowed to say that. Today, of course, being one of them."

Then the elevator doors opened, and they were in the lobby, then out in the April sun, and Marie spent the next hour roaming the streets arm-in-arm with a New York City police officer, mesmerized, for once, by everything he had to say to her.

"I know what house I'll be in. The 2-3. It's in Spanish Harlem. It's not that far from you. We can still meet for lunch."

She took it all in rapidly. The way he said two-three and not "twenty-third." House and not "precinct." It took a few minutes to process these things, but she was proud that she stopped short of asking. She also didn't mention that she had no idea that Spanish Harlem was "not far." Anything that had the word "Harlem" in it sounded eons away from her.

"*Spanish* Harlem, geez," Marie said cleverly, "I wonder why they are sending you there?"

"I guess they figure I'll blend," he agreed, smiling, lifting his head so she caught a temporary glimpse of his eyes under the blue brim, "Let's go this way. I want you to meet a couple of guys."

They walked down 58th Street to Park, where a police officer was directing traffic while two others stood on the corner.

"Rookies," Officer Torres gestured toward them just shy of reaching the corner. "On our first detail." Another word she would learn. "They're great guys, they were a pisser in the academy."

Marie stopped short of the corner, loving this, wrapping herself up in this new part of her life like a wickedly thin silk robe, but suddenly struck by unnatural modesty. "But Manny..." she reached up, lifted his cap slightly to look at him directly, "Won't they wonder why you are with a woman who is not your wife?"

He removed his hat, placed it over his heart, and grinned. "Not to worry, m'am," his grin grew broader and he leaned closer and lowered his voice slightly, "I told them you *are* my wife." And thus placed his first stone on the mythical blue wall she had heard tell about.

As it turned out, she saw lots of her officer in the days that followed. It was April 1980, the year of the transit strike in New York City. A time when taxicabs would become as prized as fine gems, and Manhattanites would learn a new word: gridlock. It was a time when new cops flooded the area, directing the hopeless flow of traffic that wearily made its way from light to light.

For Marie, the ten days that New York did without trains and buses were nothing less than a grand escapade, akin to the blizzards that crippled roads and closed grammar schools when she was a kid. There was, literally for her, no way into the city from Queens, and no way out. Therefore, the only sensible thing to do was to *stay* in the city.

"I can't miss work," Marie told her mother in her gravest of voices, "No one can. They told us we just have to pull together and ride it out."

"That's nonsense, you can't miss work," said Helene brusquely, "If you can't *get* to work, you have to *miss* work." She squashed her cigarette out hard in the ashtray to complete her sentence, then added, "Case closed."

But the case was far from closed, as Anne called Helene later to confirm Marie's stand. "It's true, ma," she said, "It's not like they can give an entire city off from work. Who knows how long this will last? I'm only able to take some time off because I've been with the bank so long."

Marie couldn't recall a time when she loved Anne more. Helene trusted her firstborn, and Anne's explanation was reluctantly accepted without question.

"So," Marie explained gallantly, "I'll be staying in the fraternity until this passes. The guys are great, they are giving me a room to myself." A fib, of course, but Helene needed that. "I'll come home on the weekend, don't worry. Somehow."

It was more than a 55-block walk from Marie's office to Psi Upsilon, but Helene didn't know that, or she might have pointed out that people were walking over the Brooklyn Bridge in a valiant effort to get home *where they belonged*. She might have expected that Marie would walk over the Queensborough Bridge in a similar effort to be reunited with her *family* each night. She might have seen right through Marie's show of team spirit for her city, and found the profuse elation bubbling uncontrollably beneath. Instead, she sighed, and admitted defeat, and Marie ran to her room to call Brendan and pack her bags.

"You are not going to believe this!" she said, breathlessly, into the receiver, simultaneously scanning her bedroom for whatever she needed to sustain her life for the week ahead.

"Ummm...you're having Captain Crunch for dinner," Brendan replied on the other end. Brendan was funny, she thought again. They had recently talked intellectually about the pros and cons of Captain Crunch cereal, how at first it was a bit "too crunchy," according to Brendan, and then, outrageously, it went against all advertising claims by rapidly reversing to soggy when milk was added to the bowl. It was one of those moments when they connected, both seeing the absurdity of the conversation, both delighting in it anyway.

"No! Well, yes, that, too...but no...Brendan, I'm staying in the fraternity while the strike is on!" She caught her voice rising and lowered it, lest Helene hear.

"Well, we will have to charge you rent, of course. It's in the handbook. Wait, let me get it." She heard him shuffle papers and giggled. "Ahh yes, here it is. No female shall invade this property without proper authorization...I can give you that...and proper compensation. I guess we will have to work that part out."

"Ha ha," Marie laughed triumphantly, "For your information, I *will* be paying you. In *cash*." It was true. Another one of the ironic perks of this "unfortunate" situation is that her company compensated people who were "forced" to stay in the city. Remarkably, they paid $20 daily to the displaced employee, and $20 to the city dweller generous enough to allow another into their cramped space.

"Forty dollars a day, for you and me!" Marie reported ecstatically, "Can you believe it? Do you know what we can do with that?"

"You can do what you like with *your* twenty," Brendan instantly replied, "I for one am going to invest mine in a high yield stock," and of course she laughed, but for some reason, wondered for a second if he was serious.

Brendan shared a room with a Brazilian guy named Aldo, and Marie reveled in being their temporary third roommate. Each night, donning her newly fashionable white sneakers and anklets over her pantyhose, she walked from 59th and Madison to West 4th. In doing this, she got her first true look at how the city was connected, and how neighborhoods changed in the long stretch from midtown to downtown. The frantic movement seemed to relax somewhat past 23rd Street, and the stores went from lavish to eccentric by 14th Street.

Marie loved walking into the fraternity, taking the stairs up to the second floor and catching Brendan and Aldo in a game of chess, or a comical conversation, or occasionally, studying or sleeping. For a second, she would stand in the doorway, just watching, taking in what college life was supposed to look like, but mostly taking in the side of Brendan's angular Irish face, softened by his deep brown eyes. "Dark Irish," it was called, referring to his warm complexion and silky brown hair. Until Brendan, she thought Irish people were all red-haired and freckled.

"Honeys, I'm home!" Marie said, Ricky Ricardo-style, and immediately dropped her bag and whipped out today's gift from petty cash, "Dinner is on me!"

And then they would walk around the Village, sometimes bundled up against the still fickle April nights, stopping at the shops that boasted incense or suggestive t-shirts, adult books or drug paraphernalia, finally choosing a place to eat. When the enchanted evening ended, Marie would settle into the thick comforter in Brendan's bed, and if she ever considered it bizarre to sleep with a man on a bottom bunk while another man slept on the top, today it was only lovely.

The remainder of Marie's "strike" time was given to Manny. Sometimes, it was just lunch times, when she would go and watch him direct traffic on various intersections throughout the city. Later, she might jokingly label herself a "groupie," or "bimbo," for what she was doing, but for now, Manny beamed to see her there.

She couldn't get enough of looking at him, awed as if the ability to stand in the middle of the street and make cars go the way you wanted them to represented the most divine of power. And then there was the uniform. She had always salivated over the uniform, even back in the day when her old cop boyfriend wore it to pick her up from Treachers. But this was different. This was Manny. More than once she caught herself wishing that it were him that she loved, that he could truthfully introduce her to the "guys" as his wife or girlfriend. This thought crept in despite the recent nights "playing house" in the fraternity. Marie always knew that somehow, loving Manny would have made the air that much easier to breathe. And now, it would also be intoxicating, because now she would be in love with a cop.

If Brendan had karate, she and Manny met for dinner instead, and she noted that it had been a long time since she had seen him in the dusky hours. As they strolled the avenues, the image of that Queens doorway came unbidden to her mind, and she looked around to see if there was another she could be captured in before pushing the thought away entirely. There was sadness in its absence.

"How's school going?" he asked, the way he always asked, the way Brendan rarely asked.

"Oh," she replied a bit listlessly, "School. Okay."

"Just okay? I thought you were getting ready to take over the Creative Department," he said, and this was another thing that prickled Marie, people's easy belief in her. It seemed to her a careless belief, one that required no effort or knowledge of the real world, and no stakes in the outcome.

"It's *not* that easy," she snapped, but he didn't wince; this was a stronger Manny, one who could change the direction of cars. She softened her voice.

"Manny, where do people get confidence from?" He said nothing; he knew he was supposed to say nothing.

"I mean, I'm in this class, right? I do my homework, I get good grades. The professor likes me. Life is good." She paused, took a deep breath. "I'm terrified of presenting anything, terrified that it's wrong. Something that I worked for *hours* on at home...I hide it in my book when I get to class. Meanwhile, everyone else is already showing *theirs* to each other. I hear them saying, 'Well, what I did is, I approached it from *this* angle, blah, blah, blah...' They are *so sure* that it's fabulous...they can't *wait* to get up there and present it. And know what? If the teacher doesn't like it, they don't *care*. They go back to their seat with this little smile on their faces, shaking their heads like, 'what the fuck does *he* know?'" She was shaking her head almost violently now.

"Where does that come *from,* Manny? I'm even afraid to show it to *Brendan*!"

Marie caught herself; she had done it. She had revealed a glitch, an imperfection in her idyllic relationship. She looked straight in Manny's eyes and almost dared him to catch it.

"Ahh, Brendan...how is the Irish Catholic lad? Giving you any good reasons to go to confession, is he?"

Marie burst into the laughter that is a narrow escape from tears, and he joined her. Manny always figured that where pearls of wisdom failed, humor worked. And he was right.

On Friday night, Brendan drove her home in his father's car, and the following week, even Anne stayed in the fraternity, and then the strike was over. People would remember different things about the 1980 strike – the new bike lanes, the sneakers, the way cabbies could pick up multiple fares – but Marie would remember two things: nights spent with Brendan, and Manny's first days as a police officer. And, in order to be closer to Brendan, she began taking karate.

******

Marie's life moved forward, and she often saw it very distinctly as a train with a programmed destination, progressing willfully but with no ability to alter its course. She felt it, always, felt in literally in her feet, the need to move forward quickly before someone told her she was going the wrong way. Marie always chose to get there first, wherever *there* was, and evaluate the choice later.

She applied for a transfer into the Creative Department in mid-August, and in October, it came through. On her final day in Media, she wrote her boss Joe Hayeck a long note, thanking him for all he had done for her, to which he replied, "Please do not write me any more notes that make my eyes water."

Although she was only moving upstairs, she left Media with the melancholy she always associated with the ending of things. She had avoided this sorrow with Treachers by fading away slowly over time, in essence allowing it to leave her rather than the other way around.

That--and trepidation. "Here we go again," she thought, and briefly imagined saying to her classmates at Baruch, 'Ya, it's reeaallly great...I'm starting in, like, *Creative*, on Monday.' She would never be like that. About the only thing that excited her without reserve about the move, was that in this department, IBM Selectrics came with extra metal balls, so you could change your font to *script*.

It also came with lower pay. Apparently the monster-sized charts that Marie typed in Media – accomplished only by folding the paper into thirds or even fourths – represented much harder work than was expected in the Creative Department. Here, it was just "straight" typing, and you were paid accordingly.

Gone was the runway; here, secretaries sat in alcoves of three, between walls that did not reach the ceiling. Enclosed offices only existed on the periphery of the floor, and were naturally reserved for the higher-paid innovative minds. Everyone else had to be inspired in a cubicle. On slow days, Marie could entertain herself by eavesdropping on one side of two or three simultaneous phone conversations, which ended up sounding like a nonsensical dispute between the individuals involved.

She sat between an older but tiny Puerto Rican woman named Maddy, who helped her out in a rapid, authoritative voice, and Kerry, a heavy-set black girl who said, "I don't need this" a few times a day. More daunting was the fact that Marie replaced a girl named Carol, who left to fulfill Marie's own dream of becoming a copywriter.

"You want to be a copywriter, too," Maddy stated in her brisk English, then went on to ask: "What is about that seat? Everyone who sits there wants to be a copywriter."

"Well, who needs this?" Kerry replied before Marie could utter a word, and Marie would get used to this; the way Maddy and Kerry talked right over her. They had been together for quite awhile: seemingly, only the middle seat experienced any turnover.

Maddy looked at Marie straight on again: "Kerry wants to be a producer."

Now Kerry looked only at Marie: "Yeah, four years of college and I start as a secretary. It's a tough field to break into. You got a book together yet?"

"Book" referred to a portfolio; a collection of well-written, well-illustrated ideas by which a prospective writer proved his or her brilliance. Marie remembered seeing the large, suitcase-like item clutched in the hands of hopefuls that shared reception rooms with her in her interview days. Zippered tightly between the leather-bound covers laid the ticket to success.

"Well, you better start getting it together," Kerry admonished, in voice that did not reveal to Marie whether she was friend or foe, "They ain't gonna just hand you a job on your good looks."

"Whatcha talking about?" Maddy scolded. They were back to talking above Marie. "Carol did it, so why wouldn't...I'm sorry, what's your name again?"

They were shushed by the arrival of one of their many "bosses," and Marie felt it, the chronic, inescapable swell of choking fear and fortitude. How *ever* could she pull this off? How could she not?

"Oh God, Manny, I need a *portfolio*," Marie whined over lunch at the Playboy Club. He was in civilian clothes; it was his day off.

"Which is?" he asked, and Marie explained. "I don't even know where to start, with my 'ideas.' I have no ideas! I want to take this class at SVA, you know The School of

Visual Arts? It's around the corner from Baruch."

Manny nodded so Marie kept talking. "It's through the Learning Annex, so I wouldn't get any real credit. But it's called, "Building Your Portfolio." Sounds more nitty-gritty than the courses at Baruch. Of course, it's $140, which I don't *have*. I told you I make less money now, right?"

Manny nodded again. He was listening, but Marie also sensed that he was patiently waiting for his turn. She wasn't ready to give it to him.

"I told my *mother*, too." Marie barreled on, "*That* was like talking to a wall. Did I somehow think she was going to lower my household contribution? Forget about it." Marie sighed; she was done. "So, how is it going with you, Officer?"

"I got to say the line that I always wanted to say." Manny sat up straighter, leaned closer. "The other night...I know this is so childish but...I chased this guy for blocks...armed robbery dude...I was dying, I couldn't catch up to him...but I'm in pretty good shape, I wasn't even out of breath. Still, your adrenaline is at the bursting point, and besides that, you're *mad*. Because you told this guy to stop and he made you do all this running. Anyway, he runs into this alley, and I know I've got him. Dead-end. And I run up behind him, and I say, "Freeze, motherfucker, before I blow your fucking head off."

Manny smiled with sheepish pride. "That was it," he said, and he repeated it: "Freeze, motherfucker, before I blow your fucking head off."

Now Manny was rolling. "It's like, this job...it's 4, 5 hours of nothing for 15 minutes of heart-racing, spine-tingling...*glory*."

"Not quite how they show it on the cop shows, huh," Marie interjected, and Manny considered the semi-question more seriously than she intended.

"Well, yes and no," he said, "It's like an hour cop show depicts maybe a month's worth of actual events. Plus, it's all detectives on TV shows, I think. We're not that interesting. Well, we are, but...a realistic show would have two cops just driving around, talking, stopping for something to eat for 55 minutes, then have something happen in the last five. Then, I guess the previews for next week would show guys doing paperwork. One incident equals days of paperwork."

"That's all me and Donna…my partner's name is Donna," Manny added, "That's all we do. Drive and talk. You have no idea how well you get to know someone when you are forced to share a car for 7 hours straight."

At this, Marie pushed her hair behind her ears, an involuntary gesture that was the equivalent of a dog perking his ears. She was suddenly on full alert.

"Your partner…is a *woman*?"

"Yeah," he answered, and if his smile was innocent, then he truly believed their days of mutual jealousy were over. "She's tough, though. Probably tougher than me. She makes fun of me a lot."

"Oh," was all Marie managed to say, and she studied Manny: his face, his entire demeanor, his *happiness*. She thought it was just the job that kept him so light on his feet, practically bouncing, but could it be something else?

She went back to work feeling highly dissatisfied, trudging past the reception desk deep in thought, and staring blankly at her typewriter for a few minutes. Manny had barely paid attention to her, she thought, barely acknowledged her current crisis about the portfolio. Why was that? She was still mulling over it as she loaded paper into her Selectric, when the front desk called.

"Marie Meyers, may I help you?" She was allowed to answer her own phone with her name, and this usually tickled her.

"There's a delivery for you at the front desk," came the voice of Gerry Brown, the receptionist.

Puzzled, Marie walked briskly back to the area she had just passed through 15 minutes before. She rarely got any deliveries for herself, and anyway, she had only been in this department two weeks.

It was just an envelope, and she opened it right there, in front of the Gerry.

Curiosity would not allow her to wait. Inside was another envelope, a bank envelope, and a note:

"Take the class at SVA," it said in small recognizable script, "so I can say I knew you when." Inside the second envelope was $140 cash.

Only Gerry saw Marie's face flush, and her stance visibly relax. Mrs. Brown, however, asked no questions, and that was good, because Marie definitely had no answers. She could never account for the relief that flooded her body, but it had little to do with the ability to take a course at SVA.

She gushed about this to Brendan later that week: "Can you believe he *did* that? I mean, I wasn't hinting when I told him about the class. I was just talking, well, complaining, but I do that with Manny all the time."

Brendan's expression was noncommittal. If he felt threatened by Manny, Marie did not yet know this. She knew that Manny had stopped by Cabrini Hospital, Brendan's workplace, in an attempt to be friends – the Academy was, after all, just across the street, so it was not too desperate a move – but one did not "buddy up" with Brendan very easily.

"Come to think of it," Marie went on, "He did do something like this about a year ago…well, summer. He asked me about biking to Rockaway, and how did I bring anything with me. I told him I wrapped a few things in a towel, and shoved it between the bars of my bike. I said I had been meaning to get a bike carrier thingy, but I never got around to it."

Subconsciously, perhaps, Marie was trying to illustrate to Brendan what love was supposed to look like, at least, the kind of love she wanted. "And then, after I was back at my desk, the receptionist called…in Media, of course…and said there was a package, and it was a bike carrier!" She paused, because Brendan looked especially disinterested.

"I guess I should just be careful what I say around Manny," she concluded.

"For instance," Brendan interjected at last, "You wouldn't want to accidentally mention that you need an item that will cut glass."

Marie laughed. Brendan was so funny, in a clever sort of way. Not like Manny at all.

*****

When, exactly, did Marie become firmly convinced that she and Brendan should be married? When had she begun the intense campaign that resulted in the .66-carat diamond, reluctantly placed upon the finger whose vein allegedly led to her heart?

The move to Creative certainly provided some impetus, for Marie had begun putting her ducks in a row, so to speak. Career. Personal Accomplishments. Marriage. At 19 years old, the "Personal Accomplishments" included things she wanted to learn, like a foreign language, or a musical instrument, or places she wanted to see, like Colorado or California. There was no order; she needed them all. She remembered a lesson her old boss Joe had taught her one frenzied afternoon in his office, about maintaining many projects at once.

Marie had politely stood and listened at the time, unsure of what question she had asked to bring on Joe's philosophy on multi-tasking. Still, she must have unconsciously absorbed the essence of her boss' message as the erroneous mantra for her life: When securing happiness, choices need not be made. Everything is important. Everything is justifiable. Happiness was a jar to be filled, not selectively, but compulsively.

Too many things seemed to slip through her hands the year before her engagement, and her "jar" seemed more like one a child attempts to fill with fireflies on a balmy summer night. Each time the jar was opened to secure another brilliant treasure, one would fortuitously slip back out into the night.

She took the course at The School of Visual Arts, of course, but it wasn't much different than the ones at Baruch; in fact, it was worse. If students in a *business* school could be pretentious about their abilities, far more so were disciples in a school with the word 'arts' in its title. Marie was there to *build* a portfolio, as the name of the course implied. The rest of them were there to flaunt portfolios already in progress.

Even so, she forced herself to get started, by walking down 5th Avenue to Utrecht, the art supply store that someone in class unintentionally disclosed as carrying portfolios; empty ones, unfortunately: encased acetate pages carrying only potential and dreams.

Marie's dreams were fast dispersing; at night she would lie in bed unable to sleep, chewing her nails and watching her fireflies escape as if their wings had suddenly acquired motors. She was not maintaining her projects, as Joe had instructed her. In fact, right now there was a new girl at the fraternity who had set her sights on Brendan, and in another part of the city, Manny was falling in love with his partner, Officer Donna Vitalino.

Brendan's girl was, of course, not really from the fraternity, but from its "sisterhood," whatever that meant. These were the girls at parties who looked at Marie with the most suspicion and near malice, the ones who most enjoyed probing into her insufficient education, and pitiful secretarial status. It didn't matter that these girls were at NYU on hopeful parents' zero coupon bonds or some other careful investment, begun on the day they entered the world. It didn't matter that these were funds about half of them would waste; in fact, were wasting right now with paltry or incomplete grades and partying nights, and later with career choices unbefitting of a New York University graduate. None of this mattered, because they were here *now,* in blazing collegiate glory, and they knew that Psi U boys belonged to the girls in its sisterhood.

They weren't necessarily wealthy, these girls, but Brendan's girl came close. Her name was Colleen Bell, another dark Irish like himself, only darker. Her hair was jet black, and complimented by emerald green eyes. Marie herself was intrigued by Colleen's looks, never once wondering what anyone could see in her. In fact, Marie's relentless scrutinizing envy was relieved only by the observation that Colleen stopped short of remarkable from the neck down; her chest small, her midsection loose, and her hips broad.

"She'd be beautiful if she'd lose some weight," Marie said to Brendan, flippantly, as if her words could make him see something he couldn't easily observe himself. She wanted to appear somewhat altruistic in her critique, allowing Brendan to think that she cared for the good looks of women everywhere.

"Really?" Brendan looked at Colleen across what passed for a dance floor in the basement of the fraternity, a building once occupied by Edgar Allen Poe. He studied Marie's nemesis hard for a few minutes, as if trying to strip her of those extra offending pounds, and Marie nearly groaned aloud. Brendan knew nothing of the games women played.

Further words dissipated because Colleen was making her way towards them. Marie felt a rush of apprehension and expectation, and she didn't try to quell her fundamental instinct to prove herself better than this girl.

"Brendan," she said, kissing him on the cheek, a first score for her, causing Marie to protectively take his hand, "what time did you finally get to sleep last night? That was some 'study' session, wasn't it?"

Marie's ground was lost, as if an entire platoon came ashore to face her army of one. Colleen used knowledge and access as a weapon; living just four blocks away in a dorm called only "Brittany," she could catch those impromptu moments that occurred long after Marie had to catch a train.

"I'm surprised *he* didn't crash earlier," Marie jumped in, depriving Brendan of a witty comeback and feigning full knowledge of this 'study' session. "He loves his sleep."

Familiarity is also a weapon of love. Marie stared into Colleen's wicked jade eyes, and moved closer to Brendan than his rules on public affection would normally permit. Horrified, Marie heard Colleen say, "I know. He was still gone when I left. I had to pull my sweater out from under his head, and even then he didn't stir."

Marie laughed knowingly, but she knew she lost, and she knew that new words for crazy had just been born inside of her: fanatical, mad, extreme, and burning, possessing no reason or thought, or consciousness of possible outcome. A quick glance at Brendan saw that a guy named Peter had stolen his attention – did Peter know about Colleen? Marie mulled – and then she plowed in. Leaning a bit closer to Colleen, Marie said, "I guess I must have worn him out earlier. I'll have to go easier on him so he can focus on his classes."

She paused to alternately watch Colleen's smile slowly dismantle, and verify that Brendan was still not listening. Then she added, "I mean, he needs to get a good job when he graduates, so we can get married."

Of course, nothing had happened between Brendan and Colleen on that aforementioned evening – she had, like many of the drunken sisters, fallen asleep on one of the depleted sofas – but the battle was on, and Marie drew her armaments, without sagacity or rationale.

From that point on, to anyone who would listen, and safely out of his earshot, she expounded on her plans to marry Brendan, *their* plans – oh, nothing official yet, but inevitable, of course, why not? Neither had ever felt this way before. She missed glances that cloistered college people gave each other, some amused and some horrified – marriage? What the hell was that? Something far from Jack Daniels and sticky floors and a paid-for apartment in the Village that only college life could grant them? Something their parents did long ago, and it was a good thing. . .for them. They would look at Brendan, and try to decipher what he had been poisoned with, and if he found this nectar sweet, or did he want to be saved? Because they would be happy to provide the antidote, if they could, he had only to show signs of distress.

This was the rhetoric she surrounded Brendan with, giving him no opportunity to dispute it, and only hinting at its possibility in his presence, and even then only in his most defenseless of moments: lying both sated and depleted after they made love, him still struggling for the breath needed to contradict her.

To maintain her dignity about Colleen, however, she went with a different tactic; that of a free spirit, a broadminded wonder.

"You know," she said one day, "if you need to do something with Colleen, go right ahead. You're only 20, and you haven't done much at all." She was worldly and wise, and selfless. "I'd understand, who could resist her? It wouldn't have to mean anything, right?"

She told this later to an incredulous Manny, who allocated her time for foolishness in between stories of Donna.

"She's tough, Donna," he said, languorously, "even though she's tiny. She's shorter than me, can you believe that? But when we chase down a perp, she's right there. Comes from a family of cops, in Staten Island."

"I told her all about you," he went on, momentarily snatching Marie's full attention, "how we used to work together, how you are my best friend."

How you love me, Marie added silently. *What happened to that, Manny? How did you leave that out?"*

"I told her we were so close, we could spend an evening in the same room, in the same bed, even, and not do anything," Manny went on, and Marie had enough.

"We *could?*" she said it more like a statement.

"Couldn't we?" He sensed the jaggedness in her voice and strove to smooth it. "I mean, don't you think we could?"

"No way," she said simply, and he probed no further, saving this particular food for thought for revealing discussions in more enlightened times.

"Well, okay," Manny said, and she was perturbed with his uncharacteristic lack of curiosity. "Okay…anyway, I'd like you to meet her. Donna, I mean."

"Sure," Marie was less than enthusiastic. *Sure, Manny. I need more women to hate right now. Let's set it up.*

They were standing; he was paying the check.

"So," he said pointlessly, "You'll be marrying Brendan." They were walking now, coming upon her office, and he saved his only poignant line for minutes before she entered her building.

"You don't really want him to cheat on you with this Colleen woman, Marie. You know you don't." He kissed her on the forehead, mentioned calling her soon, and left.

You don't know me anymore; Marie fought enraged tears with this thought, but never asked herself the palpable question. Two women, two separate men. Why, then, did she consider both females her competition when she only loved one of the males?

****

Donna Vitalino would never be cast for a main character in an 80's TV cop show, except maybe for her stature. She was petite, as Manny described, and this was necessary to offset the dimensions that police equipment added to a woman's hips. If the camera was known to add pounds, the real burden of a belt laden with a gun, bullets, radio, stick, notebook…could only exacerbate the problem. Hollywood liked its girl cops lean.

Physique aside, Donna was anything but graceful in demeanor. She had a horrific Staten Island accent – "I wouldn't believe there was anything worse than a Queens accent," Marie told Manny with mock innocence, "but there is" – and a gruff laugh. With relief, Marie noted that Donna was not pretty; with dismay, she noticed that Manny did not care.

It didn't much matter, anyway, because within ten minutes of meeting her, Marie realized that this woman was unaware of any rivalry; unlike the encounter with Colleen, there were no hidden jabs, no cozy claims on Manny's character. If anything, Donna seemed only marginally interested in Marie.

"So you're Manny's friend, huh," she said, "I tell him all the time he's nuts to come all the way down to midtown for his meal time. He's gonna get himself in trouble. But, what the hell."

"He tell you the crazy stuff he pulls at work?" she went on, just making conversation, not pulling intimacy rank, "He's nuts, this friend of yours."

"Tell her about the night we drove to the back of that warehouse," Manny said, looking from Marie's face to Donna's, proud of one or both, and they were off and running, talking with reasonable comfort.

So grateful was Marie that Donna was not openly intimidating, she found herself particularly gregarious. She mentioned she worked in an ad agency, and Donna, in a flickering moment of interest, said, "Yeah? Like you can get free magazines and stuff?"

"Sure, all the time," Marie offered magnanimously, "They're called 'comp subscriptions.' Why, what would you like?"

"Cosmo…I think I'd like Cosmo free…if you can get it."

Donna did begin receiving Cosmopolitan magazines after that, addressed to Officer Vitalino, but she never knew that Marie ordered, paid for, and renewed the subscription annually for several years. She didn't like or dislike Donna, but she knew that she chased down bad guys with Manny, and therefore had an understanding of him that Marie herself would never possess. The subscription was a misguided acknowledgement of this, and perhaps a way to own Manny by becoming friends with his friends. Perhaps, also, it was a consolation prize, for she knew she would never allow Manny to fall in love with this woman.

"So, what did you think of Donna," Manny asked before they even had begun to drive. He had picked her up from work, something she found remarkable, the ability to get home during rush hour without the use of public transportation. The train represented a mystery connection between Manhattan and Queens; you sunk low under the earth in one borough and emerged in the other. In the car, you battled the traffic and the smog to get home, but the path was still clearer.

"She was okay," Marie mused, deliberately noncommittal. "Not really your type, though, I don't think."

For answer, Manny slowed the car, pulling over to a spot beneath a sign that screamed of fines and towing and other menacing repercussions for one who dared to park there during the evening commute. Marie felt her heart skip and she hated herself for loving that Manny could do this: defy the law because he was the law.

"Not my *type*," he asked merrily, "Not my type? I have a *type*?"

Not like me, I mean, Marie wanted to say, but she knew where she was headed and was ready to rush on.

"No, I mean, well...Manny, do you love her?"

"I don't know," he answered, and she could swear he was blushing under his tan face, " I think so. I'm not sure how she feels, but we talk so well, and . . ."

Marie wanted to wipe his sheepish expression off his face, and toss it, together with his emotions, clear into the waters of the East River up ahead.

"If you don't know if you love her, you don't." Marie was efficient and certain; punctuating her sentence as if she were snapping closed her briefcase at the end of a lucrative deal.

"I don't." Manny was staring ahead. "I don't?"

She felt bad, but self-preservation ruled the day, and she couldn't be swayed. "Manny, I am your friend. And I know that when you told me you loved me, you were sure. You were positive." He was quiet now.

She asked, "How could you be sure about me, and not sure about Donna?"

"You're getting married, Marie," Manny answered, "and you're happy. And it's time for me to get real about things. I'm already married, and I'm definitely *not* happy."

Marie didn't bother to tell him that as yet, Brendan was not informed of this upcoming marriage. It was irrelevant to their debate. Instead, she had a momentary image of Manny's belt, was it called a utility belt? The one that held his gun and nightstick and what else? She wondered how he chose what to use in any given situation, when to whack a suspect over the head with a stick, when to threaten him with bullets, and in fact, when to let a bullet actually escape?

Her comments so far felt steady and numbing, like repeated bashings with a stick, but she was moving in for the kill now, and subconsciously felt herself pause before choosing something more lethal. If she attempted to find the metaphorical equivalent on Manny's belt, she wouldn't find it; for she seemed to pull out a long deadly needle, and got ready to inject him slowly.

"Okay," she said, and prepared the serum. "But," she said, and pricked. "Suppose I weren't getting married." Push. "Suppose I were free." Deeper. "And I realized that I loved you, too." The syringe was in; now it was time to insert the substance. "If that were true, and I were free, then. . .do you think that you would still want to be with Donna?"

Manny stared at her as if hypnotic, uncannily mimicking one who had truly just been poisoned. After several deathly still moments, he finally whispered, "Oh Marie. . .how could you do this to me?"

"I didn't do anything," Marie retorted, withdrawing the contaminated invisible needle and straightening defensively, "but save you. You cannot love her if you love me. Do you want to end up in another ridiculous marriage like the one you are in now?"

Marie felt no guilt that Manny believed her intentions were pure, though, like so many other things, she would one day confess to this, too. He still spoke of Donna, of the perils and pleasures of their 4-12 shifts, but he never again declared his love for her. For that, Marie was grateful.

Brendan, on the other hand, took Marie's offer and had a tryst with Colleen, bringing on weeks of misery and confusion between them. He believed Marie when she told him it was all right; he did not have the insight to believe otherwise. He even told Colleen that it was okay with Marie, which saved some small portion of her pride. Colleen told her that she was "lucky to have him."

Still, after many tears and diary entries, Marie donned her armor, waited for a perfectly lucid moment when both of them were clothed and coherent, and said to Brendan: "I want to marry you." And so set the wheels in motion for a rough journey ahead.

Chapter Six: The Creative Department

Brendan didn't want marry her; of this, there was absolute certainty.

"My parents didn't marry until they were almost 30," he explained, trying to keep it light, "My Uncle Seamus didn't marry until he was 50! He married a woman he held in his arms as an infant."

"And my mother married at 18," she said, willing him to love her, the way she wanted to be loved, without fear or contradiction, "although my dad was 27. Either way, so what? You get married when you love someone. There is no correct age. There is no right time."

"There's the right amount of money," he rejoined, calmly, though. "Meaning more than nothing. I'm still in school. I work weekends."

"Well, I didn't mean we had to do it *now, today*." Marie's frustration was mounting. "I'm in school, too. I'm getting my portfolio together, and working on my career."

She went on, "Although I don't see how my career would be impeded by marriage, exactly. But we could get *engaged* now. We could promise each other that we will be married."

"Well, we probably will be. Do you know how upset my parents would be if they found out that I got engaged without even finishing college?" Brendan's voice rarely raised then; it was just like a dripping faucet, cold and steady. He broke the meter with an occasional lacing of laughter, perhaps to soften the message, perhaps to ward off his own tension. Either way, it came out metallic and edgy, as if the figurative tap water had suddenly hit something unfamiliar in the sink below.

Marie guiltily hid her pleasure in the idea of causing Brendan's parents displeasure, although the scenario made her smile briefly. She knew they thought their son was too good for her. She knew they viewed him as the helpless victim of a shameless hussy trying to improve her social standing. She thought of the movie, "Arthur," which had just come out, in which Dudley Moore describes Liza Minelli, the woman he loves, with the following words: "She's from Queens. She's nobody." That was Marie. Nobody. But Liza Minelli got her man in the end; and so would Marie.

"It's not up to your parents, Brendan," she said. "It's up to us. Don't you love me?"

"Whether or not I love you is not the point," he answered, successfully wriggling out of the question, "I can't get married now. Or engaged. I have no job. I have no ideas for a job. All I really want to do is teach karate. Does that sound like a career choice to you?"

Marie was starting to understand the true purpose of college. It was not, as she believed, a valuable tool by which one prepares for life, no. On the contrary, it was simply a method by which one *delays* this dreaded entry into adulthood. It was an all-expense paid make-believe world that most are comfortable to remain in. During the transit strike, Brendan became the president of his fraternity, in a ceremony so comically secret; Marie was confined to his bedroom with strict instructions to avoid even eavesdropping. This responsibility, as well as teaching Tae Kwon Do at Loeb Student Center, was all Brendan sought; in fact, she suddenly realized that he rarely spoke of his classes, or of any practical purpose to college. He hadn't even settled on a major. His job at Cabrini served to keep him in grilled cheese and peanut butter, and he was truly content. While Marie sought to forge hurriedly into the future, Brendan was at ease with the present.

She quieted down, and kissed him. She sent the signal that she understood, even implied with the touch of her lips that he had convinced her, but in truth, her dreams took precedence over logic, and she could never see past those dreams. This year, she *would* complete her portfolio, and she *would* tell everyone that she and Brendan were engaged.

****

After weeks of work, her portfolio was a flop. She didn't *get* it, and none of her courses at either Baruch or the School of Visual Arts clarified it for her. Her ads were too literal, too honest and too lacking in flair. She illustrated them herself, instead of hiring an art director like so many aspiring copywriters did, tracing pictures from magazines to go with her words, and too painfully embarrassed to even ask an opinion from the plethora of creative minds that surrounded her each day.

She knew the "book," as portfolios were usually called, was all wrong as soon as she showed Gene DeCotiis, the Creative Director that had recently taken an interest in her. He just sighed too much looking through it, had too few comments, and in the end, well, he never got to the end. He shut the book only about halfway through.

"Okay," he said, tightened his lips. "Marie. Have you ever seen anyone's portfolio?"

"Some," she said, forcing herself to look directly at him, and not at the furnishings in his office or the shiny shoes on his feet, "in my classes at SVA. Not many but some."

"Well, you know, Carol…er, I forget her last name, she used to sit in your seat," he thought for just a second than waved away the need for a surname, and in truth, Marie was used to the name 'Carol Who-used-to-sit-in-your-seat,' and so urged Gene to continue, "Carol had a great portfolio. You should ask to see it."

"Okay, sure," Marie replied with invented zeal, for talking to Carol was about as off-putting an exercise as, oh…weighing oneself after a weekend binge? Going to confession? Driving through Spanish Harlem with the windows down, stopping to ask passer-bys for street directions? 'All of the above,' Marie thought, envisioning Carol. The former secretary was lithe and fast on her feet, ripping down cubicled corridors with black curls bouncing, daring anyone to interrupt her newest spurt of creative juices. She had clearly forgotten where she used to sit, had no memory of any humble beginnings, as if she one day vacated Marie's fated chair and ran away as fast as she could. Marie could not hope to catch up.

Marie stood to leave Gene's office, a real office with a window that looked out on Madison Avenue, and walls to the ceiling. She held her tears as tightly as she clutched her portfolio, willing both to stay hidden until she was safely away. Gene, however, watched her intently all the way to the door, as if wanting to see her emotions unleashed upon his plush carpet.

"Marie," he said brightly, as if a brilliant solution had just burst upon his spontaneous mind, "Why don't we go out for drinks tonight after work? To discuss your book, and what we can do to pizzazz it up a bit?"

Marie brightened as well, not because she saw a cure for her misery, but because she shamefully experienced an internal cheer that at least Gene liked her, at least he did not view her as unpromising. She was also amused by the word, "pizzazz," for Gene sold himself with a young, breezy image, so that word gave away his near forty years of age. And so she sought her depleted reserves for a clever response that would indicate that she did, really, have some way with words, but all she could do was nod and say, "Sure, great. That would be great," and then she smiled for a bit too long and left.

She couldn't find a place to cry; the ladies' room was always full of gossiping secretaries or rushing writers and art directors, stopping only for one second to adjust a stray lock of hair. It was too early for lunch, so she had no choice but to turn her tears into a ball that wedged in her throat, and a rock lodged in her chest. For the first few minutes after returning to her desk, she actually sat doodling, drawing herself as if x-rayed, with the ball and the rock clearly visible. She colored the ball and rock darker and darker, with more vengeance, and continued until one of her many bosses brought her something to type.

David Smeding, the boss that interrupted her fury, was the first gay man that Marie had ever seen up close. Correction: he was the first gay man that Marie ever *knew* she was seeing up close. Clearly "out" and unafraid, he dressed flamboyantly and when Marie complimented him on a particular ensemble, he would beam and twirl a bit and ask, "then you don't think it's a bit *too* much?" Well, it was always too much, but Marie adored him and also added acceptance of homosexuals to her ever-growing repertoire of city-savvy thinking.

"Oh my," he said, catching sight of her artwork, "I do hope that isn't you in the picture. It looks so paaaainful." David elongated his words in an almost sensual way, and put one hand on his hip as he handed her storyboards featuring a cruise ship in various places on the ocean. "Are you okkkay to type this," he inquired, dripping with concern that was difficult to accept as genuine in his tenor, "because I can ask one of the other giirrrls…" He looked around at Kerry and Maddy, who began to bury their heads in the pit of their Selectrics, where the ball twirled energetically about, like the head of a madman.

"I'm fine," Marie said, and took the storyboards somewhat brusquely from David's delicate long-fingered hands. "What time do you need these by?"

"Oh, I don't presume to put a time on anyone," David said gratefully, for even gay men are apparently not at ease dealing with moody women. "How about we say as soon as you can," and with that, he was gone.

Marie loaded paper in her machine, but didn't begin typing immediately. Instead, she read the board, which represented a sixty-second commercial about the luxury of Royal Cruise Lines.

'I could write this,' she thought angrily, 'I could *write* this. What is so special about this? How is this so different from the stuff in my book?'

"Talking to yourself?" Maddy looked up briefly, letting Marie know that at least part of her thoughts had escaped from her mouth.

"Sorry," Marie said, and typed assiduously, as if shaping each word with her bare hands instead of merely slapping it on to the page. She would not re-do her book. She had tried and failed, and a secretarial life was nothing to be ashamed of.

As if sensing that her chosen calling was swiftly losing its voice, Gene DeCotiis cancelled going for drinks with her that evening, putting on a charming smile and asking for a "rain check, darlin'." Marie finished up for the day, and having no heart to train down to the Poe house, and no call from Manny offering a lift home, she boarded the oppressive RR train, and held herself together between the throng of hot bodies on the Q39 bus. At home, she walked to the bedroom she still shared with her younger sister, and didn't even check to see if Lisa was around before collapsing on her bed, and removing each of her ads from the shiny acetate pages, yanking hard if one had the temerity to stick. Then she let the stone and the rock that jammed her insides reconstitute into the tears she had suppressed all day.

****

It would be important for Marie, and certainly for Brendan, always, to remember how that ring came to be on her finger. In later accounts, it would always seem that Brendan was bamboozled, that she had led him into a jewelry shop on the pretext of, say, getting a watch repaired, and then ransacked his pockets for whatever that jeweler required to hand over the goods. A true jewelry heist. Broken rules of engagement.

It began, pathetically, perhaps tragically, with a question from her mother. Sitting in the kitchen, in timeless fashion, poised over the crossword puzzle with her Blackwing pencil, a coffee cup on one side and an ashtray on the other, Helene waylaid an absentminded Marie in the sleepy, defenseless hours. The latter was there to accost the refrigerator, and so it was in the eerie glow of illuminated food that Helene said, "So, what are you and Brendan *doin'*," Helene said, not asked, and Marie heard the contradiction – a question with a period at the end. The inconsistency imprinted the remark; clearly, Helene didn't want to know what Brendan and her daughter were doing tomorrow or on the weekend.

"Doin'?" Marie deliberately repeated the Queens pronunciation. "What are we doin' 'bout what? World hunger? The gas shortage? Cancer?"

"Don't be a wise-ass, Marie," Helene took a sip of her coffee, "You know damn well what I mean."

Actually, she didn't, and she knew better than to proceed. Helene could easily be asking what she and Brendan were doing about birth control, or about locating places to have sex now that summer had arrived and the fraternity was closed. Marie had innocently entangled herself in unwarranted frankness before, simply by believing herself ensnared before she really was. She learned, as a result, to gauge each interrogation before divulging any secrets. And so, Marie's response was to stand there, thinking at the very least Helene could have chuckled at her clever response.

"You've been going out together, how long? Two? Three years?" Now Helene was punctuating sentences with purposeful jets of smoke blown from her lips as if they were exhaust from the mechanism that powered the conversation.

"Not three," Marie answered quickly, but she understood, and pulled out a chair, her hands void of any sustenance, kicking the fridge closed as she sunk down. "Not even two," she went on, "but almost two."

"Well, that's certainly long enough," the decisive smoke continued, "to know what you want to do. Isn't he graduating soon?"

"Yes, I guess…he has a few incompletes to clear up," Marie was now tracing the pattern on the Formica table with her finger, "but yes, he will be out soon. We want to get married."

"Well, I guess *so.*" Helene put her cigarette down at this point, as if she could run the talk on her own steam now; the subject was that elementary. "At this point it's shit or get off the pot, I'd say."

Marie didn't even wince. Shit or get off the pot. Not quite how she would have phrased it, and certainly not the words to persuade Brendan, but apt nonetheless. Her mother's particular pearls of wisdom were grittier than most, and perhaps carried the stench of some polluted bay, but with effort, a precious nugget could be extracted from the slime. Sometimes.

Marie stood to boil water for tea, the symbol of her commitment to an honest mother-daughter chat.

"I had this same talk with your sister, Anne," Helene's voice went on, softer now, the cigarette done. She gratefully sensed her daughter's submission, so rare these days, "and she was just your age, seeing Hank for a coupla years. I said, Anne, you know you can live in this house as long as you want, I don't push my kids out the door."

At this, Marie busied herself with carefully wrapping the string from the tea bag around the spoon, drawing it like a noose to extract like blood the last bit of flavor from the bag. She refrained, for once, from spilling the cynical thoughts that banged at the walls of her brain. 'Sure you don't kick us out. You just make us pay through the nose to live here.' Marie took a quick sip of tea and burned the words off her tongue, tightened her lips and listened.

"But," Helene went on, and might have faltered at this uncommon silence, and maybe she lost her stride just a bit? Maybe she was more fueled by contention than she realized? "But," she went on, "when it's time, it's time. There is no need to keep on dating a man who isn't interested in marriage."

"He's interested, ma," Marie said, but she was glad she didn't have to rate his interest on a scale of 1 to 10.

The tea was still too hot so she set it aside. "Okay, first, he has to graduate, right? And then he has to find a good job. Right?" Marie looked at Helene for confirmation.

"Well," Helene confirmed, "A job, anyway. But that's what *college* is for, you keep telling me. Why wouldn't he get a good job?"

"So," she went on, always segregating one word before continuing, and now presenting her closing argument, "You can get engaged now, anyway. An engagement is usually a year these days, anyway, so you can be married next year when he's out of school."

"That's exactly what I was thinking," Marie answered, touching her mother's hand. At some point her father walked into the cozy scene, most likely he had fallen asleep on the couch watching TV and had roused himself.

"Fred," Helene said as if something was decided, as if she needed him to get started on the paperwork, "Marie says she's going to get engaged soon. Maybe get married in a year."

"To the Irishman?" Her father provided the light fare to the mix. "Better start looking at halls, you have to book them so far in advance. I'll take you Saturday if you want."

And that's how it began, innocently, over a cup of tea that got cold before it was finished. A few weeks later, however, things heated up, because it was July, and the Meyers and the Kavanaghs found themselves vacationing again in Lake George, sans the offspring that would one day make them in-laws.

The next thing Marie knew was that Brendan was on the phone, and he was mad. Not his usual subtle wounding version of displeasure, no, he was palpably angry.

"What the heck did you tell your parents, Marie," he yelled without preamble.

"I come up to Lake George for a few days, and I'm not five minutes off the bus when my mother and father are screaming at me, 'what's this, you're getting married? Why do the Meyers' know you are getting married and we don't?'" She could hear his fury echoing off the walls of the pay phone booth he had used to call, and she pictured it, in the country diner-slash-pub, where the locals ate and drank and the tourists came laden with bag loads of coins to call home.

"I said, 'I'm not getting married,' but they said, 'oh yes, the Meyers' told us, they said, looks like we're going to be in-laws.' Marie, they said they were looking at reception halls? Are you looking at reception halls, Marie?"

It was her first chance to speak. "I didn't say we were getting married *now*," she said, "I said eventually. It doesn't hurt to just look at halls."

"So you *did* tell them," Brendan heard the key words in every sentence, and responded to them in his own version of context.

"Why, Brendan? It isn't true? We aren't getting married eventually?" Her voice was getting higher, shriller, and she imagined the bumpkins at the bar looking over, wondering who was having trouble with the missus. "What are we even doing this for, then? I mean, we should just break up if we haven't any plans for the future." It was the closest to 'shit or get off the pot' as she could muster. "Do you want to break up, Brendan?" she asked.

"No, I didn't say that," he said, calmer now, and then she heard the coins drop, and knew he was hearing the recording asking for more: 'please deposit fifteen cents for the next five minutes or your call will be interrupted.' *Please deposit more money, Brendan, don't leave me hanging like this.*

"I have to go," he said, "I don't have any more change. I'll see you Sund…no, Wed…I don't know, I have to go," and he was gone.

Her response was to high-tail it up to Lake George, uncharacteristically taking last minute days off. Her own family had already returned home, so Helene was nonplussed at her sudden availability; she had told Helene she absolutely could not get away. It was difficult to let Brendan know she was coming as the only phone that existed on the premises was in the "big house," the crumbling mansion where the resort owners lived. She had let the phone ring forlornly, imagining that the piercing sound caused the walls to further fall to pieces. There was no answer, but she knew that eventually, there would be.

She was already in Bolton Landing before someone finally deemed it convenient to pick up the receiver.

"Hi, Mrs. Henderson," she said, familiar with the voice of people she had known since she was six or seven. Sometimes, she wondered if tourists became too familiar with the Hendersons, forgetting their place as paying guests. "Can you get Brendan for me?" she asked, confirming what she wondered just seconds ago.

After an interminable silence, there was a clunking sound and then Brendan's voice, breathless; he had come from a distance.

"You're *here*?" he asked, and it was not the tone she hoped for. Not irritated, just puzzled, but either way not pleasantly surprised. Definitely not pleasantly surprised.

"I tried to call," she began, on the defensive, always, "but no one answered at the big house, and…"

"That was *you*," and now a bit of incredulous irritation had crept in, "calling over and over, like, 40 rings?" Silence. "We were sitting in the cabin wondering who the heck would let a phone ring that many times."

More silence. "Okay," he finally sighed, "Let me see if I can borrow the car to get you from town."

"I can walk," she said, knowing that it wouldn't be much fun to walk with her bag, but at least it was lighter than the other weight on her shoulders, but it didn't matter, because Brendan was gone. Propriety dictated that he not stay on another person's phone a minute longer than necessary.

Remarkably, they did not have a bad time together those few days in Lake George, nor did the Kavanaghs treat her as if she were evil. One day, Brendan rented a motorboat, and they went out on the lake with the picnic lunch that Mrs. Kavanagh had packed for them. Surrounded by a hundred thousand sparkles upon the lake, eating a tuna melt warmed further by the dry mountain sun and Marie's gratitude, she and Brendan talked. Besides expressing his feelings for her, a declaration Marie would need to hear restated in various word formations over and over in her life, Brendan also agreed that "just looking" at reception halls "couldn't hurt." This came after Marie's wide-eyed plea that if people love each other, it doesn't matter how much money they have, or if they've finished college or not. There was no need to wait for anything once you knew you loved someone. She was irresistible, and above all, presented a rational argument, full of compromise and loopholes, and he melted like the cheese in his sandwich.

And so, it was with great surprise and frustration that he found, less than two months later, Marie presenting him with possible dates to get married, and letting him know that her uncle was a jeweler and could get him a good price on a ring. She and her parents had checked out halls on their own; had chosen one in fact, and found that dates began disappearing a year in advance. They really could not afford to waste any time.

****

Marie would often in her life hear stories of other couples' engagements; how one woman was surprised by a ring left in her jogging shoes, and another glowingly reported that she had refused her husband-to-be for a solid year until he wrote her a letter that melted her heart. Her friend Jane reported matter-of-factly that her fiancé, John, had given her a ring at sunrise over Lake George, a story that brimmed with contrivance, but who could say? Marie's favorite story came years later from one of her professors, who told her that he met his wife at a party, and they moved in together two days later, married soon after, and were together still 30 years later.

Her own account, by comparison, would always be one told sheepishly, with some shame, and Marie sadly conceded that she had ruined her own romance novel. As her dishonor began to ebb, she used her tale, as would a wise old sage, solemnly offering up the moral to save others, especially her own daughters.

"Never," she would say, "ever, ever…beg a man who does not want to marry you to please do it. Don't beg and don't threaten to break up if he doesn't put a ring on your finger. It is he who should be begging *you*."

"Do you know," she continued, "that I went with your father to get that ring, even lent him part of the money to pay for it?" She'd shake her head in amazement. "Afterwards, we walked down city streets, and I gazed at that diamond gleaming in the sun, then looked at Brendan, willing him to be happy. I'd show him the diamond over and over, like some lucky amulet that could save us."

She gazed at it often, just below her chewed fingernails that she was now trying to grow to do the ring justice. Often it would startle her while typing, dancing above the keys to the tune of fluorescent lighting. It had only one flaw, according to the jeweler friend of her uncle's, but he said, "It couldn't be seen with the naked eye," a reassurance that had an opposite effect on Marie as it seemed oddly prophetic. Sometimes, witlessly, she strained to see the secreted flaw, squinting under bright lights, once through the lenses of her mother's thick glasses. It needled her that it lurked beneath the glitter, a secret jinx, a microcosm of truth.

Once, unbidden, a memory sliced through her, of a tedious shopping trip along Knickerbocker Avenue, and her mother in her heals and bright red lipstick. In a moment of aberrant empathy, Helene rewarded her weary travelers with a treat from the bubblegum machine, the ones with plastic bubbles of treasure in lieu of gum. Marie's own indulgence was a ring with a wee diamond, and studying it curiously, Marie asked a question that would end up causing her mother acute consternation.

"Mom, is this ring real?" She was perhaps six, and she knew her mother's answer would be wise and true.

Helene answered easily, "It's *real* jewelry, but it is not a real diamond."

Flummoxed, Marie assumed the disparity in Helene's answer could only be the result of misunderstanding, and so she repeated, "My ring, ma. Is it *real*?"

"I told you, Marie, it is real jewelry, but it isn't a real *diamond*," and Marie sensed that she should quit, that she was ruining the goodwill gesture, and only her silence now could restore the moment. But she couldn't let it go.

"Ma. Look at my ring! How can it be real and not real?"

When challenged, Helene's knee jerk response was not to back down, which means she did not revise her original statement by a word or a syllable. Looking down at Marie from her high-heeled height, she said, with strength and emphasis, just what she had said all along.

"Because, Marie, it is real *Jewelry*, but it is *not* a real *Diamond*."

At this Marie began to cry, and her mother reached down, and whipped the treasure off her finger. Marie, oddly, did not react or care, hurt as she was by the enigma of it. Her mother, unsatisfied, said, "If you are going to cry, Marie, then I guess you shouldn't have the ring," so she cried all the more to seal her fate.

Closing the memory softly, Marie looked again at her ring, and this time she thought of the reluctant giver, her future husband. "He is real jewelry," she whispered to herself, "but he is not a real diamond." And that was the first day she wondered if she should remove the ring and give it back.

****

Gene DeCotiis was a man that Marie would describe differently someday. She thought he was old; he was only 36. She thought he was talented, but she would redefine talent someday. She thought he was comfortable with himself, satisfied, but he was as insecure as any man whose hair was thinning and whose wife had begun sleeping with him once a month at best. Mostly, Marie thought he had taken her under his wing in the role of father figure, or mentor, but that illusion was dispelled very early.

He came back to collect on his "rain check" for drinks, but something else happened first. Carol. One day, she slowed her frenetic pace down the halls, and a second later her bouncy black curls followed suit. Marie moved to let her by, assuming Carol stopped because Marie was taking up too much space. She didn't.

"DeCotiis told me you want to look at my book," she said. She said it matter-of-factly; she had small eyes and a tired look that contradicted the vigorous curls, as if their constant motion upon her still head tired her.

Marie didn't answer quickly enough, so Carol, preceded by her ringlets, set herself in motion again. "I'll bring it by tomorrow," she said, practically over her shoulder, "when I have time."

She delivered the book with the same lack of feeling, granting Marie a glimpse of her creative psyche without comment or explanation; standing over her, alternating between shifting from foot to foot and holding very still, as if trying to control the need to run.

Marie oohed and ahhed at first, before meeting silence with silence. She noted that the makeshift ads were well executed by real art direction, and that was the only thing

Carol made a note of, because Marie asked.

"The ads were drawn by Jake Young, know him? He sits over there," she said, gesturing, "third office. I paid him $100 to do it, but it's worth it."

Marie noted the fee -- $100 – a fortune, but that was not what most filled her thoughts. Studying Carol's book, she saw cutesy lines and catchy phrases, and suddenly, finally, she *got* it. Advertising was not earnest persuasion supported by credible facts about a product. Advertising was product entertainment that made people too amused or enthralled to really bother with the facts. Marie closed Carol's portfolio – the collection of flim-flam that had gotten her a job – and thought, simultaneously, "This isn't talent," and "I can *do* this. I didn't even *need* all those classes. I can do this."

"Thanks," she said, handing the leather-bound wonder back to Carol.

Within three weeks, Marie had her own book redone, and hired Jake Young for only $75 to draw it. It was filled with Carol-style ads, like one for man-sized Kleenex tissues that said, "Now Kleenex makes it okay to be a blowhard," and other nonsense, and it was right. She knew it. Fifteen pages of playfully illustrated plays on words, and she was ready to go back to Gene.

"I think you've got it, Marie," he said, sounding a bit like Henry Higgins, sans the accent. "I think you've really got it." This time, he perused the book thoroughly, saying every now and then, "You see how this ad captures the heart of the audience," or "See how this one really grabs your attention," as if the work wasn't hers at all, as if she had absconded Carol's book, and he knew it. At the end, he closed it with an excited bang, but zipped it lovingly, like one putting a baby in a bunting.

"We need to go out and celebrate," he said, and Marie silently put another duck in her row. Engagement: check. Dream job: check. She was on her way.

****

In December, Brendan's older sister got engaged, stealing Marie's thunder with an unflawed full-carat stone, and the approval of all. The ability to justify the Kavanaghs' lack of enthusiasm for their son's upcoming nuptials dissipated when she watched Mrs. Kavanagh, yes, even she, the queen of dry Irish indifference, gush and coo over Monica's rock.

And Monica was endearing in her apparent surprise, her virginal shock at the idea of becoming contractually joined to another, as if she truly had no idea that this was where courtship led. She displayed her ring with perplexed joy, like a newcomer who has just stolen the Best Actress Oscar from Meryl Streep. Marie suddenly felt large and clumsy next to her soon-to-be sister-in-law, her own ring dwarfed by her oafish person, even her clothing feeling tight and constraining. Why did foolishness feel so *bulky*, obvious as the nose on a clown? Monica's hands were small and delicate, and Marie watched her fingers flutter, clasp, interlock, thinking crazily that these were hands that deserved gems on every finger, and not just the one.

Defenses ready, Marie's response was to bond with Monica, but she was having none of that. It was clear they would not be rushing to the newsstand together for copies of *Modern Bride* anytime soon. Still, Marie walked into the trap, allowing her clownish form to swell.

"This is so exciting," Marie honked, "Two weddings in the same...well, not the same year, I guess. Since ours is in October, I guess...you won't get married in the winter, will you?"

"Oh goodness, I don't know," Monica was still on the stage, receiving the Oscar, breathy and shy, and she regarded the question as if someone had just asked if she intended to put her prize on the mantel at home, or maybe her night table? *Please*, her voice seemed to say, *I haven't gotten that far, it still hasn't sunk in that I've won.*

Marie was self-punishing in her pursuit. "Well, you'll have to know soon," she spoke with big-sister-like authority, "because the halls book at least a year in advance! Can you believe that?"

A two-second stare, and barely a nod, and Monica was done with Marie, and Marie pushed hard for the rest of the evening to gain her notice. She felt sick inside, and she didn't know why, felt she was losing something, and she didn't know what. She would find out soon, in a few weeks in fact, when Monica set her wedding date not a few months *after* Marie's, but a few months *before,* securing her rightful place as the eldest in the family, and of course, finding and booking the perfect reception hall far less than a year in advance.

Thus began the year; not the calendar year or the fiscal year, just the *year*, or sometimes referred to as the year *before*: before the wedding, before wisdom had a fair shake. In that year Marie would run into an old friend, playing pinball in a pub near her house, laughter in every ripple on her face, while her boyfriend looked on lovingly, and learn that they were about to be married but Connie had cancelled the wedding because she wasn't ready.

"The invites were out," Connie said amidst her giggles and the discordant music of the silver ball rebounding off the posts, "and I had to call everyone. I thought Steve would kill me, but hey if you aren't ready, you aren't ready." BLING! Marie noticed that she never lost the ball, and the points kept racking up in triumph.

"I could never cancel my wedding," Marie said, envious, once again, *for crying out loud.* Jealous of those getting married, jealous of the ones canceling marriage; whenever did it stop?

"You can," Connie replied, eyes still concentrated, hips well into the fury of the game. "I'll marry Steve, eventually. I love him. And when I do, who will remember that I postponed it? It's not about *them*, honey, it's about you."

At that point the jilted fiancé came up behind her, putting his arms around her waist, nuzzling into her neck in an inoffensive public display.

Connie turned. "You made me lose my ball," she said, sweetly, warmly, and Marie felt it, again, always, that it would never be this way for her. She wasn't concerned, especially, about the invites or the opinion of people she barely knew. She was far more vexed by her own feet, following a path like sleepwalking in the light, everything bright and clear and hidden just the same. She didn't want to turn back, couldn't turn back, but if only the destination could change by the time she reached it. If only she could stop believing that it would.

****

In this restive state, Marie became an advertising copywriter, and as there were no single cubicles available, she was situated in one with a secretary that wasn't hers. She crafted first words of genius while listening to Jasmine Chavez fight with her husband on the phone two or three times a day, and when she went to the supply room to get things for her new half of an office, she was met with wry indifference.

"So, you were a secretary, is that it?" an old tired face asked her.

"Yes, up until last week, when I..." Marie was geared to tell the story.

"And now, what, you're a writer?" The voice seemed to deaden with each word.

"Yes."

"Well. If you are a writer, how can you need supplies? Pencils and paper, right? Tell me you don't have pencils and paper." Now the voice was dismissive, and coupled with the shuffling noises of pointlessly moved desk items.

"Well," Marie pleaded, "I had thought that I would at least get a typewriter, and maybe some of those special balls with different fonts so that I can..."

The face looked up but the eyes barely followed. "You're no longer a secretary, isn't that what you said?" She did not wait for an answer. "You *have* a secretary. You write, she types. Get it?" With that, weary lady banged out a cellophane-wrapped package of pads and a few boxes of #2 pencils and Bic-like pens – "I'll even give you some blue and some black," she said – and sent Marie on her way.

Thus began the proudest accomplishment of Marie's lifetime. She was 22 years old, occupying a desk that faced a partition, with only blank blue lines on yellow paper and some basic writing implements to capture her imagination. She did indeed have a secretary, a cranky college graduate named Susan who filled the now twice vacated space between Kerry and Maddy. It took Marie three weeks before she timidly approached Susan to ask her to type something, and Susan let her know that her fear was not unfounded.

Her officemate was another story: "My God," Jasmine said next to her, "My husband is a lunatic. He is the most jealous man that ever walked the earth. When you answer my phone, don't ever say I'm talking to *a guy*, okay, Marie?"

"I don't answer your phone, Jasmine," Marie said patiently, placing her head closer to her page, closing her eyes slightly to indicate some creative process interrupted," because I am *working*. I have to write this Comet ad by this week, and it has to be good."

"Oh, am I stopping you from concentrating? I'm sorry." Jasmine looked penitent and she was sincere as well. "I'm trying to work, too, but Marcus keeps calling! Know what he does? He pretends he is a different man, uses a different voice, just to see if I flirt with other guys on the phone. I mean, really."

Jasmine was erotic, truly sex in motion. She was Mexican and dark, slim and full, flat iron in some places and spilling over in others. She wore tight shirts and high boots, short skirts and gypsy earrings; her eyes and lips were large and tempting, and no one, male or female, looked at her for just a minute. She wasn't especially bright but she knew what she had. She flirted mercilessly all day with every man that crossed her path, and she enjoyed this game with her husband, of this Marie was certain.

Marie liked her, but she had to strive for status now, and whispered stories of sexual endeavors – "do you know Marcus likes when I pee on him?" Jasmine said out of the blue one day – with half-clothed secretaries could not give this to her.

****

For Helene and Marie, just talking about the wedding, usually translated into a fight about the Kavanaghs. It pained Helene that the Kavanaghs had more money to offer, and therefore, more control over the nuptials. She maintained, faithfully, that it was the mother of the *bride* that got to determine things like filet mignon or chicken Françoise, but neglected to note that traditionally, finances backed these choices.

"I simply *cannot* pay for your wedding, Marie," Helene said, pronouncement-style, upon a soap box, "I do *not* have the money. But that does not make me any less the mother of the bride. I don't care how much the Kavanaghs pay for, they are not to step on my toes."

How could Helene know that Marie barely paid attention to Helene's indignation, barely heard her sniffles of faux despair? "Maaaaa!!!" she wanted to shout, "Stop me!!! I picked out the readings for my wedding ceremony and dreamed of running far far away all in one afternoon! Be a mother and stop me, say, you know, don't get married if you're not sure, or say, wait a little while, make something of yourself first."

"I mean, right is right," Helene went on, "and those Kavanaghs don't seem to understand that."

They nearly came to blows over whether to have a ceremony or a nuptial mass. The Meyers, counterfeit Catholics that they were, wanted the wham-bam-thank-you-Reverend version of married; just get in there, say I do, kiss, and let's get our gowned asses to the reception. Marie thoughtlessly dropped this bomb to the genuine Catholics – Mr. and Mrs. Kavanagh – on a car drive from the reception hall where they had just paid to upgrade their meal to filet mignon.

"What the hell do you mean, you're not havin' a bloody mass?" Mr. Kavanagh roared, and the car literally jerked to a halt and at once filled with high-pitched Irish shrieking and low guttural Scottish bellowing as if they had just gotten into a fatal accident.

Marie patiently explained: "Well, no one in my family is really religious, and besides, we really don't have time for a mass. The wedding is at 10 and the reception is at 12, and we have to get the photos done in between."

"Jesus, Mary and Joseph," Mr. Kavanagh enunciated each name as if calling upon them to appear, "It's not a bloody wedding if there is no mass. You may as well have it in city hall."

They sat, there by the side of the road somewhere near the BQE in a neighborhood that civilization forgot, and Brendan looked at her scornfully, urging her with her eyes to fix this mess.

"I'll talk to my parents," Marie said, and she did, and Helene cried, literally leaned against the washing machine and broke down in tears, whispering, "You are becoming one of them, Marie" and, "Well, I am telling everyone on my side not to receive communion. We don't have time for that shit."

And what the hell did she and Brendan talk about, in the year *before* the wedding? It might be that all they discussed was the *wedding*, and Marie's outrage that Monica had jumped and scheduled a wedding before her, and then, lo and behold, Robert and Trish got engaged and scheduled a wedding before Monica's! But first came the stabbing.

Although he still had a few credits to complete, Brendan moved back home to save money. With the fraternity gone, Marie had two choices. After a late night out, she could either sleep at his mother's, or they would journey back to her own home via train. Brendan, thankfully, did not allow her to face the MTA alone after dark, although it sometimes meant that he nudged her to leave him a little earlier than she would like. Occasionally, he would be able to borrow someone's car, but that was very occasionally, and it had to be returned within hours, meaning Brendan had to drop her off at her front door and drive back to the city. Once, she teasingly stated that the real reason they were getting married was to avoid the commute.

They had, in fact, already located an apartment of their own in Queens, a tiny thing with only a living room, a bedroom and half a kitchen, the brilliant result of the landlord, Mr. Swendrak, getting more bang from his buck by splitting his upstairs rooms into two miniscule living quarters. To Marie, it was charming; to the Kavanaghs, it was horrifying

– "Half an apartment for $550?" Mrs. Kavanagh ranted, and in her Irish accent, it was nearly amusing.

Of course, she had already mentioned that Monica "had her bread buttered on both sides," marrying a promising accountant who, although being transferred to an office in Texas, was sure to provide Monica with a *whole* apartment. Marie, now swamped in the sludge waters of her quandaries, only took a second or two to be resentful of the comparison. And besides, her own apartment *was* charming, even if it did not have the power to charm her life.

On this night, however, they were taking the usual Number 4 train to Union Square, where they switched for the LL home. The trains at night weren't the worst thing, really; unlike rush hour, at least you were guaranteed a seat, not squished together like sardines, wondering always, if you were female, if the male next to you was only *accidentally* rubbing his privates against your butt. Nights were shared with other sleepy riders who, in New York style, barely looked at you.

The trouble was, the trains took far longer to arrive, sometimes as much as 45 minutes. Dead on her feet on the platform, sometimes suffering the after effects of one or two drinks, Marie would think of the pull-out couch at Mrs. Kavanagh's, and wonder why, exactly, wasn't she in it?

Marie slept on Brendan's shoulder most of the way, and he woke her by roughing shrugging her head into an upright position, then guiding her rapidly up or down subway steps to the next stagecoach. By the middle of this trip, she got her second wind, and began mindlessly chattering to Brendan, an unsatisfying endeavor because he was always silently scanning for possible dangers. Marie thought he was paranoid now, and admitted that once she felt protected by his fastidious surveillance.

"So, you know what my mom said about our apartment?" she bantered, "You'll never believe this. Since it's right next to the M train, she said, 'Marie, you are just doing this to be closer to the Kavanaghs!' Ha! There is no pleasing that woman. I am living in

Queens, not Manhattan, but somehow, she thinks I am trying to be closer to *your* family."

Brendan gave a perfunctory smile, and maybe a tiny grunt or mumble, but he didn't turn to look at her, and Marie went on.

"She doesn't even want me to change my last name! She said, 'oh sure, now you are a writer, and you have become somebody, and it will all be under *his* name.' I said, mom, what are you talking about? Meyers isn't *your* name, either. *You* took dad's name!"

"Although I don't know if I'll actually use your name at work," she went on, now she even knew she was mainly talking to herself, "because they all know me as Meyers now, and it's on the door, well, the wall of my office, and I answer the phone that way. It would just be confusing." She took a second to breathe now, and in that second, fear like a fierce storm tore through her, and she grasped that the wedding was only, what, four months away? And all she had resolved was whether or not to take Brendan's name.

"We're here," Brendan said and stood up, taking Marie by the arm in an impatient gesture, waiting for her to pick up her bag full of what he called, "Marie things"; papers and books and work she took home and then never touched.

They got off the train at DeKalb Avenue instead of Myrtle, since the M train ran erratically after midnight and they didn't feel like shifting from foot to foot on yet another platform. They could walk from the DeKalb station to her house, although it was a creepy reminder of just how close Marie lived to the desolate Brooklyn-Queens border.

Marie picked up the chatter as soon as they were off the train, and this was the strange part. Preoccupied, she held the cast iron gate for the man behind her, a kid, really, and she smiled at him as he took it and let himself through. Her discourse stopped for a moment, partly because Brendan had gotten too far ahead to hear her, not that he seemed to be listening anyway, and partly because there was something about the boy's face that silenced her for a second.

Shrugging it off, she caught up with Brendan, and the boy was forgotten, and they mounted the subway stairs and stepped out into the barren night. They were on Wyckoff

Avenue, a thin dividing line between the desolate streets of Bushwick and that of Queens, not that it looked any different on either side of the that boundary. The difference came when one walked deeper into either region. Marie had never walked further than a block into Bushwick, but she knew it got worse with each step. It became incrementally better the further she walked into Queens.

"God, Bushwick," she said, looking around, noticing that it was still herself filling the night air with sound, "Do you know I was technically *born* in Bushwick?"

Brendan seemed especially agitated walking these streets, his city mentality ever aware of the presence of danger. He probably wished Marie would shut up so as to keep his senses keen to each infinitesimal symptom of peril. And they heard it, too, both of them, when it came.

First Brendan had guided her across the street, and she followed like a dog on a loose leash, figuring one side of the street was as good as another, and also used to Brendan's pavement-pounding quirks.

She resumed talking, or at least, in recollection, she would only hear herself talking, but perhaps this was just the norm. And then came the sound that she only recalled clearly only after she identified it: three steps, one, two, three, the sound of footsteps speeding up, and then moving and screaming and chaos.

Brendan turned quickly; he knew they were being followed. He knew that the boy crossed the street when they did. Perhaps this saved his life, ultimately, although a few laughed and said that karate didn't help him in the long run, now did it?

Marie saw the knife, but she didn't know he had been stabbed. She watched as Brendan lifted his arms, very karate style, and said, not yelled, just kind of roared, "C'mon!" or "Let's go," something like that. Marie simply watched; she didn't run for help, she barely screamed. And the boy – the boy she had held the door for minutes before – faltered, the knife is his hand quivering, causing a strobe-like effect under the streetlights.

He had not anticipated a seemingly fearless victim, and he might have said, "Give me your wallet" but with courage lost; and then, miraculously, out of the still hours of darkness, a police car drove by. Just drove by, casually, perhaps drinking coffee in the front seat, certainly unaware of trouble, although that's not how they would tell it in their report. Marie read the side of the door, it was automatic now to check, and saw 83 Pct. Brendan began to yell, and only then did the lights and sirens start, and the boy began to run.

They caught him, of course, and cuffed him and put him in the backseat of the police car, then began questioning Marie and Brendan right there – "your name and address, m'am" – and Marie glanced at him quickly before answering, lost in the miniature prison created by the car's divider. It was then she realized what had struck her about him when she held the subway door, minutes ago: he had a dark face, a black man that really was nearly that, but his eyes were a startling green. He reminded Marie of a black cat crossing her path, his irises lighting the way.

"Do I have to answer…with him listening?" she said, and the police shrugged quickly as if she was being silly, and then moved her a bit away. She gave the boy one last stare, thinking how things change, how she had found his face intriguing but now it represented malevolence, wickedness.

It was when she moved that she noticed Brendan again, talking to the other cop, a woman. She was about to walk over and do what? Resume the conversation? But then she saw it, the puddle of blood beneath him.

"Brendan, what the h-- ," she ran to him and her hand raised and he winced in anticipation, stepped back.

"He got me," he said calmly, "just in the arm, though. But I think I need an ambulance."

"We can take you to the hospital, sir," the woman cop said, then turned to Marie and said, "Can you get home?" and then the other cop was there and said to Brendan, "Can we get her home first?" and Brendan nodded.

Somewhere in all that, another car arrived and Green Eyes was moved to that car, and then she and Brendan were the prisoners, behind the screen, and the lights and sirens began and she thought, "I wonder which signal they used" and strained to see what they touched on the control panel up front.

"What are you doing?" Brendan asked, but then they stopped at a red light, and he leaned forward and in a voice strained said, "Can you please just go through it?" causing Marie to focus again on the blood that was now escaping through his clenched fingers.

"Are you okay?" she asked, an inane question: are bleeding people ever okay? Brendan said, "Yes. I'll see you later," and Marie saw that she was home.

She walked into the shadowy house and headed for the kitchen light, where Helene was still awake and so was her father, as if they had heard already, as if they had stayed up to comfort her.

"Mom, dad," she started, and then she started sobbing uncontrollably, an odd contrast to the unnatural calm she felt before. They stood, concern deepening on their faces as she finished, "Brendan was just stabbed…in the arm."

Her sobs distorted the last bit of her sentence, and so what Helene and Fred heard was that Marie's fiancé was just stabbed in the heart. They reacted aptly, with questions and touches and bellows of concern, until they understood, it was his arm, a worry, certainly but of lesser magnitude.

Her father asked, "Which was it? Black? Or Puerto Rican?"

Marie started to answer, but thought of the boy's eyes instead, and turned to her parents and now Robert who had entered the room.

"Why is everyone awake?" she asked.

"Marie, your grandmother was rushed to the hospital tonight, with a high fever and just…she is sick," Helene finished, almost dismissing the stabbing or at least moving it over, the way one guest moves one chair over on Johnny Carson when a new guest is announced.

"What hospital?" Marie asked, "Brendan is at Wyckoff Heights."

So was her grandmother, and so the night got stranger, and Marie went to bed hoping that it would be some kind of epiphany for her; the near loss of Brendan, holding a door open for the boy that would have taken his life, and her grandmother lying in the some space near Brendan. It seemed like it should mean something significant, and Marie strained to find that implication.

That night, the phone rang twice; once to say that her grandmother died, and the other, Brendan's voice saying that he was "stitched up" and coming to her in a few hours by Lindy's cab service – "can't exactly get the same service from the hospital that I got to it, I guess, so can you have cab fare ready for me? I only have about three dollars, and three bloody dollars at that, since they were in my shirt pocket."

She stared at the ripped shirt for hours later, even took a photo of it, which Brendan thought was "a little sick." Brendan told her how he sat in the emergency waiting room clutching his arm for two hours, and when they called his name, he stood and let go, causing blood to pool on the floor in the shape of a heart. The nurse even noticed, she said, "You left your heart on the floor." And still Marie did not find any missing truths hidden in the shadows.

Chapter Seven: Babylust

"He said he did it because he hated white people," Marie told Manny later, "but the police said 'no, it was probably a robbery attempt,' and not attempted murder. We said he was aiming for Brendan's back, but they said, no, probably just trying to cut his backpack off. Why would they do that, Manny? Why would they lie?"

"First offense, maybe? Copped a plea? Good lawyer? I don't know," he answered, and then grinned, "Are you suggesting that the *police* did the wrong thing, Marie? Disappointed?"

"Are *you*?" she smiled back, "I mean, if he…Damien – his name was Damien, did I tell you that? Damien Fredericks – if Damien had succeeded, Brendan would no longer be with us."

"Did that give you a new perspective, Marie? Awaken love inside of you?" Marie suddenly realized that they were not answering each other's questions.

"No…yes…I do think, how odd. That your life story, everything that happens to you, amounts to that moment you are killed. Meaning…Brendan didn't know Damien, but if Brendan died, then Damien would be the most significant part of his life story. Whatever Brendan did, his story would always be that he was killed by a boy named Damien Fredericks, a boy I held the door for. Do you know what I mean?"

"I know that you ducked the question," he answered, "about loving Brendan. But yes, I also know what you are talking about. Destiny. Out there, somewhere is the way your life ends, and it could be at the hands of another, someone you don't even know, have no reason to know. I understand completely."

He went on, "Do you know that I sit with the guys I arrest, by the holding cells, and I talk to them, you know, just talk. Some of them aren't bad guys. I ask them about their lives and how it came to this. The other guys think I'm crazy, but there has to be something, a moment, a time where it all went bad."

Marie suddenly thought of her father's question, the night of the stabbing – "Was the guy Black or Puerto Rican?" and shyly relayed the question to Manny. "I can't believe he said that."

"I'd say it, too, Marie. I can't say this job has especially made me proud of my people. It's difficult to lock up the same dark faces night after night."

"Geez, Manny, you are in Spanish Harlem. Doesn't that somewhat explain it?" She was holding still, feeling them get past that question before, and so profoundly absorbed in where they were heading now. But it was time to go and so he returned to his original interrogation.

"Do you love Brendan, Marie? Or is there someone else you love now?" he asked.

"No," she answered firmly. "There isn't. There is only Brendan. But..." At this she took out a pen, and reached for a napkin on the table. "He is...like this..." She drew him, large, standing on a precipice, high above, "And I am...here..." She drew herself, tiny, at the foot of the cliff, looking up, insignificant. "I love him, Manny. But I can't get to him, and he can't see me." She started to crumple the napkin but he took it, folded it gently, put it in his pocket behind the shield she saw shining: 7777. A strange badge number, like something that should bring an abundance of luck.

"I *don't* wish that Damien Fredericks killed Brendan," Manny said, "I only wish that I could *be* Brendan. Only if I could switch places with him, then you would be on the pedestal, and I would be at your feet."

****

Monica's wedding heightened Marie's impatience as well as her dread. All these people; they would be at her wedding as well. Already they were giving her those meaningful looks – old ladies with soft pillowy faces dimpled with crevices for powdered make-up to settle in comfortable lines, and younger people with babies at home straining to hide the truth about lost passion – each of them in turn interrupted Marie's soulful stares at the brides and grooms and misunderstood. "It will be you next," they would nod and smile, the older ladies rumpling their cheeks still further and displaying happy faux teeth but happy, why? Because they had past the point where love was trauma? Because they no longer had questions? Because now they placed their trust in a higher truth, not passion, but habit and ease, gardening and baking and crossword puzzles? There were more of the same at her bridal shower as Marie opened pots and plates and blenders, and also scandalous negligees in virgin white, as if the garments were unaware of the shape they were in, or else they would have blushed red. The women nodded then, too, contemplating another maiden taking on the role of missus, offering the same unlikely mix of glee and sympathy.

******

The night before her wedding, Marie took a shower so hot, it scalded her face and arms into an angry red, and her mother asked, "What happened to you?" The movie, "Arthur" was already on television, and together they watched it, Marie and her mother and her father, silently except for the customary sounds of their lives – "want coffee, Fred?" – and the comings and goings of others. It's difficult to know what to do one's last night in one's childhood home, and no one had scheduled anything particularly festive for her, and so she watched Arthur, and watched him walk out on his wedding once again, only this time, Marie began to cry, and cry hysterically.

Her face was already scarlet but now she added ugly blotches as she let go, with tears and heaving, nearly gagging, enough for any mother to look alarmed. Helene asked, "What's wrong?" and Marie said, "I don't know!" but she needed her mother then, needed her to know what was wrong. Helene only smiled, flicking her cigarette, her eyes half on the closing scenes of Arthur.

"I know what's wrong. Last Minute Jitters. It's normal, honey." And Marie knew she was getting married tomorrow, at 10am at St. Matthias Church, for better or for worse, and dried her tears and stilled herself.

"I know, ma," she said, "That's all it is. Jitters." And went to wash her face and soothe her skin into a tone suitable for a bride.

****

Weddings resemble funerals, in that they offer a surreal and solemn event followed by food, as a delay into the reality that lay beyond; for one, life without a loved one, for the other, life with someone new. Both are trancelike episodes for those they most affect, and though Marie charmed relatives on both sides of the family and posed prettily for photographers, she felt far outside herself. Photographers, in fact, Marie came to realize, existed for that very reason, to prove that you were there and had done something irrevocable, and to provide a false memory of the day. They took one professional 8x10 Polaroid for the couple to have immediately, and it was this that Marie clutched some seven hours later, on a plane to Ireland to begin her honeymoon.

She and Brendan had not even the time to open the pile of gift envelopes that bulged the satin bag meant to hold them discreetly; nor did they have time to consummate the marriage before the flight. Anne's husband Hank had driven them home from the reception, then tactlessly waited in their new tiny apartment for them to change so he could drive them to the airport.

"Are you taking all these envelopes with you?" he talked through the folding doors that separated their living room from their bedroom.

"Nah, we have enough money. I just need to leave a little for my mom so she can pick up a tea cart I have on layaway," Marie answered through layers of satin and tulle she was tugging over her head.

"You have to hide them," Brendan whispered urgently, "Your mother will open them."

"She won't," Marie whispered back but Hank was also still talking through the doors, and the surreal quality of the day was drifting away as a sickening one rolled in.

She was technically home right now. With her husband. Making one of their first man-and-wife decisions, and about money. Semi-naked, with an imprudent in-law in the next room droning on and on.

Then they were on the flight to Ireland, and blessedly, they were both asleep soon after take-off. The day, a commencement exercise so long in the planning, had wiped them both out to the point of draining any will to relive it, but they did at least hold hands across their seats, and were still holding hands when they woke up descending on Shannon Airport.

Loving Ireland would take precedence for fourteen days over trepidation over marriage. It was October, hardly the best time to tour the Emerald Isle, when days were short and wet, but this was not as much a honeymoon as a visit with the rest of Brendan's family. His mother was one of fourteen children, and only four had come to the states, leaving a warm household to visit all over her homeland. Marie found them enchanting; found the whole country enchanting, in fact, and in the years to come it would be she, not Brendan, who wrote letters "home."

"You'll only be here a fortnight," Brendan's old uncle said, rocking back and forth in his chair on gray slate floors in a dim farm kitchen, "That's a shame. You'll hardly get to do a thing."

"I know," said an eager Marie, "There is so much to see, and we've barely started."

"Well, there isn't that much to see," rejoined Uncle Patrick, "It's a small country, you know."

"I know. Hardly the size of Texas!" Marie acquiesced, seeking approval through agreement.

"Well, we're not that small. We're big enough, I'd say. But it will probably rain every day you're here. It's a shame you picked October to come."

"It does rain a lot..." Marie began.

"It does not rain *a lot*. It rains as much as it is supposed to. Yankees don't usually visit in October."

"Well, that's the month we were married," Marie explained, "since Monica was marrying in July, and…"

"Well, October is a fine month to be wed," Patrick never looked up and never stopped rocking, "Just a wet one. It's just a shame you only have a fortnight."

These and other stories would be captured on postcards Marie sent home to her mother, full of enthusiasm and fondness that could only rub Helene the wrong way. She told of Auntie Bridget, her garden and scones that were always ready in her kitchen, and of younger cousins in Dublin who volunteered amusing details about their "totally daft" family. She told of cousins in Belfast, who did not find it remarkable that sometimes bombs went off there – "People shoot each other in New York City every day, don't they?" -- and of an uncle in Cork, whose wife believed she had "the power of the magic thumb, although I'd never use it!" She even told of the simple task of asking directions in Ireland:

"Do you know how to get to Adare?"

"Well, if you go straight, you'll come to a divide. On the right road, you'll pass a church, and Nellie's Pub, a petrol station and then another church, and I'm thinking there is a school after that. That's the wrong way. Go back and take the other road."

There were always times, however, on the trip that Marie found herself lingering too long in bathrooms, studying her reflection and willing herself to face reality. This was for *real*. When they returned to the States, she would not thank Brendan at the door to her old home for a lovely honeymoon. They would return and speak glowingly of their trip, and then photos would go in albums and life would begin again.

Now and then, she removed a card that had not made it into the wedding gift bag, a card from her sister Anne. On the front was a cartoon character looking down woefully at an overturned gallon of milk. Inside, were the words, "Don't cry over it." Underneath, Anne had written a short note: "I know that you have fears about all of this, but remember, there is a solution and people do it everyday." People, Marie thought. But not her.

One night in Ireland, while lying in bed, she thought she saw the Virgin Mary, or an angel, or something. She and Brendan were staying at the home of an old aunt and uncle in Cork, and perhaps it was the Madonnas strategically placed all over the house that offered some power of suggestion. She was tired, as small of a country that Ireland was, traveling the entire length of it was wearing; even though Marie only offered to take the wheel once and nearly ploughed someone over. The left side of the road, she might have been able to handle, but she had no experience with a stick shift, nor did Brendan give her a second chance. He himself was taught by a teenage cousin who met them at Shannon on the first day:

"You press this, and move that, and do this with your feet," she instructed.

"Maybe you should just drive," he offered, desperate, his jet lag already kicking in, "since you know the roads and the car."

"Oh, I don't *drive*," she laughed.

On the night of the Madonna, she went to bed before Brendan while he talked with his uncle about how people "live on top of each other in America, and was it difficult when they all left for work to get out of the building?" She fell instantly asleep, but it addition to restrooms, sleep was the other place her demons visited her. In her dream, nightmare?, she was in her new pristine, tiny apartment, only it was *her* apartment, only hers, and she was decorating it, mainly with framed photographs of Irish landscapes. She was about to make herself a pot of tea, when Brendan walked in.

"Hello," she said pleasantly, "What are you doing here?"

"I live here," he said, "Don't you remember? We got married."

At this Marie began to cry in her dream, but she also was crying in her bed, and that is when the real bedroom door opened and Mary or the angel appeared. It was someone in long white robes with a covered head, but Marie could not see her face because it was in shadow. The figure first tucked Marie's blankets around her, and then began to stroke her head, all the while saying nothing.

Marie felt stillness flow through her like a paralyzing drug, and she slept again, dreamless. The next day, back on the road, she told Brendan about it.

"Brendan, I think that Mother Mary visited me last night."

"Dammit!" he exclaimed, "I think I'm going the wrong way. Are you holding the map?"

She looked, but kept talking. "Really, Brendan, Mary came in my room last night. She touched my head and she was trying to tell me something. That things would be alright, I think. I saw her, not in my head, either. I saw her come in my room."

"Marie," he said, "I came in the room last night, to get the wedding photograph to show Uncle Dennis. You were tossing and turning so I stroked your head for a bit."

"Well, did you tuck me in?" she asked, incredulous. She believed it more surreal that Brendan had touched her so lovingly than a representative from heaven.

"I might have, I don't remember," he tossed his reply as if it tasted bad; then pulled the car over to the side of nowhere, "Now, we are due back in Clare for supper and my aunt will be disappointed if we are late. So, let me see that map."

****

Marie cried when she left Ireland, and Brendan, she knew, was also affected. Visiting relatives in another country is like glimpsing their lives on a home movie; it shows little of the problems they face or the fears they know, or even the petty things they worry about. It only shows happiness. Marie learned that the Irish do not eat huge plates of rashers and eggs and blood pudding and scones each and every day any more than Americans eat burgers and fries every day. In fact, Auntie Bridget set Marie straight the night before they left, in a rare moment of candidness:

"You know, Marie, you don't see it, what happens here, really," she said in the shaking voice of the elderly, only with an Irish accent.

"What do you mean?" Marie asked, her eyes focused on Bridget's face. Marie saw the wisdom of years in every line of her face, a woman who lost her husband to hepatitis after six years of marriage and weeks after bearing his fifth child.

"Everyone is glad to see you, and make tea for you, and we ring each other to see where you are and how your holiday is going. But when you leave, we will go back to our daily lives, and ring each other once in a while. Do you understand?" She nodded a bit when she asked that.

Marie didn't, really, but nodded anyway, and Auntie Bridget went on.

"I just mean, we all have our troubles, you see?" and then Brendan entered.

****

Home. Seven hours against the wind, and their flight landed, and her mother and father picked them up from the airport, and drove them to 68-27 60th Lane, talking all the way.

"I have a surprise for you when you get home," Helene said, pleased with herself, holding the attention of the passengers, "Wait'll you see it."

"Did you get the tea cart?" Marie asked.

"Oh, *that*. What a pain in the ass *that* turned out to be," and launched into a tragic story of furniture salespeople and deliverymen that served to allow she and Brendan to stare out the windows at the landscape of Rockaway and Ozone Park and then Glendale.

"Keep the bags in the car, c'mon up," Helene lifted her large frame from the car, and Marie had the sense she was visiting her mother's new home.

Up one flight and the front door that could not be opened at the same time as the bathroom door was unlocked, the first thing infiltrating Marie being the scent of pine from all the new furniture. It wasn't a bad way to start.

"Look!" Helene said, as her father stood, also beaming, "We got you a table for your kitchen, well, what little a kitchen you have. It was mine but I figured you could use it. And there's the teacart, whatever that's for, and we even bought you a TV stand! And we put up curtains, like them? They were mine…and look…"

Helene bustled the five steps from the living room to the refrigerator behind the counter that would serve as the divider between the rooms, and opened the door to reveal shelves stocked with food. She looked a bit like Vanna White or some other game show host, revealing the interior of a new appliance to an over reactive housewife.

"We went shopping for you!" she said, and then finally rested, still nodding, still looking around with self-approval.

Marie and Brendan were then free to move, slowly, surveying the scene more like people looking over the remains of a tornado or flood, stricken with disbelief and wondering what they could salvage. Marie felt violated and forlorn, morosely fixing on the rust fiberglass drapes that she recognized from one of her old living rooms, and wondered how long before she could take them down? At the same time, she felt the clashing of tensions in the room, as if the close walls participated in a constant ricochet of emotion, with her caught in the crossfire. Helene was seeking appreciation, she knew. Her dad was seeking approval. And Brendan, she knew, was seeking some backbone, some moral fiber that would make her tell her mother that she had no right to put together a home that Marie now shared with her husband.

"It's so…nice…you didn't have to do all this," Marie faltered, avoiding everyone else's eyes lest hers shine false, "I can't believe you went through…this all must have cost you a lot…" She drifted off; she had not a clue what to say.

"Oh, don't worry, we didn't *pay* for any of it," Helene answered robustly, lighting up the first cigarette that would be ignited in Marie's home, looking around – "Jesus, why didn't I get an ashtray?" – then finally moving closer to the sink, and blowing out her punctuation breaths of smoke. And then she said:

"You had plenty of money in your envelopes! Oh, and the cards are all in that drawer, and we wrote the amounts on each one. Ya know, for your thank you cards…" Inhale, blow, and then her father spoke.

"Yeah, yuz did good," he said good-naturedly, "Think yuz made about four grand. You got about five hundred bucks just from that old aunt of yours, Brendan. We only used, what, Helene, a thousand? On the stuff we got? Counting the groceries? Course we had to take the cash, couldn't do nothing with the checks."

"Yeah, and you had a few tightwads in there, too," Helene added, "Who the hell gives $25 for a wedding nowadays? You have to at least pay for your plate."

Brendan reached the drawer before her, opened it hard, and pulled out the cards sans envelopes and rifled through, as if to find one that wasn't ravaged, one without Helene's careful writing on the inside – "Pendola, $150, cash," "Connelly, $50, check." He put them back and now rifled his hair, leaving the drawer gaping open. Marie was immobilized, willing him not to speak while dreading what words he was saving for her.

Helene and Fred weren't totally insensitive; they felt the silence and perhaps wrote it off as fatigue or anticipation, and so Helene crushed her cigarette in the sink and Fred touched Brendan's arm and said, "Let's go get them bags," and in 15 minutes that felt like hours, they were gone.

Brendan was still quiet when they left, and finally, Marie started to speak, lightly, but he cut her off.

"I knew they would open those envelopes," he said stonily, "You said they wouldn't, but I knew they would."

"You *thought* they would," she said in feeble defense, "but you couldn't *know* they would. I didn't know they would."

"Didn't I say it?" he said, more of a statement than a question; a command, even. "Didn't I tell you?"

"And that meant you thought it, but you couldn't know it," she answered but now the argument was getting ridiculous. It did, however, become a kind of template for the arguments that they would always have, where Brendan became exasperated with her for simply not acknowledging that his word was absolute.

****

Marie is not sure why things became okay. She thought a great deal about the form in her room in Ireland, even though logic told her that it was Brendan that stroked her head that night. Her subliminal mind had obviously transformed him into some spiritual figure, or perhaps she really thought of him as bright and pure? It didn't matter, because she ignored her own psychoanalysis, and held fast to the thought that someone, somewhere, was looking out for her, and if Mother Mary had not visited her that night, well, Someone obviously wanted her to think so.

She had her film from Ireland developed and blew up the prettiest ones into 8x10's, which she framed and put around her home, everywhere some rolling green hills dotted with white sheep. She removed the offending curtains and stored them in a box, and gave back the brown and white Formica table from her mother. "If ever a goodwill gesture felt flat," Helene said with a pronounced sigh when it was once again in her laundry room, but Marie stifled her comments. She continued to put together her home, with Irish china and earthenware, and even Waterford they purchased in the duty-free shop. Contrary to all her fears, Marie loved coming home at night to the fading smell of pine, to a place that was at least, half hers, and sometimes she even found herself staring at the oddest things with delight; like the cleaning supplies under the sink, all hers.

In fact, she was so used to being a resident in another person's home, that she could not stop telling the landlord – a young couple with two little daughters – where she was going if she bumped into them leaving the house. "We're just running to the mini-mart," she'd say, or, "We won't be back until late tonight."

"Why do you *do* that?" Brendan would ask, not playfully as she would hope. "They don't care where you are going. They care about the rent."

It was the marriage part that Marie found difficult, but she was determined to fix that. Brendan, of course, was making his own transition. He had participated in the graduation ceremony at New York University, but there was no diploma inside the leather case he received. This was still riding on the completion of several "incompletes"; courses he had not failed but to which he owed work. He was not equipped to go job-hunting, and certainly not prepared to live outside the city.

"How do you like living in the city," people would ask, and he would quickly correct them.

"We *don't* live in the city. We live in Queens." He would say this to people even if they lived in Westchester or Connecticut, places that considered every one of the five boroughs, "the city." He berated his new county, saying, "You actually have to call a cab on the telephone," and "They actually think a 24-hour deli is a big deal here." He particularly despised commuting to his job at Cabrini Medical Center, a job in another department that he held full time now.

"C'mon, Brendan, wake up, we gotta get out of here," Marie would pull covers off of him, poking and prodding. He was not used to allowing at least an hour to get to work, and groggily dreamed of the days when he needed only 20 minutes total to shower, dress and get from West Fourth to 19th. It didn't seem to matter that with their combined salary of approximately $15,000 a year, they could not have touched a Manhattan apartment, anyway.

"C'mon, Brendan, I want to stop for a roll on the way," she continued to pull, "and I have to make the bed." She, of course, didn't *have* to make the bed, but there were things Helene instilled in her that would not be shaken: "If you make the bed, the whole room looks neater." Anyway, she liked to come home and see her home in its full two-and-a-half room glory.

Still, they began establishing their routines. They stopped each morning at a mom and pop deli with wood floors under the elevated M train, and ordered two buttered rolls and a tea for her and a coffee for him. "One and one?" the pleasant-faced chubby woman behind the counter asked, as soon as the bell above the door announced their entrance, and they nodded, and smiled at each other.

Because of karate, they usually came home together as well, reversing the route of the train and passing the now closed delicatessen on their walk home. And on weekends, they lingered in bed until the people below began cranking their stereo under their floorboards, and then began to stir.

"Oh my God, if I have to hear the song, 'Gloria,' one more time," Marie would whine, and began singing along, "*Gloria, I think I got your number, I think I got your alias...that you've been living uuuunnnder...*"

"*You don't have to annnswer*," Brendan joined in, "*I see your number on the li-ine, singing Glorriiiaaa*" and pulled her back under the sheets, "How can they be allowed to blast that so early in the morning?"

"Ummm, because it's noon," Marie would touch his lips, run her fingers through his hair, think again that he was beautiful, and that lying under the puffy comforter in the sun-filled room felt beautiful. "Let's make breakfast."

For the next hour, they would fashion themselves an elaborate breakfast, reminiscent of the ones they shared in Ireland, served on the china they had purchased in Londonderry, and complete with a pot of tea. They had a table now; one they purchased themselves from the Door Store, which had a pocket for storing extra chairs and a drawer underneath for storing utensils. They kept it tucked in a corner like a wee breakfast nook, opened halfway for two, although it could seat more if opened on both sides.

After breakfast, they sat around and figured out something to do, and it seemed the world was theirs. There really was nothing pressing to do. They didn't bring work home from their offices. They didn't go to school. They didn't so much as have a goldfish to care for. They had to go the grocery store and get a two-person amount of food, but that was kind of fun. They had to bring their two-person amount of dirty clothes to the Laundromat, but that was a social event as well, as they dumped the clothes and got a bite to eat next door. Mostly, they just took a walk, sometimes stopping at her mother's house, or her sister's, or sometimes just bringing a rubber Spaldine ball and bouncing it in the park. And so, gradually, life became a comfortable thing to wear, nothing flashy or conspicuous, but thankfully free of the things that scratch and irritate.

Except. Except in the dark, wakeful hours when Brendan stared at her sleeping, twisting his wedding ring around his finger as if to screw it in tighter, and once dropping it, where she heard it spin on the parquet floor until it quit and fell. For these moments, she decided to consult a priest.

Manny seemed lost in these times; these newlywed times. Marie would have to search her memory to recall where he was as she built her life. She was gaining confidence at work, had even left Jasmine behind and occupied a cubicle of her own, which she decorated with the same possessive pride she gave her home.

She worked for terrible people, mainly women, all spitfire and ambition, cutthroat and condescending. They let her know daily that she was a spare part, a tag-a-long writer that had fallen into Gene's good graces but was hardly any use to them. Merrill was the worst; an art director with long red-gold hair, who sat behind her drafting board like a queen upon a throne. She worked with a copywriter named Rose; someone Marie admired to the point of obsession. She was thin and always beautifully dressed, and words seemed to dance from her pen in effortless formation. Marie struggled for hours to write what Rose dispersed like pixie dust upon the page, making even cleanser sound like something to covet.

Then there was Audrey and Wendy, a writer-art director team hired out of college, who were about proving themselves and didn't need a secretary-turned-copywriter stealing their thunder. The art director, Wendy, was loaned to Marie as well, and did not hide her resentment.

"She introduced me to the client as 'kind of our copywriter at large,'" Marie complained to Brendan, on the train after karate, "and they just smile in that *way,* like I'm a kid somebody brought to work for the day. I'm surprised they don't hand me crayons."

Did Brendan ever really listen to her work stories, or was he too preoccupied with his own status in the business world? He was working to complete the degree he left unfinished, and frustrated daily by his own bosses, mostly Filipino women with lower education. He felt superiority over them that he could not prove, a higher intelligence that they failed to notice. Marie didn't know why she felt guilty about this, but she changed the subject.

"I'm having lunch with Father Riley this week," she announced instead, thinking that Catholicism was surely a safe subject. It wasn't.

"What for?" Brendan asked, and everything about him was prickly.

"Oh, he wants me to write for some church publication," she answered, which was true, but not really true.

"Where are you having lunch?" Brendan asked, pointedly. Like a fox on a hunt, there was a scent in his nose that he couldn't ignore.

"I don't know," Marie cowered, "Does it matter?"

"Just be careful, Marie, that's all," he answered, and now he sounded weary.

"Be careful? Geez, Brendan, he is a *priest*. He *married* us," Marie said and tried to laugh.

"I know what he is," Brendan came back quickly, "and under all those robes, he is just another man. So be careful."

And of course, Brendan was right, and Father Riley got to engrave his name in her history book, in a chapter she would forget but Brendan would remember. It didn't take long. The good father listened to her tale of uncertainty and despair, of regret and good intentions, but all he really heard were the words she spoke with her eyes: vulnerable, unsure, a perfect target.

He picked her up outside her apartment and drove her to a restaurant in Staten Island, and his hand was upon hers in no time. Marie could not even remember if he offered any godly advice about her marital fears, so quickly did he move on to his own neuroses. He was a short, dumpy man who used Vaseline to plaster strands of hair across a balding head, but Marie still felt chosen, somehow.

"What made you become a priest?" she asked, thinking of how the nuns used to say it was a "calling."

"I don't know, I think I was drugged at the time," he answered, and Marie could almost hear angels sighing at the loss of some secret. He was happy to give away more, including the fact that all priests "jerk off every single day."

The talking part went on for a few weeks, and then one day he asked her outright to have sex with him. She refused.

"But that's hardly fair," he whined, "We're friends, aren't we?"

"Yes, but…yes, but…" Marie floundered, but he was barreling on.

"And I was there when you needed to talk, wasn't I?"

"Yes."

"And now I need something. I need sex. I was there for you, and I thought you could be there for me."

It was ludicrous. She knew it was, but there was something strangely logical in it as well. And he kept on pushing his point.

"I mean, what if you need to talk and I could do anything for you but listen. What kind of friend would I be? Friends give each other what they need, not what is easy for them to part with," he said with finality, as if her clothes should come off without further ado.

"But I'm *married*," she pleaded, "and it would be unfaithful. It would be adultery, for godssake."

"Let me tell you something about adultery," he said patiently, and the wisdom he was about to impart, however self-serving and misguided, would ring true for Marie in some justifiable way.

"Adultery is not just sex with another person. Adultery is anything that removes you from your spouse, on any level. A man working all the time and leaving his wife alone, that can be adultery, more so than if he has a one-night stand and forgets the other woman. A man who doesn't properly love his wife, who denies her the full measure of his feelings, well, that can be adultery as well. Anything that cheats a spouse out of what he should expect is adultery. But if you sleep with me and get back to your life, what is the harm in that?"

It was a good argument, but she kept her own clothes on.

Her consultation with a priest taught her that "fucked up" was a gift God spared no man or woman, even the godly, and that was when things became all right, she thinks. She started going to church again, she and Brendan, and it was right there, during mass that her wedding band caught the light and shone, and she reached over and whispered in Brendan's ear.

"I want to have a baby," she said, and luckily it was before communion, or Brendan might have choked on the wafer.

****

"Why does it always have to be about money?" Marie asked heatedly, her baby idea struck down seconds after Father Riley – he was saying the mass -- said, 'Go in peace to love and serve the Lord.'

"Why can't it ever be about love, Brendan? Why?"

"Marie, please," Brendan was still assessing whether she was joking, or delusional. They were married just over five months. They were both 23 years old. They made no money. "You have to be able to care for a baby, feed a baby. You can't just toss one out there. C'mon, Marie, please." But she was crying.

She worked on him for the next five weeks. She used all the logic she knew; and some illogic as well. She cried, she wrote letters; she presented examples of people who started a family with less. But still there was a pause in their lovemaking, and she heard in that silence the condom wrapper rip.

"Why, Brendan, *why?*" It was always her plea, followed by, "We can *do* this," but he was silent, troubled. And then, one night, he went out with his friends in the city, while she slept at his parents' apartment on the pullout couch.

185

At two or three in the morning, he stumbled in, inebriated and silly, and slipped under the sheets with her. She liked Brendan drunk; he was playful and unwary, the proof of this being he got on top of her in his mother's house. In four thrusts it was over, and he pulled off her and smiled sweetly, dreamily.

"There," he murmured, "I hope I gave you a baby tonight." And he did.

****

She stared at the doughnut in the pregnancy test with a jumbled mix of emotion, akin to eating a variety of foods that simply did not belong together. Or maybe the sick feeling in her stomach was the parasite that had begun to grow, the one she had invited to share her living space. She wanted to shake the mechanism that held her urine and found the secret hidden in it, to see if the doughnut would return to stare like an accusation. "I'm here," it seemed to say, "and I'm yours now. You did this."

Anne was pregnant at this time, six months along, having waited seven years to even consider such a notion. If she minded sharing the glory of supplying a grandchild so quickly, she didn't show it. Helene, however, reacted with pursed lips.

"This was planned, then?" she said, the offensive cigarette present.

"Yes," Marie responded promptly, "and I can't be around people who smoke now. It makes me sick. And it isn't good for the baby."

"Nonsense," Helene answered, sucking harder on the Bel Air, "I smoked through all of my pregnancies."

Marie's hands went instinctively to her abdomen, a gesture invented by generations of women protecting their unborn. Did her mother ever do it? Did she ever feel it? Her lips tightened to seal in hurtful words: 'Yes, ma, you smoked through all your pregnancies. And you had six miscarriages and one preemie. Me.' Silenced, she averted her head and tried not to inhale her mother's poison.

"Why so soon, Marie? Why didn't you wait until you were more settled?" Her mother's voice held concern, in spite of the cigarette.

"I thought you would be happy," Marie faltered, still rubbing her tummy as if to keep her baby from hearing, "I mean, god, you were married at 18. You had a baby at what, 20?"

"A parent wants better for her child, that's all, Marie," Helene did squash the butt at this point, "You just got that writin' job, and all."

Marie shook her head in weariness. A parent wants better. From the start, this was the only course her mother allowed her, and now she said she wanted better for her. And in that moment, silent vows were made, the first of many, of the things that her own child would never have to endure.

Brendan's mother simply stared at them in disbelief. His father left the room.

Finally, Mrs. Kavanagh spoke: "We don't tell anyone of this until she is at least three months along. Anything can happen in the first trimester."

Then, his father spoke from the next room, which in a Cooper Town apartment was really only an extension of the room they were in. He said, "You don't even have your bloody degree, Brendan. When the hell are you going to get your bloody degree?"

"They're immigrants," Brendan consoled her on the train ride home, "You have to understand that. My uncle didn't even get married until he was near 50. He married a woman he met as a baby in the cradle." She had heard this story already, so he went on:

"Plus, my dad believes you should be financially secure. What am I saying? I believe you are supposed to be financially secure." He ran his fingers haphazardly through his hair as if to shake loose some burden.

"I guess you aren't happy about the baby, then," she said, and the bad thing was, she wasn't really sure she cared. *She* was happy about the baby. She believed it would all work out. And somehow, at that moment and forever, this baby, and all babies to follow, became hers and hers alone.

Marie was terribly sick the first trimester, and the second as well. She threw up mornings, afternoons and sometimes into the evening. She was meticulous about her caring for herself; would not even consider sucking on a cough drop during those precious months. She took a certain righteous pride in leaving the room with great ceremony when Helene lit up a cigarette, and Helene took equal satisfaction in following her to the next room, the menacing curls of smoke circling like vapors from a witch's caldron, and Helene's face the picture of blamelessness and guile combined.

She felt wise and worldly at her job; sitting at the perimeter of conference tables like one of Camelot's knights, engaging in decisions with her contemporaries who were all far older. Older, but none of them were growing life just beneath where the meeting table cut off vision.

Once, her boss entered her office spewing venom about the length of her evening commute back to New Jersey.

"A *woman*," Rose spit the word as if she wasn't one, "went into *labor* on the *train*. During *rush* hour."

"Oh my gosh," Marie was wide-eyed, imagining, wondering if New Jersey Transit trains were as filthy as the subway, "how awful."

"Three hours," Rose said, misreading Marie's look, "And it wasn't just that we were delayed. She gave birth in *my* car. I mean, imagine having to look at *that*?"

"I mean, what the hell was she *doing* on the train if she was about to have a *baby*?" Rose finished, and if Marie thought she had drained all her emphatic poison on the word 'woman,' she was wrong. The word "baby" was far more toxic.

And so Marie learned that baby-making was no source of pride for women in the workforce, on the contrary, it was something to accomplish quietly and with little fuss. Pregnancy made her even more of a child, somehow, and so she kept all the perils of procreation literally under the table.

She saved her all-knowing appeal for Manny, who regarded her with less awe than she had hoped. She didn't know him then; didn't know what hopes and dreams dissipated as her belly grew. He made fun of her immersion in baby books the way he teased her about Brendan months before. She would learn this about him, how he deflected his sorrows with sarcasm, but it would take some time, and some willingness to understand.

"I have such a cold," Marie would mention, and wait for sympathy, but he was not offering any.

"Take Nyquil," he said, but he knew.

"I can't," she would exclaim with sanctimonious awe, and add in a whisper, "the baby."

"Do you know how many drugs our parents took?" he came back with a smile, "Gimme a break. My mom didn't even bother with a…whatever baby doctors are called."

"Obstetricians," she said and that was the end of that conversation, but what else did they talk about? Whatever did they talk about during the times she was most occupied with herself?

"How are things going with Madeline," she asked feebly.

"Paradise," he answered grimly, "Maybe we'll even start a family."

Even Brendan seemed more baffled than delighted at impending fatherhood, and he spoke very little about it. They had to move, of course, and leave behind the idyllic pine-scented honeymoon suite they had only occupied for 14 months. Their new apartment had more space but less charm, and it didn't help that she began each day there vomiting into the toilet, while Brendan held her hair out of her face

They named the baby Colin, as plain and ordinary a name that could be chosen, but she had already implored Brendan for something more unusual and it was no use. Whatever she came up with, Brendan thought it was "too" something – "too strange, people will always spell it wrong," "too ethnic, people will think he is black," and even, "too Irish," although she later learned that the Irish considered Colin as Irish a name as Patrick – or he simply "knew someone" with that name and the person he knew was severely lacking in some way.

****

A baby is the sweetest form of hallucinogenic drugs. It allows a mother to see the entire rest of the world with only periphery vision, and blurry at best. It dominates like the hot flash of a camera that blinds and discolors, and reiterates with every blink of the eye thereafter.

So it was for Marie, who ceased to think about her job or Manny, or her mother or even her marriage, for that matter. Colin was born on the 14th of December, and the last effort she could recall putting into her connubial bond was just a few days before, during one of her last days at her job and in the city. She went to Barneys, a men's clothing store, and spent every penny she could spare on suits for her husband. She knew that he was soon to be their only provider, and invested in him looking the part.

Fortunately, Brendan was equally smitten. Rushing home at the end of his workday, he entered the apartment with anticipation and quickly assessed which of the four rooms held his son. Marie was unhurt as Colin received the first displays of affection, and she listened while setting the table for dinners that she had only recently learned to make.

"Was that baby sleeping," she asked playfully as Brendan entered the kitchen with the bundle in his arms.

"He was," Brendan answered, but talking to his baby in babytalk, "but I woke you, didn't I? Because daddy is home. And it's time to play, isn't it?"

Marie smiled, and placed a soggy amateurish meal on the table, but they ate with relish, as a family, and Brendan listened to all his child had done that day, even though he could do practically nothing. And this was bliss.

He was critical, though, even then, and Marie could not recall when she began dreading instead of anticipating his return. It was so gradual, a question here, a comment there, a specious laugh punctuating a well-meaning line.

"Did you burn something?" he asked after retrieving Colin from his room.

"No," Marie answered defensively, "I was just making dinner."

"That's dinner?" and there was the laugh, as he placed the baby in his seat and went to check, purposefully, as if to catch her in a terrible lie.

"Marie, this corn is practically stuck to the pot," he said, and more of the laugh, which he used to soften his blows?

"I tried to salvage it by putting it in another pot, that's all. It came out fine."

"Another pot won't make a difference once that burn smell gets through it," he kept on, then stopped and allowed a smile to crack through his face like a fault line through the earth, and allowed the next words to stifle through: "It's no big deal, I guess I'll just skip the corn."

She didn't want him to skip the corn. She wanted him to eat it, beside her and tell her how well she handled her small household in their hours apart. She wanted to be his wife, and his equal, but she seemed only capable of being that in his absence.

"What'd you do today?" he asked, not knowing the fate of new mothers to have little recollection of their days, but when did that informal inquiry begin to feel like an accusation? When did she start searching her mind for the right answer? When did she begin to feel she had to justify her moments?

"I went to my mom's," she answered after coming up with little else, "Anne was there with Tyler…"

"Oh nice," he answered, like it was a manicure or a massage.

"Yeah. The thing is, Colin cries too much, and I wanted my mother to hold him for awhile."

The laugh. Then, "Cries? Too much?" Laugh. Then he turned to his perfectly quiet baby, and said, "She thinks you cry too much. You aren't crying a bit, are you?"

"It stops around the time you get home. He cries most of the day. Well, he sleeps most of the day, but he cries when he isn't sleeping…or eating."

"Isn't that called being a baby?" Brendan asked without curiosity or expectation of a reply.

"Tyler didn't cry as much. He didn't. Colin cries a lot." She said it firmly.

"You're probably just post-partum," he said, but she jumped in quickly.

"I'm *not*. I never was. Not even for a moment," and it was true. She was immersed in the most intense form of baby lust, and never shed a single irrational tear or suffered a moment of hormonal havoc. She woke in the night to feed Colin with energized anticipation, and held him longer than she had to in the moonlit hours. Then she rose a few hours later to begin her day with him, seeing Brendan off quickly so mother and son could continue their romance alone.

But he did cry often, and she worried that this, too, was something she was doing wrong. She wanted to share her concerns with her baby's father without being the fall guy, the hidden cause of deficiency, but it was not to be.

"He's fine. Look at him." They both looked at their cherub, drifting off to sleep.

"It only happens during the day," she began again, but gave up. Whether this was her fault or merely her imagination, it stung to deal with it alone.

Two weeks later, Marie's 23rd birthday fell on a Saturday and her mother made her a cake.

"Go over," Brendan said, "Get out for a while. I'll stay with the baby." She gratefully accepted.

The phone rang four times when Marie was at her mother's. It was Brendan, looking for pacifiers, for blankets, for toys that played lullabies. Marie went home after two hours and wrapping a slice of her own cake to take with her. When she arrived, Brendan handed her Colin as soon as her hands were free.

"He cries too much," he said with finality, and now – because Brendan had said it – it was so.

They got through it, of course, the way all new parents do and go on to overpopulate the earth. Colin was colicky, and Marie was redeemed to hear that this was a common affliction that affects a newcomer to the world only part of the day. The pediatrician, an old man with old ways, prescribed Donatal, but it was really time that did the trick. It took

Marie seven months to feel like a real mother; one that trusted her own instincts and wasn't constantly trying to please people – specifically her mother and mother in-law – around her.

Helene believed that a baby was a manipulative villain, not that she used those words, but she believed that the 8 pound human could be spoiled if his basic needs were constantly met. Each wail from the young one's mouth constituted a challenge, a game of wits, as if crying were code for "I'm fine. But I'll bet I can make you pick me up if I want to." In her mother's presence, Marie had to grit her teeth and bear the sorrowful sobs of her flesh and blood, because if maternal instinct caused her to shift in his direction, her mother's hand restrained her: "Let him cry awhile. You don't want to spoil him."

It was quite the opposite in the Kavanagh house. There, Marie was not permitted to *ever* put her baby down, not even if he were comatose, dreaming of whatever is stored in the unconscious mind of one just weeks old, curled tight with a last trickle of milk rolling down his chin. She was, of course, allowed to place Colin in the arms of another, but never in the artificial confines of a crib or baby seat. And if she did manage to detangle him and set him down, then God forbid he whimpered. Marie would at once be subjected to the Irish howls of the elder Mrs. Kavanagh, a sound far worse than any sound a baby could produce: "Marie! Your *son* is crying! Go get him! Now! Pick the child up! Can you not hear that?"

Miraculously, Colin thrived in spite of the dichotomy in his upbringing, and Marie remembered the moment she felt like his mother. It was in Lake George, in fact, in a cabin where she and he were alone, Brendan having returned to work for a few days, and the clashing grandmas in other cabins. Colin woke up in the night, a stranger in a strange crib, and cried out for something familiar.

Marie picked him up and held him, soothed him, then wrapped him up in a blanket and walked down to the lake to sit on the dock. There, underneath a moon bright against a blue-black sky, Marie let them both feel the rhythm of water kerplunk against wood until

Colin was fast asleep against her chest.

"You are my son," she whispered to the delicate curls on his head, inhaling the clean smell of untarnished skin that we only have once in our lives.

"*My* son," she went on, "and I am your mother. And I am going to take care of you. Because I know how to do that. *You*... are the one thing that I am sure of."

****

Soon after, Monica shifted the focus by producing a son, and even though he did not bear the Kavanagh name, Monica reminded her mother that her baby was the true "child of her child," as if Marie's involvement was in question. Marie's maternity leave ended and she asked for and was granted a 3-day workweek. Her sister Anne took care of Colin since she was home with Tyler, and everything settled into life as predicted, except that Marie's periphery vision always included Manny, and he would soon squeeze himself back into focus.

Manny was wonderful when the baby came. What he held back before, he gushed now, so taken with wonder at the life Marie had created. From the start, Colin provided an acceptable outlet for Manny's desire to lavish; what he could not give to Marie, he gave to Colin instead.

"What do you need for the baby?" he asked eagerly, "I didn't give him a gift yet. Name it. I'll get it."

"Anything?" Marie asked, finding greed for another equally justifiable.

"Yeah, anything, c'mon, name it, what?" He was impatient because he had found it, his secret way in, and he was ready to break the door down.

"Like, how much are you willing to spend?" she asked, fighting for diplomacy, for some sort of restraint.

"Marie, what do you *want?* I know that you know, now tell me."

"A dresser. It's beautiful. Walnut. A baby dresser. It's $300, but it has a little closet and drawers." She went on to describe a dresser that had all the features of furniture by that name.

"Done. Good. See, wasn't that easy?"

She never thought a $300 gift would aggravate Brendan; she never thought at all when she wanted something and especially something for her son, as if some of his early distress came from the inappropriate placement of his wardrobe. The dresser was delivered within the week, and she showed it to her husband with pride, as if she had gotten it with her own resources. Actually, she believed she had. Manny's love had always been her reserve.

Marie knew nothing of male pride, of territorialism, or of the need to provide. She saw Manny's gesture as innocent, and never suspected him of attempting to gain ground. And so, in the months ahead, she and he would shop happily for things that Colin "needed," all over the city, as Marie's lists grew longer and more elite. They shopped on her two days off, they shopped at night when Brendan went to karate, and eventually on Saturday when Brendan took a second job to make ends meet. In stores like "Toys R Us," or "Kids R Us," or Childcraft, or smaller boutiques on side streets in Manhattan, amidst Fisher-Price toys and Osh Kosh overalls, they established something that could no longer be denied or changed.

And so it was in a mall parking lot, 8 years after the first time, that one of them kissed the other again.

Chapter Eight: It Was Only a Kiss

Marie could never say how it happened. They would argue, mischievously, that it was the other that provided the impetus – "Oh no," each would say, "I had no intention of doing anything. *You* were the one that started it." They would reach no conclusion, but sit back with eyes shining, breathless, feeling that fate had truly been in charge, and that this, forever, would be the climax of their story.

Honesty, ultimately, played the primary role, the honesty that seeps through unintended through proximity. They spent hours together now, and they talked. It was no longer the polite banter of a lunchtime interlude, or the constrained chat of those keeping their dirty laundry hidden. Marie allowed discontent to enter descriptions of her life, and to Manny this was like chinks in the walls of Camelot.

"Brendan says we don't have sex enough," she said over lunch that day, and Manny could not stop himself from leaning closer to soak up his salvation. "He says it all the time, how I used to want it all the time. He brings up that goddamned pool table at least once a week…"

"Pool table?" he asked for clarification, but with as few words as possible. Manny never disturbed the air when it was fortuitously blowing his way.

"Oh," she laughed, "I'd never mentioned the pool table? 'Twas long ago, and if only I had known it would haunt me for all my days." And she described the moment she had 'taken' Brendan beneath the billiards in her basement.

"Of course, we don't have a pool table, but we do have a baby now, and I don't mean that as an excuse." She looked up sharply, checking that he understood. She was still young and vital, and she in no way had lost interest in sex.

The floor was hers so she continued, "But…I need *help,* not always but sometimes. And he thinks, well, he works and that is enough. He *provides*. But shit, I work." She glanced quickly at Colin as the offending word came out, but he was playing with his corn niblets and oblivious.

Manny was still silent, as was his gift to her, to never interrupt, to wait for the sentence that sounded final, and even then allow her words to settle like softly falling snow on warm pavement. He only spoke when they dissipated, leaving space for more.

"I never curse anymore," she mused. "Anyway, it's not a big deal, just sometimes I really can't think about sex when the sink is full of dishes, but I can't think about doing the dishes because I'm exhausted, I just got the baby to bed... and isn't it funny how, now, a man who does the dishes is like, foreplay to me! I see that Lemon Joy and I'm there, baby." She finishes with a laugh, but a troubled expression returned immediately.

"Do you know what I mean," she asked helplessly.

"Yeah," he said, but would he say anything else? Two minutes of silence, and then, "Madeline won't get a driver's license."

"She's 28 years old, and she can't drive. I know, I know I did this, made this helpless blob that...well, anyway, she has a hair, *one* hair, that grows on her shoulder..." He looked tortured now, shaking his head and squeezing his eyes tight shut.

"And when I get home from 8 hours of chasing bad guys up and down the street, she doesn't say, 'how was it today?' She looks at the clock and gets this face, this *face,* Marie. And she says, 'Are you still gonna be able to take me to electrolysis?'"

"She goes to electrolysis, costs twenty-five bucks, to get rid of *one* hair. Or sometimes it's ceramics. She goes to ceramics and she *has* to go, has to make another fuckin' cookie jar." Now he glanced at Colin, who was staring at his face, the niblets forgotten.

Now Marie was silently waiting, a new skill for her. With her new perception of disappointment and disillusionment, she no longer felt pleasure in hacking away at Madeline's integrity.

"You saw where I live, Marie," he said, "behind the mall. Do you know how many trains and buses go by there every fu…every day? It's the Mecca of mass transit. But do I tell her to get off her fat ass and get on a bus? No. I get up and drive her to fu…freakin' electrolysis, or ceramics or whatever else she needs to do in her useless life." He finished.

Marie still said nothing because words sometimes only trivialize things, so instead she turned to wipe Colin's hands of the mashed potatoes he had dabbled in. "Wanna go?" she said, half to her baby and half to her friend, but she knew she had to go since she knew that babies in restaurants, even 'family' restaurants, carried non-negotiable time limits.

"Can we still walk around for a bit?" Manny asked, repentant since he believed he had taken too much of her time, "We can stop by Starlight and see if they have that Norman Rockwell statue you like."

"Okay, but you have to watch Colin outside until it's time to pay," she said, "or he will break everything in that store."

"Ten-four," he smiled.

She was only in the store a few minutes when it happened. Whatever Colin had fingerfooded into his tummy at TGIF's did not agree with him, and he chose that moment, in Manny's care, to expel it, all over himself, and the stroller and the mall floor, and who knows, maybe even a few horrified passers-by.

"*Oh shit*," she said, loudly, and Colin was definitely not listening now. Guilt flooded her, the first of many moments of culpability she would feel after this day, "I wasn't paying attention to him at the table. We were talking and he was socking down whatever…well, whatever you see right here."

"Relax, m'am, I got it," he said and she couldn't say how the mess disappeared and they ended up, within twenty minutes, sitting calmly in the car with an almost fragrant baby sound asleep behind them.

"Thanks," she said, emotionally exhausted, not from the mishap, but from the draining of her soul in the moments leading up to that sorry pinnacle, and perhaps from the draining months before that day as well.

He was still in cop mode, oddly enjoying the moment. "M'am, I deal with the very scum of the earth. That was nothing. We live to serve." And with that, he put the key in the ignition to begin their trip home.

Something flooded her, a series of images – so much he had done for her – and comparisons, him to Brendan, or Brendan's reaction to throw-up in the mall, he would have been screaming! And more images, of their lives and her despair, and him, always him, there to catch her, hold her, hear her, back her, spot her, everything but judge her. She turned to look at him but his eyes were straight ahead, so she leaned over, saying it again, "Thanks," only this time really thanking for so much more.

She intended to punctuate the word with a kiss on the cheek, but he turned and there was the controversial moment forever up for clarification. There was not even a split second of hesitation, no awkward moment of misunderstanding. He turned, and both mouths opened simultaneously and met deeply as if it was the intention of the gods and they would be forever blameless.

Intensity is not measured in seconds, and their lips fell apart in a time both short and full. Neither said anything, and Manny started the car as Marie checked that Colin was still sleeping, and then settled herself in her seat.

The world began to race past the car and their thoughts raced forward, but as sights became more familiar, she made a decision.

"Manny," she said dryly, breaking the spell but speaking directly to the windshield, "I think we have to stop somewhere. I think we have to do that again."

He didn't answer, and he didn't stop, and she was rebuffed. Later, he explained that he was stunned enough to think he misheard her, that surely she said she needed to stop for milk or medicine and that the part of his heart in charge of his hopes had granted him another illusion. He may have left it at that, and dropped her and her child at home without another word, if she didn't have the courage to try again. This time, she looked at him.

"Don't you want to stop?" And he did.

"All I did was kiss him," she told herself, many times that evening and throughout the next day. "That's all I did. That's nothing," she repeated even though with Manny, a kiss felt more like a culmination. It was a heady sensation, to give someone treasure, a hint at a million hours of dreams.

"Just a kiss...a few kisses," she said as she carried Colin up the stairs and into her apartment. There was a package in the hallway and she noted that it was from Ireland, and she knew what it was: a Royal Albert china teapot she had ordered that matched cups they had purchased in Derry on their honeymoon. The pattern was called, "Colleen," and it cost as much to mail as it did to buy, but she had wanted it so much. She opened it and rinsed it, and when Brendan came home, there was tea steeping and a table set, and she took a picture of her husband sipping Earl Grey, on the day she kissed Manny.

Colin, as it turned out, was actually sick, the incident at the mall not simply a reaction to one negligent meal. The proof of this was that he repeated the act once again in his crib and several times the next day before settling into lethargy and a low fever. Marie actually enjoyed his weariness, which allowed her to both care for him tenderly and think about what had happened. She took a picture of that as well, Colin snug in a chair with crackers and books and a blankie, on the day after she kissed Manny. She would remember because the phone rang right after she snapped the shot.

"Marie?" he said, and she knew everything from why he had called to what he was feeling. She *knew*.

"I just called to see how Colin is doing," he said, and she heard indiscernible background noises.

"Where are you?" she asked, more to deflect the words she heard behind the words he was actually saying. It didn't work.

"Actually, you aren't going to believe this, but...I'm in Spain. I forgot to tell you that Madeline and I...it's a trip we do every two years. I'm sure you forgot we did this, I've told you about it before, anyway, well, how is Colin?" He spoke fast, and when he did, it came out in mumbles.

"Manny, let me get this straight. You called me…from Spain…to see how my son is doing…is that right?" She was enjoying this for one reason, a reason she only recognized when she started agonizing over him: she believed it would never happen again. She believed she was in control.

"Well, he was sick, and…I forgot to tell you that I was leaving in all the…confusion, so I thought I'd call." His voice trailed off.

"Manny, can you hear me okay?" she asked and he affirmed. "Okay. Manny, you are not calling me because you are worried about my son. You are calling me because you kissed me yesterday, for the first time in 8 years, and now it's all you can think about."

There was quiet on the other end and then she thought she heard Madeline's return to his side from wherever she was. And then his tone changed, and she could hear the smile in his voice, back in the game, in the company of secret-keepers everywhere.

"I have to go, Marie, and I want you to know something. I'm gonna worry about your son every single day that I'm away. And the minute I'm back, I'm going to come straight there to make sure he is alright."

He hung up, and she held the phone a minute, smiling like someone who is loved without conditions. "No, he isn't," she said to herself, and hung up the phone, because she was in control of this. She was.

****

He was gone ten days, which was enough to reorganize her thoughts several times over, and plan some line of defense. 'No doubt,' Marie thought, 'that he believes we have begun something, but we haven't. He has to understand that.' She never stopped to consider who she was convincing, or why she felt so good inside, just genuinely good, the way one feels after reluctantly exercising, or slipping on a light cardigan on a cool night, or eating only a healthy salad at a fast-food joint. Kissing Manny had fed some part of her; a part that obviously hungered, and now she told herself that only one meal would be enough.

She also wanted to hear his desires before she crushed them; after all, it had been eight years since he had placed his lips on hers! She wanted to know how she felt to him, what it was like to taste her once again. He certainly kissed better now than he did then, but how he felt to her was secondary. It was always how she felt to him that fueled her.

For ten days she maintained her life, saw it equally as something threatened and something treasured; something she would not give up for someone who loved her but could face better because of that love. She dropped off Colin at her sister's and boarded the bus for work and felt vital again.

Her account now was one no one else wanted: P&G Productions, which was, in short, the soap operas. Although she was writing ads for television shows, it was a print only account – and mainly black and white ads since they ran in TV Guide – so it held none of the glamour of television commercials.

Marie loved it because nobody, not even her creative director, seemed to care what she did with it. The agency side of Procter and Gamble Productions was lodged on the fourth floor of the building, and it was directly to them – specifically, one pregnant woman named Debbie LaSalle – that Marie reported. As a new mother and a mother-to-be, she and Debbie hit it off instantly, although Debbie was older and far more sophisticated, a Manhattan resident with a husband who designed toys for a popular company.

Debbie was happy enough with Marie's work, but she was bewildered and vaguely insulted that her account only merited the efforts of one lone copywriter, and a green one besides. She was aghast that Marie's concepts reached her desk unrefined by more experienced hands, and that together she and Marie had to dig up any art director that was momentarily free to execute those ideas. Still, ads were made and presented by Debbie alone to the client, and Marie's portfolio filled with the sensual faces of teenage boys with lines beneath that said things like, "He's free this afternoon."

It was an account that allowed Marie to leave each day at 5 o'clock, and leave her work behind; and then to get on the RR train to Long Island City, and then the Q39 bus to her sister's house in Glendale to get her son, strap him in the car that she left parked there 11 hours earlier, and drive home for the precious last hours of his day.

"I fed him already," Anne said, and Marie was grateful. It meant that all she had to do was play with Colin, guaranteeing the quality time she read about in all the magazines. She also noticed that Colin's face was washed and his hair combed, as it rarely was in Marie's presence. Anne was more Helene's daughter than Marie ever would be, and their priorities were different.

"What should we do tonight, Col?" she asked him, looking at his face in the rearview mirror as she drove. He was just beginning to talk, and she recorded every word in a baby book she had been keeping since his birth.

"You wanna do some puzzles with mommy? Is that what you want?" She was speaking absently as Colin's vocabulary had not extended to the ability to request one recreational activity over another.

Brendan was already home when she arrived, and she felt a quick pang of disappointment; always she needed that time, even if it were only minutes, to adjust to a different image of herself before she faced him. It started with a fast self-assessment: Was she carrying something she purchased that day? Did she neglect to do something that she should have? Was she late? How did her parallel park look? Sometimes she envisioned it as "suiting up," putting on some imaginary armor, taking one breath in for courage, and then going out to meet her righter of wrongs. But there was no time for that tonight.

"Hey," he said softly, addressing the baby, of course. "There's my boy," and he relieved her of his weight although she would have preferred to keep clinging to him. Brendan kissed her quickly on the lips as well, and if she didn't consciously count the seconds, then her breaths counted for her, the moments before something would be wrong mingled with the hopes that tonight everything would be right. She counted the hopes with her heartbeats.

"Manny called, by the way," he said nonchalantly.

"Oh really...when?" she asked, matching his off-handedness.

"A few minutes ago," Brendan answered, playing 'clap hands' with Colin and watching the news at the same time.

"Oh. Was he at work?" and here was the only place her heart fluttered because she knew he was still out of the country. *'Please, please don't let him have told Brendan he was calling from Spain,'* she silently begged, and someone answered her plea.

"How should I know? What do you want to do about dinner?" he asked, his face alight with the television's glow. He was watching the Rangers, not the news.

"Well, what do you want?" she asked, jumping, feeling absurdly like Edith Bunker. That's who she was. Edith Bunker, perpetually afraid of displeasing. She looked at her husband, holding her son, and she *wanted* that, wanted that beautiful, smart man whose liquid brown eyes matched her baby's, and then she thought of Manny's eyes, also deep and brown, only his were filled with her. She looked at him and saw herself gleaming without the armor.

'Why can't I have both?' she asked the same entity she had pleaded with moments before. *'Why can't I have someone to love, and someone to love me? How could that be more than is allowed?"* And then she realized she had both, just not in the same man.

"I only have frozen pizza," she said out loud, "It's in the oven. Now me and Colin have some puzzles to do, don't we, honey?" And she sat down beside him, and they were together, a family.

****

Manny didn't really come directly to her when he returned. He was as married as she was, and in those early days, it seemed to matter. He also had a job to return to, however, and he was someone else there; still married, of course, but the NYPD seemed to have its own law book on the bonds of matrimony.

He called her his first night back at work. "Marie?" Manny's conversations with her always began with questioning if she was who she was. In the simple questioning of her name, he was asking a few things at once, firstly, "Are you alone?" and after that, "Are you busy?", "Can you talk?, "Is the baby asleep?", "Do you even want to talk to me?" and later, even, "Are you okay?"

"Yup," she replied quickly, and her confirmation answered all those questions.

"Ummm...how are you?" he asked anyway, and she smiled. She stopped to consider Manny in that moment. He did not possess the voice or stature of a confident man. He was not much taller than her, maybe 5'6'' or so, and he used to be skinny, there was no other word for it. Skinny, that is, in an unappealing way, as in, lacking muscle anywhere. That changed after he got on the job, and his arms seemed larger each time she saw him. His voice, however, did not change; it was unintelligible at times, like he spoke with cotton in his cheeks. She didn't think she was faintly attracted to him physically, but she always understood him, nonetheless.

"I'm *fine*, Manny and you?" She was deliberately formal, laughing on the inside, wondering how long they would dance around like this. "How was Spain?"

"Very Spanish. Spanish people everywhere. Just like every other time I've been there. 'Cept I hate Madeline more. In any language. How's Col..."

"Colin is fine, too," she cut him off. And then there was silence. Was there something they were supposed to say now? If so, what was it? Was he supposed to apologize, or re-declare his love for her? Was she supposed to say they made a mistake?

"Can I come over?" he asked, point-blank, "Like, soon? Tomorrow? What is tomorrow? Are you working...yeah, yeah, of course you're working. Well, then, can I drive you home?"

It was already the danger zone, the place where innocent comments go to die. He didn't ask to meet for lunch; he asked to drive her home, and once, that was as innocuous a request as any. He had driven her home many times, and it was a treat to leave her office and step into a car instead of train, chatting peacefully over the 59th Street Bridge and beyond, using the time they saved to park and talk a bit more.

Now it was different. Here was the moment to make or break the circumstances, and it all rested on her reply, because they both knew what they were avoiding.

In one last desperate plea, he attempted to obscure the issue. "I can't get away any sooner, I just got back from vacation and there's stuff to do, and Madeline needs lifts." It came out rapid fire and hoarse.

"You can drive me home, Manny," she answered, and she was no longer blameless.

It was an unfamiliar thing, anticipating the arrival of Manny with anything aflutter within her. She had experienced anticipation itself before when he came to pick her up, but it was a quiet kind, serene, filled with images of his smile upon her cheeks. Peaceful. That is what it always was with Manny, the peace of never having to decide what to hide and what to show. Of course they had moments where they were less than forthright, but it always seemed in the interest of some greater good, and never the result of fear. And so she awaited his arrival in the past like one who knows a cool shower is waiting after a humid beach day; soon the grit would be gone and something naked and clean would take its place.

Her metaphors for Manny were always like that. She always saw him as something comforting and uncomplicated: the soft touch of any fabric you wear after you squeeze your work clothes off, or the wispy brush of Colin's baby curls against her cheek. Something so subtle, she didn't feel it even if it enfolded her; she just had that wave of inexplicable well-being that surely is exclusive only to those in touch with God.

It was a shock, then, today, for Marie to glance at the clock over and over, and then the phone, and then the clock again, her thoughts matching the direction of her glances: 'He will be here soon,' and 'I should call to cancel.' It was a respite, then, when it became too late to call and she had only the clock to play tag with. 'Too late,' she breathed in a resigned whisper, as if all the years to come would have been different had she only picked up the phone and cancelled that ride.

He was downstairs earlier than five because he had to be. Parking was prohibited and so was double-parking or standing; and these offenses carried heavy fines in New York City. He always had to circle the block continuously until she arrived, and she had to be ready to jump in as soon as she spotted him. The traffic cops were harsh group.

"What are they called," she asked, gesturing the officer in the brown uniform.

"Called?" he asked, maneuvering through rush hour, and using this as an excuse to keep his eyes glued to the road.

"Yeah, you know. You're 'New York's Finest,' and my brother is 'New York's Bravest,' what are those guys called? New York's 'Nastiest?'" She finished with a laugh at her own joke, and wanted him to laugh as well. He didn't.

"Ummm...I know...I forget...All's I know is that they are cop wannabees, just like the transit guys, you know, on the subway." He continued studying the road.

They were making conversation. She knew that.

He used a moment of gridlock to glance at her. "You look nice," he said quickly before turning back to the windshield.

"Thanks," she said back, and knew that this was going to take time. They were saturated with emotions aching to spill, and they could not be satisfied allowing them to seep out in interrupted trickles. They needed to gush, to flow without fear of embankment, to give justice to the power of these new sensations by giving them the space and time to surge unheeded. Until the car stopped, his attention had to be divided, and that meant this trip from Manhattan to Queens would be the longest drive they ever took.

There was nothing to do but stick with silence. It was no use attempting to fill it with the broken obsolete utterances of a time now past, so she satisfied herself with looking out the window, and waiting for the car to finally stop. When it did, she knew they wouldn't be home, but somewhere bleak and isolated, a place with factories and graffiti, and maybe some barbed wire, the kind of place she would get used to as background for her rendezvous' with Manny. Once, so long ago, it was a peeling doorway.

The quiet felt like hours of inhaling, without letting anything out. Many years later, Marie would have an asthmatic daughter, and would learn that asthma was actually the inability to breathe out. The ability to breathe in was unimpeded, but the air just stayed there, trapped. Her thoughts were like that, that day in the car. They kept collecting with each mile, and inflating, but without the escape of words, they had no place to go.

And then, finally, the car did stop. They were somewhere in Maspeth, Queens, minutes from her home but on the opposite side of Metropolitan Avenue. It was an industrial area, and they were in the loading area of a plant long closed for the day. She saw Manny check it out, giving a small nod of approval, and then he said, "This okay?" very low because maybe he didn't expect an answer. Maybe he, like she, was thinking, "Okay for what?"

He killed the engine and didn't immediately turn to her, still concentrating on the details of their location, but finally he pulled away from the wheel, and settled his back against the door in a semi-twisted position.

It was a small car, Manny's, a two-door with bucket front seats and a stick shift standing between them like a chaperone. It was the first she realized that he didn't drive an automatic. She had made a note of it, on the long drive, watching his brown hand fall continuously between them.

"So," he said. He would open many future talks with that ineffective segue.

"So?" she said, and she was smiling now. They were friends, after all. They would always be friends first.

"So, how was work?" he asked lamely, but he was getting it now, too. Yes, something had changed, and would stay changed; but the change was only verification of all that remained the same, and had so forever.

"Work...okay...work, let's see," she was fully playing now, in command of him, as she had always been, "Do you really want to know how work was?"

And he shook his head. Slowly, with head moving and eyes fastened, and it was one of those many moments she thought she had scripted. She would never again call Manny's eyes the same color as her husband's. Brendan's were beautiful, shining brown, but they were a mirage that offered nothing up close. Manny's eyes were long endless channels that contained all their memories, and all their ideals, and all of her.

They were going to solve nothing today with words, so they stopped trying. She met him halfway over the stick shift, found his mouth on purpose and didn't let go. Marie felt his kiss everywhere; like the glass of liqueur she once downed too quickly that heated her fingertips and toes and even the tops of her ears. Manny's hands touched her nowhere else on that first day, but she felt them, anyway, as surely as if he had.

He pulled back only to look at her and begin again, kissing her eyelids and cheeks and moving back to her mouth. Every cliché she knew came to surface, every worn out phrase about passion and love, but it irked her to use them for what was happening now. This could not have existed for anyone before today.

"We are going to have to think of new words for this," she murmured softly, but he didn't understand or try to. He just didn't want to stop, and he knew she would be the one to pull away.

"I have to get my son," she whispered, and he nodded, but moved in harder, closer, a thirsty man squeezing the last drop of juice from an orange. He kissed her now like there was just a certain amount he had meant to steal by a certain time, and he was nearly done and time was nearly up.

Then they were back to the silence, nearly the same silence as before except that this time it had inhales and exhales, as they each filled up on new inspirations and discarded unattainable principles. Instinctively, Marie knew this was all going to be easier for Manny, because he was sure and his motives were true.

Marie picked up Colin and looked at his big eyes, also liquid brown, and still felt relief that nothing had actually "happened." Not yet.

****

Diligence and routine are the dual harnesses of wild thought. In Marie's younger days, the latter encumbered the former; that is, the reviewing and reflecting of her sins and indecisions slowed an honest day's labor almost to a halt. She well remembered the migraine-like pain of "solving" boy problems, complete with the blurred vision, slowed reflexes and insomnia that made her daily life impossible to achieve; and then how failing at everyday living only compiled her misery and pain.

It was not this way with Manny. Perhaps she had determined that it would not be. Perhaps she was older and stronger or maybe just more in denial. Or maybe, just maybe, Manny was too a part of her life all along to wreak havoc with it, and what they were experiencing now had always been there.

He drove her home nearly every day now, and they stopped in the same spot. In between, she carried on, renewed again by the knowledge of love, and allowing once or twice during the day the reminiscence of a look, or touch, or especially words. Marie's life was words, and she was lulled, intoxicated, and stolen by them.

They had only just begun to resume casual conversation, but behind even this was the new vigor of passion; their friendship energized by a renewal of belief in their own theory of everything. They were both peaceful and fierce philosophers, fueled by the validation they found in each other. Many years later, Marie would still think of Manny's car as both her safe house, and a container where dynamite goes to explode.

In between, there remained life with all its petty jealousies and frantic schedules. Marie was still very content with her three-day week and her soap opera account, which was starting to gain some recognition. She felt worldlier, and knew part of that came from Manny's eyes, but much of it was genuinely earned. She was a writer, and a mother, and the manager of her household, and she no longer burned any dinners. And if Brendan sought to tear her down, Manny was the fiber that kept her from flinching.

They were sitting on the steps by the fountain just outside of Central Park, and he watched her agitation with contentment as uncomplicated as the water rising up from its origins only to cascade in a sunshiny curtain back upon the pool. The fount and Manny were both singular in their purpose, to keep feeding into and drawing from a well that would never run dry. They both knew nothing else to do.

Marie didn't know that she was already cheating, in the way she brought her days of successes and disappointments straight to Manny's ears and stopped troubling Brendan with them. If she had an inkling of her indiscretion, she also had a ready excuse. Brendan never speculated about why people behaved one way or another; or why time seemed to simultaneously move and stand still, or any of the other things that vexed Marie. He cared about money, and survival. He would only semi-listen to her woes, and then begin to 'help' Marie by pointing out the errors of her argument.

It had been a few weeks since the mall, and Spain, and they fell into a most unusual arrangement. They talked by day, over lunches. They kissed three times a week, on the drive home. And they made love on the phone.

She was always at home, and he at work. He called, religiously, in the small space between Colin's bedtime and Brendan's return from karate. With the protection of plastic and wire, he told her, unrestrained, how he yearned for her. He described the feel of her lips in trembling detail as if they were a holy experience; he described the touch of her tongue as if mysteries were solved in her mouth. And he said the words that pulsed liquid through her; he said, "I want you, Marie. I want you so much." Best of all, he said the words with no hope of ever having her; he said them like a prayer to a god that only listened to greater men. This, more than anything, excited Marie beyond stability. This was her aphrodisiac.

"He's still sleeping," she told Manny one day when he arrived, and she looked at the clock in a way he would memorize. "We have a little time."

They went into the living room, the room farthest from Colin's, and she closed the curtains in another gesture he would forever commit to his mind. Then they were on the sofa, mouths parted and pressed; only this time, for the first time, his hands took a chance on her acceptance.

She wore a white shirt that day, a button down, collared blouse. If she had to describe it as evidence in a crime, she would be able to supply each and every detail of that shirt; where it puckered or wrinkled, where it had the slightest residue of Colin's saliva. She would see that shirt in her dreams, and she would never throw it out, not even after it became unwearable.

She knew the shirt because she watched it unbutton, each pearly fastener released by one brown hand. It was the contrast that startled her, the contrast that stilled her and soaked her. Brown on white, in slow descent down her body, followed by her eyes, the only part of her still moving. He watched, too, alternating between her face and his own fingers, begging her not to stop him and still going slow enough so that she could. Button by button, she watched her skin revealed, and she counted those buttons later, sure there were a hundred. She was also sure no woman in history had ever been undressed with such assiduousness, and knew what she had in him.

When each side of the material parted, she saw her breasts, covered by the thin material of her bra, also white, so the battle of hues deliciously continued. She was fully swollen now between her legs, aching with her own blood flow, and she kept her eyes averted from his face and fully focused on his hands. She wondered, briefly, if she should tell him that her bra opened in the front, both sides connected by a tiny precarious hook. She wondered if telling him would change the moment; if her help indicated a consent that would ruin the flawlessness of her vista, or interrupt the serrated sound of her breath.

He didn't need her help, and with one more look in her eyes, he undid the hook and then both of them were transfixed by this ultimate contrast: her pale breast under his dark hand. It stirred Marie so hard that she shook, and then felt something else, felt herself orgasm silently and deeply within the confines of her jeans, and she gasped, and he knew.

His hand instantly went to the button on her jeans, and this is when reason interfered, because he was hasty now, and she didn't want that. She wanted something withheld, wanted time to savor where they had gotten so far. She wanted to force Manny to have something still to yearn for, as if attaining it once would cut off all desire. She even had the nerve to think him presumptuous to believe she would give herself to him so quickly.

"Stop," she said, and he stopped, and it was *he,* she would always remember, that carefully closed her bra and slowly buttoned her blouse. "It's just…too much…too soon," she whispered, and he nodded, although they both knew instinctively that whatever would happen between them would happen soon.

There was wild energy between them now, restless and tangible, and just waiting for its chance. Marie would continue to deny this to herself, but her body would mock this contradiction and would remain perpetually ready for Manny to enter it.

****

Marie marveled that there was so much of life that is forgotten. She remembers a timeline she had to make in grammar school of some famous person, Abraham Lincoln, perhaps. The line supported a series of goal posts, six or seven, with the white space of the paper in between dominating most of the assignment. Six or seven, two of which included birth and death, and one that mentioned marriage. What were the others? Presidency, of course, and writing the Gettysburg Address. The point was that even a great man's life was reduced to a just a short series of events. No one would ever know how he felt waking up in the morning, did he ever have a bad hangover, and how often did he make love to his wife? Nothing about his daily life was really very important, even though everyday life really *is* life, isn't it?

For Marie, the time between the day Manny unbuttoned her shirt and the time he made love to her was just such a white space. She didn't know how many weeks it was, or really much that happened in those weeks. She assumed it was all the same: she worked, went home to Brendan, took care of her son, probably got together with her sisters and some friends, but it was mostly blank – white, white paper.

Manny also continued to take her to toy stores all over New York, and once even brought Colin up to his precinct and let him play there. She knows this because there are also photos of the day: Colin on top of a police car, Colin in front of a "Wanted" poster. They would be photos that Marie would search desperately for, through albums and shoeboxes, in the days after Manny was gone.

They didn't talk too much about "that day," the day he unbuttoned her, but they did mention it. Strangely, he finally brought it up after a complaining session about Madeline. It was about the amount of money she spent on clothes.

"She has to have all the name brands – Jordache, Sassoon, Calvin Klein – why? They don't look good on her! It's like dressing a cow in silk; it's still a cow. I tell her, why don't you spend the money on losing some weight, huh?" He wasn't really mad, not the way he used to be. The change in their own relationship soothed Manny a great deal. Their feelings were reciprocal in that way; they each made it easier to live with their spouses.

"She buys all this designer lingerie, expensive bras, geez, for what? All the lace in the world won't make her look like you did in that plain white thing," and then he stopped.

"God, Marie, your breasts are perfect," he said, and she wanted to hear more but he was lost in envisioning her upper anatomy.

He came straight to her now on Mondays and Fridays after his 12-8 shifts, mainly to sleep, to catch a few hours before Madeline began assigning him chores. Soon after Brendan left for work, Manny arrived, and she carried on her day with Colin while he napped, and she felt she was doing her duty for society, giving up her bed so that a cop could sleep.

And then, one day, it was *the* day. He walked in, jumping with energy, with no rest in him. He told her about a foot chase the night before, which was really just a few hours before, and how he was still semi-pumped from it, his adrenaline taking time to lull. He was in the middle of the story, talking fast and pacing, when suddenly he stopped, and took everything in.

"You're still in your pajamas," he said.

"Wow, Officer, you should be a detective," she answered.

"Where's Colin?" he asked, incredulously, like he was interviewing a perp who had just committed the most heinous of crimes.

Her eyes locked with hers, then dropped, and he moved closer in an almost menacing way, but really he was watching for the second her answer left her lips. It was a suspended moment, like waiting for the bell to sound at the racetrack, allowing edgy horses to sprint. Her words would either open or close the gates, and he seemed like he would almost shake them out of her.

"He's not here," she answered finally, but that wasn't enough, and he moved closer. "He's gone for the day. Brendan took him to work. There was this thing going on in the city, and…" She never finished. She had supplied the key piece of information – *he's gone for the day* – and his mouth was on her fast, pulling her away from the kitchen counter where she was about to make him coffee.

Does anyone ever remember how they make it to the bedroom? In movies they show a long line of discarded clothes, but Marie's cotton pajamas were still on when she found herself lying on her bed with him above her. There are no clothes in the world easier to remove than nightclothes, however, and they were gone in an instant. The lack of hooks and buttons and clasps this time was in sharp contrast to last, and it almost seemed part of the plan, that she come to him so unencumbered.

He did not take his time. He kept his eyes on her as if she were a leprechaun's pot of gold, and would surely disappear if he looked away. Holding her in place with his stare, he managed to take off his own clothes, and she never saw his under things. They just seemed to vaporize and then the man she had known since she was 16 was naked, and it was so surreal to her that she had to close her eyes. One dark hand against a pale breast she could take; a long dark body against the length of hers exemplified the start of sins unforgivable.

There was little foreplay, unless she counted the way he looked at her, absorbing her, studying her, checking all his dreams of her against the final reality. She would notice it then; she would notice it always: Manny could make passionate love with the desire in his eyes. She was soaked, drenched, engorged and aching, and she didn't care a bit if he touched her as long as he got himself inside of her.

She exploded on contact; she knew she would. Again, she felt that it had never been like this, not for her, not for anyone. It was effortless, the way her walls closed around him and almost sang for the joy of it, the way she felt that the rest of her body was drowning in this one small section, like she had jumped in some electrifying pool of pleasure. She didn't believe anyone else could do this, and she never would.

"Manny," she whispered in his ear. He was not a tall man, and their bodies perfectly aligned. "I knew you would feel this good. I knew it."

It didn't take very long, and she yelped a bit when he came; then tried to stifle it. Her apartment was on the first floor, after all. He got off her gently, and she was dimly aware of his movements, including the removal of a condom she never realized he had donned. She didn't even know where it went because he didn't get up. Police officers know not to flush things in another man's toilet.

"Remember," she broke the silence lazily, her eyes half-closed, "years ago, when you said, if you were ever...you know, 'with' me, that it be over in seconds, that you would come before you even got in me?"

"Mm-hmm," he answered, stroking her hair, still in a state of wonderment, "I was kind of afraid of that, today, before, actually."

"You lasted longer than you thought," she smiled to herself. "I'd say you lasted long enough."

"I'll do it better next time," he said, and lifted her arm and kissed the inside of her wrist.

That was when Marie began reaching for her clothes, except it was an awkward reach, because it seemed a little ridiculous to put pajamas back on. She didn't want to stand stark naked, however, and mundanely pick out what she would wear that day. What if she caught herself in some mirror, and had to face so soon what she had done?

She lay back down, and he resumed stroking, but she was afraid now, the cold fear contradicting the warm ebb of blood flow back from where it came. She was still swollen, and would actually spend the entire day and even the next acutely aware of her own vagina, as if she was wearing it inside out and exposed.

She was afraid, because he had mentioned next time, and there would be no next time. He looked so sublimely happy, as if he had finally come home, but this was *her* home, and this was not a beginning for them.

There could be no next time. And then again, how could there not?

****

He began talking of love, and of leaving, right away. His gentle explanations of why he could not leave his wife were now replaced with solid arguments of why he had to.

"I'm leaving her," he said, nodding confirmation to himself. "I'm going. I can't take it anymore." They were sitting in his car.

She was torn. She always thought he should leave Madeline, but *now*, now it was different. Why was he going now? What did he expect?

"Well, I'm *not* leaving Brendan," she said vehemently, "You know that, don't you?"

"I know it's hard," he said, touching her lips, "with Colin and all…"

"Manny, it's not that! I'll never leave Brendan!" She shook her head, made his hand fall. "Why do you think that I would?"

"I dunno," he mumbled, his confidence with her was easily shaken. He could race toward an armed man, but he backed off Marie as if shot. "I thought that this…that we…I love you." He finished with a punctuated sigh.

"I don't know what this even is, this *thing*. It's just a thing, and that's all. I won't say it was a mistake, because…because it wasn't. But it's just a crazy thing that I can't figure out, something uncontrollable. I love that you love me. But I don't…love you. I love my husband." She finished.

"You don't love me," he said, more as a confirmation than a question.

"No. No, I don't," she answered.

"Marie?" He looked at her face, and now he was unafraid, staring at the barrel.

"What?"

"Yes, you do. You do, Marie." And he reached over and kissed her and touched her until she begged to have him, right there in the car, in daylight, and climbed over the stick shift and lifted her skirt, and pulled her panties aside. He unzipped and quickly looked around for interlopers, but she knew it didn't matter. What if someone called the police? He would be congratulated if caught in such a position.

She didn't voice her thoughts in the fast drive home, in the semi-silence of post euphoria. She was thinking that today was Thursday, and she would spend the day tomorrow with her baby, and by Tuesday, their next drive home, well, she would have this thing all figured out.

Chapter Nine: "Mam-ma"

Manny left Madeline a few weeks later. Marie, in the context of friendship, helped him pack, going with him to his apartment in Middle Village and helping him fill a few boxes with the things he would need. They were alone, but lust was put aside. Marie had taken a long lunch to do this, and he had picked her up from the train station. He was jittery, and barely kissed her.

"It's the right thing, Manny," she said to calm him, and didn't add, 'no matter what happens with us,' because it wasn't the time.

When he dropped her off at work, he thanked her, sincerely and profusely, for her help, then went on to his sister, Naomi's, apartment on 34th Street, near NYU Medical, where he would be staying for the time being. It would be months before Madeline learned who had helped her husband leave her; she would blame Naomi and hate her for it. She would also write a letter to Marie, begging her, as Manny's good friend, to help him see reason and return to her. The letter would arrive on the same day as the third time they 'had' each other – Marie still had trouble calling it 'making love' – and Marie would discover, oddly, that she felt no guilt about this.

She felt little guilt with Brendan, either. This was the magic of denial. There are no books that define how many sexual encounters amount to an affair; no equations that show how such a thing can be undone. She made certain rules about it: they could never again do it on her marital bed. They also could never get a hotel room since that was too sleazy, and in fact, they weren't permitted to 'plan' it at all. Each time had to somehow just 'happen,' accidentally, even after Marie started meeting Manny at his sister's apartment during her lunch hour. Most of all, Marie had to keep uppermost in her mind that this would end, that it would never be permitted to get uncontrollable; and this was probably her biggest denial of all.

There was another reason for the lack of guilt. More than ever, she noticed that Brendan did not treat her right, and she finally had the nerve to be indignant.

"What did you get?" Brendan asked one day after she returned from the avenue, Colin on one hip, a small bag in her hand. She set her son down on his feet, a gesture she loved, feeling his small form grasp the ground and steady himself, then opened the bag to hand him something inside.

"Oh, it's just a little toy Colin liked in the store. You should have heard him, he talks amazing. He said thanks to the saleslady, and she said, 'how *old* is he?' in this shocked voice," she finished, beaming, a proud mother sharing with the father of her child.

"You bought it for him?" Brendan asked in his dead calm voice, "Why? It's not his birthday. It's not Christmas."

The truth was that Manny had bought it for him, but that just put her in between a rock and a hard place. She thought quickly, but the only wisdom that entered her psyche was a line she would hear like advice from angels: *Manny would never treat me like this.* Manny would listen to her story. He would laugh. He would be proud. He would kiss her.

"Yes, I bought it for him, Brendan. It was $5.99. Do you want me to take it back? C'mon, let's go tell Colin it isn't Christmas." And with that, she stormed away.

That became the pattern of her life; to have one man's love be her adrenaline and validation so she could go home and face another. Manny infused her with self-belief and quiet certainty as if they were contained in his saliva or his semen, or maybe in some ultra-violet form that emitted from the intensity of his gaze. And yet, she would continue to deny it, to deny him anything but the evidence of her feelings in the form of her body.

"My sister says she hates that we meet in her apartment," he said one day, smiling, so very happy. "She says she hates helping me cheat on Madeline. But I explained to her that we are in love, and that…"

"Stop it!" Marie nearly shouted and he drew back. "Stop saying that! We are *not* in love. You explain that to her. I love Brendan, Manny, okay?"

He held both her hands and studied them, and she did too, always the contrast. Then he said, in a low voice, "I'll tell her anything you want, Marie. But we are in love. Why else would you be with me?"

She had no answer, but a few weeks later, she stopped being with him. She didn't stop out of guilt or loyalty or fear. She stopped for a simple logistic reason: she wanted another baby, and she had to be sure that the child belonged to her husband.

****

Some day, Brendan would ask her if she was out of her mind. Knowing all she knew then, and doing all she did, she still thought it perfectly reasonable to continue adding people to her family. The truth was, he just didn't know her mind, or the magnetic, ambitious course it took. She thought like her old boss, Joe Hayeck, and the multiple projects he kept forever running on his desk, alternating between each and ever on top of them all. Her addiction to Manny was one project; something she would have to analyze, decipher and file away. The continuation of her 'real life,' or the façade of it, could not be put on hold while she washed away her sins. Both projects had to be worked simultaneously, or she would lose precious time. Colin, after all, was nearly two years old.

She could not discount that her compulsion for Manny was potent. He was an extraordinary lover, and an extraordinary friend. When she saw him, or even when she knew she would see him, it seemed that every liquid in her body either roared or stilled, concurrently; the tumultuous waves that crashed in her brain calming into a reflective pool while below her fluids heated and rumbled like hot springs. The combined effect was toxic, for who could ask for more than peace and passion?

Sometimes, in the midst of a sunny stroll or a riveting talk, she would look at him and see everything he had done to her and everything he could do to her, and then her liquids became some broken pipeline that burst and coursed hard through her, nearly buckling her with its impact.

Marie wondered, absurdly, if she could teach Brendan the things that Manny did to her. She read it in magazines all the time; about telling 'your man' what you wanted, showing him, and guiding him. She began, during their lovemaking, to watch what he did, studying it intently, but she learned there is no technique in passion.

"Manny," she would shudder when immobilized by her own flood of unrestrained pleasure, "why? Why is this so good for us?"

"Because you love me, that's why," he would answer without hesitation.

"That's not why," she would reply serenely, without any fight. When standing on her feet and lucid, she would go on: "This can't be love. It's too…raw…animalistic. This is something different."

Still, she memorized his 'skills,' if for no other reason than to sustain her through the dry spell ahead, when she had to keep her Fallopian tubes clear for conception, and forever after that, she reminded herself. She lay beside Brendan's sleeping form at night, evoking the images that set her on fire. The way he always insisted on undressing her as if opening a delectable but fragile gift, and watched every move his own fingers made as though he might miss the first moment her body was bared. The way he gave her a fast, final look before entering her, to ask if he could, even though he could have assumed so by now. The way after he entered her, he held perfectly still for a moment, and oh, this sent vibrations exploding through her blood and she felt like she would orgasm through the roots of her hair or the tips of her fingers or even her teeth, because she knew what he was doing. He was savoring her, memorizing her, and thanking her all at the same time, and maybe even saying goodbye as well. It was his moment of silence.

And then, of course, there was Manny's mouth, a holy instrument for her deliverance. He kissed her in places that were previously ignored, the insides of her wrists, her eyelids and forehead, her upper and lower lips separately and in turn. And…when he placed it between her legs, he gripped her clitoris like it was a tiny but life-sustaining fruit, a jewel full of secrets. She always had to beg him to stop, but shortly after, she begged him to continue. She had taken to wearing skirts now, nearly all the time. A skirt let her be ready for what time and space might not permit.

Each time, every time she was with him, it was a multi-dimensional thing, as if Marie had become both him and her, and an onlooker as well. She felt in full what he did to her, and the effects of her touch on him; but she experienced also what pleasuring her did to him, and it was this that most electrified her. It was intoxicating that sex could be this, a constant gift to another, and it agonized her to take it away from him even more than it killed her to deny herself.

This is what she would give up, to begin the mundane and humiliating task of asking Brendan for another baby. This is what would stop so she could stand in front of her husband and prove why it was right, why they could afford it, and how it was what other people did. This was the price for a normal life.

******

Helene was working now, having decided the year before that her nest was emptying and she was needed elsewhere, at a local John Hancock office, as a part time office assistant. If Marie popped in after picking up Colin, she would inevitably find her mother on the telephone, pots steaming on the stove, cigarette polluting the steam, engaged in the joy of office gossip.

"Well, lemme go, my grandson just walked in and I hardly see him," Helene concluded her conversation.

Marie had her back to Helene, investigating the food on the stove, when she allowed her eyes to roll. Their relationship had softened with Marie's own advance into motherhood, but there were still things that Marie could not let go without comment.

"Ma, I know you saw him yesterday," she said.

"That was different," came the predictable answer. "Anne brought him over yesterday, when you were at *work*. *You* haven't brought my grandson by since last week."

"Oh, so he looks different when I bring him, is that it?" Marie smiled, though, thank God; she could finally just suck it up.

"Well, of course he is better behaved when Anne brings him," and at that second, an excited Colin patted his grandmother's face, and quickly, Helene slapped his hand, "No hit, Colin. No."

Marie removed her startled child from her mother's lap. "For godssake, ma, he is 18 months old. He is *not* hitting you. He doesn't know what hitting is."

"Well, that's why you have to teach him, Marie," Helene said sternly, with deep concern, as if saving the world from future violence. Anne slaps Tyler's hand when he is bad."

"Well, Anne is the perfect mother, and I am *trying* to raise a delinquent." '*More than one delinquent, I hope,*' she thought.

"It's not funny, Marie. You have to teach them," her mother baited, but Marie was okay. She knew her mother was from a different time and place. Just last week, a hungry Colin went into the kitchen, climbed on the chair and pulled down the Cheerios, which opened and surrounded him with hundreds of little toasted oat circles. Nonplussed, he sat down and proceeded to eat them off the floor with his fingers. Marie was delighted with the scene she came upon, and ran to get her camera. Helene was shocked by the photo.

"Did you holler at him at all?" she asked.

"Oh yes," Marie answered, rubbing her mother's arm. "After I took the picture, I beat him to a pulp."

"Oh Marie," her mother surrendered, "We should never had made you on the couch," referring again to her moment of conception.

Marie's smile faded then, because her mother didn't know the half of it. Her sins went far beyond allowing her child to eat multigrains off the linoleum. And worse, she missed sinning, every second of every day.

It took less begging this time, and by summer Marie was pregnant. It was the summer that Colin learned to say "Mam-ma" for grandma, and also the last summer of Helene's life.

****

Preoccupied with pregnancy, Marie resumed friendship status with Manny and almost reached some reconciliation with it. She felt "cured," saved from certain disaster, and purified once again. He, in turn, did his part, playing the supportive ally, and she tried to ignore the yearning in his eyes. There was only one thing that spoiled her illusion of redemption and restored honor, and it was one slip up – one last time after their official last time – during the "untouchable" time in which she was trying to conceive. She knew why God had told Joseph to know Mary not until she had borne Jesus. Manny had known her once, and it created nine months of havoc.

"Manny, what if, what if you made a mistake," she asked him countless times.

He was clearly hurt that his possible offspring could be referenced as a mistake, but he rallied and reassured her again, slowly, with patience: "Marie. I used something. I was careful. Nothing…unusual happened. Stop."

And she would ask again, next time she saw him, and the next, envisioning a bitter and possibly violent scene in the delivery room when a brown baby left her loins. He repeated his assurances, but every now and then, he said something different.

"Would it really be so bad, Marie? Then everything would be out, and we could be together."

She shook her head violently before he could continue, and he sighed deeply, and reiterated, "Well, it couldn't be, anyway."

Even so, the way Marie continued to cling to the possibility of carrying Manny's child endeared him to the unborn, even more than his adoration for Colin. The baby showed up in May with pale skin and wisps of red hair, and Marie whispered a silent thanks to God above, and vowed to be good.

Helene died before seeing her third grandson. She had begun feeling ill in the summer before Marie was pregnant, after a time Marie considered the most peaceful with her mother.

"Guess what?" Helene asked her family one day in early June when they somehow ended up in her presence at the same time. There was never a pause to actually guess what, so they all looked silently at their matriarch, and waited.

"A girl at work, she has this place in Pennsylvania, a house," Helene's pride was obvious; it would be hard to let her down if there was a reason to, "and she said she isn't using it in July."

"It's near a lake, in the Poconos, and we can use the house for a week!" Helene finished, and looked at her children's faces.

"Well, I still go to Lake George," Marie verbally meandered, which was true, at least. The Mcyers had given up on the five-hour trip but the Kavanaghs remained faithful, even though the original resort had been sold for condos and they had to move on to another.

"Well, when are you doing *that*?" Helene asked accusingly, and it was the old competition, Marie choosing her in-laws over her parents. The stakes were higher now that there were grandchildren to consider.

"I'm sure I can manage a few days in the Poconos," Marie said quickly, and it was settled.

God or fate had a certain way of speaking to one at times. They spoke in whispers, and took on the face of coincidence, and were often unwisely ignored. They spoke more urgently and obviously when the potential for loss was greatest, which testified to some sort of caring on the part of the divine or the universe. They told you to be careful. They told you to watch. They begged you to listen.

And so it was that Marie had a beautiful few days with her mother, and sisters, and the grandsons. Brendan drove her to Pennsylvania but didn't stay as he had to work, and Marie took an extra day off from her 3-day workweek, which gave her four days.

She remembers her father as background in those 96 hours, but sees her mother front and center, splashing in the lake with Colin and Tyler, and pushing them on the swings. Walking with them in the stores in town, and buying trinkets. Looking on as they took their bath together, four shining eyes amidst a sea of iridescent bubbles. Lovingly putting on their pajamas and holding each powdered body on her lap, alternating kisses on baby clean cheeks, and reading them a story. And then, when they lay fast asleep on thin vacation beds with guard rails from home, Marie made coffee or tea, and her mother and sisters sat up and talked.

They took Marie and Colin to the bus stop in Carbondale when it was time for her to leave, and Marie knew it was possible to get another day off from work. She recognized a moment that might never return, but she was steadfast about maintaining her life; and so she boarded the bus.

Colin sat near the window and pressed his hands and nose against the glass to see his grandparents, waving outside. That was when he said it, "Mam-ma," over and over, and the voice of God or fate began screaming at Marie to get off the bus, to get off *now,* but she followed tradition and ignored it.

"Yes, Colin, that is your grandma," she said, as the bus pulled away, and settled him into his seat.

Until the rocking of the bus lulled Colin to sleep, Marie read to him the books her mother bought him, little 39 cent Golden books that Marie would never have chosen. She was into only Newberry and Caldecott winners for her son's literary culture; but she fondled these books all the way home, and never threw them away.

****

In September, Marie knew she was pregnant. By then, her mother was in pain, mostly in her abdomen, and popping Tums all day. The doctors assured them that Helene was very sick, but remained unsure what was wrong with her, and were constantly running tests.

Anne took over in parenting the parent, and Marie went into complete and utter denial. She assumed it would all be figured out, somehow, sooner or later. One night, she even had the audacity to ask her mother to baby-sit so she and Brendan could go out, and her mother looked sadly at her.

"I can't, Marie," she said, "I just don't think I'm up for it."

Even Brendan knew, she thinks. He asked about Helene more than he asked how his wife was doing. Marie cannot remember how they got along during that time. She knew there was no joy in the new pregnancy any more than there was in the first. Brendan reacted with the same sort of distanced distaste, as if he was sorry he could not blame her condition on her alone. Her morning sickness was raging, and he stood back, seemingly in the hope that this alone would discourage her from future procreation.

Helene's decline was rapid. In October, she wrote a poem for Marie and Brendan's 3rd wedding anniversary, but a few weeks later, she could not hold the pen steady to write a note to her insurance company, nor hold her mind steady to form coherent sentences. One week she was at the beauty parlor getting her hair done; the next she needed help walking to the car.

She was diagnosed, finally. Marie got the call at work, to come straight to Mount Sinai Hospital, where her parents were.

She called Manny, and he drove her. That day she learned that the cancer, which had begun in her kidneys, had already metastasized, and there was nothing anyone could do.

"It's not fair," her father said in the white walls of mystery and doom.

"It's fair," her mother whispered through her tubes. "We've had 35 wonderful years. Most people don't get half that." Marie was struck by her words, because with all the disapproval she held for her mother, the truth was she had managed to love only one man, and love him well.

They gave her two months, but she was gone in ten days. Absurdly, Marie still held some vague hope that a cure could be found within 60 days, and she rushed to her mother's house each day armed with that futile optimism.

She helped Helene dress and move to the living room, to greet whatever visitors came to see her, but it was mostly just herself and Anne. It occurred to her once, in this maternal act of taking off her mother's clothes, that she had never seen her mother naked before, and she stared at her body. *This is where I came from*, Marie thought. *This is my mother.* Once, as Marie moved a heavy ottoman to put beneath her mother's legs, Helene said groggily, "You shouldn't be doing that. You're pregnant," proving to Marie that she was *still* her mother.

One day, Marie's mother was weak but alert, and aware of her short time to impart wisdom. With Anne and Marie at her bedside, she sat up, and looked at each in turn.

"Anne," she said sincerely, "I want you to know that I always knew you loved me. You didn't say it much, but I always knew." While Anne's tears fell, she turned to Marie:

"Marie," she said and stopped, whether stilled by weakness or introspection, Marie couldn't say. "Marie," she went on after a breath, "You never listened to me." And stopped again, looking down and talking more to herself now. "But I guess I never really listened to you, either. But will you promise me something?"

Marie nodded, for who denied a dying woman anything?

"Promise me that you will never allow the child you are carrying," she stopped again, "to eat mashed potatoes with his or her fingers." And so Helene remained true to the end.

Early on the day that Helene died, a visiting nurse came from Cabrini Hospital to see if she qualified for hospice care. At noon, she called her office to tell them that Helene did not qualify; by five she called to change her professional opinion. By six, Helene was in an ambulance, rushing to the emergency room.

Marie had taken Colin apple-picking the day before, and was in her kitchen, making jars of applesauce and apple butter with him. She always allowed him to pick far too many, her camera there to capture the moment, and so she felt the need to use each one lest Brendan make a special note of the waste. It was with the syrupy sweet smell of boiling apples in her nostrils that she answered the phone and learned that her mother was en route to the hospital.

Brendan was at karate, just blocks from Cabrini, and something made her do something that she would never consider. She called the school, interrupting the ancient mystical warriors, and asked that Brendan come to the phone.

"My mom is on her way to Cabrini," was all she said, and he said, "Okay."

Marie's mother died beside her father, and her husband, who had changed and rushed to be there. "I think she's gone, Brendan," her father had said, and right then, a bond formed between the two fathers in Marie's life; her own and the father of her children. It would take decades for the bond to finally break.

******

Helene's children all thought their father would fall apart after his wife died. He didn't. He spent hours gazing at her photos, and crying, but that made sense. He cried with each grandchild born that she would never see, beginning with Marie's son Daniel in May – "the first redhead," he lamented – and then Lisa's daughter, born in August, a mere ten months after her wedding.

"She only seen three of 'em," Fred would say often, even up to the 16th grandchild born. There was a photo of her on his wall with those three, Anne's son, and Marie's, and Robert's daughter, born just a few months before her death.

He didn't crack up, but he spent his survivor benefits madly for a while, as if it hurt him to have them. He bought bicycles for the grandchildren that they would not be big enough to ride for years, and clothes for them, and the following year, a house in Pennsylvania, not far from the one where they had spent their final summer.

He lavished gifts on the only child still living with him: 16-year-old Louise, who would feel most potently the effects of growing up without a mother. Fortunately, he also bestowed on her a gift no other Meyers child received: a college education. The baby of the family would be the first to hold a degree, and it would set her life on a different course than the ones the others had traveled, as would the absence of Helene. Louise would grow up not free of insecurity, but certainly more equipped to cope.

Marie was back on maternity leave. At first, she was disappointed that she didn't have a girl; seeing her chance to provide the first granddaughter on at least one side of the family, but maternal instinct kicked in, and besides, Daniel was special. He was content and peaceful, with a smile that said he had seen beautiful things before his appearance in the world. He could amuse himself for hours with a rattle, and of course, he stopped people in the street as only a baby with the light of dawn upon his head could.

His timely birth allowed her to be off all summer, and so she spent a few weeks with the Kavanaghs in Lake George, and a few in the Poconos with her own family. It was strange, the photos taken at that first vacation without Helene, photos of her dad alone with *her* grandchildren, for he would always call them hers.

She saw very little of Manny and not much of Brendan, either, as he did not have the luxury of maternity leave and weeks away in the mountains. When she saw her husband, though, she noticed his caring ways with her bereaved father, and she was proud of him, and loved him anew. She had made a mistake with Manny; she knew this. She was lucky to come out unscathed and unpunished. She had her life back now, and it would be normal.

"I'm going back to Madeline," he said one day out of the blue, looking not at her but at Daniel, the baby he adored. It was early September, just prior to her return to work.

"What?" she dropped spoons, cups, whatever she had been washing at the sink in order to evade a moment of accidental intimacy. "Why?"

"She wants me to come back," he said, still touching Daniel, his soft plump arms, his curled toes, "and I…need a life. I need what you have. A family. I don't want to get old alone."

Marie was only staring, so he went on. "I see what you have here. I know why you won't ever leave it. These kids are your life, your breath. Madeline isn't the worst woman in the world. I want...what you have. It isn't ideal with Brendan, but look what you've got."

"But...but..." she began, but there were no "buts." What could she say? But this is mine, and you are mine, too? But I can only survive this because I have you? Or should she play traitor to herself, and say that maybe he had a chance to meet someone else if he stayed out there?

She didn't finish, because he placed her baby in his little seat, and said something she didn't expect.

"Can I kiss you, Marie? Just kiss you? Because I have to tell you something. If I don't kiss you, I think I'm gonna throw up." And she let him, because she needed to hold and defend what was hers. And her life was once again impure.

****

Manny indeed went back to his wife, and began the arduous task of impregnating her. He kept Marie posted on each attempt and the effort associated with it, and Marie wondered why she didn't burn with jealousy at the thought of his body with hers. She guessed it was because he found the task so unappealing.

Marie returned to work, but it was not the same environment she left. In her absence, a go-getting youngish copywriter, Randy Seifarth, took over her soap opera account. He was senior to her, as were most people at the agency, even now, and he was determined to keep his job in a rough economy. His wife had just had their second baby in 18 months and wasn't dealing well with it. In fact, one day he had to leave work early because she had accidentally locked both babies in her running car in a mall parking lot.

Babies aside, Randy was creative and aggressive, and once Marie considered him a friend and ally, but he had a family to support and his need for friends in lower places was slim. In Randy's hands, the worth of the account was discovered, and the Creative

Director was appalled at the lackadaisical way it had been handled previously – "how could we let this one slip by us? It's inexcusable," he said – which basically meant, "How did we let a kid writer do this alone?"

Now they looked upon the work done so far with criticism, but it was *good* work in concept, Marie maintained. It just lacked the resources for a great execution, and now resources were marching out like reinforcements to a drained troop. She went down to complain to her friend Debbie LaSalle, only to find that she, too, had been given a supervisor.

"For months, they don't pay attention to this at all," Debbie said caustically, "and now it's like a freakin' Volvo account or something."

"But you have to tell them it's *my* account," Marie said to her, sensing that Debbie wasn't unhappy enough. "You have to say how well I've done it."

"Oh, they know, Marie, they saw, and I said," Debbie went on, "I'm sure you are still going to work on it. But you are a part-timer. And no one down here is going to be sad that the Creative Department is finally paying attention."

"There's a big celebration on the 4th of July, out on one of the piers," she went on, "All the stars will be there, and you're invited. It's the 50th anniversary of 'As The World Turns." She was throwing out a bone, but Marie only nodded.

"Cheer up," Debbie said, "So how is it with two kids? I can barely handle one."

Marie was undeniably still on the account, but the problem was, Randy wasn't *off* it, and he wanted all the glory. During those months, Marie came to work each day and did absolutely nothing for 7 hours. After awhile, she began getting in at 9:30, taking lunch from 11 to 2, and leaving at 4 for the day. No one noticed, and she collected her paycheck every two weeks.

It was demeaning, to read at her desk while around her the hubbub raced on, writers blowing hair out of their eyes as they whizzed past to meetings, producers talking loudly on the phone. Sometimes her own inactivity was so apparent, that she could hear different halves of phone conversations over the cubicle walls, and played her old game with herself in which she connected them to each other.

After a few weeks, they hired an official junior art director to the account, and for the first time, Marie was made to share her office.

It was at this low point in Marie's career that Manny called her and told her that he had "made Sergeant." She left work immediately, said goodbye to no one, and spent the rest of the day celebrating with him.

"They'll probably think I'm just a 'quota' sergeant," he said, explaining a system in which a certain percentage of minorities had to be chosen, regardless of their actual ability, "but I got a hundred on that test, Marie. Studied for weeks, even with Madeline moaning about not taking her anywhere."

He wasn't upset about this injustice. Manny accepted many injustices that would have enraged Marie. She was the only thing he took seriously.

"After the ceremony, we had this lunch with the other guys, and I stood up with my glass, at my table, and I said, 'this country be berry berry good to me. Me only get fifty percent on de test, and now me a sergeant.' Most of the guys laughed, but one just glared at me."

"Manny, how could you *do* that? How could you let them *think* that?" Marie wanted to rush down there, wherever there was, and tell them the truth.

"It's no big deal. The guy who was mad is already a good friend. Jerry. He looked up my scores and told me I was an asshole. I'm gonna be working with him at the Civilian Complaints Review Board. CCRB."

"You're not on the streets anymore?" Marie was disappointed.

"Negative. No more uniform, Marie, sorry. Madeline is ecstatic."

Manny came over, to Marie's house; after the ceremony and the festivities, to present himself in full regalia. Brendan spoke to him for a bit, congratulated him, and Marie went to get her camera. She took a picture of him, there in front of her apartment windows, turned slightly to the right to display the new stripes on his arm. She could barely contain her pride. It was in late November or December. She knew because she had a Christmas wreath up, and the corner of it jutted into the picture.

She made tea that night, and the three of them and her sons sat around talking, Brendan mostly asking questions as Kavanaghs do; ever deflecting attention from themselves, and Marie mostly soaking in the scene. This was the man she loved, and the man that loved her. One was soft spoken, smart and beautiful to look at. The other was also smart, but it was not as apparent in his presentation, and beautiful only because of the uniform that Marie glorified. His voice was not so much soft as it was muffled and fast, giving him a demeanor of nervousness. Marie knew both of them. She needed both of them.

That New Year's Eve, Manny and Madeline had a party, mostly for family and close friends so Manny invited Marie. She showed up late and alone, having attended a family thing of her own, and immediately told Manny that there were drunks all over the road and she was afraid to drive back. To Madeline's displeasure, he offered quickly to drive her back, and she could get her car in the morning.

They left before midnight, and rung in the New Year in his car, innocently in the moonlight, in one of those moments where the breadth and impossibility of their lives mixed with the wonder and the magnitude of it. They talked in the moonlight, where all faces are beautiful, and all expressions are illuminated.

"What are we going to do, Marie?" he asked her, with a sigh underscoring every word.

"I don't know," she answered, and then they heard the shouts and noisemakers, and it was 1987.

****

Marie thought about quitting her job each and every day. Most people told her she was crazy; why quit a job because it was too easy? The art director that shared her space was fresh out of college, young and sure, and saw Marie already as a has-been. Marie couldn't stand it. She was too young to be washed up.

She had other issues as well. She hated her new babysitting situation for Colin and Daniel. Anne declined to watch Colin after Marie's maternity leave, as her own son was in preschool, and she had time to herself. She was also pregnant again. Marie yearned to put Colin in preschool, but it was only half day. She couldn't find affordable, suitable childcare for a baby and a 3-year-old, so they went to separate places. Colin boarded a minivan each morning, crying, to attend a woman's home childcare center. Daniel went to another woman's house, Patty, a safe but unstimulating environment that had only one benefit: his cousin, Robert's daughter, also went there.

Marie hated seeing her firstborn drive away with tears in her eyes, and hated to see her second born plopped in his seat in front of the television set. She hated spending 45 minutes on a bus and another 20 on a train, to sit at a desk and feel humiliated while her children were cared for by strangers.

She met Manny at CCRB now, at the Puck building downtown, a glaring red stone affair adorned by some gargoyle or nymph. It would be her custom to visit him at each place he worked, to know his life and to stake her claim in it.

She had plenty of time to make it down to Soho and back since no one, save the astute but tight-lipped receptionist, noticed her comings and goings. And then one day, upon her return, there was a message on her desk on one of those preprinted, pink papers. It said simply, "Laine Dupre called."

Laine Dupre was the personnel manager, and Marie's heart hammered in her chest. At first she thought someone finally noticed her extended absences, but then she knew what it was about. There had been, in the last few weeks, a lost account, and what the business world morbidly called a "bloodbath." The account was a huge lost of revenue, and the ripple effect was wide. Marie was lower level, and part-time besides. She joked with others that firing her would not make a difference. She was obviously wrong.

Laine was a good woman, and an older one, a person who had seen many changes throughout her 25 years with the company. Marie did not return her call, but walked to her office instead, and her sorrowful glance up confirmed Marie's suspicions.

"Sit down, please, Marie," she said, and finished up something quickly, before speaking.

"As you know, we have been dealing with the lost of the Crisco account, and there have been mandatory cutbacks," Laine said, in the voice of one who had given this speech too many times.

"I know," Marie answered, looking at her straight on, "and I know you are going to fire me. It's okay."

"I'm sorry, Marie," she recited, but Marie stopped her.

"Laine, this is good news, not bad," and then it was all logistics.

"You'll receive a settlement package, plus a month's severance pay for every year you've been here, and then, of course, unemployment."

Marie was hardly listening. *I'm free*, she thought. *Free.* She would take care of her own babies, and could even now register Colin for preschool. She was lost in her own reverie of possibility, when she heard Laine's concluding sentence.

"And of course, you can use your office for two weeks, to establish contacts, you know, use the phone. We don't usually allow that but we can in your c…"

"I don't need it," Marie said, first to herself, and then she looked up. "Laine, I will be gone today. I'll be packed up by five. I'm going home."

She walked back to her office in a daze, past the junior art director who said only "hey" without looking up. She picked up her phone and dialed.

"Manny," she said slowly, "Can you drive me home today? I'll have a lot to carry."

She went down to Childcraft on 59th Street and spent a chunk of money on wooden unit blocks. She had read in a parenting magazine that if a child could only own one toy, it should be these. She couldn't carry them back to her office, so she told the clerk she would pick them up soon.

Although not really hers, she took the lamp on her desk, and cleaned out her drawers. She was outside with everything when Manny pulled up on the side street.

"What's going on," he asked, taking in the scene, "You quit?"

"Nope! I was *fired*," she said, for the first of many times, said it with gleeful expression, even though Brendan would correct her and say she was merely, 'laid off.'

She was beaming. "They said I spent too many lunch hours having sex," she added, and loaded the trunk, and got into his car, again. So much began and ended in Manny's car.

"Hi Colin, hi baby," she took her son off the bus; full of news he wouldn't understand. His nose had been running, and it looked like he had been wiping it all day with his sleeve. There was a streak of dried mucus running from his nostril to his ear.

She had already picked up Daniel, and tears filled her eyes at the sight of each one of them. No more daycare, she wanted to say to them, no more, but all she said to Colin was, "I bought you something cool!" and carried him inside to see the new unit blocks.

She was with Compton for 8 years, and so would get her full salary for 8 months, and half her salary for 4 more. Full pay without commuting costs, or lunch costs, or childcare costs, and she could begin to live in jeans instead of having to update her work wardrobe. It was miraculous.

Marie sat Daniel next to Colin, and together they played, Colin making buildings and allowing his baby brother to knock them down. They were still there when Brendan came through the door.

"Hey," he said softly, happily, and she had to admit that the sight of his sons did make him smile, and gave him a voice rich with love. He put everything down and came into the living room and began playing with the blocks, too, and Marie tensed because they were new, and expensive.

Marie had taken to saying that Manny bought the toys that appeared in the house, which was usually true, but she said it no matter what. She thought it the lesser evil, as if Brendan would not mind if gifts came from Charles Manson as long as they didn't upset their own family budget. She was wrong about that, but right now, they both seemed content to keep the peace, and he didn't ask about the blocks, and she didn't offer.

"Guess what?" she said softly, and she could swear he blinked, or winced, as if afraid of her words, but if he did, then he recovered quickly.

"What?" he asked, keeping his gaze upon the boys blissfully amusing themselves.

"Brendan, I got fired today. I'm going to be home with the boys from now on, well, for a while," her voice began accelerating in speed and volume, "and I get *paid*, I get paid for a long time. And now Daniel doesn't have to go to that stupid hot apartment anymore, and Colin...Colin can go to school!" She finished and looked at him hopefully.

"Slow down," he said gently, "You don't even know how much preschool costs. But congratulations, I guess. Never congratulated anyone for being laid off before."

They sat there, for a long time, playing with their sons: a family. They were a family. Eventually, they loaded the boys in a double stroller and went out for pizza, and Marie for once did not worry about money, and got ice cream afterwards, even for Daniel who had not yet had this taste sensation. His face was covered with it, and he smiled with brand new teeth.

The next day, Marie marched straight to her nephew Tyler's preschool, only to find it full and not taking any more students. Undeterred and impatient, she continued up the Avenue to St. John's Evangelical Lutheran School, and found a place for Colin there. It would prove to be another one of those life-defining turns, a subtle intersection that changed her direction, but she wouldn't even feel the shift, nor would its impact be immediate. Not until much later, when she figured out what 'evangelical' meant, and how it affected sinners like herself.

****

Colin began attending preschool, and Marie became a stay-at-home mom. Better than that, she was also a "freelance writer," as she liked to call herself, having obtained jobs through Debbie LaSalle, whose husband worked for, of all things, a toy company.

"Can you believe it?" she said to her sister over tea. She hung out with Anne now, mostly, but she also set out to develop new at-home friendships. "Toys. I'll be writing about toys. Not commercials, just, like, box copy. I don't care. It's work and it's toys!"

It was a remarkable life; taking a child to school, and working, and caring for her baby, and it was marred by only one thing. She had time, and she had opportunity, and she still had Manny.

****

Who wouldn't, one day, think of Manny as nothing but a dishonorable man, a liar and a cheat and a coward? His wife was heavily pregnant, due soon, and he used all the moments he could to get away from her. He held Daniel as if he were his own son, removing him from the bath and wrapping him up, and laughing when once the naked baby peed all over him. He strapped both children carefully in car seats, and walked lazily around with her, pushing one or both boys in a double stroller.

"I can't imagine loving any child like I love yours," he said to her sincerely one day, and she did not rush to correct him with platitudes. She didn't want him to love any child like he loved hers.

He brushed against her at the zoo, or the children's museum, or in store aisles; a nearly imperceptible hand on the side of her breast, or a press from behind to show that he was hard. The effect was always instant, shooting heat to her groin that in turn diluted through every pore in her skin. She would look directly into his eyes, over the heads of unknowing babes, and gasp.

"It's intense, isn't it?" she said, but not as a question.

"It's intense," he agreed.

Their chances were concentrated and swift and unplanned; a naptime shared by both boys, or an engrossing Disney tape. Manny never missed one. He was like a heat-seeking missile in her home, and she could feel his heat rise as forces in the cosmic universe merged to give him the moments to open her legs. He felt any shift in her that might be a sign; a cursory glance at the clock, or even if she kicked her shoes off under the table.

He was also invasive, and she would never know if this was just his personality, or if he could not shut off the cop in him. He arrived, and checked everything: her calendar on the wall, her checklist of things to do, her mail. He would not allow himself to miss anything, anything he could help her with, surely, but mostly anything that would free her to be with him.

"What can I do?" he would say upon arrival, and this alone made her flush with pleasure, that his first utterance would be to ask how he could serve her, and especially that he wanted her enough to work for it. It wasn't like that with Brendan.

She could not stop comparing them. Brendan had taken a Saturday job with a sanitation company privately owned by a friend. It helped to make ends meet, and also to increase his irritation at home. It never dawned on her that his angst was due in part to finding two cups on his kitchen table with the remains of tea in the bottom, indicating that he had worked and his wife had played.

Marie passed Manny off as a nuisance to her husband, a clinger, a guest who wouldn't leave.

"God," she would say, "He asked to stop by and then he wouldn't *leave*. I had *things* to do today. I barely got to any of them." But of course, she had gotten to all of them, because Manny had helped. All of her household tasks, and then ten stolen minutes that even now she could feel, engorged and saturated and scented with pheromones.

Manny's baby was born in August, and it was, to Marie's dismay, a girl— Ariella Torres, Marie's first competitor.

Soon after, Brendan quit his job at Cabrini and began working for Doubleday, the first rung on his climb up the corporate ladder. Soon after that, Marie found Jesus.

Chapter Ten: Life in the Spirit

It was the yearning for a house that started it, the way all journeys to God begin with greed and wanting. Oh, Marie noticed that the people at her son's preschool were different, but in a way she both forgave and ignored. They talked about Jesus daily, as if he were a neighbor, as if he had recently borrowed a cup of sugar or came through with a Tylenol one late headachy night. They would say, "I was thinking of quitting my job, but I really have to talk to the Lord about it," or "I didn't know what to do about my son's teething, but the Lord told me to have patience." Once, to Marie's amusement, a woman with bad teeth showed up at school wearing a fancy dress and make-up. When asked, she happily replied, "Oh, I just felt like gussying up for Jesus today."

There was no kind way to say it: Marie thought they were plain stupid. Stupid as in; uneducated and slow, and naïve and ridiculous. But, what did it matter? They were nice enough and harmless although not friend material, and Colin liked his school days, and Marie loved watching him learn.

Sometimes, Colin said things that made her laugh, like the day he asked how Jesus could be born in a staple when staples were so little. And once, he began to sing a song, and then stopped himself. "Singing is wrong, my teacher said," he explained. Marie immediately began to extol the virtues of singing, when it dawned on her that he meant, "sinning." She wasn't sure the pressures of sinning should be borne upon the shoulders of a 3-½-year-old, but she approved of the acquisition of knowledge in most forms, and let it go. She got used to 'sinning' talk and 'Jesus' talk. It had very little bearing on her busy life, except in the quiet moments when she realized that she might soon have to take some stand on religion.

She didn't believe that Jesus should be called upon to find parking spaces and relieve menstrual cramps. She thought he existed for a higher purpose than this, and so had no need to call upon him. At the same time, she felt her own sins to be far beneath his notice. Jesus was for capitalists and murderers; he did not have time for two-bit thieves.

Marie was a writer, and that is how they sucked her in, God's angels appealing to her pride. They needed a new writer for their monthly newsletter, and the principal, Mr. Johnston, approached her.

"We heard that you used to be a journalist? Is that true?" he asked her one day. He was a diminutive man but emanated certain strength, perhaps stemming from his obvious education. He seemed scholarly, and gentle, the way Marie imagined Jesus' disciples to be.

"Not a journalist," Marie replied quickly, "More of an advertising writer."

"Oh. Hmmm..." Mr. Johnston looked at some papers and Marie wondered if he were quietly consulting Jesus.

"I've written brochures," Marie offered, hoping that the Lord did not give up on her already, at least not until she knew what the mission was.

"Well, you see, we need someone to write the newsletter. Just once a month. Generally, we like it to be someone from our own church, but I thought we could make an exception here." He looked puzzled, but that was part of his daily countenance.

Marie didn't know if she wanted to write anyone's monthly newsletter, but she knew they wanted her and she couldn't ignore that.

"I can do it," she said, and so it was settled.

"I heard you were writing the newsletter," one mom, a mother of six, said at the dismissal doors that day, "I didn't even you were a writer. Amazin' how the Lord knows how to find the people he needs."

Marie smiled weakly, and nodded just as ineffectually. If the Lord really cared to find her, she would have some explaining to do.

Guilt likes to be noticed. It tolerates only for a short time the bliss of ignorance, but this respite is granted only to give it a chance to fester. It camouflages in the hopeful colors of justification, and then permeates like the aftertaste of a far too delectable meal. Beyond the voice of reason, guilt is the voice of indignation. It whispers first and then it shouts, "You can't have this. You shouldn't have this. You must give this up."

Justification, on the other hand, is a weak and whiney voice that is merely fighting for time. What it lacks in stamina, it makes up for in repetition, placating the conscience with a barely sustainable level of credibility. It is a mantra that monotones, "You deserve this. You only live once. It is different for you."

Brendan never treated Marie right, or at least, not her version of "right." She did not stop to consider whether there were flaws in her expectations, because justification is a blind friend. Marie felt submerged by the sheer force of Manny's emotions; she deemed it unimaginable to be immune to such an onslaught of coveted perfection. Indeed, Manny's love was a work of art, capturing both the romantic and the erotic in a display that kept her helplessly rooted to the spot. There was no way to refuse him, because he *loved* her. He loved her, and it didn't matter if she loved him in return. Justification stated that it only mattered that she deserved love, and if she could not get it from her husband, she was entitled to take it from someone.

Each time Marie surrendered -- and it was always surrender, in some form, whether to a look in his eyes, or a sigh or even just an internal struggle -- and led Manny to stolen chances that only she could choose; each time she lay back and closed her eyes to see if she could distinguish between the instant he actually pushed inside of her and the sweet heightened pain of anticipation that directly preceded it, like the way she liked to see if she could feel the second a plane left the ground after rushing down the runway; each time he made short, gasping love to her, the rhetoric of justification began: he loves me, and I need this, and I deserve it.

Mixed with justification was another unreliable bedmate: rationalization, the language of denial and misguided hope. Marie told herself daily that she could fix this, *would* fix this, just as soon as she figured it out. She maintained that spending time with the problem, that is, Manny, was the key to understanding and eliminating it. Unfortunately, she knew the clock was ticking, and every second brought her closer to the day she made a mistake, and was discovered. This added another frenzied element to their already laden lovemaking, as if each orgasm brought her closer to a cure.

"I wish," she said breathlessly after one such time, "that we could do that once and for all."

He said nothing. She began pulling up her panties, and had another wish, that she could just once sleep it off, revel in the post-climactic glory until she drifted off.

"Do you know what I mean?" she asked, and he shook his head.

"Well, when you do something incredible, you don't usually have to do it over and over. Like, if you climbed Mount Everest, you wouldn't say, 'I gotta do that next week and the week after, too.' You'd say, 'okay, I did that, and it was awesome,' and you would put a picture of it in a frame and look at it, and remember, and that would be enough."

He was still only looking at her, as if she was crazy, as if she was beautiful, as if he were trying to find a way to give her Mount Everest.

"So, you're saying you want a picture of this in a frame? Me, too."

"Seriously. If we had hours and hours and just went at it all day, no eating or sleeping, then, do you think we could do it once and for all? Like, work it out of our systems? And then, say, okay, done. Do you think that's possible?"

He was helpless now; he hated telling her that anything she wanted was not possible. So he resorted to humor, and said, "Tell you what. Let's give it a try. When do you have hours and hours?"

She smiled; too, because on some level, that was always the answer she wanted. She wanted to hear that this couldn't be stopped, that *he* couldn't be stopped, because if he could give her up, for even the noblest of purposes, what good was he?

And so, rationalization and justification held innocent hands, not with each other, but with their mother, Bliss. Marie's days, at least, her weekdays, were blissful hours of womanly completeness, beginning with the early morning when she placed her baby on her breast, and stroked his chubby legs as he nursed. Daniel was becoming beautiful, and she thought herself objective in this since she didn't think he was born that way. He was the first grandchild on both sides to possess the golden red hair of his Brooklyn grandpa and his Irish granny, and that alone seemed to stop people on the street. He was a calm baby, with huge brown eyes and an easy smile. Marie admired him each morning as she nursed, already anticipating the day ahead. Her children were always her first thought in the morning. Manny was usually her second.

He worked 4-12's now, which was perfect. It allowed her to live a perfectly dual life. She rose and fed her babies, then dropped Colin off at pre-k, chatted about newsletters and Jesus for a bit, and then went home to await Manny's arrival, perhaps doing an errand on the way. She made tea, and first they sat, and talked. There was even an order to their talking, first the concrete and then the philosophical. He talked about his job at CCRB, the Civilian Complaints Review Board, a paradoxical organization run by civilians -- "non-uninformed members of the police force" -- and police together, its simultaneous goals being to mollify the complainers while at all costs, defending the officer involved.

He spoke of his friend Jerry, who had come to like him after his comment about quota sergeants, and went with him to CCRB. Jerry was a happily divorced father who occupied his time chasing women half his age.

"I tell him, 'do you have to hold their hands when crossing the street?' Manny told her laughing, "I never stop ragging on him. I say, 'What do you order for her in bars, Similac and Seven?'" It occurred to her later that Manny was a different man at work than the one she knew, and also that he wanted her to appreciate that man as well. Sometimes she did, but mostly she was content with only the single focus of her version of him.

After a bit, they would talk about life, as they had always done. They talked about the phenomenon, which of course, included sex, a simple act of flesh meeting flesh that was performed with, what? The heart? The mind? Marie held nothing back, even asking him how it was that she found Brendan infinitely more attractive than Manny, and yet, this did not in any way enhance the experience. Manny could take talk like that and speak objectively without any hint of damage to his ego. They talked about people and what makes them good, or bad, and they kept talking until Daniel's naptime, all the while pretending to have no stake in its arrival.

Sometimes, now, he brought Ariella, and Marie would be rankled by this. She tried to keep her irritation in check, since there was simply nothing honorable about resenting a child. She was never afraid of Manny's opinion of her before, so here was another needle: the need to tell him how she felt, and the need to protect his untarnished image of her. Ariella also was, quite frankly, another nap that needed to be coordinated.

After all respective siestas, they bundled whatever babies they had and took to the streets, sometimes heading for a nearby park where they pushed little ones on swings, other times finishing up the days' errands together. Either one was a backdrop for further exchange; and they soaked up each other's words with the pleasure of a child with a Popsicle dripping sweetness down his face.

Then Manny had to go and Marie had to get her son from pre-k and ready herself for part two of her day, the part that was both more and less secure. Brendan would arrive home and they would be the family she cherished, mingled with the fear of her own inadequacy in that role. She ran her fingers through her husband's hair and listened to another account of a workday while she selected what news to share in return. She made love to him, many nights, for the single purpose of clarifying that she was taking nothing from him by giving it to another.

And so Marie might have nearly accepted her own circumstances, abnormal as they were, as simply the way it had to be. It was self-preservation, it was survival; it was a way to face the days, and would have remained as such, if Guilt hadn't grown tired of being ignored.

****

The evangelists say that Jesus knocks on your door several times during your life, but he knocks softly and unobtrusively, and so many simply don't hear. Right away, Marie should have found some problem with that theory, because if the Lord God was coming to provide respite from a life of meaninglessness and misery, he damn well should knock hard and insistently. It should not be some inner heavenly joke that some alcoholic or murderer or any hopeless soul could have been delivered several times 'if only.' "If only I had heard when Jesus knocked, my life would be so different," some of them would say. Well, Marie thought, Jesus is Jesus, for Godssake. He shouldn't play this little game of chance. He should knock with all the authority of police on a raid, even breaking the door down if need be. Salvation wasn't something to play with.

Nonetheless, Marie bought this fluff when she first heard it, because it seemed to hold true. When guilt began its slow and treacherous hold of her senses, unrest soon followed. She began looking in the mirror, and seeing what she was: a liar, a cheat, a charlatan in the role of wife and caretaker of her family. When she and Brendan had other couples over for dinner, she played her role, with playful stories and heartwarming glances, but she also watched other wives with their husbands and felt herself die inside. They were so loyal, and good. The men could joke about the white lies their wives told about how much they spent on curtains or baby clothes, but there always followed a look of pride that said, "She sure did pick good curtains, though," or "Look at my kid in this outfit." The women, too, shook disapproving heads over some male peculiarity, but there was privilege in knowing it personally. And there was love. And, Marie thought, there was certainly no backup spouse in the shadows, waiting to catch them when they failed each other.

She wanted to get out of Queens, far from buggy apartments and loud, uneducated people. Once, Daniel fell asleep in the baby swing at the park, and she gently placed him in his stroller and took the opportunity to read her book in the shade. Within minutes, a sallow-skinned woman with bleachy hair sat beside her. To Marie's disgust, she started the conversation with, "I won't bother you, readin.' You gotta do that to look smart, right?"

She was tired, also, of living at the mercy of landlords who let her freeze in February while their own heat was still blasting, and complained about children blowing bubbles on the front steps, or putting a bird feeder on the window ledge -- *iffa you gotta birds, you gotta bird shit,* her new Italian landlord said. She was tired of alternate side parking regulations, that forced her sometimes to park blocks away from her home and then walk back with groceries and children, or that forced her to find a good spot a day in advance and then commit to going nowhere for the next 12 hours. She was tired of heavily alarmed sports cars that inevitably went off in the middle of the night.

Marie wanted a house, and she wanted normalcy. It became her daily obsession. She began to talk of little else, and Brendan began to tell her why her own spending habits precluded saving for a down payment. This included her desire to have children so quickly, over and over he would say, "Well, you wanted these children" as if their sons were extravagant vacations or Lamborghini's. They were already paying back a debt consolidation loan. The word, "budget" lived inside Brendan's mouth and spilled out like bad breath, making Marie draw back every time she knew it was coming. "You have to budget," he would say, and would add, "I don't even buy a morning paper, and I never go out for lunch. I figured out that seven morning papers a year and five lunches add up to at least $900 a year. $900! You don't see money going, Marie, but it goes in bits and pieces." Her argument back was that he could do this, skimp on himself, because he only had himself to think about, and he was at work all day. She was at home with children, and children needed things, but then she remembered, she had wanted these children. And so they had no house, and it was all her fault.

And then, one day, she walked down the familiar corridor to her son's classroom to drop him off. Her head was down and she was preoccupied, and so she nearly walked head on into a door she expected to be open. It forced her head up, and there in front of her, was a sign, a literal sign, most likely a bumper sticker. It said, "God has a plan for your life."

If nothing else, the words gave her at least someone else to blame, and she adopted them quickly. In testimonials some day, she would describe the feeling of peace that entered her upon reading these seven words.

After this everything happened quickly. Jesus came knocking, only he didn't look like the Messiah; he looked like the wife of the principal, Mrs. Johnston. And when Marie let him in initially, it was probably because she didn't recognize him.

Mrs. Johnston did not possess any of her husband's subtleness. She either didn't speak to a person or she did, and if she did, she spoke her mind directly. She taught the 4-year-old class, which Colin had recently joined, and had never said a thing to Marie until the day she spoke for Jesus. Marie would drop off Colin, with Daniel on her hip, and Mrs. Johnston would quietly take her in as if stillness gave her a clear view of another's soul. Marie wouldn't have liked her except she was good with the children; from them she got her animation. There was a piano in her classroom and she could play it, and Colin often came home singing -- Jesus songs, granted -- but singing happily.

It happened when Marie had been writing the newsletter for several months. There was a buzz around the school that she wasn't doing it right, a hum Marie only heard because it stopped when she was near, and instantly smiled at in a pained and patient way. It was true she had been trying to add flair to the document she saw as largely unread, but she didn't think she compromised any truth in doing so.

Still, when Mrs. Johnston walked purposely across the room to confront her one morning, Marie was certain it was about the newsletter. She had been joking to Manny for two weeks that she was about to be fired from a volunteer position, after already being fired from a Madison Avenue ad agency –"laid off," Brendan's word instantly popped into her mind, "not fired." Of course she pretended that the absurdity of such a thing was the medicine that kept it from hurting, but she still felt its sting. And so, when Mrs. Johnston approached, Marie considered leaving the room.

Mrs. Johnston learned what all teachers know, that parents are a touchy bunch, and that their children are the way to their hearts. She spent the first few seconds complimenting Colin; how articulate and energetic he was, which someday Marie would understand as the positive version of loud and fidgety. Now, it sucked her right in, digesting each word hungrily, because, of course, she knew her son was special.

At the end of the toast to her eldest son, Mrs. Johnston leaned in closer, which was an impressive feat for a woman who seemed to define claustrophobia, and said, "Listen, a friend of mine and I would like to come to your house one evening. Just to visit."

Marie found herself nodding as if drugged, first by the sweet syringe that attacked her maternal pride, and then by raging curiosity. She checked her calendar mentally and came up with a date, then stayed rooted to the spot waiting for another hit of whatever drug the principal's wife was injecting. When nothing came, she shifted Daniel to her other hip, and turned to go.

"Just a short visit," Mrs. Johnston said, and then turned her attention back to her class.

"What could she want?" Marie asked Brendan several times all week. She cursed herself silently again for choosing a date so far in the future.

"Well, you know, we are Catholic, and it's a Lutheran school," Brendan mentioned. He was untroubled by the things that troubled Marie, and the distinction between what affected each of them grew wider since she took on the role of a stay-at-home mother. Brendan had to worry about providing for his family while Marie's fears were far more frivolous.

"Oh my God," she said, causing Brendan to do that thing he did, that imperceptible pulling back, the way one does from an unexpected sneeze, unwilling to inhale the breath she exhaled when she said something foolish, "Could that be *it*? Are they going to say we have to convert in order to keep Colin in the school?"

"Well, we are not going to *convert*," Brendan said simply, as if the point was as moot as changing his skin color, "but I doubt that's it anyway. Not with the tuition that school charges. I'm sure they don't care what we are as long as the bill gets paid."

Marie noticed it; the tiny dig that said preschool was just another indulgence of hers, and the hint that next year when Colin started kindergarten, they would have to go the public school route. Which is why Brendan was unperturbed by the possibility of losing St. John's, for whatever reason.

They came a week later, Mrs. Johnston and a Pastor from the church, a skinny man with large teeth and big glasses. That was another thing that marked the Christian community at St. John's. So humble were they, it never dawned on them that there were certain aesthetic elements about a visage that could be fixed without offending God. They didn't wear contact lenses; they didn't get their teeth fixed. Mrs. Johnston herself wore no make-up, nor did she fuss with her hair. Together they looked like an act from a play about deprivation, except that Pastor Smith's glasses magnified his eyes absurdly, and his teeth made his smile eerily happy, and so he might have been a starving circus clown.

"Sit down," Marie offered, nervously, checking all around for signs of sin. Brendan also sat, complying with the odd request that they both be available for this special talk.

They fumbled through the protocol of drink offerings and the like. Both visitors wanted only water, in keeping with their colorless prudence, and then they were settled.

"You probably wondered why we came by," Mrs. Johnston began, and Marie stilled her characteristic rush to restate to exhaustion just how that feeling of curiosity felt. It would only delay the gratification of knowing.

"Yes," Pastor Smith chortled, and that is exactly what Marie would call it, a chortle, because the word itself was as absurd as the goofy sound that came from the good Pastor, "I was saying to my wife before I left, 'we must seem pretty strange to folks' just barging in, but our message is pretty important."

Marie winced, of course seeing them through Brendan's eyes, their simplicity glaring and counterproductive. These were people he would be kind to, but would never call friends.

"Anyway," Mrs. Johnston tag-teamed, "What we want to know is, 'Do you think that you are going to heaven?'" When one spoke, the other nodded, on the off chance that the listeners could possibly think they weren't in agreement.

There followed the kind of silence that is felt in a classroom when the teacher calls on someone who hadn't been listening, and the befuddled stare on both her and Brendan's face matched that scenario. Brendan, however, was like the student that recalls the answers suddenly, and knows he will be saved.

"Yes," he said assuredly, "I do. I am a good person, and I try each day not to hurt anyone." He smiled in the way that would win over businessmen in conference rooms for the rest of his life.

The two evangelists nodded knowingly; they had heard this answer before. But instead of enlightening Brendan just then about the true road to salvation, they turned to Marie.

"I don't know," she stammered, and this brought a tiny smile, because it was closer to the correct answer. "I'm not sure. I don't think of God as existing for me. I'm neither very good nor very bad. I'm like the mediocre student who falls through the heavenly cracks. Pretty much off of God's radar."

"Mm-hmmm," the two assimilated together. They were pretending to consider these answers carefully, but like good God salespeople, they already had their response. It was in the Bible, and Mrs. Johnston pulled one out of her bag, and began to read, even though she could well have quoted from memory.

"It is by faith that you have been saved, and not by works, so that no man can boast," she read, and gently put the good book down, and closed her eyes.

"This means," Pastor Smith said, "that it doesn't matter if we are good or bad, it is only through belief in our Lord that we are saved. Have you accepted Jesus Christ as your personal savior?"

"I have," Brendan answered, "I've believed in God all my life."

Marie didn't answer. She was liking that line about no man being able to boast, seeing suddenly a kind of happy socialist heaven, where everyone had an equal claim to the pearly gates. Even the noble Brendan could not cut her on line.

The messengers swooped on her hesitation, pulling out brochures for her to read, and talking excitedly about the goodness of God. Then they stood to leave, the message delivered, and Marie saw them out. Before they reached the door, however, Mrs. Johnston turned to Marie and said softly, "We're beginning a 'Life in the Spirit' course next week. You should come."

Inside, Marie sat back on the sofa near Brendan, and said, "Well, I guess they aren't expelling our son."

"I guess not," he responded, but his eyes were on the television.

"Are you really sure you're getting into heaven?" she asked him.

"Reasonably. But that's not why I said that. I know exactly the answer they wanted. I just wasn't going to give it to them." With that, he clicked off the news and said, "Want a cup of tea?"

****

A week later Marie was in the "Life in the Spirit" class, and three days after the first meeting, she spilled her guts about Manny to Mrs. Johnston and the good pastor.

She and the good sergeant were having a nice day, a glorious day, in fact, when the synchronization of their motions, both physical and mental, was uncanny. Marie felt always their smooth moves and transitions, and felt something sensual even in the innocuous act of handing him something; a diaper bag or car keys. She felt that they breathed in unison, her out to his in, and he felt it too on this day especially. It was always present but today they noticed, against a serene cerulean backdrop, how fluid they were with each other, how even their words to each other flowed back and forth like a gentle wave pool.

Marie had parked in the lot behind the Queens Village mall, which was so close to Manny's home that it seemed a lot for the apartment complex as well, a misunderstanding so common that signs all over warned against it. They had taken his car down to Rockaway, to let the children sift sand between their toes in the pleasant chill that was early autumn. Now they were back, after a 30-minute ride in a car filled with sleeping babies and hushed contentment. When the final set of eyes drifted closed in the back seat of the Toyota, Manny's hand reached across the console that separated them and held her hand, and there was nothing to say that they didn't already know.

Now they were back in the parking lot, breaking the spell with each awakened child that had to be transferred into her own car, and the one that had to be placed in the stroller for the walk to his front door. The children were cranky to be so unceremoniously disturbed, and responded with immediate requests phrased according to their language limitations: "Want a ba-ba," or "Can we get ice cream?" or just simple crying. She and Manny tended to them, and when they were settled, and it was time to say goodbye, they found themselves looking deep into each other's eyes.

Manny felt compelled to speak, and he breathed deeply first, but didn't say what she expected.

"I want to thank you, Marie," he started, "for everything. I was thinking about it the other day, how because of you, I know what I know. I can joke with the guys at work because I know what I know. I mean, not about sex, 'though it's good to have a healthy contribution in that area, too, believe me." He smiled and let images fill them for a moment.

"I mean, you're there, with me, in everything. I keep your photo under my hat, but I keep you in my attitude towards, well, everything." He grimaced, ever frustrated at the limitations of words in transcribing a day like today, which was a microcosm of the emotions that lived inside him.

"Anyway, I just wanted to thank you, for being with me. That's all."

"You're welcome," she said, and they pecked goodbye like illicit lovers do in public places.

Marie drove away dreamily, not yet willing to make the transition to the other life, the color-in-the-lines life, far from the untamed ocean waters that crashed defiantly in front of her today. She saw Manny's eyes in the sun, glimmering in a way no one could imagine a hue as dull as brown could. Suddenly she shuddered, and even her sons felt the quake because it affected the sinuous movement of the car winding towards home.

"Why are we stopping, mom," Colin asked.

"We aren't, honey. But we will soon. We are almost home," she answered.

We aren't stopping, she reiterated in her head, and knew what had caused her to disconnect with euphoria. In Manny's eyes, there was love, always love, and wanting and wonder and even gratitude. But there was never guilt. There was never fear, and there was never remorse. These, she had to bear alone. And it was that thought that released the confession that evening after her Holy Spirit class, after which she would call Manny and tell him that she could never see him again.

Mrs. Johnston acted like she had heard many a soul-baring like Marie's, but it was clear that she was out of her league. She marched Marie straight to the pastor, not the one who had visited her house, but the senior pastor, a spooky ethereal man who seemed to live in the dark, and whose name, incredibly, was Angeles.

"Tell him what you told me," she demanded, gently though vaguely excited. "Don't be afraid."

Pastor Angeles had perfected his starry prophet-like gaze, and so Marie had the impression he already knew what she would say. There was no condescension in his face, but it was a practiced look, and Marie thought judgment surely lurked beneath. But she was there now, and there was no turning back.

"I have a friend," she began, "a male friend."

She started the story the same way she always started it, and would for years, until one day she changed the focus and centered first on the void in her marriage. Either way, it was a preamble that begged for understanding if not forgiveness. What followed was a slow analytical assessment of where she was, a confession as honest as a puppy's hunger or a baby's cry, but she needn't have bothered offering up so much. Analysis is wasted on true Christians.

"The answer is clear," the good pastor said like a well-timed recording. One hand reached for King James while the other hovered over Marie's like a hesitant healer. Did he think adultery, like leprosy, was highly contagious, or was he afraid that his holy flesh would sear hers? Either way, the burden of the Good Book required both hands, and he pulled the other back.

"It says, right here, in first Corinthians, 6:18, 'Every sin that a man does is outside the body, but he who commits sexual immorality sins against his own body." He finished by somberly closing the book.

"Do you see?" he asked in his ethereal voice, and briefly Marie wondered if, upon discovering that he had a voice like Marley's Ghost, did he feel he'd never make it in the corporate world? Did that account for his vocation? Did he speak to his wife like that in bed?

"You have to end it," he rumbled, snapping the book shut. "Today."

Marie panicked, because the meeting was over, so she grabbed his arm and nearly rattled the stained glass with her anguish.

"No, you can't do that. You can't just say what to do. You have to tell me how. I don't know *how*."

Mrs. Johnston, mesmerized and participating only through affirmative nods until now, stepped in as if to protect her leader.

"It's easy," she said, "Just stop. No phone calls, no letters, no visits, no contact. Nothing."

"That's how," Marie asked incredulously, a question without a question mark at the end.

"That's how," Pastor Angeles nearly whispered, and added the line would become a taste Marie would spit like bitter herbs from her mouth: "Remember, God never gives us more than we can handle."

"Okay," Marie said, wearily rising, "That's God. But you don't know Manny." And she left the scent of death and incense and walked out into the sun.

****

She told Manny that night that it was over. She told him point-blank in between his "I love you's" and how at work, they all knew he loved her, and reminiscings of the afternoon, and warm breathy descriptions of how she made him feel, and spine-tickling anecdotes of adventure, NYPD style. She could barely find a place where her rejection would fit.

"Manny," she disrupted, like an ugly paperweight dropped hard on delicate figurines, "I cannot see you anymore."

And then there was silence, and she explained. All of it. The awakening knowledge of God. The reading of the Bible, which, of course, he knew about. The guilt. The meeting with the pastor. The verdict.

"They said, 'no phone calls, no letters, no visits,' nothing," she finished, almost in a self-righteous voice.

She cannot remember if Manny said another word after that. She doesn't know how they got off the phone. She only knows that the next day, he began the stakeout. From that day on, she never left the house without glancing around to see where his car was sitting. Except for the hours he was at work, he was always there, waiting.

They say alcoholics are never really cured; they only replace their addiction. They find a new thing, a more acceptable thing, to embrace obsessively. Marie plunged herself fully into her Bible, and in it she found a truth she would just as fanatically deny one day.

Right now it worked.

In the "Life in the Spirit" class, she learned that all good things come from God. Therefore, it was pointless to fault her husband for his inability to make her happy. It was not his job. It was between herself and God. So taken was she with this concept that she raced home one night after class – with Manny's car following her in the shadows – and walked in the door, breathless.

"Brendan," she nearly shouted, and he was flipping channels on the television. "I have to talk to you. It's important."

"Okay," he said, without the interest that a bright-eyed woman bouncing from foot to foot should generate. "I'll make tea first."

He went into the kitchen and she paced. She didn't want tea first. She wanted to tell him that it wasn't his fault. She wanted to say she had the secret to their relationship. She wanted to say they would be okay.

So she started, "It's about our relationship. I learned something tonight. I know why we have troubles communicating with each other," she said, "It's because…"

"Well, wait a minute," he stopped her, "The kettle is about to boil. Hold that thought."

She left the room, just to keep moving, and checked on her sleeping sons. They were beautiful asleep, cheeks like pillows cushioning their little faces, and rhythmic breath that filled a room with sweetness. You can smell a child slumbering and it is the true scent of peace. They still have nothing real to fear.

The tea was done when she came back. Brendan was sitting, with a paper in his hand and she sat across from him and waited for her moment, a moment that she considered a pivotal one in their marriage.

He never looked up. He kept staring at his paper, which, she realized, was their bank statement.

"So," she started, but she was again interrupted.

"Well, would you look at this," he said with wonder, "I think this is the first month ever that we avoided fees for not maintaining enough in our account."

Perhaps Marie gave up too soon for a moment that was supposed to be fundamental, but hurt welled inside her like liquid from a burst blood vessel. She quietly picked up her tea, and cradled it as she left the room. She hoped that he would stop her, but he did not. A few seconds later, she heard the television click back on, and she opened the Bible on her night table and began to read.

****

The stakeout thing became a game. One day Marie would know for sure that it was a game that she never wanted to win. She became holier each day, avoiding Manny as she should, but she made sure that he was there. Her heart pounded hard when she saw him, and she quickened her pace like one eluding death.

If forbidden passion is a heady emotion, then lust restrained is a reckless animal that kicks and strains at the walls of his prison. That he wants to escape is obvious; that he is not enjoying the fight to be free is not as clear. The combat alone keeps his adrenaline pumping, and the potential for victory keeps his spirit alive. There is no chance of quelling his ardor without fulfilling it, and so the quest alone feeds the passion.

Maybe Marie knew it was inevitable that sooner or later, the being inside her would release itself; maybe she knew that Manny would never give up. Each day only brought her closer to a more potent surrender. Perhaps it was this, and not God at all, that allowed her to stave off the inescapable.

She left the house now two evenings a week, once for the class that was soon ending, and once for a Friday night worship service. This of course gave Manny two possible ways to follow her, that is, if he happened to be off work.

Once, on the way home, she stopped at a red light and in a flash he parked and opened the passenger door, getting in and slamming the door before the light turned to green.

"Manny, you scared me," she said, and she wasn't lying. She was scared, because she had lost.

"Going to church, Marie?" he asked.

"Yes, to a worship service," she answered, and felt ridiculous. These were the words that were leaving their mouths, but this was not what they were really talking about.

"Worship service," he repeated.

"Yes," she said, and now she was driving and wondering how he was going to get back to his car, so she pulled over. "It's so different from Catholic Church. People here are so into God. They're passionate. They shout and sing and are full of joy…"

"Charismatics," he nodded, "I know the type."

"You don't," she said, "They aren't a 'type.' They are people who…"

"Marie, I understand. You don't have to explain." He put his hand on the car door and began to open it, then closed it again and looked at her.

"Go to your worship service, Marie. But I'll bet you never shouted for God the way you've shouted for me. I'll bet you never whisper his name the way you've whispered mine." And he opened the door and got out, leaving Marie to continue on to church feeling damned.

By the fourth week of "Life in the Spirit," they began talking about 'the gift.' Apparently it was a very coveted gift, one that invoked jealousy among modern Christians because it was given only to a few.

Mrs. Johnston looked serenely blessed when she spoke of it, because she, of course had it.

"The gift of tongues," she explained, "is a special prayer language. It is for communicating with God in a way that goes beyond our earthly language. It is speaking the words that He wants to hear."

Marie didn't get it, didn't understand it at all, but the others in the class nearly salivated, their glowing eyes resembling those of the last round of finalists in a beauty contest, waiting to see who would be eliminated.

"The apostles received the gift as a way to spread the Word to all," she said, "but we receive it as a way to speak to our Lord."

"So," Marie said, "We don't even know what we're saying?"

"Well, you can. The Spirit also grants the gift of Interpretation. But, not all who receive the Gift of Tongues also receive the ability to interpret. So, if a word is uttered in tongues, it may have to be interpreted by someone else."

Marie saw no gift in this, because she already had many thoughts she did not understand, and saw no sense in being able to vocalize semantic chaos. She knew what she wanted from God, if He were indeed all-powerful. It was what she wanted since she was old enough to stop wanting Barbie dolls and snow days off from school. She wanted peace. She wanted satisfaction in what she had already.

The culmination of a course entitled "Life in the Spirit" was to actually receive the Spirit, a Pentecostal appointment in the chapel. There was a service, and then, in confirmation style sans the Bishop, they were to go up and be anointed by Pastor Angeles. It was too exalted a job for the messenger pastor that had visited Marie's house seven weeks before.

When it was Marie's turn to approach the altar, her prayers were fervent and ingenuous, hopeful and austere. She called upon God as if he were car salesman about to close the deal, and begged him for honesty.

"If you are real," she said, "You know what I want. And if you know what I want, then I am asking to show me that you are real, and that you are listening."

She walked back to her seat and buried her head in her hands, and then it happened; something that she couldn't explain, something that she would never be able to account for long past her holy roller days. Was it power of suggestion? Hypnosis? Or just group dynamics?

Whatever it was, when she opened her mouth to continue her unadorned prayer, out came a string of utterances that definitely had syntax, but was in a language that was certainly not her own. She paused, twice, to check its validity, or at least she tried to pause, but the words – were they words? – had a life of their own and surged ungracefully but sure from her tongue.

Marie was hooked. It was simply inexplicable, and the inexplicable could only come from God. She left the service walking in some foggy bubble; she wanted to tell someone what had just happened but she didn't really know. She crossed to the deli across from the church, remembering there was something she was supposed to pick up, but once in the store she could only walk up and down the aisles, admiring the graphics on cookie boxes and raviolis. She could not remember what she needed.

"Weren't you supposed to get milk?" Brendan asked upon her arrival.

"I was!" she answered, and sat down beside him on the couch, grabbing his hand. She had never really done drugs as a teenager, but she imagined this nonsensical feeling to be akin to some illicit stimulant, and she relished the moment.

"It's only real if I can do it again," she thought to herself, and so, the next day, in the confines of her room, she tried. Could hypnosis reach her there? On her knees, she simply started and her vocal chords once again took control, and it was true: she was praying in tongues.

God works in mysterious ways. Even a seemingly useless gift becomes powerful simply in the possessing of it. Marie wanted a house in the suburbs; she wanted to be free of the force that ensnared her with Manny, and she wanted Brendan to love her. But now she could speak to herself in words that sounded like an old reel-to-reel tape played backwards, and this was the language of God.

People came straight up to her at St. John's the next day. Some were there the night before and saw her, and knew that she received the gift. Apparently Mrs. Dermody, one of the aides, had been aching for "the gift" for quite some time, and she was jealous.

"You got the gift, didn't you, Marie," she spoke sadly, and Marie was proud, and chosen. She exchanged a look with Mrs. Johnston, who was beaming at her prize student, her face lit like a Christmas ornament.

"I did," she whispered, "I didn't even want it, but it happened." At that moment she did what many Christians do with their faith: she used it as a medal of honor, one that separated her from common folk. She perfected her look of sympathy for the damned, and became practiced in quoting the line from scripture about just how narrow the road to heaven sadly was.

The language of God was not going to keep Manny away, but Marie waved it before him like a cross before Dracula. Believing herself armed, or pretending to be, she allowed Manny to get closer. Maybe she wished to share with him the glory of her salvation, or maybe she needed to test God's power within her. Maybe she just missed him. Whatever the reason, the next time she found him lurking beneath her windows, she went down the two flights of her apartment stairs, through the vestibule door and then the front door, and up to the side of his car, where she startled him by knocking on the window.

"Why don't you come up for a cup of tea?" she asked benevolently, and although Jesus lasted forty days in the desert, Marie would quench her thirst within forty minutes, and not with Darjeeling. She would wonder on that day how God had failed her so quickly, and would spend the next years both loving Him and despising Him at the same time.

****

Now she and Manny had a new word to add to their vocabulary of guilt and justification, and that word was "sin."

"We're sinners, you know," she would whisper to him after, always after, when sin was fully represented by moisture: the sweat on their bodies, the mingled fluids drying on her thighs, and the tears in her eyes. Sin had an undeniable scent as well, a pheromonal toxin that soaked the air as they panted, and lingered accusingly when their breath returned to normal. It clung to Marie daily now, like damp clothes left too long to stagnate in the dryer, and it seemed the only way to escape its staleness was to keep it fresh.

"Sinners," she would repeat, "damned to eternal exclusion from paradise."

He looked at her more intently now, and touched her more deliberately. "If this," he said, pushing his fingers inside her, "keeps me out of paradise, then I'm ready for hell." And Marie immediately blamed God for the injustice that made one man, the wrong man, able to make her feel like this, when it certainly had to have been in His power to fix it. This was not war. It was not famine or drought or political corruption. It was one man's touch, a no-brainer, and God need only have snapped his own divine fingers to free her.

In the meantime, she walked the walk. She read the Bible to her children, and laid her hands on them at night, and prayed over them. She traveled with her new cohorts, and attempted to evangelize the world, starting, of course, with the head of her household.

"Come on, Brendan," she begged on Sundays, "You don't even *go* to church. How can you say you're Catholic when you don't even go to church?"

"If I'm going to church, I'm going to my own church," he would reply patiently, "and that is where my children will go. I'm glad you found something that helps you, but we're not Lutheran. We're Catholic."

"Do you know that Catholics are idol worshippers? They pray to *statues. Statues.* The Bible clearly forbids this. I've read the Bible cover to cover, twice now, Brendan." She wanted him to acknowledge her as an authority on this, at least *this,* because she knew more than him, dammit.

"And they worship *Mary*," she went on, "when she was no different than you or I! She was simply chosen by God. We aren't supposed to *pray* to her. Look. 'There is only one mediator between God and Man, and that is Jesus Christ.'"

"There is imperfection in every religion, Marie. Even your pal Billy Graham said so, remember?" And she cursed herself for convincing her husband to accompany her to see the great preacher, because he did say that, sort of. He said, 'If you find the perfect religion, it will become imperfect just by you joining it,' something like that. It was conceivably the only thing Brendan actually heard all night, since he was probably still shaking off the icky feeling he got from traveling on a holy rolling bus full of misfits to the stadium where Mr. Graham appeared.

They couldn't go to St. John's on Sundays, nor would Brendan come to any of the midweek worship services, and again, Marie held God accountable, because she certainly did her part to make her life righteous, and it was only Manny who snuck into the back pews. He wanted to be part of her life, and if this was part of her life, he was not above even sharing the thing that wished for his demise.

He even went to visit Pastor Angeles, on his own, telling Marie about it only when it was done.

"I told him that I love you," he said simply, "and that I do not believe that God could disapprove of a love so pure."

"And he replied...what?" she asked, attempting to keep worldly derision in her voice, but failing, because a man had just basically defied God in her name. She could not get Brendan to embrace God with her, but Manny was ready to take Him on to keep her.

"Oh, you know what he said," Manny said and his derision was real, and he spoke in a singsong voice. "That my love for you was actually the work of Satan. That Satan is the great liar, convincing all that evil is good when evil is just evil. That if I truly loved you, I would leave you alone and not take you down this path to destruction." He paused for a minute, thinking, as she nodded.

"Bullshit," he said, finding the word he was looking for. "That's not what I said to him, but ... bullshit. The guy's an asshole. I'm a cop. I'll show him what evil looks like any night he wants. We can have a contest, in fact. Who can find more works of Satan in one 8-12 evening. Don't tell *me* that Satan is some genius that can hide all the crap he pulls. I look it straight in the eye all the time."

Marie was staring at him, tingling in the surprising delight of defeat, and he stopped his sermon to look at her again.

"I love you," he said, "and I'll do anything for you. But I will *not* leave you alone, and I will not let anyone tell me that loving you is evil."

"Okay," she said, but they continued to talk about it, and it was their new thing to talk about, God and religion and sin and scripture, and the prayers she could now utter. And she loved dissecting the phenomenon with someone who found it at least valuable enough to engage and battle, instead of denying it and moving on. Manny took hold of her passions no matter how misguided, and made them his own, and their mutual ardor remained alive and nourished.

****

Marie was never one to stay still in her life, and her restlessness infiltrated on a day she was putting wash out on the line, straining out her kitchen window and maneuvering the pulley attached to the distant telephone pole. She realized that she was comparing her line-up of towels and t-shirts and socks – her white wash – with that of neighboring lines, noting how hers was neater because her mother had taught her the "small-large-small" rule. It was a special rule that ensured that the largest items would end up dead center, thereby absorbing the most sunshine for the duration of the day.

Marie took this rule to the extreme, attempting a fully symmetrical gradual growth and decline of items, and was frustrated if sometimes she missed a towel in the stack and ruined her pattern. Hers was the only washline around with karate uniforms on it as well, and they never really hung neatly.

On this day, she was using utmost care, flattening the karate gi's just so, her eyes reverting from adjacent geometric arrangements and back to her own, when she realized that she had had enough. She loved being a mother, but she needed more, needed the career she had persisted so strenuously in attaining. She loved mothering, but there was too much in it that was simply about keeping things clean: the home, the clothes, small noses and faces.

She wanted other things, too, and everything swirled in her head like a tornado of desires; the house she yearned for, and something else: a daughter. She wanted a little girl, but it had to be a girl this time.

Marie closed the window with a bang that day, and the sound was like a gavel making a final decision. She bought a book called, "How to Choose the Sex of Your Baby," and began scanning the classifieds every day. She began the process of luring Brendan into yet another fertilization scheme, carefully keeping Manny away; and at the same time, began going into the city, to review the advertising red books at the library.

She sent out 90 resumes, and the day after she was offered a job, she realized that she was pregnant.

Brendan reacted to neither accomplishment with great ceremony. He asked her what she intended to do, much like a teenaged boyfriend might upon finding he had knocked up his girlfriend a month before she was to go away to college. How was she going to handle this? There was no question that she would have the baby, but what would she do about the job? His position was one that was ever-growing in their marriage; that she had reaped what she had sown, and was not at liberty to complain or even comment on her quandaries. She would simply have to handle them.

Marie wanted the job. It started at $38,000/year, the highest starting salary she had ever known. Brendan was up to $50,000 now, and she saw herself catching up with him. Even if she didn't, their combined earnings would be close to $80,000, which was close to a hundred. How could anyone not afford a house on such a staggering salary?

She liked the office, too, a small unimpressive environment situated on a side street in the garment district, where the doorway to the building was barely noticeable in the continuous row of fashion picture windows. Unlike the agency that had fired her months before, it emanated warmth over bitterness and desperation.

The man who interviewed her owned the place: Dermot Gregory, of Gregory and Glass. Glass, she would learn, was Robin Glass, his business partner and nothing else, a woman with a vivacious demeanor, reddish hair, and a stunning figure. Dermot interviewed her with a smile built into his face, a kind of Johnny Carson look that defied natural interest. He had eyes too blue to be real, and since colored contact lenses had recently surfaced on the market, Marie doubted that they were.

"This is obviously a small agency," he told her with almost self-effacing pride, "Mostly print. Print ads. Brochures. Lots of brochures."

He was paging through her portfolio with mild concentration. "It isn't really what you've done before," he added and began to gesture to the wall behind him, a wall filled with the agency's work, but Marie cut him off with the promise that got her the job.

"Nothing I've written is like anything I've done before," she said simply and honestly, "but I've done it. I wrote a 20-page booklet for log cabin builders; how wood breathes, benefits of different trees, et cetera. I knew nothing about it, but I researched, and I wrote it, and that taught me one thing, that I can write *anything*."

He closed her book and pierced her with eyes you imagined swimming in off the coast of some magical island. "That is exactly what I think about myself," he said, and stood, and said the usual; that he had other interviews, that she would be hearing from him. But she knew.

She dutifully wrote her follow-up letter, thanking him for the interview, and this too impressed him, even though to her it was protocol. That week she would land yet another job a few blocks away, and would wake up with a familiar feeling of morning sickness.

"Two job offers in one week, and I'm pregnant," she told Manny, with feigned displeasure, ignoring the fact that his own discontentment was real. It was tumbling down once again; another baby brewing, another job to fill Marie's days, and more obsessions to keep them apart. He always accepted that he was not first in Marie's life, but sometimes couldn't stand be relegated to positions further and further down on her list.

"The office is miniscule," she went on, because this is what she did; she kept talking as a pretense and a shield. Manny was sad, but Manny had to deal with that. She would not acknowledge it.

"I mean, I'm not in a creative department, I practically *am* the creative department," she babbled. "There's me and one art director. One media person, one producer. I mean, I haven't met everyone yet, but I didn't see more than seven offices altogether. Oh, and one secretary. For everyone."

"I guess it's back to meeting you for lunch," Manny said, and it came out like a sour note on an old Christmas record album, a bright sound distorted by warped ridges and the crackles of age. He was happy for her, really, but he also ached for some sign that she felt a loss as well; that she would miss their unscheduled days and stolen moments.

"Well, not right away," she said, and even wondered herself if she were cruel, or if she hated him on some level for everything: for both showing her perfection in a partner and lover, and keeping her from it, for loving her intensely and keeping her from God, for sharing her dreams but never her shame.

He looks brave, she thought, like someone delivered a terminal diagnosis but determined to fight it. She took his hand. "Come on, Manny, it's a brand new job. I don't want to blow it. It will be bad enough when they find out I am great with child. I doubt my new boss Dermot has ever seen a child up close, let alone understand why people keep making them."

Marie was enchanted from the first. It was the corporate world without the corporate politics; a warm and fuzzy family of workers with no hierarchy or competition. Marie sat in her office that had walls that touched the ceiling, and she wrote. When she finished writing, she showed Dermot, and he said, "This is great," or "I don't think we're quite there yet."

Most of the time, he took the finished product to clients himself, and Marie was content with this. She had never enjoyed presenting work. She liked writing, only writing, watching the words appear on paper and feeling instinctively when they were lyrical or convincing or clever. Dermot was her audience of one, and he was an easy, amiable audience. Once he gave her a particularly unattractive assignment, writing about some trucking company, and held up his hand when she began to whine.

"What was it you said on your interview? Oh yes, I remember. You can write about *anything*," he said.

It was a place to be good, to be both successful and safe, back in the city she adored and bringing home a paycheck to justify herself with Brendan. She even spent more time with Brendan, meeting him halfway between her office on 38th and his on 53rd, for lunch at least once a week.

"Look at us, Brendan. We're on a date."

She had no recollection of whether these midday rendezvous' pleased him. As much as she would rack her brains later to recall some sign in his visage that he enjoyed her company, all she would ever come up with was some look of strain. Did the lunch cost too much? Did it take too long? Was she not particularly interesting, even with her career back on track? It wasn't that he seemed displeased, either; it was that if he looked happy or proud or in love, well, *that* she knows she would have remembered.

The most difficult part, however, was leaving her children every day, dropping both off at respective sitters and running to make the bus, a task that was always hers and never Brendan's. It killed her to see their faces get smaller as she walked away from them, knowing how many hours it would be before she saw them grow closer again, and worse, knowing how tired she would be when "quality time" was expected of her.

"I have to do this," she whispered to herself as the 39 Triboro brought her to Long Island City, where she would pick up the train for the rest of her journey. "I have to do this so they have a house and a backyard, and so we can get a puppy and blow bubbles wherever we want."

Everyone was buying houses now. It was 1988, the year of her family's mass exodus into the suburbs. Monica was the first to go; announcing her house purchase with the same aplomb and startled pleasure with which she had delivered the news of her engagement years before. It was just something she could do; a grown-up thing, and Marie could barely stand to hear her ease as she passed around photos of the house.

"It's in New Jersey," she said, "in a pretty neighborhood with good schools. We looked at 10 different towns and we wanted a really good school system."

Of course, Marie thought, Monica would make sure the school system was good.

"We'll definitely miss the city, though," Monica added, singsong, forming a smile Marie associated with the models in her TV commercials that had just removed a very bad stain from the sink. All Monica's spot needed was a tag line.

Marie's brother was next, and he did what Queens people do: he headed straight for Long Island. She had no idea how Robert threw together the money on his fireman's salary, but he managed to swing a flat uninteresting house in a neighborhood of houses quickly constructed for returning veterans of the second world war. Marie didn't like the place, but it was a house.

Perhaps the most difficult for Marie to take was the migration of Lisa, her little sister. Her stockbroker husband gave her a checkbook and told her to go house-hunting the way you would give someone a shopping spree or a day at the spa. Actually, Marie had never been handed even those two things, but Lisa got into her car and went to find her perfect house each Sunday while her husband watched football.

In no time, only Marie's father and sister Anne shared with her the neighborhood she despised, but both of them already owned the house they lived in, and had options. Soon after, her father would sell his house and move into a cozy apartment just up the street. Anne stayed on just a little bit longer, but something unprecedented happened: her husband left her for a young cocaine addict and a Harley Davidson motorcycle, and Marie knew someone could be worse off than herself.

Marie never visited any of the new houses for many months. She didn't want to see them; didn't want to see other people's children playing in the yard or showing off a room or planning a garden. Her father, a genuine stranger to envy and perhaps a believer in

Marie's good character spoke glowingly of his new homeowner offspring every chance he got.

"Oh, you oughta see Lisa's new kitchen cabinets," he would say and went on to describe them in detail, including the cost and any problems with the installation. He did this with paint and swimming pools, pets and azalea bushes, and in the end Marie felt like she had witnessed each house being built, brick by brick. Visiting could hardly be worse.

Mostly, she bonded with Anne, listening to the story of what separation is like, and renewing her resolution that this could not and would not happen to her. She shuddered looking at Anne's little sons, the older of which said that "daddy was always at work." And she was ever conscious that she walked a tightrope over a minefield, and if she fell, something was bound to explode.

Months went by, and the pile of money Marie thought she would accumulate by working didn't materialize.

"I don't understand it," she complained to Brendan, "I make a good salary, but I can barely save anything. It wasn't supposed to be that way."

"Well, you spend it," Brendan answered quickly and it was as simple as that.

"I *don't*. On what? Child care? Work clothes? The bus?" She had answered her own question, but it was inconsistent with her convictions, because she believed that justifiable purchases did not fall under the category of "spending."

"Oh, I *know,*" she added sardonically, "it's that buttered roll I buy each day in the coffee shop in my building," she finished, and realized Brendan was nodding.

"You think it isn't?" he said and actually inhaled before continuing. "That's the difference between you and me. You don't realize that small things add up. Like, how much is that roll? Must be eighty-five cents in the city. And you get one every day. So that's, let me think…" He began mental calculations in his head.

"Could be $17.00 a month on buttered rolls, which sounds like a little, but a lot of littles make a lot. Also, if that $17.00 was in the bank, it would be getting interest. So you lose that as well."

"And what about the money you spend on the boys on the weekend because you feel guilty that you work? McDonalds and trips to Toys R Us? Ten dollars here and ten dollars there? See what I mean?" He leaned back in his chair satisfied, and looked at her crestfallen face.

"I'm only trying to help you, Marie. I don't think you see what you're doing here."

Marie began treating herself to a buttered roll only once a week, but she could not reduce her weekend indulgences with Colin and Daniel, because Brendan was right: she felt guilty. They deserved for their lives to be good *now*, today, and each day, and not have to wait until mommy and daddy had a house. And so she bought tickets to children's plays in the Village, and took them to petting zoos and museums, and got them Happy Meals when the prize inside was really good. And she paid for all of this herself, because it wasn't possible to enlist Manny's help on the weekends.

Marie had morning sickness with this baby as she did with the others, and her belly was growing, but her boss Dermot didn't seem to notice. For this, she was both relieved and insulted. On their rare cab rides together to photo shoots or meetings, Dermot kept his eyes fixed to the windows, and commented on every beautiful woman that wasn't a blur once the cabbie slowed down. He gave no sign, however, that he even regarded Marie as female, and his blue laser beam eyes held no hidden lust. The secretary was the first to say something, but Marie denied it. Rosalie was a single mom herself, barely 25 with a six-year-old daughter, and she grew up in an environment where matriarchs dominated.

One day, she looked up as Marie was walking by her desk, and in her quick Puerto Rican accent, said, "Some guy named Manny called. Here's the number. Who is Manny?" She handed Marie the pink "While you were out" slip, and added, "And when are you due?"

Marie snatched the slip, and feigned indignation. "Thanks a lot," she said, "I guess you are saying I look fat?"

"I won't say nothin'," Rosalie eyes were back on her word processor, "but don't even try to tell me you don't have one in the oven."

That was September, just after summer's end, so she was safe. She wanted to be sure that she got her weeks' vacation in the Poconos, where her family had rented a large house. This year, she surprised herself by asking Brendan that they take back to back weeks so that her sons could be away for two, and they could overlap on the weekend. It was a request born only of love for her sons, and because it was just that innocent, she didn't realize that she had given herself a week home alone until she got on the bus home leaving her family behind.

Someday Brendan would wonder about that week, and what her true motives were for planning it, and that is the oddity about lies and truth. You often don't know yourself which one governs your purest intentions, but what does it matter when it is only the one that oversees your actions that anyone even cares about. Marie sent Brendan away for a week so that her sons would fish and swim and catch fireflies under the stars far from their apartment with one air-conditioned room, but she still spent time with Manny in that room while they were gone, and there was no purity in this; and the lie prevailed.

At the end of the week, she went straight to the Port Authority and got on a bus to Pennsylvania, and two hours later got off to see Colin and Daniel in matching Osh Kosh overalls, and Brendan holding each hand. He was beautiful, Brendan, always was, and she wanted beauty to mean more than the right configuration of sparkling pieces. She wanted them it to be a genuine display of something good and useful, something from which you would never look away for fear of losing it.

Their first daughter was born that December, just four days after Christmas. She, too, was beautiful; so beautiful, in fact, that as Marie laid back on her pillows in the recovery room, she heard the nurses talk about her daughter. Dark hair and dark eyes, she had an intense inquiring look that would cause people around her to work harder just to see her smile.

Dermot had not been pleased to learn, two months before her due date, that his writer was leaving, and vowed he would never again hire a woman, coming out with a statement about pregnancy and PMS that he would surely be sued for had he been serious. Still the entire staff held a shower for her in the conference room, and fully expected her to return after her maternity leave. She never did.

Instead, she continued to work for Dermot from home for her entire leave, at last getting the hang of typing her words directly instead of writing them by hand. Once or twice a week, she left Kristin for a few hours to go deliver her work and meet with Dermot, or gathered her up in a Snugli and brought her along. It worked so well and saved the little company so much money both in salary and benefits, that Robin suggested that she continue to work this way permanently. And so Marie once again "had it all."

She had something else, too: a plan. Some day, she would say that her life, or part of it, anyway, changed in a cab ride downtown, akin to the way priests say they received their "call," but not as noble as the way Mother Teresa made her decision to help lepers while riding on a train. Revelations aren't always world shattering. Sometimes they are obvious but simple things.

They were headed for Scholastic, a company that created curriculum materials for schools. They had two such clients, Scholastic and Random House, and Dermot felt that Marie needed to meet with their people directly in order to better understand what they were looking for. The executives, writers and other corporate people at both companies weren't what Dermot was used to. They were all former teachers.

As a mother, Marie warmed to these people, and was able to converse in their jargon in a way that she never could with the cutthroat corporate types on their client list. Sure, they were salespeople, but Marie thought their product was somewhat nobler.

Her boss felt differently. He was out of his element with these teacher types, and could barely maintain his affect around them. His eyes nearly dulled beneath the bright blue contacts when speaking to them, and he allowed Marie far more latitude in meetings with them.

He complained about them on the cab ride over, and changed Marie's life. He was not complaining exactly about them, but about their false humility in pushing their manuals and textbooks. They were educators, first, but Dermot was not impressed with educators, either.

"Yeah, teachers," he said, "They have it made. They get off a week in the winter, a week in the spring, every Jewish holiday and the whole damn summer, and they still complain that they don't make enough money."

Both of Brendan's sisters taught, but Marie had never heard them complain about the salary and she had no idea what the salary was. She knew they both sounded like teachers, wherever they were, or whoever they addressed from their spouses to their offspring. Marie imagined them in bed with their husbands sometimes, gently but firmly offering much needed instruction, perhaps saying, "good job!" with proud cheer when they reached a desired goal or milestone. There are people, Marie once told Manny, that you would never be able to imagine having sex and Brendan's sisters were definitely the first two that crossed Marie's mind.

Marie began to offer up her sisters-in-law to Dermot for some comic relief, but something made her commiserate silently, while attempting to locate some hidden gem in his lament. She had never really noticed that Monica and Tara were off all summer; had not, in fact, thought to be jealous of that. Actually Monica had quit working years ago to be with her children, and since Tara did not have any children, Marie didn't make the connection.

It was Dermot's final comment that hit Marie the hardest. Before leaning forward to instruct the cabbie where to stop, he closed his diatribe on educational professionals by saying:

"I mean, let's face it, teaching is a part-time job. That's why it pays a part-time salary."

Teaching is a part-time job. Marie heard it and knew that any teacher would dispute it; would point to work they brought home at night, papers they graded, planning they did on weekends, not to mention workshops and meetings they were required to attend. Tara often mentioned "teacher burnout," so Marie knew there was more to it than 8 to 3 with summers off, but she still heard the words over and over in her mind: Teaching is a part-time job.

She decided then and there, that after she had this baby, as soon as she could after she delivered, that she was going back to school to become a teacher. She didn't really know how it was possible now, but the seed was planted, and Marie rarely let even the smallest kernel of possibility go unnourished. It made even more sense to her now as she reviewed her passions – reading, writing, and of course, children – her own, right now, the ones she needed to be near, but also children in general.

Marie didn't bother to tell Brendan; it would be foolish to offer up yet another dream for his disheartening scrutiny, but she filed it away as one gently storing bridal treasure in a hope chest. When the time was right, she would take it out, and activate its dusty, dormant promise, always remembering that she had located it in a yellow taxicab speeding down Fifth Avenue.

For now, however, she had two sons and a daughter, and a freelance writing job. She kept one foot on either side of sin and redemption, walking an everlasting tightrope of happiness that needed to be clung to, or lost. Life around Marie became the blur of some circus audience as she struggled for her own balance. Anne's husband returned to her, and Lisa had another baby, as did Monica, and her father had his summer house in Pennsylvania, where he placed a painted portrait of her mother over the mantle. More families left Queens to purchase houses elsewhere, and still Marie stayed on, her desperation quietly becoming a dripping faucet that nobody really heard anymore.

And so it went for the next two years, until one day she knelt in the chapel at St. John's, and prayed for nothing. Tired of asking God for gift-wrapped virtues and a fairy tale life, this time she relented, and took Him for what he had.

"I'm accepting this life, Lord. I'm accepting these ugly gray streets and my horrid orange vinyl wallpaper and seeing my son play soccer on a mud field surrounded by graffiti, and never giving my children a puppy for Christmas. I'm accepting a bank account that will never grow faster than house prices and interest rates. This is the life you gave me. It is what you intended and I will not ask for more. Anyway, I am a sinner and probably deserve no more."

That night, Brendan came home and sat her down, and took both her hands in his.

"How would you like to go house-hunting this weekend?" he asked.

When she said nothing, he went on.

"I had lunch with my father today. He is giving us a down payment for a house."

Chapter Eleven: "I Am a Jealous God"

Much happened the year before Marie left her final apartment dwelling and it was difficult later to place them in proper order. Perhaps the first was the chest pains, knifelike jabs that came and went for no apparent reason, and had, according to her doctor, no definitive cause.

They actually began a year earlier; soon after Kristin was born, a dark-eyed, dark-haired serious child that would forever draw looks from passing strangers. "Black Irish," some would label her, while her own granny called her "Dagger Eyes," for the long seething looks she delivered when she did not get her way.

She was a baby who would not drink from a bottle; even rejecting Marie's carefully pumped breast milk if it came through a rubber nipple, steadfast even through hours of hunger. If Marie dared to leave her behind to attend some meeting in the city, she returned to a full Playtex nurser and a screaming baby, and had to sit down immediately and unbutton her blouse to silence her.

As Kristin grew, she kept Marie on her toes, because she could not be trusted with even one unsupervised moment, lest she get herself into something.

"If this one is quiet, watch out," Marie told Manny proudly, giving tales of goldfish stolen from bowls and bouncing on the living room floor as Kristin intently watched, or Ajax cleanser carefully sprinkled all over the sofa and chair. The boys in the house dubbed her, "Kristin the Destroyer," but Marie saw her stubbornness as strength, and her refusal to please others as confidence. Marie would not raise a frightened, weak daughter.

"She isn't going to be like me," she continued, watching Kristin squirm from Manny's arms, and watched her wistfully as she traipsed off.

Still, Kristin was exhausting; in fact, life was exhausting, and at first, she chalked up the pain in her chest to stress. She was running two children to school each morning, and lugging her third to New York a few days each week. She did all of her work for Dermot in the evening after all three were sleeping because Marie could never write if there was even a chance of being interrupted. She could not ignore the sounds of her home, even the harmonious ones, and so her new work time was approximately 10pm, after she cleaned up the remains of the day, until about two o'clock in the morning.

Brendan offered little help, but her resentment of him was quelled by her pride in herself for single-handedly "having it all." It was also eased by their weekend house hunts, and the promise of a different life that looking inside someone else's life held. Each home, with its flower garden and Little Tykes toys strewn on the lawn, was a microcosm of another existence, and Marie would not jeopardize her chance to seize it with negative emotion.

Marie barely had time to give Manny during this time, her fatigue was that debilitating, and when he stopped by she would immediately ask him to keep an eye on Kristin so she herself could take a nap. Sometimes he brought Ariella, and so the two children played as he hovered nearby.

He began to brush Marie's hair during these months, she remembered. Perhaps he was only looking for another way to touch her, but when she sat across from him wearily sipping tea, he would rise up and find a hairbrush in the bathroom, and stand behind her running it through her mane, lifting it off her neck like a burden. He would do it literally for an hour straight, or until it completely lulled her and she could no longer keep her head up.

Love has many forms, and lust has many reasons. During those months, love was Manny's hands on her hair, and lust was something that rose from appreciation. Her desire was not strong then, but rose like the succulent scent of some delicious recipe, gently luring her near as it quietly simmered.

"Why did you stop talking?" she asked him sleepily, because in between the rhythmic strokes on her head, he was telling her a story about work.

"I only stopped for a second," he answered. "I saw you glance at the clock."

"And?" she asked, but she knew.

"And Kristin has fallen asleep," he went on slowly, "and I am trying my best not to breathe. Because I know that there is a chance that you might make love to me and I am not going to even move a molecule in this room that might shift the cosmic universe as it stands. What if I say something stupid?"

"Well, that definitely wasn't stupid," she whispered, and succumbed even though she had a thousand things to do and Kristin's rare nap times were precious. There were some things that simply could not be denied.

The house-hunting assured Marie of another thing: that she would end this "thing" with Manny, by putting geographical distance between them. They were searching for residence in Monica's town in New Jersey, approximately an hour away from Queens, and surely that would be the yoke that would break them. Marie placed much hope on this, and her "new" life full of suburban moms and green soccer fields, and husbands that discussed trips to the new Home Depot. Manny could not follow her there, could not be allowed under the nose of her sister-in-law or the view of pristine neighbors.

She told him this one day, bluntly and nonchalantly.

"You know, when I move away, it's over. Completely over. It's for the best. I have to finally straighten out my life. You know we can't keep doing this. At least when I'm far away, it will be easier to…resist." She kept rambling because he had said nothing, was simply staring at her.

"I mean, my life will be different. There will be no highs too high, but there will also be no lows too lows. It will all be just even, calm, you know? That's what I need, just calm."

"I am not even going to tell you my new address," she finished.

At this he spoke, giving enough silence to assure himself that she was through. "No highs too high. Hmm...that's what you need?" She nodded but he went on. "Well, I doubt that is what you need, but you know I care about your happiness. I care a lot. I've proven that, I think. But Marie?" She looked at him and he continued.

"If you don't want me to know your address, then you better decide not to drive in the Garden State, or any other place in the United States for that matter. Because if you have a driver's license, I'll find you. It won't even be difficult, just a matter of typing your name on my work computer. And once I know where you are, I will come there, even if it's just to brush your hair."

And Marie, once again, felt both defeat and triumph sing in unison inside her.

*****

The search for a house, however, was mostly defeating. They were told that rates were down, but sellers seemed in no hurry and just as happy to relist at a better time rather than lose their price. They looked at 6 or 7 places in one day, climbing new flights of stairs, three children in tow, until Marie felt ready to collapse. And still there was nothing large enough in their price range.

"You should consider a less expensive town," Monica offered in characteristic singsong, and this burned Marie and increased her determination. They stopped there sometimes for lunch in between trekking around her neighborhood, and Marie stared at her home with longing and grit, even though she didn't really like the house much. It was in the middle of a busy street, and had virtually no charm. They had purchased when prices were at their highest, and had to bid against two others for their home.

"No, we like it here," she said in equally false tenor, "and the cousins will be near each other."

"I'm surprised you didn't want to be near your sisters, though," Monica came back, never giving up. "Your kids have cousins there, too. How many are you up to on that side?"

It was true that Marie liked Glenfield. It had a small town look, with a center full of quaint shops in low-story buildings, and an elevated railroad dividing one side of town from the other. It also had a river running through it, and a place for renting canoes, and even its own farm. Marie loved it, and wanted one of the old houses there, with a wrap-around porch and a detached garage. Even in her desperation, she would not settle for a house she did not love.

It was also true that Marie liked the idea of her children becoming closer to their cousins on the Kavanagh side, and of Monica, perhaps, seeing her as an equal, even a friend? But first she had to find a house they could afford.

One day, in the midst of this, Marie watched Kristin toddle to the door of her brothers' room, smiling mischievously, only to have the door slammed in her face. She crumpled to the floor, screaming, and then she began to bang furiously for entrance.

"Kristin can't play with us!" Daniel's muffled voice exclaimed to Colin. "She will wreck our guys and our tower."

She needs a sister, Marie thought, and then decided, and within a few months, executed. She barely had to beg this time; Brendan caved easily, and Marie was pregnant for the fourth time.

Russian immigrants moved into the apartment below Marie's that last year, a family with two young children. The parents spoke little English and the little boy and girl none at all; yet they got together and the children played blissfully without words. Kristin touched a hot iron that year and was rushed to the E.R., where Marie was subjected to suspicious stares from hospital personnel and intensive questions about possible abuse.

Marie got a high-paying freelance job that year, writing about something she had virtually no understanding of: foreign exchange management systems. Eleven pages for nearly $3,000, a rate that would secure her mortgage even though it was a one-shot deal. The bank multiplied the amount by 12 and jotted it down as part of her projected annual income.

Mostly, though, all she could remember about the year was the pain, and the nausea, the cough, and the everlasting fatigue, and her desperate reliance on Manny. She didn't tell Brendan that she couldn't handle things, that she felt faint just zipping her daughter's jacket or tying her son's shoes. Marie recognized the futility in this. She wanted this baby, and she wanted this life, and Brendan did not want to hear about her difficult days.

Manny picked up her sons from school; and Marie stopped caring about the appearance of this. He took Kristin with him, and Marie slept, sometimes standing up only to feel her head spin and lay back down again.

People noticed. They asked questions, and Marie brushed them off. "How much weight have you gained?" and Marie said, "I don't know" because she had not gained any; on the contrary, she kept losing weight. "We thought we would see you at worship," and she said, "I was worshipping that porcelain god again."

"This is my worst pregnancy ever," she told her sister. "I've been sick before but this is ridiculous. I can barely stand up."

"What's all over your chest?" Anne asked.

"Who knows?" She pulled her shirt down to reveal blue lines, dark as the ink of a Sharpie, criss-crossing above her breasts. "Well, I know. They are obviously veins, but I don't know why I can see them so well, and my doctor doesn't know, either."

Marie felt a change in Manny in that time, a change she welcomed because it revealed him as less than perfect. He was angry. He was angry because she would find a house sooner or later, and she would leave, and she wanted to leave. He still took meticulous care of her but he was suppressing resentment, and it showed. Their physical relationship stopped; she could not spare her physical self on anything but the care of her children, living and unborn. He did not know she was sick; he only knew she was retreating.

One day, he led her to his apartment, and filled a bubble bath for her, placing Kristin down for a nap. He came in, and washed her hair and sponged her down, and even lifted each leg and shaved them. He wrapped her in a bathrobe and brushed out her hair, then guided her to his bed and tucked her in. It was beautiful and selfless, except that it wasn't. He stood over her, and waited, but she gratefully fell asleep and stayed that way until she heard her daughter call out for her.

Afterwards, they fought over a most ridiculous thing: a Cabbage Patch doll dressed like a clown. He had mentioned that Ariella never played with it, was afraid of its ghoulish grin, and so Marie put it in her bag to take home.

"You can't have that," he said, blocking the door as they were leaving.

"I can't?" she laughed, a feeble sound. "Why can't I?"

"It's my daughter's," he said, and there was something in his voice that simultaneously panicked her and ignited flames of fury.

"She doesn't like it. You told me." She faced him squarely, her eyes intent on him. She knew they were not really fighting about a doll.

"That doesn't automatically mean you can have it," he answered but he tried now to avoid her eyes. "You didn't even ask me. You just took it."

"You're kidding, right?" She leaned down so she could recapture his gaze, hoping that was all she needed to recapture. She laughed again. "Since when do I have to ask you for anything?"

"Maybe you should ask me for things, Marie. Or ask me something. Ask me how I feel about you running away from me, and don't say that you're not. Or ask me if I miss you, if I miss you holding you, or maybe ask me if I think Brendan will take care of you when you are tired, or for that matter, ask me if there is any man in the world who will do for you what I will do."

If the plea was intended to move her, it succeeded, but it did not move her the way he intended. It aroused neither pity nor love. With those words, he had failed her, and she delighted in the disillusionment. She had to leave him, and she didn't want to suffer the loss. She looked at him, head on, and all the energy she lacked rallied like a sleeping giant who finds his home invaded.

"Thank you for that. Thanks a lot. Thanks for sounding just like Brendan. That's exactly what I need from you. I need a love that is completely conditional. I need to stop believing that there is any other kind."

Usually, he crumpled under her ire, but her speech missed the mark, too. He walked two steps to her, and pulled the instigative doll out of her hands.

"You're still not getting this," he said simply. "Come on, let's go get your kids."

****

They found a house in May, one that was better than they could have imagined, on a street that was only one block long. They had looked at 42 houses in two different towns with two different frustrated weary realtors. The latest was an overly friendly older man named Calvin who had begun to run out of platitudes, and both she and Brendan got the clear sense that this was the last day he would waste on them.

He showed them a house that was not for sale, only for rent, and explained that the family lived in England, and that this was the perfect way to break into the neighborhood. They barely listened. Marie was suffering from a mix of hopelessness and nausea, and all she wanted to do was sit down.

The rental house was at 22 Avalon Place, and the next house they were going to see was at 8 Avalon Place. Marie headed urgently for the car in anticipation of just a 3-block ride in air-conditioning, but to her surprise, they began crossing the street.

"Yup, 8 is just across the street," Cal chuckled falsely, "even though it's number 8. I don't know why that is. Avalon's just a block long. Just five houses total."

When it was their house, their own, and full of their stories, they would learn that once upon a time it carried an 18 on the door, which made sense since number 20 was next door. One day the 1 just rusted and fell off the wood, and rather that going through all the trouble of nailing it back up, the house number changed. It was a charming story, and it became part of them.

Right now, however, all she and Brendan could see was yet another house that they would never be able to afford. It was huge. Built in 1901, it had three floors that held 7 bedrooms, and a basement where a drummer practiced. It had a family room and a living room and a large kitchen, the first large kitchen they had seen in 42 viewings. It had stained glass and oak pocket doors and a front porch and fireplaces, and a detached garage. Basically, it had everything.

By the third floor, Marie had stopped looking. She felt sick and really, what was the use of falling in love with this place? She told Brendan she had to get outside for a bit, and she sat in the backyard, where she promptly threw up. Perhaps that was a sign, she would say later.

"You like it? Make an offer," Cal said fervently, and it felt like he was going to reach out and shake them.

"What are they asking?" Brendan asked, and Cal began shaking his head.

"Make an offer. Just make an offer," he said again.

"We can't afford this place," Brendan said solemnly, and Marie felt sorry for him, this child husband of hers trying so hard to remain the voice of reason.

"You do not know how motivated a seller is," Cal said, and they wondered if he had this planned all along; this showing of a rental house as a bluff before showing his real hand.

"Our offer for this house is the same as our offer for every other house we've looked at," Brendan said, "because it's all we can afford. We can't go up even a thousand dollars over that. That's it."

"Got it," Cal said, "So I can tell them you made an offer, then? Come back to my office and make it official."

Marie wanted to go home. It was over. She couldn't bear even another minute with sunshiny Cal. She wanted her bed, even if her bed was in a cramped apartment. She liked the Russians downstairs. She liked her sons' school. And she would find another way to stop Manny. But first, she needed to sleep.

They stopped at Cal's office, signed some papers, and drove home in silence. The kids slept deeply and Marie fitfully.

An hour after they arrived home, the phone rang. Brendan answered, and talked rapidly, writing furiously. Curious, Marie left the couch and came beside him, and then he wrote, "WE GOT IT!" on the page, and she didn't dare to understand.

"That was Cal. They took our offer. We got the house." Marie sunk against Brendan and vowed that their life was just beginning. Then she went to their folder full of papers and pictures and maps and rummaged until she found what she was looking for: a gray listing photo of 8 Avalon Place.

"Our house," she said to herself, and cut the picture and pasted it in her journal.

Manny became even more aloof after she told him about their offer, and Marie became even more determined to ignore this. The house represented to her a multitude of things: forgiveness from an understanding God, a purity restored, and a talisman for a bright, untainted future. It was redemption and salvation covered with aluminum siding and surrounded by trees. She carried the picture of it around like an amulet, or a holy cross to ward off vampires and anything else that wanted her flesh. She would not do this wrong.

Shared goals and renewed hopes allowed her to share her thoughts with Brendan. Marie probably didn't see that the house represented many things for him, too, like his renewed belief in himself as a provider for his family, and as a husband who could make his wife feel no need for any other source of happiness. He gazed at the picture with her every chance he got.

"You know that we placed that bid on Mother's Day?" she asked, touching his shoulder, "You got me a house on Mother's Day. Can you believe that?"

"Yes, I returned the flowers as soon I knew we had it," he answered, and it was the voice she wished she cultivated more in him, the one she would always remember and yearn for.

She became serious. "I keep thinking," she said, "that there's only so much happiness you're allowed, and that this is way too much. I worry about it. Like, know what I dreamed the other night?"

"What?" he asked, still gazing at the picture, and – could it be? – he was stroking her hair.

"I dreamed that I was talking to the devil. And he warned me, that this was not good, getting everything I want. And then he said, I would see. And then, the day I moved into the house, I found out that I had cancer."

"Did you die?" her husband asked her, and drew her closer.

"I don't know. I woke up." She answered.

"Good girl. Showed the devil, anyway," he said, "Want some tea? Decaf?"

Marie pushed herself to shake off the fatigue and pain, and take care of her family without Manny's help. It worked for exactly six days, and then she collapsed in the middle of the hall of St. John's, after bending down to tie Daniel's shoes and standing up too quickly.

In the emergency room they determined that she was severely dehydrated, and admitted her for two days to pump her with fluids. Remarkably, no one questioned why a woman six months pregnant weighed so little, or ran any tests, or asked any questions at all.

"You have to eat more," a nurse mentioned at discharge, and Marie promised that she would. She had only three months left, and she would manage, and then she would raise her completed family in a place with trees and flowers, and they would get a dog, too.

She began zealously packing her apartment, surrounding them with a maze of boxes that grew ever taller, and tossing out anything that did not merit a place in her new home. The act of disposing with the extra baggage of her old life was purifying, and she kept track each day of how many bulging black bags shone with the weight of her efforts. She imagined herself stepping over the threshold of her new home with only the things that mattered, only the things that truly belonged there.

On August 13th, they closed on the house, and though the movers were hired for August 17th, Marie did not wait even those four days to leave Queens. Renting a mini U-Haul, she and Brendan packed whatever was necessary for short-term survival and that very night, she and her family slept on mattresses in the room that would become the dining room. Brendan made more trips for more items, but Marie never went back.

"This is our home," Kristin asked, bewildered, waking up in the echoing vacant space of her bedroom.

"Yes!" Marie exclaimed, picking her up and twirling her as if they were refugees that had found their way to the Promised Land.

"Oh," Kristin answered, wiping sleep from her eyes. "Are there Rice Krispies here?"

There was. There was no refrigerator yet, but a cooler of ice kept milk cold and there were a few snack tables to eat on. Marie took photos of those days; hot summer days with barefoot children, exploring bugs and blades of grass and learning words for rooms they had never needed to know before.

"Give this to daddy," Marie told Kristin, handing her a cup of iced tea and hearing her stubby legs patter away in anticipation of providing a service.

She was back. "Where is daddy?" she asked.

"He's on the porch," Marie answered.

"Oh. What's the porch?" she asked.

It was the same with the garage, and the attic, and the basement, and the driveway. Day after day, Marie was charmed by Kristin's acquisition of the words that signified the change in her life; a change she was too little to appreciate, but Marie held solemnly as fulfillment of an unspoken promise made at her birth, made at the birth of all wanted children, really: I will take care of you. I will give you the best I can.

The movers arrived, and the boxes that towered in their apartment now filled one room of their new home. Day after day, Marie pushed herself hard to empty them. Everyone told her that it did not have to be done all at once, but of course it did. Brendan rushed home at the end of each day and smiled his approval at the home that was unfolding. Then, late at night, Marie lay back on her pillows and placed her hand on her pregnant stomach.

"Move," she whispered to her unborn child, "C'mon, let me know that you are still there." She kept her hand there, in the silence, until she felt the flutter of a tiny foot, and breathed her relief.

Three more months, and I'll be back on my feet again, and everything will be wonderful, Marie thought, but wonderful was a word that never asked to exist in real life. It was a ridiculous word, reserved for storybooks and rarely used for every day conversation except in a rhetorical sense. If and when one got a sense that everything was wonderful, it was time to question one's perception.

****

The rest of the summer was an amalgamation of emotions and physical states. Marie was impatient to immerse herself in her new community and especially to find her children some friends, but the streets of Glenfield were deserted in late summer. Her sister-in-law Monica seemed determined not to help in this regard; she barely hid her vexation at Marie's intrusion into her town, and more so since Marie bought a house nearly twice the size of her own.

"Everyone is either at the pool or on vacation," she offered in a voice that implied that Marie should have known better than to choose a town where this happened, and ignoring the obvious fact that Monica, with pool membership, could have invited Marie and her children to the town's social hot spot. With only a few weeks left in summer, it was not possible or fiscally feasible for Marie to join.

Finances, in fact, were another source of mood-altering havoc. They had a house now. They had a mortgage. Brendan cautioned her to distinguish her wants from her needs now more than ever; and so deep was Marie's gratitude to lie in bed at night hearing only the crickets singing, she complied. Still, she looked at her windows and saw curtains that should be there, and through her windows to a backyard that must have a swing set and a picnic table and all the other decorations of suburbia.

She had arrived, but her life simply could not start. Monica suggested that she just "get out, take a walk or something" as a way to meet people, but there lied the other snare: Marie was tired. She felt the way her daughter's Italian ices looked when the sugar-starved child had been sucking the juice free for over an hour after the substance itself had dissipated. Even a walk seemed a daunting task; and a walk with her children was insurmountable.

She found the beach one day, on her own, pouring over her Jersey guidebooks to choose the one most family-friendly and coming up with Avon-by-the-Sea. She summoned up every vestige of energy to load her three children in the car, with all the blankets, buckets, sandwiches and safety products needed for 5 hours under the sun.

I just have to get there, she whispered to herself, *and then I can rest.* And it worked. Eight-year-old Colin and five-year-old Daniel shouldered their share of beachware, and she balanced Kristin on her hip while loading the rest in the stroller and walking two blocks from their parking spot.

The day was rousing and satiated with hope and satisfaction. Three children engaged themselves in a thousand particles of sand while Marie soaked up the vista of the shore – it was no longer the beach – and took photos of the everything with her memory since she had forgotten her camera.

They stayed until after 6, that magical time when the sun changes personality and shines a whole new way, and Marie started thinking that she had some obligation to be home.

This time, she left the bulk of their belongings in the comfortable hue of the evacuated boardwalk, and walked more freely to her car with only her drunken, sun-soaked children. She was satisfied; she had done it. For the rest of the summer, she would haul her cherubs down the shore.

"Oh no," she said as she reached her car.

"What, mommy?" Colin asked, snapped quickly from his lassitude by the sound of his protector's distress.

"I can't believe this," she kept going, lightening her tone with a mother's instinct. "I left the crook lock on."

It was something she used in Queens and still did instinctively; applied the auto-theft device across the steering wheel as soon as she put the car in park. It wasn't a new car and it wasn't a nice car, but on a Friday night a group of Queens youth might steal anything for joyriding.

"Just take it off, mom," Colin continued while the others just waited for the solution that adults, especially parents, were supposed to provide.

"Use your keys," he said simply.

"I can't. My key to the lock is on my house keys. My house keys are still my Queens house keys, and I don't use those anymore. I moved my car key over to the new house keys but I forgot this one." She realized that this was too much explaining for even her eldest child, so she changed tact.

"Pray," she said to all three, looking at them with earnest trust in their ability to reach God, "Pray to God to send us a police officer." She didn't know where to find one nor did she have the strength to walk around town with the children.

They knew how to pray and did so fervently, but no squad car appeared, so she joined them, her head one minute bent and one minute searching for God's response.

Ten minutes later, a truck drove by, a Plumbing and Heating truck, and Marie ran up to it and explained her plight, a sunburned pregnant woman with three small children in the middle of the street. Although skeptical, the plumber stopped and took out what looked like large scissors.

"All I can do it cut it," he warned, "It won't be any good after that."

"That's fine," she said, and minutes later she was in her car, racing to retrieve her things that remained abandoned under the setting sun, and ignoring the palpitations of her heart above the tiny heart beneath.

The children were asleep before they even reached the Garden State Parkway, but she kept talking to them anyway.

"You see, that is how God works," she said to them, "In his infinite wisdom. You may pray for a policeman, but he sends a plumber instead. But either way, we are okay now. We'll get home safe."

Traffic slowed almost to a halt at Exit 129, which Marie knew was about seven miles from home. "A mile an exit," she had reminded herself. The lull in motion caused a disturbance in the inertia of sleeping children and they woke, shaking sand from their eyes and hair.

"I'm hungry," Daniel said.

"Let's stop," Marie answered because the request came just before the Cheesequake rest area. She unloaded them once again with excruciating effort, and prayed the restaurants inside took Visa because she didn't have a cent on her.

She was aware again of how she looked; heavily pregnant with three scantily clad little ones clinging to her skirt, asking if a fast-food joint took Visa. They did.

Sitting there with her family, they learned that traffic had slowed because a toll-worker ahead had been fatally struck down by a heedless car, and everything became part of some mystery of life – the shore and the plumber, and the family somewhere that would learn that their father would not be coming home.

****

Marie did not admit that she missed Manny, or that her days were more tedious without him. She willed him to be part of a past life, a time entangled with all the things that would never be again, like sneakers that dangled over telephone wire, or graffiti marring a freshly painted warehouse door. She left him with those gray and gritty things that gave birth to her but did not own her; things that hid behind her eyes but could no longer be in her line of vision.

They had a last time, out on the Brooklyn piers; one she swore would not happen but at least recognized that she was lying to herself. He came by earlier that day to help her pack boxes, and seemed reconciled to her leaving by then, his voice edged with brittle cheer and an artificial lack of hope.

"I guess you won't be needing this anymore," he said, holding up a shopping cart she used for her walks to the grocery store. "Not in the 'burbs. You'll drive everywhere, won't you?"

"And I'll actually have a garage, so I won't store everything I own in the trunk of my car!" she answered sanguinely. It was a good day. The pain in her chest had dulled to a constant but bearable weight, a silent marauder content to sleep for a bit. Even more assuring was that she was with Manny, but not torn up by his presence. Her defenses had thickened around her like a rubbery cocoon harboring the brilliant possibility of passion but allowing it no release. She was safe, and she was moving away, and would be gone before the next inevitable rebirth of sensation.

Placing her faith in the fiber of her insulation, she turned to him and said, "Want to go out for a little while tonight? Just kind of let me say goodbye to the neighborhood while I feel well enough to do it?"

Sometimes Manny looked at her like he didn't know whether to hate her or to love her, or whether he believed in her innocence or merely pretended to, but he faltered before he answered her. How many words fit into the space between reaction and response? How many choices appear before one even utters a sound? What words did he reject before he answered her?

"You hate this neighborhood," he said.

"I know," she said softly, spinning another silken thread around her armor. It was good that he didn't want to go. It was wise. It was better, and –

"What time?" he asked.

The plan was to say goodbye to Queens, so they drove past a series of backdrops that held her memories in the foreground. Her high school, her old street, and, of course, Arthur Treachers, which was now a Hallmark Store. They drove under the elevated trains and past the gratings of the subways that blew dust and candy wrappers when the train screeched by. The ethnicity of Ridgewood had changed a great deal since her childhood, but the ambiance remained the same.

They said nothing, but when Manny got on the ramp for the BQE, she knew they were headed for Brooklyn and the protest that entered her throat lodged there and refused to budge. Instead, she watched out the window as the scenery changed in a way that only a borough dweller would notice; a difference in architecture, and atmosphere, familiarity and unfamiliarity rolled into one. And in the distance, Manhattan blazed like some holy city, staring down at its unworthy cohorts.

It had started to pour by this point, the lights of Manhattan now trickling in pools down her window, and the smells that rise from dampened slummy streets now permeating the car. She thought of a million lame conversation starters; comments about her childhood, or comparisons about the neighborhoods they passed, or jokes about the immense Jehovah's Witness tower that loomed ahead of them – "Jehovah Central", Manny called it – or perhaps a bit of reflection about what she would and wouldn't miss. All of it gridlocked behind the still unuttered protest; until she reconciled that, there was nothing to say.

They were out on the pier, across from the Seaport and the World Trade Center, and Jersey way out in the distance, somewhere. Marie had seen her small world framed in Manny's windshield so many times before, but tonight it seemed to surround some juxtapose of her being, some things behind her, some in front, but everything that would ever mattered sealed within the confines of these four doors.

"Looks like you could swim to the city from here," Manny murmured. He was sad, and sadness was a thick emotion, viscous and cumulative, as if every atom of unhappiness ever born still existed, joining with new ones to form a dense unbreathable air.

"We never completed our list," she said, freeing her vocal chords and destroying the protest. They had an unwritten list of things they would do together, which, of course included places that they would make love. They referred to it often, the list, and made mental checkmarks when something was accomplished.

He looked out the window and knew what had provoked the thought, because one of the things on "the list" was doing it outside in the pouring rain, and here were the heavens providing the chance. Still, he said nothing, recognizing always that he would have to wait for her to define the moment, waiting as always for her to decide what she meant.

Marie wished this wasn't true; wished fervently that it were not always up to her to maintain which side of hell they occupied, but in this Manny had made up his mind long ago, and in fact, his borders were so much more clearly defined. So Marie looked through the sheet of water at her old life, closed her eyes and whispered to herself, *how could one more sin possibly matter?*

"You know how much I love my checkmarks," she said out loud, and within seconds they were on the hood of the car, and he took off every item of clothing she was wearing. The rain was colder than she imagined it would be, and the metal from the car scratched her back, and she had a split second's concern about the baby she was carrying, but all that was fleeting because she started to come almost instantly, and kept coming.

She savored it by envisioning how it looked, her pale skin under the lights of looming buildings, shimmering with rain and fully exposed, and then it was a dual experience; the one that she felt and the one that she watched. When he got on top of her she heard the buckle of the car's hood beneath his knees, a creaking that would continue for the duration of the act, mixing with the pummeling sound of the rain that concentrated and pooled in the places where their bodies allowed it, and ran off in rivers everywhere else. She knew she was never going to forget this moment, and would remember not only with her mind but with all the neurons that were ignited and inflamed, and etching the moment in the secret place where forbidden memory is stored. This would never happen again, they said, but they didn't just mean the physical logistics of this moment. They meant it would never feel like this again, and so it needed to be retained somewhere in her being.

When it was over she was both shivering and trembling, and she would never again think that both words meant the same thing. The last words of Christ ran through her head – "it is finished" – and she stood on legs that wobbled when they touched the ground. In spite of the rain's iciness, she refused the shelter of the car and walked to the edge of the pier, still seeing herself from another place: an Adamite in female form, a woman naked before God with a vulva so swollen and bruised it seemed to eclipse feeling in every other body part. She imagined that it was the only part that God could even see as it rose to meet Him, scented and gleaming with the product of their ejaculate, hers and Manny's, drying faster than the rain could even hope to dispel it.

Marie remembered when she was a little girl and her mother made her change out of her bathing suit right on the beach, ignoring her protests and promising her that no one could see. Marie always rushed, but for that split second in the open air, she felt it, the scrutiny of some unknown eyes upon her, and she was embarrassed. Now she invited those eyes to look upon the evidence of the sublime pleasure she felt, and apologize to her for making her give it up.

"They can see you," Manny murmured, coming up behind her and running his hands along her hips in a way she knew, like he wasn't sure the moment had passed yet, and he was already wondering if he had damaged her. "I mean, across the water. The lights are pretty strong. If anyone is awake or outside in this horrible weather, it's pretty easy to see across."

"I don't care," she said, but he led her back to the car.

"You're freezing," he said, and searched for a blanket once he settled her on the passenger side. When he found one, he wrapped it around her shoulders but kept it open in front and stared at her form.

"More?" he asked and reached over and put his fingers inside her, and lowered his head to meet them with his mouth.

"More," she answered, and shifted to accommodate the small space, this time feeling the door handle against her back. She looked through the window once more at the clouded heavens, and thought it again – "it is finished" – then added, "but not yet" as Manny held her swollen fruit in his mouth and licked away the rain.

Two weeks later, she began her new life across the water in New Jersey.

****

The signs were strong that she was sick; that this was not something that would pass with pregnancy; that it was not because she was older and weaker this time around or that she had more to do with three other children and a new house. These were the excuses Marie gave people for the tangled blue veins that shone like iridescent ink through the papery skin on her chest, and for the weight loss that continued to sap her arms and legs while her belly bulged only a little.

"Were you born with a heart murmur?" her new obstetrician asked her at her first New Jersey check-up, and she asked her father if she was but he said only, "One of you kids was…your mother knew that…I don't know" and she let it go.

And then there was the article in *Cosmopolitan* titled, "Do you have Hodgkins Disease?" and Marie, in her OB's waiting room, did what she always did while aimlessly perusing: read only the first paragraph:

If you are suffering from night sweats, extreme weight loss, chest pain, a dry hacking cough and fatigue, you might have Hodgkin's Disease.

Marie didn't know what made her move on to the next article without reaction, but later she would remember the article; later when three doctors failed to diagnose her accurately and when a fourth one finally did and said they had found it too late. She would search for a way to get a back issue of Cosmo, because, she thought, "I was diagnosed by a sex magazine, and didn't even know it."

She woke up screaming with pain once, and Brendan rushed her the next day to the ENT in Queens because they had yet to find any Jersey doctors. Brendan look frightened, and Marie was taken aback at how he looked – almost caring, almost loving, almost intense – but the ENT had no great insights and things settled back once again.

And then the baby came. Grace was their tiniest, fighting for life inside a body that was depleting instead of burgeoning, and weighing in at only 6 lbs., 2 ounces. Her eyes, however, were bright blue and wide open, and right away she seemed to claim a large space with her small frame: her space as the baby who would ever remain the baby in the family.

They brought Grace home and Marie got ready for those magical first days of a baby's presence – the inimitable lone cry, the distinctive scent on soft blankets, the heroic feel of motherhood – but she was tired and something else: her fever had soared to 105, and she was popping Tylenol like candy just to get through the day.

She kept making mistakes, and it troubled her. She showed up at National School week on the wrong day, and embarrassed Colin, and when Grace started to cry and needed feeding, his eyes warned her not to reveal any body parts in his classroom and she had to leave.

People came to see the baby, but Marie wasn't up for it. This too frustrated her so she forced herself into making lunch and serving guests and participating in the celebration of life she deserved. The wait was supposed to be over. It was time to begin living.

"I'll never forget how you looked that week we came," her sister would say later, "trying to make that soup on the stove for us, with these little stick arms and this white face. You looked barely alive."

She visited doctors to no avail, follow-ups with the OB-GYN, and some other guy she found in her benefits book, but they found no cause for the fevers. One even sent her away because Tylenol had calmed the fever to 102, and he told her to come back when it returned again to 105.

Thanksgiving came when Grace was two weeks old, and they drove to Pennsylvania to celebrate with Marie's side of the family. On the way back, the car broke down, and they sat in a cold that was thankfully bearable for late November, and waited for a tow truck. It took hours to come, and the children fell asleep, while Marie clutched Grace through layers of fleece and realized the Tylenol was wearing off.

Sitting in the dark by the side of a still Route 80, under eerie lamplights spaced far apart, Marie felt again the clarification she noted a few weeks before. As she put chilled hands to her blazing forehead, she whispered softly into the supple ear of her newborn: "I'm dying, little one. I know it."

She wasn't entirely wrong. A week later an unworried doctor sent her some prescriptions for tests, and everything moved quickly after that. The lab was in Glenfield, and Brendan dropped her off, but afterwards she decided to walk home to get a good look at the town that was still new to her. There truly is the utmost calm before storms, because she felt it as she strolled, looking at the quaint shops that would be replaced by different quaint shops before the year was over. It was her first moment in weeks without children in tow, without an infant at her breast, and she savored it. It was late day and the train passed by frequently, dumping out what seemed like hundreds of the same men with the same suit and briefcase into the streets. It was all so cliché-ish and Mayberry-like, and she loved it anyway.

She walked up her driveway smiling to herself, the tests not forgotten, but pushed like fertilizer into a place in her mind that would only yield colorful flowers. Unlike the night in the motionless car, she had no belief that she was very sick, let alone dying; in fact, she was equally sure she was not. 'Whatever it is, they'll find it,' she thought, and smiled bigger when Brendan came out her front door holding Grace.

"Where were you?" he said, and she began to explain, indignant – was it 30 minutes she had given herself? Should she have hurried? – but he kept talking.

"The doctor called with the test results. He said you have to go to an emergency room. Now." He ignored her outstretched hands, reaching for her baby. "I called my sister to baby-sit. We have to leave."

"But...I can't go now, I have...there are things to do...there are...I feel better...why do I have to go?" she sputtered.

"Marie, they said that your sedimentation rate is 250. I don't know what that is, but normal is 125, and if it goes to 150, you're very sick. If it goes to 180, you're dead. You're at 250. Let's go."

****

It was the day she became an irrational patient and the beginning of a denial so solid, the word was written in dark uppercase letters across one of her charts: DENIAL. She took hours to leave for the E.R., putting everything in place carefully and calmly getting her children ready for bed. Brendan was frantic and pacing, helping little, and almost literally pulling his hair out, but smiling in a contorted attempt at reassurance whenever she looked at him.

"We have to be back in four hours," she stated in the voice of a dictator – "So it shall be written, so it shall be done" – and justified her edict in a way that suggested she didn't have to: "I just fed Grace. I have to be back for her next feeding."

"I bought formula," he began but her eyes flashed a warning that suggested he would be sent to the gallows, and he fell silent.

"We'll try," he said but she wasn't having it.

"Four hours," she said, "And also I have to stop on the way. I wasted too much time at the doctor today and I need to stop at Toys R Us for something."

"You need to stop."

"Yes."

"On the way to the emergency room."

"Yes."

"At a toy store."

"Yes. I'm sure I have time. I'm not gonna die on the way, am I?"

"Okay," Brendan croaked, and his fingers rifled hard once again through his hair, but at last she was ready and they got in the car.

Marie had an acute sense of her body's demise in the past weeks, but tonight was the first of the two times that she would feel a break with her own sanity. They stopped at Toys R Us so she could purchase the latest collector tin from Crayola Crayons, and she continued to browse just a little, smiling at Brendan and chattering like anyone on an adventurous shopping spree of Christmas and what the children wanted and how it was their first in their new home. And Brendan kept listening and smiling weakly and nodded hard, and jerking his hands again and again over his scalp.

The psychotic break would continue through not one, but two emergency room visits that night – the first hospital she was sent to was apparently incorrect – and needles and poking and prodding and answering the same questions over and over – "The pain has been going on for months, even years," "I don't know if I was born with a heart murmur," "Yes, I have been experiencing high night fevers." All questions asked and answered for no ostensible purpose or feedback because the nurses and technicians "were not doctors" and "knew nothing."

One technician put her newly acquired chest x-rays up on the eerily glowing screen, then ran to her side with a panicky question:

"Have you lost a lot of weight recently?" he demanded, and Marie thought the word "Eureka!" should have preceded it; such was the tech's energy and certainty.

"Well, sure. I had a baby." And she waited for the diagnosis that would send her home because they were just passing her 4-hour limit. She was grateful that Brendan could not share an x-ray room – the poisonous rays only ironically unsafe for anyone healthy – because at least she was free to answer questions herself and omit facts at will.

"Why?" she asked expectantly. *If you have some secret, spill it right now. My baby is hungry and I have to go home.*

"No reason," he answered, his demeanor so suddenly nonchalant, it was like air let out quickly from a robust balloon, leaving a sagging heap of wrinkled rubber. He returned to his x-ray and Marie began to screech.

"I asked you *why*," and she felt it, a crack along some fault line of her brain, beginning the separation like a scalpel in an evil hand, or even a random pen roadmapping the break in a spidery path.

She sat up. "You see something. I know you see something. So, what do you see?" she begged and squinted at the gray murk that obscured the milky portions of chest as light gleamed through it. *"Tell me,"* she threatened, but he was retreating and knew she couldn't follow.

"The doctor will be here soon," he said and was gone, but the thin lines continued across her skull at irregular angles, and the first trapezoid they formed became the first chink of reason that fell away from her.

Now her brain was an excavation site, because the truth was, she was not going home at all. "They" had decided to "admit" her. She was surrounded by enemies, and Brendan was one of them, all of them involved in some conspiracy: to keep her away from her baby, and away from her Tylenol as well, so that her temperature soared as her breasts engorged with the missed feeding and images of Grace's red wailing face tortured her. She cried when the milk began leaking through her shirt; the liquid that sustained her daughter's life ebbing away with her strength, and she refused to answer any questions from that moment on.

"When did the night sweats begin?" another disinterested face, another white coat with a head, asked, and Marie turned on her in venom.

"I have to feed my baby," she said, and offered up her soaked shirt as evidence, but the nurse just turned, and told someone, "She needs to get into a gown. And maybe someone can get her some nursing pads from maternity?"

From maternity. Where she was just a few weeks ago. She was even at the same hospital, she realized deliriously, but then she was here for birth and now she was here for death. In a moment of semi-lucidity, she grabbed the bored woman's arm and said, "And a breast pump. I need a breast pump, too. Or my milk will dry up and I won't be able to feed my baby."

The woman gently unlatched her arm and her smile appeared to Marie as amused. "Oh honey," she crooned, "You don't need a breast pump. You're a very sick girl. You won't be feeding that baby again. Concentrate on yourself."

They kept her for three days during in which time her anxiety mounted and further geometric shapes of reason fell away from her like homes in a mudslide; once so solid and now lost as something trivial. Her upper arms ached and Marie gazed at them hard, searching for the baby that should be in them. Flowers appeared on her windowsill in big cumbersome vases and she stared at them, too, wondering if her windows opened; wondering if she could drop them one by one to crash on the ground below – or maybe even hit some innocent stranger? – if she did this, then would they let her leave?

She snapped at anyone who came near her, attempted to touch her, because they were dim-witted and could not prioritize. She was the *mother* of *four* young children. She had just given *birth* two weeks before. She was *needed* at home.

They "ran tests." They took fluid from her spine. They took blood and more x-rays and pieces of her neck. During the latter, four white-coats discussed their ski vacations as they cut into her, making jokes as they removed a sample of tissue that would determine that she had cancer.

Her dad and sister visited her in that time, and so did Manny. She was silent for most of her family's visit, accepting their platitudes like homemade gifts from children who can offer little else, but she never saw Manny. She was asleep when he slipped in, and the only evidence of his aura were the things he left behind: a breast pump, for one, and candy, and the photo Christmas cards that she had left at Drug Fair for developing. These articles restored her wits in fragile patches, as she both emptied her breasts and stimulated them to keep producing, a measure of optimism and hope, and began to write out her Christmas cards.

"You shouldn't be doing that," a nurse said harshly.

"What?" Marie asked, a single word poisoned with sarcasm, "Writing out my Christmas cards?" and continued to bemusedly gaze at the photo on the front, her first of all four in reds and greens and whites, in front of their first fireplace in their first home. "Want to see my kids?" she went on, the sarcasm mixed with unfounded pride.

"Actually, you *shouldn't* be writing or whatever you're doing, but that's not what I meant. First, you should be resting. Second, you should not be sapping your strength with that machine. You need your strength to fight your illness." The nurse spoke robotically, like one on a commercial for pain relievers.

"What is my illness?" Marie asked, but the nurse didn't answer, and Marie knew she wouldn't, so she went back to her cards and waited for her to finish her rattling about and leave.

I'll be home soon. She spoke with her mind to the four in the glossy print. *And I will feed you again, Grace Tara. So don't get used to that formula.*

****

Marie was right. She did get to feed Grace again, and not just once. She fed her for 7 more days, right up to the day of her first chemotherapy. She wept silently all through that final feeding in the wee moonlit hours of morning, just before the sun appeared with a babysitter so she could leave for St. Barnabas Medical Center.

Her tears and her milk left in chorus, one nourishing her child and the other wetting her tiny head. To Marie's distracted surprise, Grace's thin downy hair was truly soaked with tears, and one salty drop even wandered into the infant's eye, which caused her to yank her head, startled, from the nipple. For a moment, Marie watched as the drop ran down Grace's face and joined the milky trail that trickled from the corner of her lips, diluting the product that ended its journey on the baby's chin. Bemused, Marie struggled to find some meaning in this joining of her fluids upon her daughter's dewy skin, but she was far too resentful, and sorrowful, and angry for this type of reasoning.

The diagnosis had come three days after her return from the hospital. It was Hodgkin's Disease, and because of the absence of the word, "cancer" in its title, it would be weeks before Marie realized that it certainly was.

"So, what do I do about it," she asked the doctor on the phone.

"We just have to get rid of it with a little medicine," the Korean woman replied.

Marie was relieved. "So I don't have to do chemo?"

"You do," came the reply, "That is the little medicine."

"I don't get it," Marie said to Brendan later, "Why do I need chemo if I don't have cancer?"

The office visit was equally vague and ambiguous, because Dr. Shin liked to give the facts straight only to Brendan, and dress them up a bit for Marie.

"You start chemo on Monday. Side effects are nausea, vomiting, and you won't be able to have another baby. You'll be sterile."

"I'll be sterile," Marie said flatly, "Sterile. And you think this belongs on the same list as nausea and vomiting?"

Brendan shushed her, begging her to be grateful to those who attempted to heal her, as if her irritability would cause them to reconsider. She was no better with those who attempted to cheer her up, offering up comments like, "Hodgkin's is the best cancer to have," and "well, at least you've had your children," and then of course, the prayers and platitudes of her old holy roller friends. The fact was, she had a rare strain of multi – or was it mixed? –cellularity Hodgkin's that had hidden itself from diagnosis for three years. The good doctor told Brendan – not her – that she only had a 15% chance of surviving. Marie cared nothing for that. She was unable to feed her baby and unable to have any more. This and only this consumed her.

She bit off their comments until finally; she just refused to take anyone's call at all. Then something happened. Her old friends stopped calling, but the friends she searched for high and low in her new neighborhood appeared from nowhere, in the form of fully cooked dinners and babysitting offers, and knocks on her door from someone about to run an errand and did she need anything?

One of these Samaritans was a pastor's daughter, from a charismatic church in a neighboring town, and so there you had it: God's reasons revealed. Marie was sick and suffered her losses, but through it she gained friends, and a church, and one more thing: the feeling, at last, that her husband might actually love her.

Marie would remember, forever, how precious Brendan was in those months. How he held her hand when the needle filled with the mustard gas that would destroy every egg in her ovaries went into her vein. How he touched her face and his eyes glistened, and he had to stop frequently when he spoke to keep his tears in check. He cared nothing about money then, encouraging her to purchase ridiculous gifts for the children that Christmas with no mention of the dreaded word, "budget."

"Promise me you will fight this," he would say, possibly a bit too dramatically, but he was an Irishman, after all, and as such found his place in misfortune. Of course she would fight this, but was she really the one doing the fighting? Wasn't it the doctors with their vials and chemicals, pills and regimens?

She would not say this to the man who finally looked at her with something unguarded and flowing. She only reached behind his neck to the place where his hair fell femininely soft, and drew him close as her fingers united with the strands.

"I'll fight this," she whispered, and added with her mind, *"because you do love me. I'll fight this and I'll fight Satan and I'll fight every form of temptation. You just have to keep loving me, just like now, just like this."*

****

Ten months of chemotherapy is a long time, and two months of radiation an eternity, but one year is nothing at all, and in that time, children grow and life does what it was asked to do; continues without care or remorse.

Grace grew on formula; all Marie's determined attempts to locate someone who would let her nurse failed. Even LaLeche League, the people who advocate breastfeeding no matter what – "even if you've had a double mastectomy," Marie would joke – advised against it, although they did hedge a bit.

"W-e-lll," a shiny sounding person said on the phone, "if you fed her, it probably wouldn't harm her to-d-a-a-y. But she might never be able to have children of her own."

At one point, Marie decided to opt for faith healing, something she read about, and told Brendan she would not go on with chemotherapy. He panicked, and brought in leaders from her new church in Elizabeth, one the father of her neighbor.

"Have you heard directly from the Lord about this?" they asked.

"Well, yes," Marie replied, "I mean, I think so."

"You can't 'think so,'" was Pastor Arnold's quick reply, "You must be sure that the Lord spoke to you about this.

"Of course," Pastor Cleo jumped in, "We do know people who have gone this route."

Marie brightened. "Can I talk to *them?*" she asked.

"Honestly, most of them have died," Arnold said, and like a tag team, Leo joined in, "But very peacefully. They were not unhappy with their decision." And behind her, Marie heard Brendan crash a cup into the sink.

Her friend recommended a good chiropractor, and her new organic neighbors some juices and natural remedies, but in the end Marie took her chemotherapy, and with it her sorrows, and also with her joys – good friends, a husband who devoted himself to her, and a sin that finally blurred into the background, like the taste of lemonade on a hot day long ago.

Grace did thrive on formula, although she was the sickliest of her children, and Marie would never chalk that up to coincidence. She was nearly hospitalized at six weeks with her first of many asthma attacks, and she was the first of four to suffer from ear infections. Still, she blossomed in other ways, cared for as she was by others who came when Marie was in the hospital. Grace became a serene and joyful child, held by many, and in love with the world.

Marie's house was filled with people then, Brendan's parents and her own father; Brendan's mother who held Grace all day and sometimes fed her at night, and both grandfathers who alternately mopped the kitchen floor "the right way" until they stripped it of all life. Marie only minded the company when she couldn't be part of it; that is, when she was in the hospital and Monica visited her own parents at Marie's house, and stayed for dinner with her children. It was only then that Marie felt the loneliness of her affliction.

And so the year passed. The children grew, the house became home and Marie became a suburban mom, chatting with the others of her kind outside the school doors. She got to pick easily then from the line-up of possible comrades that came and went while she was sick, her favorites the women somewhat out of the Stepford mold of suburbia: an earth-defending naturalist named Sonya, and Claire, the woman who would rush to Marie's side for any…well, anything. Claire did not bring pot roasts wrapped in tin foil or offers of cleaning services, but she did not bring platitudes, either. For the next year and the rest of her life, Claire would bring humor and nurturing and intelligence and perspective.

Brendan also kept true throughout the months, his eyes illuminant with wonder at Marie's ability to keep on living, and another thing: promise. He promised her that Grace would not be her last child; that they would try again, as soon as they were certain Marie was better. In the meantime, they acquired a puppy, a wee West Highland terrier named Bonnie, just like the one they met in Ireland on their honeymoon.

Brendan's parents reprimanded him for buying the dog, and other people – friends! – laughed at them for this new acquisition; a family of six with a brand new baby and a dismal cloud of disease over their heads adding to their workload so recklessly.

At a boy scout event, one dad said, "I hear you got a puppy? What, was life too easy?" and laughed and Marie laughed, and thought about it.

In fact, life *was* easy. In the face of all adversity comes life with clarity, and with clarity, contentment. Marie was certain she understood mysteries that had previously escaped her; saw them without seeing them, with some extrasensory vision. People asked her in that time if she had "found Jesus" and she would smile and give an answer later used by Forest Gump: "I didn't know he was lost." She did not find Jesus, but she located another piece of herself, and made the mistake of believing that it could never be lost again, and that her new, tree-lined utopia would cocoon her for always.

Life understood is in fact life misunderstood. Even Socrates confirmed his intelligence solely on his ignorance. Life is static, wriggling uncomfortably out of anyone's grip of comprehension, and perfect knowledge is just a wall blocking further exploration; but for Marie, it was safe. She got better, if not completely well, and a few weeks before her final chemotherapy – she always had difficulty calling it anything as cute as "chemo" – she began making plans for the next phase of her time on Earth.

Her wheels were always turning before anyone suspected, and her decisions made and confirmed without consultation. And so, when Brendan arrived home from work one Indian summer evening, ambling up the driveway and entering through the side door – thinking, what? That he was a lucky man? That the worst was over? Or was he ever worrying about the bills now that Marie would live? – she was in the kitchen.

"I registered for classes today at UCC. I am going to get my teaching degree."

****

Marie wasn't sure when the romantic candle began to burn low in Brendan's eyes, but she knew it was happening, and she knew when it was snuffed out completely. It was the day he began yelling again, taking off his cushiony demeanor and meeting her again with all promise forgotten. It was like some superhero movie, where the hero loses strength with every good deed, while the victim becomes empowered, never realizing what she has stolen. As the months went by, Marie would almost believe that her IV was connected not to a clear plastic bag full of cancer-killing fluids, but to a plump vein in Brendan's arms, sapping the life out of him as it killed the evil cells inside of her.

She knew she had been irrational but he supported her. One day, the oncologist said her red cells were too low and she needed a transfusion. Marie stated that she did not have time, and insisted that it be done at night while she slept and her children slept, and that she leave the hospital first thing in the morning in time to bring them to school. The oncologist complied with Brendan's approval and he said nothing when the bill arrived, charging him for a night's stay in a hospital when insurance had only approved an outpatient procedure.

The fact was; Brendan could deal with Marie in a weak and dependent state, relying on him for carrot juice and reminders to take her "meds." He could not deal with her robust and able, speeding once again head-on into her vision of life and dragging him along like a reluctant stowaway.

The first day he yelled, it was because the dog had an episode of diarrhea all over the rug.

Marie's sister Lisa was over, and they were talking intently in the kitchen about Lisa's pending divorce, and so when a child's voice yelled, "There's cra--, I mean poop all over the living room", Marie made no move to clean it. Brendan was watching TV on the porch, and she knew he had ears, too, not to mention the olfactory organs that were surely taking a beating right now.

Lisa looked at her, but Marie smiled a little and said, "Keep going, Brendan will get it" and stopped herself short from saying again how good he was to her, in light of the fact that Lisa's husband had walked out on her.

When no action was apparently being taken, Marie interrupted Lisa's diatribe of injustice with a touch on her arm, then queried aloud, "Brendan?" and then again, louder, "Brendan?"

"Yes?"

"Did you hear the kids? Bonnie went on the floor."

"I heard."

"Well, you can't just leave it there. Aren't you going to clean it up?" she asked, still smiling at Lisa, who was impatient to get on with her story.

And then he shouted: "Jesus Christ, Marie, why don't you clean it up? This is the dog you wanted!" His voice got louder with each syllable, punctuated with hard purposeful steps as he approached the kitchen, pulling paper towels off the rack with a force so implacable, the towels themselves refused to rip but the holder came undone from the wall.

Lisa's breath caught; her eyes rose, and her thoughts of finishing her own tale of woe temporarily stilled. Marie knew well what her sister was thinking, for she was thinking it as well. The cancer honeymoon was over, and they were back home again, where Marie was very much alive and no longer a cherished porcelain doll void of white cells.

Marie always tried to see past her hurt to the place where Brendan was. She tried to remember that cancer happens to everyone; it eats away at the cells and physical body of one while it devours the patience and tranquility of all who helplessly watch. Marie knew that she could never do what Brendan did had the situation been reversed. She could never devote so much mental energy to his care. She would want it over. She would want to move on.

Brendan's mother was next; her symptoms beginning soon after Grace's birth, but only diagnosed after Marie was in remission. She died that December. He took it hard, and would remain cancer-phobic for the rest of his days, scrubbing vegetables from the market diligently, and avoiding oddities like tin foil or later, excessive cell phone use. Death would always affect him more deeply than it affected Marie, for he considered life a gift to be stolen, while Marie always thought of it as a challenge to be conquered.

At the wake, four-year-old Kristin walked up to the casket to gaze upon her granny. Her grandfather, rushing to her side, spoke solemnly to her.

"It's okay, Kristin," his Scottish burr a whisper, "Your granny is in heaven now."

At which point, wise little Kristin looked around at the musty room, filled with flowers and old ladies with tears running through their heavy make-up, past the nuns struggling to hide the strain of chastity pasted in their eyes, and screamed a question-like statement through the gloom:

"This is heaven???" Heads turned. Her disappointment was apparent, and Marie was proud of her little girl, while Brendan stood, aghast.

Chapter Twelve: The Upper Hand

When did Manny re-enter? This was always blurry to Marie, but as it would always be, Manny came on the heels of her disappointment with Brendan, like some comic book hero that shows up in the nick of time. Not that Manny was ever completely gone; he always lingered in the periphery of all Marie's life paintings so as to sense a change in tone, a darker hue, a reason to seep across the pages and dilute the shadows.

Brendan's metamorphosis from caring husband to disgruntled provider was complete as soon as Marie got well, and all the promise his eyes once held disappeared as quickly as the removal of tinted contact lenses. Marie, who had written in her diary and even in a letter to her newly in love sister-in-law, that she had found love and passion again with Brendan, was hurt. She was floored. She would someday say that Brendan only knew how to love sick people.

He would not consider having another baby. That was the hardest thing to bear among his broken bedside vows. She could barely take that he had returned to scrutinizing every purchase she made, or that he no longer looked deeply interested in her when she spoke, but the baby thing was the ultimate betrayal. She needed to recover what she had lost.

Her ob-gyn told her not to believe assertions that she was sterile. He said it as a precautionary measure, to let her know that she should still use birth control: "as long as you still get a period, you can still get pregnant." Marie took this as a ray of hope, for her cycle had indeed returned after the valve being shut off for the past 11 months. She didn't count on a shutdown from her husband.

"Why?" she spit fire at him, "Why, why, why? You *promised.*" Marie no longer argued coyly. If anything, cancer had given her that. She spewed the full wrath of her damaged and repaired spirit, with the dauntless fumes of a survivor.

"I just don't want another baby," Brendan said, "and besides, what if it kills you this time…"

"No!" Marie retorted, "The last pregnancy did not bring on cancer and you know it. In fact the pregnancy stopped its progress. Don't change things. The oncologist said she had never seen such an advanced case stay in one spot. The baby *stopped it from spreading*."

"But you are weaker now, and…" Brendan said and she was an unstoppable tirade.

"*I am not weak.* Remember? I fought this."

"It's selfish to have another baby."

"Oh Brendan, it's selfish to have any baby at all. It's selfish to have the ones we have, and it's selfish to have no babies at all. Everything is selfish, Brendan, because we do everything for *ourselves*. Give me a break." She finished and stormed off.

The argument went on throughout the months ahead, increasing in intensity and racing against the clock, for Marie's menstrual cycle slowly tapered off.

"Another thing they don't tell you," Marie complained bitterly to Claire, "is that you aren't sterile all of a sudden. It's something that almost literally leaks away. Your period comes back like some ray of hope, and then recedes."

Claire was a registered nurse, but there was nothing ever clinical in her reactions. "Well, yes. It brings on menopause. It sucks. I'm sorry."

Meanwhile, her Bible friends told her, "Just pray for him," while her other friends told her, "Maybe he is really worried about your health," and her family asked, "Why do you want another *baby*? You've got *four*."

Marie read about ways to trick her husband, things you can do with a turkey baster or ways to mislead him about where she was in her cycle, but even she experienced some unease in such tactics, not in any regard to Brendan's feelings – for he had promised her, after all – but because she held a true Christian's belief in repercussions. What if the baby was born with birth defects? What if the cancer returned? She knew God punished those that obsessively pursued what they wanted, and she had little trust in His unconditional love. Marie knew that the Lord giveth only so He had something to take away; it was the small print on every divine contract, and it was also untrue that the Lord only gave and took what you could handle. The simple fact was, it was impossible even for God to please all of the people, all of the time, and the good Lord made very broad assumptions about what His children could live without.

"Why can't you be *white*, Manny?" she lamented one day, "Then I could steal a baby from you."

"Need I remind you that my semen is as white as the next guy's?" he came back quickly, and it was of course a joke, but something quickened inside her for the first time in months.

"And has anyone been the recipient of that semen in these last months, Sergeant?" she asked cautiously, "Because I must remind you that it is mine forever, whether I use it or not."

"Ten-four," he said with mock solemnity, and thus, another seed was cultivated; sewn in the fertile soil of Brendan's betrayal, watered with Marie's tears of bitter disappointment, and tended always by Manny, who never stopped watching over his dry, quiescent fields for seedlings of hope. Each root gripped its rich surroundings with unseen familiarity, working steadily and silently, and in a few weeks when Marie let Manny back inside of her, she would swear that it "just happened."

"Sin," the preacher boomed, "is just like a weed in your garden. At first you just don't recognize it. It looks mighty interesting, pretty even, and you figure you'll leave it alone, see what happens."

He paused for emphasis, and Marie watched the nodders and the squirmers around her in the congregation. Everyone knew where he was going with this but some were free of the feeling that the good pastor was talking directly to them.

"So, you have this pretty little weed growing taller in the garden, and you're just waiting for it to flower into something good…and of course you figure that you always have time to pull it if it amounts to no good." Again he paused.

They were at church, a large abandoned theatre in a questionable neighborhood where Brendan checked three times to see if he had locked the car or left anything valuable on the seat, then held his children's hands tightly right up to the entrance under the marquee.

"My friends, you do *not* have time to pull those weeds later! Underneath the ground, they are establishing their roots, and each day you allow them to remain, they take a firmer hold on your garden! Your richest earth will soon be ruined! The roots of sin will take hold beneath and *choke everything that is good, until your garden...dies!*" The pastor was sweating on his stage-like pulpit, and in his audience came cries of "Amen!" and "Lord save us!"

They stilled, and now he spoke in a hush. "Check your garden daily. Search it for signs of weeds. Be diligent in your discernment. Leave not the tiniest sprout of sin untouched." Pause. Nod, nod. Squirm, squirm.

"You will be rewarded, my friends. Your garden will be lush with God's vegetation. Purity and grace and righteousness will color your world. They will soon crowd out the weeds until there is no room for them to sprout again." He finished, and sat down and the music started and the audience was on its feet singing, "My God is an awesome God, he rules with power and love…"

Marie stood, too, and sighed. Of course it would be the weeds that needed aggressive removal. Never the flowers. You had to practically beg the flowers to grow. You tended them like a maniac as you gazed hopefully at the pictures on seed packets of what they could be. Or sometimes you purchased them already as established plants; with the vain hope that someone else's rectitude will crowd out your wickedness.

But it didn't work. You watered, and fertilized and pulled away at those weeds. You even yanked a lot of weeds that could well be flowers, just in case, and then missed the opportunity to know one way or the other. Still those wild plants reappeared, and you realized that you would be struggling with this eternally, until ironically you ended up beneath the ground with the whole conglomeration of roots, seeing nothing at all. And of course God took no responsibility for inventing the weeds in the first place. He only claimed the flowers; only claimed the weaker thing that barely stood a chance. For this he was dubbed "all-powerful." For this, all the people around Marie came out to praise him.

"So I supposed Satan invented the weeds?" Manny would ask later with some glee and some speculation, after she filled him in on the sermon with all the earnestness she could muster. "And of course all those wildflowers on the sides of the highway are pure evil?"

"No, stop," Marie defended her ideology, but she was always begging to lose the debate. "You are oversimplifying."

"*I'm* oversimplifying? Me. Not the pastor?" He smiled, touched her face. "C'mon, Marie, you're a college girl now. Aren't you supposed to be rejecting God by now? Bucking the system? Writing home to your parents to tell them everything they taught you is wrong?"

"I've only taken six credits," she surrendered and they walked on. "'Bucking the system 101' comes later."

"Well, if you want the AP course, come to work with me. Lotsa weeds there, Marie, on the streets of Brooklyn," he mused. "Lots of godforsaken weeds."

That conversation took place at Turtle Back Zoo, where they had brought three girls – Kristin straight from preschool, Grace in the stroller, and Manny's daughter, Ariella – and allowed the animals to amuse them so they could focus on each other. The zoo was near Marie's pediatrician's office, and it was small enough to squeeze in a visit before the girls' check-ups.

This was how Marie maintained her life; ever mixing the mundane with the miraculous, the untainted with the corrupt, the weeds with the flowers. She knew the difference, but it was too late to do any separating, for all was intertwined now in a life-sustaining pattern.

She would remember this day as one of *those* when everything mixed together into some reckless aromatic cocktail, or an impetuous Pollock painting. Everything thrown together yet somehow belonging together, imprisoned as some bizarre portrait of existence that could be interpreted any which way but never disregarded altogether. A miasma with meaning, that's how Marie would always remember days like these. Microcosms of what her life had become.

They walked around, nonchalantly guarding their children while intently guarding each other.

"Look, Ariella! An alligator!" Manny would point his daughter's attention, but it was Marie's hand or waist he lightly brushed; it was her eyes he held above the heads of their collective offspring, and so they were always holding two conversations at once.

"Kristin! You are too far away," Marie warned, but it was like the babes all knew in their childlike wisdom that they were only on the periphery today and could stretch their limits; and so Kristin ran still further before her own prudence brought her back. She was dark – brown eyes and hair, olive-skinned – and so she and Ariella looked like sisters on a fleeting glimpse and maybe even after full scrutiny.

After verifying Kristin's safety, Marie came back to Manny. "Well, all I can say is that you will not make it to paradise with your way of thinking, Sergeant. You are destined for hell."

"Ha!" was his quick reply. "Like I haven't been to both places already. I think we've had this discussion already." And managed to press her up against the cage of – was it an orangutan? – her pelvis tight against the bars and his holding her in place. "This is the part I call paradise," he whispered in her ear, and pressed harder, "and hell is just when you take it away from me…from us."

Later, he would use another metaphor, referring to the stretches of time she allowed him in completely as "summer," and the inevitable times of guilt and shame in between when she held him at bay, "winter." "I feel a long winter coming on," he would say forlornly, but then added, "But, Marie, I never stop hoping for the summertime. It never fails to come around again."

When the microcosm expanded, it was what suburban moms like to call "hectic," with dramatic emphasis and appropriate head shakes. At least fifty percent of it was lived inside a vehicle, toting children in car seats and booster seats and finally plain old seat belts to and from everything the children never asked to be part of: softball and soccer, art and piano lessons, gymnastics and baby swim classes. The idea seemed to be to schedule the young ones for so much as to create an inevitable conflict, which you would then regard with incredulity before you solved the issue creatively and had something to talk about at the next coffee clutch that nobody "really had time for," but never failed to show up.

Marie dove into this lifestyle, forgetting how she once put her children on the subway to take them to museums and plays in Manhattan, and in fact, disregarding that there was a city she once loved across the water at all. It was all here now, in Glenfield and its outskirts, and it's not that Marie stopped seeking cultural experiences for the kids. She found new museums and plays and even a circus that came to town each year. She just didn't venture far out of her white bread town.

In the summer, there was the town pool, a literal watering hole and oasis for the middle class moms. There was no need to call each other in summertime; there was no need to do any arranging. Everyone would end up at the pool sooner or later. Lounge chairs were saved in spots in the shade; food was shared. Blankets and towels and strollers were set up for a long day that often began with early swim lessons for the kids and ended with someone deciding to order a pizza at dinnertime.

Even this, Marie found both enthralling and amusing. She valued the pool as something that she would never have had in Queens; wholesome relief from the heat, barefoot children risking bee stings to play ball out in the field between dips, and friends to chat with in the sunshine. Baby Grace amused herself with the dangling earrings from the lobes of all the women who insisted on holding her; marveling again at the miracle of her existence; a baby that grew in a womb with a tumor above her that grew just as fast.

What amused Marie at times was the conversation. Women sitting in resin chairs while lifeguards minded their children, still found ways to be dissatisfied, almost competitively frazzled.

"I have so much to doooo," one wailed, and others joined in.

"*You.* I have a contractor coming at 5, and Jeff has soccer, and I haven't even a thing in my refrigerator."

"Don't even talk to me," another joked, "I have a new baby. I haven't slept in weeeeks."

Marie would mentally record the conversation and add a note to thank her husband later. She often would arrive at the pool just after dropping him off – his body sheathed in clothing that was almost inhumane for a day that was already sweltering by 8am – at the train station in town, amidst a throng suited exactly the same way; knowing the kids would be swimming long before his last connector made its way to midtown, then stay until he boarded the first train for home some seven hours later. Marie knew she was lucky. She worked hard; she cared for her children well, but she was fortunate to be where she was.

Once, she decided to bring everyone to meet him for lunch, and Marie was exhausted by the time she arrived at 57th and Lex three trains and three harrowing platforms later.

"How do you *do* this?" she asked. "You can't even sleep on the train or you'll miss the connection. At least we could sleep on the bus going to work in Queens."

"And who invented that monkey suit, anyway? It's 99 degrees and you're buttoned all the way to the top with a tie around your neck. May as well be a noose! I mean, granted I had four kids with me, but it's grueling getting here. And then you actually have to begin work once you arrive. And do the whole thing *again* later!" She finished.

Did he look grateful when she spoke like this? She wasn't sure. She seemed to recall him only looking at her quizzically, as if there were things he wanted to ask but thought better of it. She knows she thanked him, more than once, for providing for his family. It was what he knew. It was what he was good at.

On the weekends, there were garage sales and estate sales, an early morning adventure that got them the things they need for their home. Families were always moving, children were always growing, and people were always selling off something. Marie was perfectly content to purchase things secondhand and it was consistent with Brendan's sensibilities as well, so each Saturday in three out of four seasons they would arise, make coffee, and get in the car to drive around. In this way, they acquired picnic tables and furniture for indoors and out, curtains, and a barbeque grill and even a baby grand piano. Oh, and toys: Marie noted that every child in town owned a Little Tykes Cozy Coupe car, and was delighted when she picked one up for $15.

They spent much time in the yard they never before had, cooking on their cast-off grill, and watching the children run around with the dog or play on the swing set which was one of the few things they had purchased brand-new.

Brendan took videos of these times, and Marie piles of photos as well; Kristin in a sandbox, Grace in a baby swing, the boys with wiffle balls and bats or with a hockey net in a street that cars rarely came down. Ruddy, spoiled, happy children, oblivious to the struggle it took to get where they were.

Marie watched her family with glossy eyes, and would view the photos later the same way. She knew they had been happy; she had proof that this was so. Still, there were things that were not in those photos, except maybe in the strain in Brendan's own eyes, and this was forever her cross to bear. It is difficult to reconcile happiness, and difficult to explain why it isn't present when it should be. It is difficult to justify the need to find it wherever you can, because some things simply aren't justifiable.

Should anyone have privy to her life in its entirety, they would be most perplexed;

for it was a nonsensical blend of conformity and lack thereof. She ran a bi-weekly Bible group in her living room, but in between her best friend was Claire, a proud Unitarian and probably the only one that existed in Catholic Glenfield. While their children played, she and Claire spent hours over tea philosophizing, and Marie always found Claire's perspective far more refreshing than that of the pool groupies or the Bible-thumpers. What's more, Claire possessed traits that seemed lacking in the carbon copy crowd: Lack of judging others. Genuine caring. Humble insecurity. Sharp-witted intelligence. Marie did not disclose every detail of her conflicted life to her friend immediately, but she worked up to it over the years and by the time she offered a full-blown confession, Claire seemed to already know.

The other thing that consumed Marie's thoughts and days was her slow but steady progress through school. She began by taking only one course per semester, one night a week, at the community college less than a mile from her house.

College gives the opportunity to redefine oneself. This is true of the wide-eyed 20-year-olds who filled most of Marie's classes, but it was not untrue of herself. Marie knew she was filling in some gaps in her understanding. She felt as if she was living in reverse, like a person who assembles a complex piece of furniture as well as she can, then goes back to check the instructions to see where and how she has failed. Marie was married, a mother of four, a homeowner and a freelance writer. Now she sat among fresh idealistic men and women on the brink of what Marie had already accomplished, and they were not only reading the instructions; they were personalizing and perfecting them. In their precious innocence, they were soon sure that they could do a better job than what's been done so far; better than their own parents and certainly better than Marie.

They had the same voices, especially the girls. They stretched certain words for emphasis that was not needed, like it was a random choice of every third or fifth sound.

"The other *da-aay,* I was at the *stoo-ore,*" a clean, bright face holding ivory teeth began a story for her professor, sure that it was pertinent, sure that it was interesting. "And this *mo-om* had her child with *he-er*." And proceed to tell a tale in which the unqualified parent treated her child inappropriately by not allowing him to climb on the glass at the deli counter.

"I mean, he was just *exploooring*," she finished, "and kids *neeed* that."

'*And grown-ups need deli counters that do not have children attempting to sit on them*', Marie smiled, but kept her thoughts to herself. Sometimes she wished she could take down the phone numbers of all the optimistic reformers in the room, and ask them to keep in touch so she could check back with them after they had lived a bit.

She turned to the person she had strategically sat near; the other "older" student in the class, and whispered, "Yeah, I remember when I swore I'd never take my child out in his pajamas. Now I practically have a breakfast bar set up in my car."

The woman snickered but finished with a gentle smile. "They don't know," she said amiably, "The whole world is out there, for them, just waiting. And they are so sure they know exactly how to navigate it."

Even more amusing were those that openly renounced God or their religion in class, as if they were the first ones ever to do such a thing. Like frustrated rebels that had missed the 60's, they spoke out angrily against the "bullshit" doctrine that had thus far governed their lives, as if hurt by hours wasted in Sunday school. Or they used newfound knowledge to at last criticize the government, stating the obvious in a new way. They loved the word "anarchy" and used it frequently and with gusto.

Marie took all this in wistfully, for she herself had been denied the chance to approach the future with so much hope and information. She marveled at the strength of their convictions, their lack of embarrassment or discomfit, and wondered if it took a strong perfect body and their parents' blind adoration to reach such a confident state. They looked at Marie resentfully when she spoke from experience and crushed their dreams. They were not interested in the world that came before them, only the one they would create.

"Of course they hate you," Marie's friend Deirdre told her one day over coffee. "You're the "adult" student. I always hated the adult students. They always got "A's." They always wrecked the curve."

Marie sensed at times that her professors sometimes took her silence more seriously than the anecdotes of the young set, but she still was somewhat intimidated by them. For all their youth and inexperience and drawling syllables, Marie knew they possessed something that she did not: they were all sure they would graduate and instantly get jobs. They were all sure they would make great teachers, while Marie, as always, wondered if she would reach her goals at all.

****

In addition to examining their lives on a timeline, people tend to divide them into sections, beginning with childhood and going on to include different locations and states of feeling or maturity, some marked by deep trauma and some just by a few fine niceties, and some seemingly by nothing at all.

Marie would note later that the most traveled and faultless of roads would be the most difficult to remember or describe afterwards; so crowded as they were with details that seemed not to matter. The only thing that really mattered was how that fragment ended, and then only its end would define it.

The next section of her life would be the final section, although she would live long after to mull over it. All time after this would be a new story, another person's story; that person being the ghost of who she was now, one tortured with the chains of memory and regret.

Right now, she likened her life to a verse in a Dylan song; a verse she wrote long ago in her best friend's 8th grade autograph book: *To dance beneath the diamond sky with one hand waving free.* She assumed that the Tambourine Man could only have one hand unencumbered because he clung tightly to all that was precious in the other: his tambourine, which supplied the music of his life. Still, as prized as it was, it couldn't possibly be enough for him, or he would not be so adamant about keeping one hand ready to grab something else. Her friends hung on to their precious lives -- filled with lawns and fences, L.L. Bean backpacks and fathers with leaf blowers – with both hands, while Marie convinced herself that she had enough strength in only one arm to keep this perfect life intact, no matter what the other limb ended up ensnaring.

What else did she discuss around suburban tables and later relay in a skewed picture at her dinner table to Brendan, or in a complete picture to Manny as he brushed her hair? Did anything but the monotonous struggle with sin stand out in those steady, sturdy days?

There were changes in her family around her; as Lisa divorced and almost immediately remarried, Anne's husband gave up his Harley Davidson and returned two years later, and her brother's marriage began to fall apart. Meanwhile, Marie's baby sister, Louise, got married, and would surprise them all by being the most durable nuptials in their family.

"You see, Manny?" Marie analyzed, "She did it right. She went to college first, then graduated. They both graduated. Then they got jobs and then they got married. That's how it should be done, I guess."

"And if you did it that way, everything would be different?" he asked, not challenging but sincerely, because they enjoyed tossing thoughts around.

"I don't know. If I did it that way, would it still be Brendan? I don't know. But I do know that if it were Brendan, he wouldn't dominate me. We would be on equal ground." She paused.

"But you know, the only reason that Louise got to be this way is because my mother died. I'm not talking about the survivor benefits that paid for college, either. I'm talking about that voice she never had, telling her what she couldn't do. She lost her mother at 16…traumatic, yes…but probably the best thing for her."

"Uh oh. You're taking psych now, right?" Manny smiled. "Back in college, everyone who took psych suddenly had all the answers."

"Far from it, Sergeant. But I am figuring out something. I'm taking child psych now, actually. And I'm realizing that Brendan is not a good father." There. She said it out loud.

Manny listened, and waited. There was still time for lovemaking, and he watched for signs like a predator alert to the slightest movement of its prey. Marie admired this in Manny; the simplicity of his pursuits. It was not complex for him, loving her, nor riddled with inconsistency or discord. It was just was. Marie wished it were that way for her, so free of entanglement or maddening thought.

The other thing that still drew Manny's attention was any negative assessment of Brendan, and so he asked immediately, "Not a good father? How so? I mean, how not?"

"Well, I always hated the way he talked to his kids. Because he talked to me the same way. Demeaning. He calls them stupid, he calls them jerks. He screams at them over nothing." She shuddered for a second, fighting tears.

"He will stop the car and cause all their heads to jerk forward, just to turn and scream at them. I just say nothing, because I feel like he's yelling at me too, and another thing, that he told me never to contradict him in front of the children."

"But I *disagree*. I always disagree with his approach. And I'm forced to just sit there, and let him do it. But I asked the psych teacher about it, cause he has his own private practice. He said that verbal abuse is just as damaging as physical abuse. Like I don't know that, huh?"

It was a startling discovery for Marie, the days she began doubting Brendan's superiority in all things. No matter how she felt about it, it was something she held as solid truth, that her husband was better than her, purer than her, and knew more than her, about money, surely, and politics and humanity; in all things, he had the facts while she operated purely on misguided instinct.

She remembered a particularly pivotal day the winter before, when she coaxed her family into a ski trip in the Poconos. The vacation house her father purchased was in Big Bass Lake, which boasted a man-made lake, swimming pool and tennis courts, and in the winter, bunny slopes and a t-bar for skiing. The rental shop was cheap for homeowners, and the slopes perfect for teaching young children, but there was no snowmaking apparatus and so a good time depended solely on the good graces of Mother Nature.

They watched the snow and planned weekend trips accordingly, thwarted only by another siblings' first dibs on the place. For this particular trip, the snow looked promising mid-week, but began a steady meltdown and seemed all but lost by Friday.

"We should cancel," Brendan said like the voice of doom. "There is no snow."

"Well, that's *here*," Marie countered, "not *there*. It could be entirely different there."

"It's one state over, Marie," Brendan said ever so patiently, but she would not be stopped.

"New York is one state over, too," she said weakly, "but we don't always have the same weather as my dad, right?"

Still, he had planted the seed of doubt and worry, and the cloud that hung accusingly. The weather was now her fault, and as they drove with a car packed with winter clothes and sleeping children, Marie stared out the window anxiously. As was their habit, they had left at the childrens' bedtimes, so as to secure a more peaceful trip, and it was in silence that Marie scrutinized the sides of the highway for white powder and found none.

"See?" Brendan spoke like a validated prophet, "No snow. Oh well. We'll have to think of something to do with the kids."

They arrived at 10pm, to mountains of snow. Snow plowed into high walls on the wooded sides of the paved roads that led to her father's house; snow not yet beginning to melt or lose its pristine whiteness. Snow that so fully blocked her father's long driveway that they had to park in the road and carry heavy unconscious children through drifts up to their knees.

The next day, they had to hire a plow to come and clear the driveway. Marie said nothing, holding her tongue the way she held her hopes, waiting for permission to allow a release.

Brendan had only one comment: "Well, the plow cost fifty dollars. I guess there is no such thing as a free vacation, huh?" And Marie's children all went skiing, for hours in spring-like warmth, while she beamed and held a single thought: *he is not always right. It is time to start trusting myself.*

****

He was right about one thing, though: they were always in debt. Brendan's salary kept on increasing, and he continued to make sound career moves that advanced him in the corporate world; but they never came out from under, and they had different policies for attending to life. Marie believed that you had to enjoy the moment; she was raised by folks who no doubt purchased her with a Sears charge card and had only finished paying for her recently. Brendan, of course, was raised by people who squandered nothing; his father still possessed the first dollar he ever earned in America. Brendan saved for the future at the expense of the present so that one day Marie imagined that her children would be rich and bitter, wondering why they hadn't had a childhood.

In such cases, a loving balance would be ideal, but it was not to be had in the young Kavanagh home. Marie believed that she was doing her part by purchasing things secondhand, but it wasn't long before purchases of any kind irritated Brendan. Like a child of the depression, he denied himself everything, reading only a morning paper left behind on the train as he commuted, and never going out to lunch in the streets of Manhattan, not even to a hot dog vendor.

"I leave the house with $10.00 in my pocket, Marie," he said, "and usually come home with it."

"Well, that's easy for *you*," Marie sighed, so tired of the attacks upon her character, "because *you* don't leave the house with four other people. Children need things. You can't say no to everything."

"Children *want* things," Brendan answered, "and you *can* say no. You don't want to say no, Marie. Look at their toys. No one has toys like that. You aren't getting all of them at garage sales, honey."

"Manny buys a lot of those," she shot back, and instantly regretted it. It was the truth that Manny was the benefactor of all things unnecessary and frivolous, but it was still not a good answer.

He came up close to her, an inch from her face, with his index finger punctuating each word on her chest: "Manny should buy his own child toys. Leave mine alone."

It was at instances like this that she continued justifying Manny's existence, or rather *over*justifying his *over*existence in their lives; brushing him aside as an inconvenience, assuring Brendan that he was nothing. "He's just a friend," she told him in a voice that she hoped was tinged with a mix of nonchalance and disdain. "We have been friends forever, and he is in a bad marriage and just needs someone to talk to sometimes."

At times Brendan seemed to accept this, or Marie decided that his silence was acceptance. At times he even seemed to encourage it, outlandishly suggesting that she "go out with Manny" on a night she seemed distraught about something. If her signals were mixed, then so were Brendan's, although neither should have been so naïve. Marie knew that Manny was not nothing; but she still, after so many years, did not know what he was, and she would not compromise her marriage in the discovery process.

At nights she lay in bed wondering how all this would end, attempting to envision this cast of characters in five years or ten or twenty. She was aware that something had to fracture somewhere because it was ludicrous to think that this double-life could continue on indefinitely. How would it end? Would she get careless one day and leave something incriminating around? Would Brendan come home early from work and play out some dramatic movie scene in which a lover is hidden under the bed or in a closet?

In one of her psych classes – or was it simply Cosmopolitan magazine? – she read that women who are discovered having affairs are only found out because they *want* to be exposed, perhaps because they were only doing it for attention in the first place, or maybe because they couldn't take the guilt anymore, or their intention is to punish their mate, or whatever. These sinners subconsciously leave clues or take risks, then unload their dirty little secrets in a tsunami of pelting truths, relieving themselves and drowning their mates in icy cold unretractable reality as they shake their heads from side to side begging for it to stop, pleading for the calm ignorance of bliss once again.

Marie knew that she was not that kind of adulteress. She had no intention of opening any floodgates, not ever, and to that end she was true and meticulous. She kept no photos of Manny, not anywhere, nor any sentimental keepsakes. She did not allow him within inches of her until she called Brendan at his desk and verified that he was a solid distance away, and so that phone call itself became another molecule that Manny would not disrupt. She didn't introduce him to anyone she knew except Claire, and she did not allow even their hands to touch unless they were unseen, and even then it was a luxury that lasted only seconds. This stark scarcity of proof that they as one existed would haunt her someday, and that someday doesn't wait very long to arrive.

"If something were to happen to me," he said lightheartedly, "what would you want? Like, to inherit?"

"Your credit cards," Marie answered immediately, and then they started immediately on a possible scenario.

"I would be shot and bleeding in the street," Manny jumped into the game, "and I would call for you, and you would say, 'yes, I'm here, Manny,' and I would say I loved you, and…"

"And I would be like, screw that, what's the Amex number, Manny? The Amex number!" She laughed and so did he.

"You'd be like, 'there's a new line of American Girl dolls and my daughters don't have the whole collection! You can't leave me now!'" They enjoyed a fit of their own brand of humor, and the subject was dropped for a time.

"You are not going anywhere," Marie said finally.

Marie realized they did not discuss Manny's job enough, the nightly reality of it. Manny only talked about the people he worked with, or the jokes that they told, or how it compared to Hill Street Blues or NYPD Blue. He mentioned proudly that when he lined up "his guys" for a tour, he used the line from Hill Street – "Let's be careful out there," - and how he liked saying it. He talked about this guy or that as being "a really good guy," or how the term, "do the right thing" was a special kind of cop jargon. Once he told her that he was a completely different person at work; one she might not recognize or like.

"I never stop joking on the job," Manny told her, "but it's sick humor all the time."

They talked about cop culture and how cops are friends with cops and only cops, and sometimes Marie resented the exclusivity of it and tried to get him to deny the blue wall was anything more than an exaggeration. He would not. She still made it a priority to visit every precinct or office he joined for whatever amount of time, to lay her mark upon him there; to keep as familiar as possible with the world he knew. She recognized names when she called him at work –"84. Officer Santiago" – and said hello before asking for Manny.

"They all think I am just a cop bimbo, right?" she asked and waited for him to deny it.

"Nope." He said it firmly. "They don't. Do you notice they always get me? Wherever I am? Let me tell you something. They don't get me when my *wife* calls. They know the deal."

She nodded, satisfied, but he felt the need to enlarge the proof of his devotion.

"They all start by thinking you are a thing on the side. Let me tell you something, they all…no, most…have things on the side. They will tell me how much they love their wives, but that doesn't mean there can't be a side thing. It's allowed. It's okay." He stopped, setting up the next verse of his balcony scene.

"So, they are like, fine with me, er...having you. I tell them you are gorgeous, that you have a killer body." At this she winced.

"So, it's all good, right? But then I tell them our story. I tell them I love you. I say, 'if she would leave her husband, I'd leave my wife in a heartbeat and marry her.' This they are not cool with. They make fun of me then. Call me Romeo."

"If you hear them laughing when you call, it's not cause you are a 'cop bimbo,' as you said. It's because they are getting me with all these kissy noises. They are calling, 'Romeoooo...Juliet is on the phone.' Sometimes they stand around and listen to me talk to you, and say, 'awwwwww...true love,' shit like that. They say that they can always tell I'm talking to you because I look goofy."

"Sorry," Marie interjected happily.

"The thing is, Marie, I don't mind a bit. I should mind this disgusting misrepresentation of cop macho-ism. I don't. I love it. I love that they know who you are." He finished.

"Well, Manny, stop telling them I'm gorgeous and stop telling them I have a 'killer body.' I can't visit the precinct after you set me up like that. I could only be a disappointment." She wasn't fishing for contradiction or compliments. It was a real concern for her, to walk in there, on display, and not fill their expectations.

"You know, I know what I want from you, you know...should anything...happen," she said with uncharacteristic shyness.

"Recovered drug money?" he joked. "Diamonds from a jewelry heist?" He kept it up, but she was serious.

"I need a letter. I need proof of your feelings...in black and white. Something that I will always have, can always read again." She stared at him with what seemed like premonition, but it was only deep regard for the past and not fear of the future at all.

"A letter? I can give you that right now. You don't have to wait for my demise to get that from me. I'll have a sworn declaration by the end of the week, signed, sealed and delivered." He touched her face.

"No," she answered quickly. "You can't give it to me now. I won't have anywhere to keep it. I won't have any place to hide it. You have to write it, and you have to give it to someone you trust. That person will give it to me when...if...it ever becomes necessary."

"I'll keep it in my locker," he said. "A cop's locker is sacred ground. It's where I keep everything you ever gave me, sent me...everything."

"But..." She wanted to be done with this conversation but she had another question, "How will I get it? Will someone know who to give it to?"

"Someone will know. I tell someone at every house I go to. Fret not, Juliet." He was not as anxious to leave this touching demonstration of her feelings.

"Okay, then, Manny?" She touched his arm and looked into his eyes.

"Yes?" He moved in closer.

"You might as well wrap the letter around a wad of cash, then. Nothing says 'I love you' better than a pile of thousand dollar bills." She started laughing again.

"You suck," he said, but said nothing more, because her eyes had flitted across the clock and the molecules aligned.

****

The guilt had become a steady bass drum, beating on her consciousness slowly and unrelentingly, with no reward of blessed composition – its intention being only punishment – and constant enough to be ignored sometimes; while the passion still remained a sensual tango pulsation, always new, always taking her by surprise, always luring her to dance. Sustaining everything was the melody of their friendship; begun so long ago and seemingly unending.

Marie wrote the church newsletter, led Bible study in her home, and silently searched like a lawyer for loopholes in the Word of God, but it was no use. Even if the good Lord carelessly let her off the hook, there was still basic morality to contend with, and lying and cheating even offended the doomed nonbelievers. At best it could be understood but never really condoned, and Marie knew she would never come out of this unscathed or unpunished.

Her own father sometimes offered input, but it was not so very different from the kind of advice he imparted in her teenage years, completely free of judgment or guidance.

"How's Manny doin'," he asked most matter-of-factly, as if he were the only one in the universe who suspected nothing decadent in their alliance; allowing her to talk about him with the pride and ease of a devoted lover.

"He's good," she replied, and went on to impart the latest cop story or show him a gift Manny recently bestowed on her daughter; a large handcrafted doll house, which he admired and put a dollar value on – "Hey, those things ain't cheap, you know" – before nodding his head in satisfaction.

"He's good to you, that's for sure," Fred Meyers said in all his purity, with all due discretion.

"You don't think it's bad to have him around? I mean, like, bad for my marriage?" Marie asked him as a child begging a parent for discipline, but like any child, she was not providing her parent with enough information for any wise decision to emerge.

"Well," he said, "I'd imagine it burns your husband to have him around, don't you think?" Her father could do that. He could state the obvious without reprisal or judgment, tossing the moralizing right back into the lap of the guilt-ridden. He had not led the life of the saint, and instinctively knew without even being familiar with the verse what Jesus meant when he said, "Let he who is without sin cast the first stone."

"In my Bible group, they call it an 'unhealthy friendship,'" she coaxed him in his parental role of guidance and management, but he only looked again at the beautiful dollhouse with its tiny lace curtains.

"Seems pretty healthy to me!" he said and laughed, and she laughed, shaking her head at him.

"Yeah, we go furniture shopping every week to get things for the dollhouse," she conceded, and then they were talking about how expensive the miniature furniture costs and did she know there was a place right in Pennsylvania that had "nice stuff?"

Then, late at night, she looked at the dollhouse with its perfect country décor, emerging slowly like the dreams of some hardworking homeowners, and wondered what kind of family lived there. There was probably no adulteress at this fanciful address. There were no rooms corrupted and stained with illicit lovemaking. Marie touched the stairs, walked up them with her fingers. She and Manny had even done it on the stairs. He had pressed her there one day, out of view of any windows, and far enough from the front door that she could compose herself should a visitor drop by. Marie shuddered even when her finger caressed the miniature step that represented where the deed had occurred, as if stuck by some voodoo force, while her eyes traveled the rest of the house where normal life resumed.

I'll never be normal, she thought, and felt cheated. Instead of taking responsibility for all that stood between her and normalcy, she blamed whatever unknown forces there were for her deviance.

God has a voice that penetrates storms and rock and fills the expanse of the desert, and Morality sneaks its opinion into the ears of the unwilling, but it was the curious voice of Marie's children that began to unglue her. They were growing and they, too, had an emerging picture of what was customary.

"Mommy, is Manny your boyfriend?" Daniel asked her one night at bedtime.

"No, silly," she answered while every one of her senses stood alert, as well as her skin and hair and the marrow in her spine.

"Oh. I like him. Why isn't he your boyfriend?" Daniel persisted.

"Because I'm married. Married people don't have boyfriends. Manny is just my friend." It was a truth she bought for the price of denial, but it rang false against the simplicity of a child's candid perception.

"Oh. But he is your friend and he is a boy." Daniel bestowed on her the look that mother's cherish: he was completely untroubled and trusted entirely her ability to sort this out for him. He only had to wait for her mouth to open.

"Yes, but it's not the same thing. Like, I don't kiss him or hug him or live with him. It's different." She finished, failing him and failing herself.

"Oh. Right. Do you kiss daddy?"

"Of *course* I kiss daddy," she said, tickling his arm. "You know that I kiss daddy."

"Yeah. But not so much," he settled into his pillows and gave the signal that he was ready to close his eyes. "I kiss a girl at school sometimes. But we aren't getting married."

"Good to know," she stood, looking at his red curls that seemed to glow in the dark.

Not so much. Not so much. Not so much. She heard the words in her head for a week afterwards, keeping time with the beat of the unremitting drum.

Later, it was her daughter who sent out a sign, in the form of a disappointed look upon being picked up from preschool.

"Hi mommy," Grace ran toward her, "Can we go for ice cream?"

"Maybe," Marie asked, hugging her daughter. She was always moved by pickup time from school, after those brief but significant hours of separation. She loved the light that came into her child's eyes upon catching her, waiting outside the school doors, a light that may be more and more hidden as they grew older, but never really disappeared. Years later, as a teacher, she would watch parent-child reunions at dismissal time, and feel the same small lump in her throat as their arms entwined.

But today she spoiled it. She told Grace, "Manny is in the car," and Grace stopped walking.

"Oh," she said, just "oh," but there was so much disappointment in that single syllable.

"We can still get ice cream," Marie tousled her hair: *Give it back, Grace. Give back that sweet moment when all was good.*

Grace was walking slowly now, so Marie kept talking: "You like Manny," she said like every parent she didn't want to be.

"You guys talk too much," Grace declared, and said nothing more; not in the car, and they got ice cream the next day instead.

****

Brendan changed jobs, working for multi-millionaires who owned more Manhattan real estate then Trump. He was exactly what they wanted: handsome, white, charming and sly in a business meeting. He knew how to "play the game," as he would put it. His salary would increase steadily, but he would remain a penny-pincher, forever thinking of the future and rarely placing any value in the present, unless enjoyment could be obtained for free. There were sometimes free box seats from clients to Ranger, Yankee or Jets games, and these he bestowed upon his family.

Around the same time, Manny got a promotion of his own: He was made lieutenant. Marie knew that he had taken the test but not much more, so it was with some surprise that Marie got a late night call at home.

"Manny?" she asked incredulously. Brendan was away on business, but she still looked around to see who was listening. Manny did not call at this time.

"Marie, can you get out? Can you get out right now?" he asked, breathily, and she heard accompanying hoots and shouts around him.

"Er...well, I don't know. The kids are sleeping and...Brendan isn't here, and..." she let herself trail off.

"Marie, I did it. I was made tonight. I'm a lieutenant. They are all having a party for me, right now, right tonight. I want you there. Can you come?"

She could. She would. She found a way. She asked her single neighbor to come over, said she had an emergency, and could she stay in her house for a few hours? And then, Marie fled to Brooklyn, pride and tears creating a potion that accelerated her trip, and all the way she wished she were prettier, wished she was a knockout so that the cops would envy Manny. She wanted them to see what he saw, and understand.

She met them in some bar near the piers, and he grabbed her hand as she entered.

"I'll be sworn in, in a few days, and there will be a ceremony and a party, and all that. But Marie, *this* is the party. This is the real thing." He squeezed her hand tight and led to a group of people, most of who were familiar to her either by voice, name or appearance, but he named them again, one by one, and attached an anecdote to each.

And Marie listened and strove to belong, but a cop crowd is difficult to infiltrate; such is the nature of their lingo and their pride in keeping it that way. Still, she reveled in being there; and a few of them came up to Manny and patted him on the back.

"Look at him. He's got his beer. He's got his Tostitos. He's a lieutenant, and he's got his lady. Life is good."

She drove home in the wee hours of the morning after spending hours in his car, talking over the night's events, and then driving to some secluded spot to celebrate properly.

"I'll be sent to a new precinct," he said happily. "You know what *that* means."

"What does that mean?" she asked but she knew.

"Oh, let's see. New people to tell our story to. New dark places to scout out for absconding you. New nicknames, new adventures, new…"

She interrupted. "But you'll be inside now, right. I mean, lieutenants don't really go out, do they? Don't they just drive around and sign those little blue books? The ones that say they 'visited?' or something."

He loved when she paid attention, but he was shaking his head.

"Not me, Marie. I don't like to be inside. I'll be out there for as long as I have legs and a heart that can handle a mad foot chase." He smiled. "A few weeks ago some lieutenant died of a heart attack sitting his fat ass in a patrol car. That will not be me. I will go out in a blaze of glory, I swear."

"There's a ceremony," he told her again, "the 'official' one. Do you want to go?"

"I dunno. Is Madeline going?"

"Well, that's just the thing. If you want to go, then, well, there is always reason I can tell her that she can't come. Cops lie, did you know that?" he asked.

But she thought, and said no. Tonight was enough, she said, and he reassured her that it was; it was the real thing, like visiting a true local pub in a foreign land instead of one of the tourist attractions.

"Okay, call me by tomorrow if you change your mind," he said, and then they both felt that the night had ended, that she had to go.

"I'm assuming you won't let me book a room somewhere and spend the night?" and stopped. She had to go home.

Three days later, on the morning of the ceremony, she cursed her decision to stay away, and died not to be beside him, in a public display, on his arm. She called the precinct; she wanted to know where it was but they said it was short; she would never make it, and so she envisioned it, and cursed herself again for not choosing to go.

And then, in the early afternoon, the phone rang.

"Marie, look outside your door in three minutes," he said.

And there he was, fully uniformed, his new ranking shining on his arm, and behind him, a *police car*. He had driven a New York City police car over the Verrazano and the Goethals, and down her suburban streets, causing her neighbors unseen to stir, she was sure, but he was *here*.

"I knew you would be sorry you didn't come," he said, and she tried hard not to touch him, right there out on the street, to run her fingers as she used to over his shield. She closed her eyes.

"I would like a picture of us, both of us, together," he said. "Can we do that?"

She nodded, and they walked down to her single neighbor's house and she took the photo in front of her white fireplace with a Polaroid camera. She took it twice; one for him and one for her, and this became the only photo that existed of them together.

"Mommy, does Manny not have his own wife?" Now it was Kristin.

"He does, honey."

"But he likes you better? Does he like us better than his own kid?"

"No. But he likes you just as much as he likes Ariella."

"I know. That's why he brings us so much toys," Kristin finished with satisfaction, but Marie floundered in misery.

Manny had a beeper now, and gave her exclusive rights to the number. It was reserved for every matter she considered urgent, from the arrival of a hard-to-find toy that he must search for, to a persistent thought in her head, and of course, to warn him of any change to their plans.

"You rang," he called her back within minutes. "I was in the middle of chasing a mass murderer, but I stopped to call you."

"You don't chase anyone," she teased, because they had put him in the 63 Precinct, and he was, indeed, "inside." The NYPD didn't seem to care about his personal thoughts on this.

"I will be. This is temporary. What's up?"

She "beeped" for a reason: "Manny, I think we have to see each other less."

"Less? Less than practically never?"

"My kids…people…they are starting to ask questions."

"People? What people?" Manny's voice had an edge now, perhaps the edge of fear but also defensiveness. He was always ready to guard his position.

What people? Well, her organic democratic friend Sonya was sweet about it; saying that she thought it was "great" that they had such a good "friendship," and how it was also "great" that Brendan could be so "good" about it, and how every time she drove past the house, Manny's car was there. The pastor's daughter said a lot by always saying nothing at all, just smiling in a way reserved for the godly. Others just made little comments – the words, "second husband" came up quite a bit – and some were genuinely innocent, but the guilty do not interpret them as such.

And Claire...she had finally just told Claire the truth. Their friendship had reached that level where Marie figured that Claire knew, anyway, and was just being polite. Once it was out, Claire made a comment that stuck with Marie, and made her think, and made her cry.

"I figured as much. You are always very settled with Manny, very peaceful. You are never that way with Brendan."

She wasn't settled now. She couldn't solve this; could not find the equilibrium between right and wrong. It had been years – years! – and after each and every one of them she thought she would arrive at some solution. Marie wanted *something*; a crack of lightening, a cosmic shift, or maybe a severe bout of amnesia, something, *anything*, to stop this daily, weekly, monthly *failing;* failing her husband, her children, God, herself, and even Manny. She failed him as well, never really giving him what he wanted; only giving him a sampling of what it might be like.

"Okay," she sighed into the phone, "Okay, Manny. Just...maybe we have to be more...discreet...or something. I don't know. Forget it."

Manny sighed louder. Then he hung up.

A double life is just two roads headed for a breakdown lane. Marie was now speeding; waking each morning with her mind so in motion, it seemed to shake her body as well. She wanted to close her eyes again but it didn't stop the vertigo, any more than it would in any vehicle out of control. She needed to put her foot on the brakes, but she didn't know which road should be the one not taken. She couldn't know until she saw them both, but she could not see them both until the end.

More things happened during that time. Marie had nearly acquired her associates' degree, although it had taken twice the time to get this two-year degree. She held transcripts that she fondled like trophies, full of grades of "A" like lines of little teepees. She was fiercely proud of those grades even as she chided herself for placing so much value on them. Manny said she was "all about the validation," and it was true, and said affectionately, whereas Brendan said she was on an endless quest for reassurance, and it was said quite differently.

Another publication contacted her; asking if she would be interested in writing for them, and of course she agreed instantly. It was a free local paper, written for families, with a calendar of community events and regional attractions. It did not carry a name like Forbes, but it paid $75 and anyway, it allowed herself to keep calling herself a writer.

She also wrote her church group's newsletter, complete with photographs, for one day Brendan brought home a digital camera, belonging to his office but available for his use. Marie immediately begged him for a color printer as well which seemed almost magical to her to own, and he reluctantly agreed and off they went to The Wiz.

She made "to-do" lists each day, she studied them and checked them and fretted over them, and her time became constricted: school, and the church and the children and jobs tightening hard around her. When Manny stopped by now she had a "to-do" list ready for him as well, and he picked it up dutifully. His objective was still to buy them some time.

"What can I do to have five minutes of you?" he asked wearily, because he had a life to lead as well and Marie didn't take that into account. He drove from Queens to Brooklyn to work, then Brooklyn to New Jersey to be with her, and then back again; he had a child of his own, and a wife for better or for worse, and his own heap of bothersome daily matters, the small ones that strain the memory as well as the time.

"I can't catch up, Manny, I just can't," and he didn't say the forbidden thing, the thing that Brendan said, that she had taken on too much, and that perhaps she should give up something. He didn't sneer, and say that the things she did were largely insignificant, anyway, and existed only for her ego and not to put food on the table.

"You'll get it done," he said. "I'll help."

****

It was around this time that Manny began talking about Aileen O'Brien, a woman he worked with, and Marie, being too immersed in her own quagmires, took a bit of time to hear the warning sirens in her head.

"I dug a girl's car out of the snow the other night," he said and she should have wondered why this was significant, but she didn't. Manny liked women; liked them far more than men and not for the obvious reasons. He told her once that men are far too boring, and talked of nothing but food, including beer, and sex and sports. He said only a woman had the ability to provide deep and meaningful conversation.

Women, naturally, gravitated towards Manny for the same reason: he was caring and nurturing and safe. They sighed at his romantic tale of lifelong, undying love for one woman; some yearned to protect and care for him while others became more helpless upon discovering his need to nurture them.

"It's because you have too much estrogen," Marie told him earnestly. "That's what it is, Manny. We all have testosterone and estrogen, and if a guy has a high amount of estrogen, it makes…well, you."

"Great," he answered good-naturedly, "Could you share that with the guys who work under me. I'm sure they will be thrilled to hear my estrogen is high."

"Well, it doesn't mean you're *gay*," Marie educated him, "It just means that you are every woman's dream, but they don't know it. They don't find out until it's too late. When women are young, all they seek are testosterone-laden dudes who are out to abuse them, one way or the other. They ignore guys like you. Then, years later, they see you again, and think, shit, this is what I needed. Why didn't I ever notice him before?"

"Does this mean you're leaving Brendan soon?" He took her hand as if to propose.

"No," she answered. "It means that women are stupid."

But Aileen did not seem stupid and her motives did not seem innocuous. Her name began to pop up often in their conversations now, much like Manny's first partner Donna did long ago. Aileen was what was known as a "non-uniformed member of the police force," engaged to be married and dubious about the whole idea. She was Irish but not Kavanagh Irish, not staunch and gloomy and Pioneer pin Irish. She was fun-loving, stay-late-at-the-pub Irish.

"Aileen asked me to go skinny-dipping in the reservoir after my tour."

"Oh. And did you?" Marie looked up and Manny found gratification in her concern.

"Would you have cared if I did?" he asked her.

"Manny, let me make you understand something. I would have beaten the living crap out of you if you did. I would knock you down and kick you until you bled to death."

"Well," he said, "I guess we're clear on that, then. Can I hang out with her now and then?"

"Yeah, yeah, Manny, sure. Just don't start fucking reading Trinity, okay? Take it from me, it will not lead to anything but heartbreak."

And then came the fireworks; everything that happened next occurred in quick succession; boom, first one thing, and boom, then another, so close together that it was difficult later to distinguish which thing came first. Boom! Marie went to see the pastor of the church and then boom, Manny left his wife again, and then again, boom, she and Manny "broke up," for lack of a better term. They stopped. The end came and there was silence and dullness and the smoky scent of leftover brilliance. And she and Manny were apart, at last.

It was not her fault that the incessant drumming of shame and self-reproach and culpability grew louder and that the drumsticks themselves seemed to be held by those she loved the most. It was an illness, and it needed a specialist; a wound that needed a surgeon. And so, once again, Marie went to see her pastor. This time, she wrote to him first, to spare herself the long, tiresome story about how she "had this male friend." She wrote, and hoped Pastor Arnold, her neighbor's father, would not respond. She would take that as God's permission.

He took less than a week to call her.

"Marie? Darling. I got your letter." She would give him one thing: his voice was full of compassion; it brimmed with genuine concern and, dare she think it, sympathy? Could this be someone who might confirm that this was God's mistake; that although he was all-powerful, there were times when he let a few fall by the wayside?

"We have to meet," Pastor Arnold said. "We have to get you back on the right road."

Back on the right road? she thought. *Was I ever on it? I can't recall the scenery on that road at all.*

"Yeah," she said lamely, because every patient resists the treatment even if she asked for it.

"I'm a bit busy this week," he said (*Good, she thought, good*), but maybe sometime the middle of next week?"

"Oh, there's no hurry," she protested feebly.

"Marie, I think there is. I wish I could meet with you sooner. How about Wednesday? Say, 10 am, here in my office?" And it was done.

Now sin had an expiration date; and so she counted the days that she could use it freely before tossing it out. She did not spoil it more quickly by telling Manny about its diminishing quality, but instead drank it as fully as she could. He was surprised, to say the least, at how she set other diversions aside to attend to him, and misread the reason, and chattered even more about Aileen O'Brien.

One day he brought her a photograph, of himself, at a recent cop funeral. He was standing in front of a platoon of erect blue men, saluting on some random street in Queens. It was still easy for her to tell Brooklyn from Queens in any backdrop.

"Look at this picture," he breathed with expectation. "What do you see?"

"Ummm...an ugly Queens fence?" she answered.

"C'mon, really, look. Do you...see something?" She looked harder but he was asking the wrong question. He *was* getting to the point, however.

"I see cops, Manny," she answered, handing it back to him, and he took with a nod and tight lips.

"Aileen says this picture gives her goose bumps," he said. "The way I am at the head of this squad of men, and the way...well, forget it."

Marie was honestly sorry for giving the wrong answer, especially since she knew it was not the answer she would have given years ago, but they were older now, and more familiar. Then, suddenly, stricken, she realized something.

"Who took the picture, Manny?" she asked.

"Aileen did. She was there," he said, stating the obvious and then producing more shots, one of him alone in full regalia, including the black band across his shield that signified the loss of one of their own, and one of he and Aileen together.

Marie studied the latter one more fully. Aileen was certainly pretty but not beautiful. She was blond and freckled and her demeanor strutted fun and carelessness. Manny's arm was not around her, but they were standing very close.

"Manny, there is something that you should know," Marie said slowly.

He waited, and she began her rant.

"Give me the other picture." He did.

"First of all, I don't react the same to pictures like this because some things are assumed. You got that? You know how I feel about you, and you know how I feel about what you do. We've had jokes our entire lives about my reaction to you and this uniform.

She paused. "So I don't want to hear about how someone else gets goose bumps, and I don't want you assuming that your...magnetism...has worn thin. Got that so far?" He nodded.

"Okay, now is when you have to listen and listen hard. Your life is yours and I'm never leaving Brendan and you know that. But make sure you know this. If you sleep with someone else, you must come and tell me. And you can never, ever touch me again.

Not ever."

"And don't even try to keep it from me. If you are with someone else, I'll know. I'll see it in your face and I'll...smell it on you, Manny. I've known you for, what, 16 years? I'll know, and Manny, I will forgive you. But, I don't want you if you have been with someone else."

Her eyes filled with tears; she was being so unfair.

"This is not an equal partnership we have, you and me. You have always given more than I have, and I have always expected you to give more. But you are still the purest, most unspoiled thing that I have. The only relationships in my life that have not disappointed me are the ones that I have with my children, and the one I have with *you*. I don't *want* you with someone else's mark on you, you get that? Well, I know there is your wife, but..."

At this he finally interrupted.

"Marie? Stop. I get it. I've always gotten it. But Marie? I left Madeline. I mean, not yet, but I just got an apartment in Brooklyn. And I'll be out by the end of the next week."

****

Of course the pastor said exactly what she expected. There were no new pearls of wisdom in the spiritual realm. The Bible was written thousands of years ago, and translated and interpreted again and again, but there was no version that said, well, under some circumstances, some sins were permissible. There were no clauses or ambiguities there. Aramaic, Greek, King James, Good News for Modern Man, it didn't matter what version you preferred. All forbid the taking of the love of one man while married to another.

It was no use replaying the entire conversation with Pastor Arnold. It had been replaying in the background of Marie's consciousness her entire life. The only thing that really mattered was how it ended.

"There can be no further contact," the pastor said, "No phone calls, no letters, no visits...oh, and I guess I should say no emails nowadays, huh?" He chuckled like this was a simple thing.

"But pastor?" she was like a paying customer, and wasn't leaving without the full service. "Pastor, you aren't helping me. You are telling me what to do. You are not telling me *how* to do it."

"But I am, child," he said gently, "and so is the Lord. No phone calls, no letters, no visits, no contact of any kind."

Marie left, and she was angry. God was a wimp. She remembered that expression: "God helps those who help themselves." He was like the soldiers in the story that made soup from a stone. Of course the villagers were so fascinated by this power to make something from almost nothing that they came running with vegetables and meat and seasoning to enhance the miracle; but there was no miracle. There was only cunning and deceit, and a soup that in the end was made by themselves.

But it was delicious soup, nonetheless, and Marie had to begin to warm the pot. There was no better time. Manny was about to be a free man once again, and he had a chance at being happy with someone else. She had to do this, for both of them, and so she began to plan how.

Step one was arming herself with defenses, and for Marie, that meant enough love and passion to see her through. She began nudging Brendan more in the middle of the night, sometimes to make love to her and sometimes just to grill him with questions.

"Do you love me, Brendan?" she would ask and she didn't exactly hear him groan, but it wasn't his favorite question.

"Yes, Marie, I do," he said.

"Why?" He had been through this interrogation before, and floundered for the correct answers, but Brendan had always relied on books and experts and never on personal experience.

"Because," he said finally, "you are my best friend."

"Am I?" she asked him incredulously, noting how familiar his shape was on his side of the bed, a window behind him framing him in the moonlight.

He was silent now. He didn't want to play this game. Usually she either stopped or continued to ask why, but the stakes were higher this time around, so she continued.

"I am not your best friend, Brendan. You don't even like me." He tried for a moment to pretend he had fallen asleep and then he turned to her.

"You don't." She spoke softly and simply; she was only making a point. "You don't like anything about me. You don't like that I talk too much, you don't like that I spend too much money. You don't like my religious convictions or the job I do. Really, never mind what you don't like. I'll bet if I asked you to come up with just one thing you *do* like, you wouldn't be able to."

He touched his head as if it hurt: "I like the way you take care of my children."

"Ha," she went on. "I knew you would say that. It's a good answer. But you don't like that either. I am too laid back with them. I talk to them, I negotiate with them. I don't lay down the law. No, you don't like that, either."

Now he was resolutely silent. If he was permitted to say he hated her in that moment, he would have.

"You see, Brendan, you are like someone who says you think another person is beautiful. That you love her face. But then, you immediately start saying how you hate her eyes; they are too narrow, or you hate her nose; it's all turned up weird. And those lips...and then you realize that her complexion, the entire setting for her features, is mottled and ugly. But no matter what, you maintain that the person is beautiful. You refuse to acknowledge that in the breakdown, you don't like a single thing."

"Marie, I like things about you," he said, almost harshly, into the darkness, "but it's 2 o'clock in the morning. I don't like that you talk to me at 2 o'clock in the morning. I work. I need to get up in four hours. I have to look good. You don't work. You can look like shit. Goodnight."

Marie was stung and lay awake with her thoughts. *Actually, you don't have to get up in four hours. You will get up in closer to six, then monopolize the bathroom so my kids have to go downstairs to pee. Then you will beg me for a lift to the last possible train that will get you in on time. And I'll drive you because I, of course, don't work. And when I get back and the kids are at school, I will call Manny and ask what he likes about me, and he will have a list, and this is what I have to give up, a man who has a list of thing he likes about me.*

After that moonlit conversation, Marie began to summarize, like one assessing the value of a stock portfolio. Okay, she thought, so the spousal affection is showing no significant returns. But look at the rest of the packet: the children, the house, friends around the pool. Brendan was the loss leader that secured the other goods.

He had met them at the pizza house in the town two nights ago; Marie and the kids and two other couples and their kids, and he walked in late, and people beamed at him. It was a long table – actually it was several pushed together – full of animated children and spilled sodas and scolding adults, and Brendan walked in with his Irish cap on his head and a scarf around his neck and smiled a greeting at everyone, and Marie, sitting at the furthest end of the tables, got to survey the whole scene. People would think she was crazy, she thought. People wouldn't understand. He's beautiful and funny and intelligent; the perfect package. No one here would know that he is a package that was not possible to open.

****

The day Marie ended things with Manny was unplanned, of course, in the end. He visited; they talked. He was mostly full of news about his apartment and the scene with Madeline; how this time she had sat in front of the door and clung to his legs, begging. This drama thankfully supplanted any anecdotes about his Irish friend, although he did mention that she was having second thoughts about getting married. Big surprise there.

"Don't you have things to do?" he asked. "Don't I have things to do for you?"

"Nah," she said with resignation. She had been up all night, writing an article because nights were still the only interrupted time she had. Marie couldn't write a word unless she was sure that no one would call her name, by any title, whether it was "mom," or a cry or the barking of an unwalked dog. Sometimes, on the weekend, she would ask Brendan to man the ship so she could get something done but it never worked, because she would still hear the kids, calling for her, and the exaggerated sound of Brendan's voice saying, "Mommy is busy right now."

"I need a break," she said, and listened to him for a change, describing the moving process and hinting at the times he and she could have in his new love nest.

Finally, she stood, and took him by the hands. She hadn't looked at a clock nor removed her shoes, or locked a door or made a phone call. She had given him no clues, but led him upstairs to one of the guest bedrooms, and began to undress.

"You love me, Manny, right?" she asked as she took off everything; no mere lifting of skirts or blouses but a complete baring of her flesh and essence.

"So very much," he said, and she started undressing him now.

"If you love me, you have to do something for me," she said softly, and ran her hands from his shoulders to his hips, the stood back to look at him. She rarely saw him completely naked, only in disjointed states of undress, and it was a wonder that she could even associate his face with his body as she never saw them as one unbroken line. She never thought of him as a handsome man, one who would stop a table of people from their next bite of pizza with his salutation, but she had stopped thinking of his looks at all. What did it mean when you looked upon someone's face and all you saw was his soul?

She thought of a toy that her brother had years ago called Mr. Machine, a transparent walking robot whose gears were clearly visible through his plastic flesh, allowing all to see how he worked. In spite of the blatant exposure of everything inside of it, Mr. Machine never lost his appeal, and Marie watched his gears go round and round every time her brother wound him up. Marie could see Manny that way, not in separate parts but in a mix of mechanisms spinning together, and if there was one that wound him up, then she was that one.

Now she forced herself just to look at his surface, at the bronzed expanse of him, at the curious way a light brown penis looked when it was erect; the color of autumn leaves trapped between life and death. She took it in her hands and rubbed it against her belly like a dark pen on pale parchment, then took his hand and placed it on her breast to see again the stark difference in their color. She kept him standing there, wanting and wondering, while she performed her experiments, and completed her study. Why was *this* the ultimate betrayal, the fatalistic sin? She and he had shared thousands of thoughts, had meshed their minds in a delectable collision that had surely reached climax over and over, but nobody punished that. Manny could see through to her gears just as she saw his, but there was no shame in that. It was only this; the unveiling of clothing that remained evil. Ask Adam and he would tell you: God placed a great deal of consequence on attire.

She led Manny to the bed, never losing contact with his skin, touching some part of him with every backwards step she took, and finally, laying back and pulling him on top of her. She reached down immediately to take his organ in her hands, and placed it at her entrance; hovering, poised like one standing outside a room in which people were deciding his future. In fact, this is what Marie was doing: deciding Manny's future.

"Anything, Manny? Right? You would do anything for me?" she begged with her breath out of control.

"Anything," he responded and thought his confirmation was the key to his entrance, and pushed so that his tip penetrated her and she stopped him in the vestibule before he could get any further.

"You have to promise me that you will not see me anymore. Not at all. You have to get out of my life. Completely. Promise me and you can have me right now. I don't have to go anywhere. My kids all have playdates. Brendan is away on business. You can have me for as long as you want. Only promise me that this will be the last time."

What could he do? He promised, and he pushed, and he was in, and his future was decided.

****

Marie became a girl scout leader. Someone asked; and she said yes, and began immersing herself in the acquisition of merit badges and the ability to cook breakfast on a tin can. She did like the girls, but it was just another thing for the "Who's the busiest of all?" contest. It was also another brick in the foundation of the structure called, "normal." Marie was normal now.

The thing was, Manny kept his promise. He didn't call after that day. Not once. They had stayed in that room for many quivering hours, and if such a thing could be done "once and for all," than this was the day it happened. It was days before she stopped feeling him inside her, as if he had left some ghost of himself behind as a placeholder until he returned. But he never called. Not once.

Of course she told herself that she was relieved. Of course she never believed that he was capable of life without her. And of course, a pure life was easier to lead. There were no longer two roads headed for a breakdown lane. There was only one road with predictable scenery painted on each side, pristine and faultless with every leaf in place, and it was headed only for more road that looked exactly like it.

She kept her head higher these days. There was no longer a scarlet letter upon her chest. She belonged with everyone now; she was not self-excluded from the wives that spoke with possessive edges about their husbands or the bible thumpers that spoke with pride in their God. Her descriptions of herself no longer ended in "if" or "but." When they looked now, people got the entire picture of her; and even if it was a painting with its luster removed, Marie was still satisfied with the image.

Did Brendan even notice? She would ask herself that many times later when they sorted out her misdeeds; could he even tell her naughty from her nice? Could he sense her resolve or her pride or her devotion? It was doubtful. Marie would learn than Brendan considered nearly everything to be an affair: the time spent on her schoolwork, or getting ready for a girl scout meeting, or writing an article. Anything that evoked passion and dedication in her was cheating, in Brendan's mind.

She had taken to long bike rides at 6 in the morning, before anyone rose, to clear her mind and get into shape, although the latter seemed hopeless because she was now caught up in the life of bake sales and coffee clutches, and she was gaining weight. Marie noted wryly that not only was she on a straight and guiltless road, but she was also becoming a very neglected vehicle plodding along. There was something to be said about using one's body for the total satisfaction of another: you kept it fine-tuned for the occasion.

Did she please Brendan in bed, even then? She didn't know. She knew it was much more of an effort; and just this exertion alone simmered the ardor. One didn't want to think of sex as a step-by-step procedure that, when followed correctly, obtained the goal of orgasm, especially when one had the curse of knowing that it was possible to climax with one touch. Still, when Brendan did get on top of her, and entered her, her biggest excitement came from purity alone, for in her head came the whispered voice: This is my husband. There is no sin in this.

Did the children notice Manny's absence? Sometimes, but they were kids after all, ego-mongers engrossed in their own worlds, and unaware of the curse of time. They might say, "Next time Manny comes, can we go to that toy store?" but didn't notice the minutes passing without his arrival, and they certainly didn't notice the mourning in Marie's eyes.

And so Marie wore her sacrifice like a Superman suit; biking each morning and stopping on the footbridge each morning to pray to the God she had pleased. Staring at the brown waters of the Rahway River, she prayed in tongues, and called herself blessed, and finally, free. But she was still amazed that Manny had managed not to call her.

"Where is Manny these days?" Claire asked one day, as the children indulged in the freedom of afternoon play.

"He's...gone," Marie answered.

"Gone?" Claire's eyebrows raised. "Gone...where? Is this something we aren't talking about?

"Gone, out of my life," Marie answered, and in the face of a true caring friend, Marie's voice broke. "It had to be done."

"Well, yeah, I guess something had to be done," Claire answered, and miraculously, added, "I'm sorry."

Marie smiled bitterly. Claire was sorry. Would she find anyone in Bible group who would say they were sorry that Manny was gone? Or would she watch them wide-eyed and nodding, noting the beautiful power of God to restore such balance to Marie's life?

She had fought with Claire once, about religion and it was something that she would never do, not ever, again. It began with what should have been a harmless conversation with her daughter Kristin, who was growing up clear-eyed and blatantly honest. A serious child, she saw and she questioned, and even at a tender age, weeded out the drivel. Once, she asked her mother point-blank if she was a spoiled child, because, she said, "I have more stuff than my friends." Kristin did not accept palliative responses, either – "Of course not, darling, you are not a bit spoiled" – but demanded of her mother facts supported by evidence.

"Mommy?" Kristin probed one night. Whether the obscurity of nightfall inspired young philosophers, or if children just sought to delay the separation between themselves and their parents, one thing was certain: bedtime was the time for deep inquiry.

"Does everyone believe in God?" she asked.

Marie placed herself next to her child in bed and readied herself for a long explanation; how, no, not everyone believed in God and it was their loss not to do so, and in fact, we should pray for those who do not.

"I want to pray for someone," Kristin responded graciously, and again, her motives may have been suspect because her bedtime had now long past.

"Well," Marie yawned, "Let me think. You can pray for Claire. She doesn't believe in God." Which wasn't necessarily true, Marie thought later. In fact, her dearest friend only didn't believe in *Marie's* God, which may have amounted to the same thing to Marie; but such was the ego of a "true" Christian.

She wasn't prepared for Kristin's aggressive curiosity or her desire to fix the world, but the very next day, outside the schoolhouse doors, in front of all the pious and righteous moms of Glenfield, Kristin asked her friend's mother:

"Claire, why don't you believe in God?"

The argument that resulted was not severe, but it was Marie's first feeble attempt at evangelism. Claire stated once again that she placed her belief foremost in science, and certainly gave no credence to the God that punished and the religions that divided, and Marie explained to her that it was wrong to think this way and that she would be denied salvation. In the end, of course, the matter was dropped, but Marie couldn't help but feel jealous of those unburdened by the constraints of God; basking only in his love if, in fact, he existed at all.

And still Manny did not call, and Marie told herself that she was thankful; and also, that this proved something, didn't it? Manny had given her up, had let her go, and for what? One afternoon of lust. That was all it had taken. He agreed to no further contact with a woman he supposedly loved, and all it had taken was a day in bed. That proved something, didn't it? Marie allowed one day to negate some 16 years of testimony, because that was the only way through the bleak moments without him.

After three weeks, she gave up. Three weeks of throwing herself into her tasks, 21 days of complete attentiveness to her husband, placing him under 24-hour surveillance for some sign that he could love her as well, or as much, and then she gave up. She had an excuse: she had misplaced her license. It had happened once before a few years back, and she had replaced it without fuss because Manny was able to look up her license number. The DMV actually asked for this number on forms for lost licenses, as if one kept the 15-

digits in one's head. Without it, they required myriad methods of proof of identity.

Marie told herself she needed to call Manny; it was necessary, because he could do this for her, could spare her wasted time. It meant nothing; it was necessary, and he would be glad to oblige her. She beeped him.

And waited. Because he still did not call her back. And Marie began to panic.

Two more weeks had gone by, and Marie was beeping Manny daily. She was paralyzed. Images filled her head: he was not answering her because he was in his new apartment, having mad sex with Aileen; he was, in fact, hearing the beeps of desperation and laughing. "There she goes again," he was saying to his new uncomplicated lover.

Marie was frantic. Images pushed in front of her eyes as she attempted to write an article about the benefits of gardening for children. They sat like bricks upon her brain as she listened in biology class to the logistics of a chemical reaction. They knotted her stomach as she played in the yard with her children, and they seared her chest when she made love to Brendan.

It wasn't possible; she would not believe it. There had to be an explanation. It wasn't possible that Manny was not miserable; was not waiting for her to end his sentence, was not ready to call her back and say, "I waited as I always do."

After seven weeks, she called the precinct. The police officer that answered was one that Manny had mentioned was transferring out, so in her most untroubled voice, she began the conversation:

"Hey, Officer Rollins," she struggled with her heartbeat as she spoke, "I thought you were gone."

"Hey, Marie," he answered and she could hear his grin, the everlasting smirk of cops, "I thought *you* were gone."

She giggled, and said deliberately, "Oh, you know how it is. I'll never be gone," and then was stricken by his silence.

"Is Manny there?" she asked.

He wasn't. He was out on patrol, and Marie realized that this meant that she would have to call back later, and that everyone there would know that she had to call back and that he hadn't called her. Did they all know about Aileen? Were they all rooting for him? She wasn't a cop, per se, but she was one of them, wasn't she? And she was free: free of all the drama and misery that was Marie's package deal. Hell, she even lived in Brooklyn.

Mercifully, Manny did call her back. His voice was business-like; he sounded as though he were responding to the distress call of a battered wife.

"Did you need something, Marie?" he queried, and for the second time that night, she was struck down. There was nothing familiar in his voice; no tiny seed of tenderness for Marie to snatch and cultivate. She was never so out of her element and she wanted to say something babyish, like, "Talk to me the right waaaaayyy." Instead, she described her license dilemma and he said he would take care of it.

"I'll call you back in a day or two when I have it, okay?" he said and then she started to ask how he was -- *did he miss her?* -- but he abruptly ended the call, saying, "Gotta go, I'm on patrol tonight."

A quiet hysteria filled her like fluid in her lungs. Her breath squeezed by in tiny gulps and her head spun as if oxygen-deprived.

"It's over now," she whispered, "Over. I need to leave him alone. This is what I wanted," but the next morning, in the dawn hours, she reached a different conclusion.

It was like a mathematical equation. She had just recently been required to take algebra again, and although she claimed to hate math, Marie enjoyed the neat solving of those equations; skillfully maneuvering the numbers like organizing a messy room until only one each remained on opposite sides of the equal sign. It was satisfying to see something so long and complex and seemingly unfixable could be reduced to something so safe and obvious.

On that morning, Marie didn't pray on the footbridge. She analyzed the sixteen years of Manny, from Arthur Treachers to the phone call yesterday, and she put every aspect of their bond in its proper place, discarding nothing, because you couldn't do that in algebra, either; simply toss out the numbers you couldn't get to fit. One thing had to cancel out another, until only the barest proof remained. She sat down on the bridge and early morning walkers stepped around her, and she calculated, methodically, looking for the simplest term.

"Oh my God," she said to herself at the end, but she still wasn't praying.

He is my first thought in the morning. My first thought when I see something interesting, good or bad. He is my best friend. He is the only one that I feel safe talking to, or being irrational in front of. Physically, he is the most satisfaction that I have ever received. He reads my body, he reads my thoughts. He never criticizes me; and he is both security and excitement at the same time. He is...a soul mate?

"Oh my God," she whispered to herself again, "I love him. That's what it is. I love him. When you love being with someone, and love talking with someone, and love sleeping with someone, then, you love him."

At this, she stood, and lifted her bike, but didn't mount it. She slowly began to walk it home; noting that it was getting late and it was time to wake her kids for school. She should have ridden, but continued to walk, dazed, and whispering the words again and again in time with the spokes turning on her tires. *I love him. I love him.*

Then she turned her attention to the sky. "Listen, Lord. I love Manny. I love him. And there is nothing that you can do about that." And got on her bike and sped the rest of the way home.

****

Apparently, there was nothing Marie could do about it, either. After the initial exultation of discovery, reality came in to bite at her heels. She left her bike in the driveway and went upstairs to wake her babies.

Colin, at 12, was quick and humorous, but he could argue like an attorney, always finding the chinks in anyone's armor and invading them relentlessly. His teachers called numerous times to say, "He will not accept my authority. He follows me around the room to argue," and Marie would have a "talk" with him, and then he charmed her, admitted she was right and promised to be better. He had a wealth of friends and was out the door each day with a glove on or a football in his hand.

Daniel was now 9 and he was the sensitive one. He seemed to know when Marie was tired, and offered to help her with something. He came into her room at night to brush her hair. He bought her gifts, like a little butterfly necklace he found for $1.00 at a street sale. He, too, had Irish wit – actually, they all did – but it was tempered with compassion, and a need to do the right thing. His teachers told her that "Daniel will never have an ulcer" because he was calm and sure. "Ms. Kavanagh, even if he is late in the morning, he never walks any faster. I watch him from the window and he just ambles along like he's got all day."

Seven-year-old Kristin was her bull, but she was sadly unsure of herself. Learning disabilities had made her self-conscious, and she sat in her room memorizing whole books so that she could read them to the class at snack time and pretend that she really knew the words. She was analytical and evaluated herself and the world daily.

And Grace. Grace was only four. She was Marie's co-survivor of cancer, growing under her tumor and depleting her mother's system as she took the life that was given her at conception. She was positively joyful. She smiled all the time. She loved everyone. Grace stood out from the rest of the four, being the only one with blond hair and blue eyes, as if she was destined to radiate sunshine.

Marie woke them, one by one, to start the day, summarizing each in her head, calculating the upset to their lives individually should Marie do anything to act on her newly revealed emotions. She watched them leave the innocent, protected haven of sleep and enter a world that they assumed would be equally safe. It was their parents' job to see that this was so.

Marie sighed as she woke them. *There was just no way, no way.* These feelings were nothing more than another curse, set down upon her. Still, she felt liberated by them, because at least she *knew*. She no longer needed to hate herself for the sick fatalistic attraction she held for Manny; she no longer needed to spend hours trying to figure it out so she could defeat it. What she needed to do now was tell him. However futile her feelings might be, she needed him to know they existed.

This also proved to be a challenge. She couldn't reach him. She beeped him but in pressing the numbers she could not convey her urgency, and so he received the sound from the instrument in the same tone as any other. Perhaps he wondered what else she had lost that he could help replace. *Oh Manny,* she telepathed hard, *it's different this time. Please know it's different this time.*

He didn't, and another week went by. Marie hadn't seen her friend in three months, and she missed him in muscles that felt atrophied and underwent spasms of sharp pain. Where *was* he? What was he doing?

Brendan, unmindful of her months of devotion, now noticed her defection.

"What's with you?" he asked, "You seem...crazy."

"I don't know," she answered wearily, "I guess I have too much to do."

"Well, stop doing some of it," he answered quickly, "There is no need for you to bite off more than you can chew."

Too late, honey, Marie answered silently, *my whole life has been more than I can chew. In fact, tomorrow I am going to swallow some pride.*

She hated doing it, but she called Manny at the precinct. She closed her eyes as she held the receiver, thinking of what she would say to whatever officer answered; how would she convey that this was not a call for their entertainment? As the tone stung her ears repeatedly – one ring, two rings, three – she prayed for someone anonymous to answer who would have no incentive for jerking her around. Someone who did not know "the story." Someone who...

"63 Precinct, Lieutenant Torres," and she felt herself jump.

"Manny? It's me. We need to talk. When can I talk to you? I need to talk to you." She had never felt so uncertain.

He sighed long and deep. Finally, he said:

"You want to talk. Okay. When can you come to Brooklyn?"

Marie did what she had to do, farming out all her children to separate resources and getting her affairs in order like one contemplating suicide. She told all the appropriate lies to free herself for an afternoon, then got in the car and headed for Brooklyn, to Manny's apartment. He wanted to meet there.

They did not talk immediately. Marie got lost along the way, literally and figuratively; she had difficulty navigating the one-way streets of the borough that once was her neighbor, and she had more difficulty finding her way with Manny. She entered his home – a sun-filled, sparse but pleasant abode – and immediately began looking for signs that he had shared this space with another. She found nothing, but what did that mean? Had he hidden things?

He did not help her. There were only three rooms to his apartment – bedroom, living room and kitchen – and one could take it in with one panoramic glance, but in such snug quarters, he still managed to keep his distance, side-stepping her like a boxer in the ring when she approached. And he waited for her to break the silence.

"It's nice," she said at last. *Did you have sex with anyone here?*

"Yeah. I like it. Want something to eat?"

"No." *Was she better than me?*

"Drink?"

"No…thanks." *Do you still love me?*

She had called this meeting but now she didn't know how to put it in session, none of the questions rattling her mind being appropriate. She had freed her afternoon, but it was not enough time; travel time alone had stolen half of it and she was losing her chance.

Marie walked up to him and captured him in the corner. Like last time, she began to undress him, and he watched, and she was afraid she saw only amusement on his face. She had an odd, unpleasant flashback to her teenage days, when sex was all she had to give and no boy treated it like a gift; only the foolish offerings of a girl he would never call again after it was over, and in fact, he would be thinking of something else to do before his penis dried and resumed normal size. Had it come to this with Manny? Was she just a freebie? How strange to be so unsure of someone she was once so sure of.

"Make love to me," she said, and he did.

It was deliberate but not earth shattering; like an initiation but not a celebration. Afterwards, he made her an omelet and she willed herself to speak and state her purpose, but it was late now and there was too much to say. Naked, she went into the bathroom to splash water on her face, leaving the door open and checking in the mirror to see if he watched her. He didn't. She needed some sign of yearning but he would not give it to her.

Slowly, Marie dressed. "I have to go," she said, and her frontal lobes screamed, *Stop me, Manny! Tell me not to go. Beg me to stay!* But he didn't even watch her dress, nor did he dress himself entirely, and she realized that he was like the boys from long ago who didn't even walk her home when they were finished with her.

She made the short distance to the door, then turned, because this was it; the deciding moment between claiming him again or doing another round of futile calls to his beeper that actually seemed sent to empty space.

"Manny?"

"Hmmmm?"

"Will you see me again? I can't keep coming here. You know that. Will you come to me again?" She was going home but she was already lost.

"Marie? Do you want me to see you again?"

"Yes, I do. I do, that's why I'm asking." She put her hands up to touch him again but he took a step back.

"You're sure?" he asked as if speaking to a child making some final decision on a flavor of candy.

"Yes, Manny, I'm sure." Her eyes filled with tears but he remained unmoved and she was again stunned by his resistance, and brushed them away.

"Then, Marie, I will see you again. Call me." He finished, opening the door to let her out.

She lingered. "You don't answer when I call you," she said desperately trying to hold some apparition.

He kissed her lightly on the cheek.

"I'll answer," he said, and there was nothing else to do but leave.

****

In love, someone always has the upper hand. This isn't deliberate; it just is. Throughout a partnership, each lover has a turn when he or she is the needier, or the more insecure. One of them will have a time of requiring more validation, more assurance, or maybe just more snuggle time, and this essential puts the other in a place to give or not give; to bolster the wanting loved one, or instead, to sit back and use another's naked need to feed his or her own ego. In fact, "upper hands" are delegated by the one who reveals desperation, and are kept by the one who revels in it. The only healthy bond, then, is one shared by two people who have already secured their own individual confidence, and feel no need to play the power games.

Marie had never been in the upper hand position with Brendan. She had lived their life together as a small insignificant beggar at the foot of his large throne; begging for love, and compliments, appreciation and babies and money and permission. If she captured his positive interest, even for a moment, she noticed the way you notice one tiny cool breeze on the hottest day of the year. Instantly, your head turns, and you try to stay in the line of that breeze for as long as it cools your clammy neck, knowing full well that it will not be long. One day, in class, Marie found herself absentmindedly doodling on a notebook margin and saw she had drawn herself and Brendan, he larger than her, and higher up, and contained in a box of some sort, sealed away from her; similar to how she described him to Manny years before.

With Manny, Marie always had the upper hand, but if she had drawn them in a doodle session, it probably would have looked different: she would imagine herself high up but only because his arms had held her there, above him. She would picture him as small, perhaps, but not his arms, for it was always his strength that kept her on that pedestal.

Now those arms were gone, and Marie was left to jockey for position. She discovered that with loving him, she no longer wanted him to deny himself to please her. She did not want to feed upon his insecurity; giving him the firm impression that should his arms fail, even for a moment, that he would lose her. She no longer wanted to thrive on his day-by-day lack of guarantees from her, always fearful of disturbing the air in the room in which she breathed.

And so, when Marie returned home from Brooklyn that day, and tended to the needs of her flock, and waited for nightfall and Brendan's departure to bed; she sat down and wrote Manny a letter, and told him finally, that she loved him, and how she came to know that this was true, and how sorry she was to have never known before. She had always written far better than she spoke, and she summoned all the eloquence and precision she possessed, to run through her veins and be spilled in ink form upon the page. She did not check it for errors because she knew there would be none, but sealed it in an envelope as soon as it was complete.

Marie mailed the letter to Manny's Brooklyn address on her 6am bike ride, and that week, she didn't call him at all. She waited, and three days later, he called.

"Okay," he said when she answered, "What day can I stop by?"

Was that April? – Or May? – when Manny finally entered her kitchen through the side door, and leaned against her counter. He had a cassette tape with him, the song

"Everyday" by Phil Collins, and he popped it in the player on the counter; then folded his arms as it played. He seemed to have difficulty looking directly at Marie, as if he were shy of her blatant affection. He just folded his arms, and leaned back, and the music played, and Marie noticed that he had very muscular arms. She had never noticed that before, and wondered if she were blind in this as well, or had he been working out these last few months? She didn't ask him. She was pleased just to notice them; to notice *him* at last.

They went through all the motions of her day, and didn't talk until Marie got all her children to bed; Brendan was fortuitously away again. Then they talked, partially like old friends, and partially like new lovers, and partially as partners negotiating the rules of a new deal.

He was cautious, and she could feel it. While Marie wanted nothing more than to convey her joy in her transformation; Manny wanted to search for flaws in her contention in order to determine its ultimate value.

"But Marie," he interjected, "You made me make a deal with the devil. You tossed me out of your life like trash."

"I know, I know," Marie nodded, "but…"

"And I went," Manny continued, not allowing her to brush this aside, "because it was what *you* wanted. And I swore long ago that I would never be Brendan. That I would never drag you down. And this was what you wanted, and I would be a fucking hypocrite if I didn't give it to you."

She started to move in, to hold him, but he held her back, looked into her face, and kept talking. "Because I told you that I cared more about your happiness than my own, and that sounds like bullshit, but it wasn't, Marie. So if you wanted me to go, then I had to go. But Marie?"

She waited, keeping her hands dutifully at her side, nodding slightly to indicate that she was listening.

"Marie, you can never do this to me again. Never. I'm not asking you to leave

Brendan, I know how you are about your kids, and maybe I love that about you, too. But you can't do this to me again, toss me out and ask me back, and toss me out again, not for God, not for the neighbors, not for anything. I'm pretty sure I never demanded anything before, but, well, that's it."

She promised, simultaneously breaking so many other vows she had made to others, and herself. They talked in the dark for hours and then he left, and at the door, he asked, "So where does this leave us? What do we do now?"

"We do our best," Marie answered, "and that's all. We just do the best we can."

Marie called that time the "courtship." She told Manny that at last, he was going to know what it was like to be on the receiving end of ridiculous, uncontrolled affection; that she would seek ways to win him over as if he had not been already won. She sent gifts and cards and letters, some to his apartment and some to the precinct. He loved a song called "Broken Arrow" by Rod Stewart, and she managed to find a gold pin in the shape of a broken arrow and sent him that, as well as an ornate bottle of rainwater. She sent him photographs of the recent solar eclipse, writing something goopy equating the obscuring of the sun with the feelings she had never shown, but nonetheless, the sun had been there all along.

He took much flack from the boys in blue with the profusion of mail that kept arriving and one day, he called her up.

"You gotta cut this out," he said, "They're killing me here."

"Awww, c'mon, Manny," she replied, "You can't tell me you don't enjoy this."

"Oh, I love it," he admitted, "but we need to temper all the gushy stuff with a little hardcore. This stuff passes through at least ten sets of hands before it reaches me."

"What are you suggesting, Lieutenant?" she asked sweetly.

"Write about how great I am in bed," he answered, "Be very descriptive. And of course, send *postcards*, Marie. *Postcards.* That way at least thirty people will read it before I do."

She didn't know if he was kidding or not, but she complied. She basked him in an avalanche of risqué eloquence, some original, and some from others who had known the satisfaction worth writing about. Marie sent them, and half the 63 read them, and Marie had never known Manny so happy. He was on the top of the world; he had nearly everything he wanted. Are we always destined to lose something once we acquire too much? Everyone talks about the misery of "rock bottom," but people rarely mention the danger of the other extreme in escalation. There is, at least, an end to plummeting; but a heady, reckless rise knows not where to stop.

"Other" things happened during that time, and Marie would always remember them as "other" things, and would forget in which order they happened. It wasn't that they weren't significant: they *were*. It was just that Manny was a constant, thereby regulating everything else to being a series of unrelated things; things to take and overcome or experience one at a time. It wasn't that Marie stopped feeling guilt. It was that she stopped feeling that there was anything she could do about her guiltiness. Loving Manny removed her culpability and self-reproach and became simply the card she was dealt.

She began sharing him more, mostly with Claire, as if he were now a boyfriend and no longer an illicit affair. This, too, brought Manny a parcel of joy. He felt normal. He talked freely, told stories of the past, and made fun of Marie's religious convictions mercilessly with Claire on his side. He had something that he never had before: someone in Marie's life that *knew*; knew, and did not judge or try to save Marie's soul.

One day, over precious tea time, a Claire asked her a question: "You know, you and Manny always talk about Queens. I would really like to see it. The place where you grew up."

Marie was delighted. Now far removed from the scene of her childhood, she had become immensely proud of it, as if it were the scene of a battle she had won. She could not believe that anyone else would express any interest in the place, however, and set a date to visit the following week.

Driving her friend around, Marie passed the place of her birth, her first home, street corners and alleys that carried a piece of her past; all the while matching each landmark with an anecdote of some kind: "This is where I was first kissed," "This is where Ray worked." Inevitably, she led Claire to Arthur Treachers. It was still a Hallmark shop, but bore the same yellow and green colors adorning the brown glass where Marie first checked out her reflection before entering 17 years earlier.

She stopped and stared, and held back her tears as painfully as if she were inhaling water. "And this, Claire, is the place I'll never be sure about. Whether it was a blessing or a curse that I walked in here. What would be different if I had just kept going."

Claire understood moments such as these, and never spoke just to fill an empty space. They went on from there to a diner on Jamaica Avenue, and Manny met them there, an aura of excitement tingeing the air around his skin. Manny was perpetually excited then; a man who seemed to jump out of bed in the morning, perhaps sleeping with one foot on the floor in the first place.

"The neighborhood's changed, huh, Marie?" he asked, but she didn't think it did. Only her perspective had been altered. She did not want to live back in her old borough, but could not help but see that it was a place full of life and substance, where people struggled with more than their lawns and the police actually had real work to do.

He kept talking, trying to draw her into a memory lane trip, but she shushed him; always leery of conversations that became too personal between them and left her friend out. Claire, however, seemed impervious, even genuinely interested, so Marie leaned back against the red vinyl of the booth, and watched them; her two closest friends, one old, one fairly new, surrounding her like some plush cushions in an asylum designed for those deathly afraid of sharp edges.

Manny was headed for work, so they followed him for a while before he exited in Brooklyn, and although she and Claire were contentedly engrossed in conversation, Marie watched her lover leave the Belt Parkway on the ramp until he was completely out of sight.

It was one of the images that stayed with her; watching Manny first leading her and then disappearing from her sight, and feeling his presence nonetheless.

Claire noticed, and stopped mid-sentence to look at her. "Something you want to say?" she asked.

"Yes," Marie breathed, "I want to say, want to ask…Claire, how does anyone give something like him up? How do you let something like him go?"

"I don't know," Claire acquiesced, "but it doesn't appear that you are ever going to let him go anyway. So I guess the point is pretty much moot." Months later, however, she would once again be driving with Claire and the issue would arise again, this time demanding a more solid answer.

Marie's father had a heart attack "in that time," and she would rush to his side, full of fear that she would be soon be an adult orphan. He survived but the brush reminded all his children of his mortality, and like anyone with aging parents, Marie began to fear her telephone if it pierced the silence of her home at an odd hour. If the instrument rang late at night or before the waking hours, Marie heart jolted, and she stared at the instrument like an enemy she was forced to touch; tentatively separating the receiver from its cradle.

"You know what I was thinking, all the way, on the drive to you, dad?" she would tell him later. "I was thinking, 'Not yet.' It can't happen yet. I'm not ready yet. I know it's out there, but not yet. I was afraid you would be happy to be joining mom and give up the fight."

Her father laughed boisterously, as nonchalant about death as he was about life: "Don't worry, Marie. I ain't ready yet, either. There are still things I gotta see. I gotta make sure that your sisters end up okay. I have to see your baby sister have kids of her own. And other things…" He drifted off, then said again with more conviction: "So…*not yet.*"

Fred Meyers would end all his conversations with Marie with those two words – not yet – from that day on, always and thankfully listing more things he needed to see or do before moving to the other side. At times, he would add other phrases, like, "Any day above ground is a good one," a line he picked up from an Irish writer and actor named Malachy McCourt. Her father's optimism would reassure Marie, as if vows and platitudes alone could keep a person's breath in his body.

Still, there were many reasons for her father to stick around, as his family was in constant flux; instability becoming the cornerstone of their lives. There were divorces and remarriages and more marital discourses the second time around, and babies arriving like broken branches in a storm. The discord kept her father a parent, still needed by his grown children for babysitting, and emotional support, for fathering and grandfathering.

"If your mother was here, she'd have known what to do about this," he'd say often, but the truth was, she wouldn't have. Often there was nothing at all to do but listen and sympathize, and Mr. Meyers knew how to commiserate without advising or "I told you so's." His belief in his own shortcomings as the wise parent made him all that much wiser. And, as always, he accepted Manny the way Marie now accepted him: as a simple fact of life.

"You know, your pal came to see me when I got back from the hospital?" he semi-asked, a surprised pleasure in his voice. "Came by after dropping his wife at Roosevelt Field to shop. Said he can't take walking around the mall."

Marie smiled secretly, knowing two things: first that of course Manny had visited her father and also noting that with *her,* he could walk around a mall for hours. Still, she listened to her father's version of the visit, noting where it coincided with Manny's account, and then stopped when her father asked a question:

"I thought Manny wasn't with his wife anymore, though? Didn't you tell me that?"

She had, but this was another thing that happened during "that time." Manny returned to Madeline. He asked Marie first, and said it was temporary, but Marie understood the strange phenomenon that affected them both when they became so happy together: it made it all that much easier to deal with the parts of their lives that were imperfect.

In any case, Manny wanted to be a good father. And so, he dismantled his haven in Brooklyn and deposited all his worldly goods in Marie's garage, a hope chest of items kept as insurance of a different future: one that they might share in the same space. Marie spoke of it now as a possibility, a remote one, for sure, but at least one that existed. For now, they both had children to think about and Manny moved back home.

Then one day he arrived at her door with his usual fervor heightened, and words in his mouth waiting to tumble out like flowers in a fallen vase. He walked deliberately close to her, took her hands and squeezed them hard, trying to make her feel the unrestrained thrill in his muscles.

"I'm getting transferred, Marie. I'm finally out. I'm going to the 7-0. You probably heard of it, it's been on the news a lot. It's one of the busiest precincts in Brooklyn. And Marie? I'm going to be back on the streets."

Chapter Thirteen: "Let's Be Careful Out There"

Now Manny was full of stories, and since they had both recently joined the age of technology, he often shared them by email as soon as he arrived home after midnight. Or, if Marie happened to be online herself, he sent an instant message and they would chat for hours; Marie climbing into bed with only a small amount of time left to sleep.

Last night was a night to remember, he wrote. *We had a guy who committed suicide by hanging himself off a tree. He was probably "hanging around" (a joke I used all night) for two days before a guy on a nearby elevated subway noticed him and lead us to him. Note: I also used the joke, "I'm sure he was well hung" all night…I know…I know childish at best.*

Of course one of my Sergeants did manage to pull a groin muscle in the process of going over the fence so we could get to this suicide victim…and of course when I visited him in the hospital I joked that I didn't think he had any balls that could get pulled anyway. He threatened to kick my ass when he's back on his feet. I've got to be careful since he is 6 ft. 2inches tall and weighs about 260 lbs. I'm not that brave, so I threatened to never let him borrow my jeep again. He loves to drive my jeep, I guess because of his large size. I forgot to tell you that I always drive or am driven in a Blue NYPD Bronco (OJ type vehicle). It's the lieutenant's vehicle but I sometimes trade with one of my Sgts, because you can't turn corners too fast in a jeep, and trying to beat my younger cops to jobs makes the night go by a lot faster.

There was another incident where another Sgt and his driver were struck by a vehicle that ran a stop sign. The vehicle attempted to leave the scene and was pursued by police cars and subsequently on foot. He was apprehended. Oh yeah, he didn't know he struck a NYPD vehicle because it was an unmarked vehicle. I had to go to the hospital again because that Sgt and his driver were slightly injured.

Then there was an armed robbery of a Chinese Food Store by 3 masked (hockey) black gunmen. Two sector cars just happened to be a block away and a tremendous footchase took place. I'm happy to say that two out of the three bad boyz were caught and both were armed w/handguns. I can still run pretty fast for a 40yr old guy.

There was a big accident near the pct. (No dept. vehs involved) No major injuries but very visual. I never saw a taxi w/a brand new (29 miles on the odometer) car sitting on the hood. I'm not kidding, all four wheels were on the taxi's hood.

And last but not least I got to torment the Midnight lieutenant, because one of the midnight officers was involved in an off-duty incident in a Lover's Triangle with his apparent male lover and another male. I renamed the midnight platoon, "Pedro's Homos" after their leader Lt. Pedro Sanchez. He's a great guy. We went to the academy together and worked together as rookies in Spanish Harlem…you know…those days when I wore my hat visor so low over my eyes. Don't say I'm childish, he torments me at every opportunity.

Well that's about all the high points, as you can see it was the kind of night I live for. If you tell Claire about this letter be sure to tell her about cop humor…we are not insensitive to people killing themselves and we are not homophobic.

Did you get all your work done? Didn't you have a bio test? I hope today is less stressful for you. Pardon the typos but I just got home, it's 3:30am and I'm tired. When can I come by?

Marie printed the email; saved it as an example of irony. She had also been up until about 3am, writing an article about catering. What were the ups and downs of having a party catered versus doing the work yourself, and where can you find the right caterer for the event you're having? Marie smiled; shook her head. She had barely left her computer, but Manny hoped that today was less stressful for her; while he had just finished the "kind of night he lived for."

We sometimes think that words can guard us or save us. Children think so; feeling that putting 'please' in a sentence will achieve the proper result of candy or a toy, or that by 'calling' the front seat in the car, no one could dispute their right to be there for the entire length of a boring trip. This assertion does not disappear with maturity, however, because mothers will still tell their children not to run on a concrete surface or not to forget their lunch or not to lie, and believe it enough to ward off these behaviors, or at the very least believe that saying them alleviates them from all blame when a mishap occurs: "Didn't I *tell* you not to do that?" a shrewd mom might say, never relenting until her offspring takes full responsibility for his or her own pain. Only then is she redeemed.

At some point, grown-ups realize that spoken words can fail, and they begin to write things down, get them notarized, or pay lawyers to phrase them properly and send them by registered mail. A man could no longer claim that "his word was good," or his "words were his bond," and a woman who believed in the strength of her declarations would soon find herself robbed blind.

Soon after Manny entered the 7-0, Marie began admonishing him to be careful. She did not make a big deal of it; she merely stated the words as punctuation for all talks that preceded his leaving for work; or at the end of mealtime calls made during his tour. Sometimes she softened it, using the words of the lieutenant from Hill Street Blues – "Manny? Let's be careful out there" – a line he had taught her since she had never actually watched the show. With each dynamic description of one of his typical nights, Marie armored him anew with auto-piloted words of caution. Even as she chastised herself for being silly, she experienced a niggling unease if she forgot to say it, and called him back, and put it out of her mind. She had told him to be careful, and he would be.

Grace was hospitalized with a severe respiratory infection while Brendan was out of town, and Manny rushed to baby-sit her other children while Claire accompanied Marie to the emergency room. Marie spent days with her, gazing at her tiny sleeping body in the oversized bed, her small belly retracting with each jagged breath she took, and the strip across her index finger registering oxygen levels that teetered dangerously below normal.

Marie feared that she was getting careless; having established that there was nothing one could do to stop loving another, she prayed that she was not forsaking the others in her life that needed her. She swore silently to herself that nothing whatsoever could happen to her children while she was with Manny. "God help me," she said to him, "if one of them gets hurts while I'm in bed with you, Manny. God help me. It cannot happen." And redoubled her efforts to be ever vigilant.

Brendan surely felt helpless being so far away while his child was suffering, but when he got back, he expressed different concerns.

"He slept in our bed, Marie. The kids saw him."

"He slept on our bed, not in....and so? He was taking care of our kids, did you get that?" Marie's confusion was partially forced.

"There are sofas all over this house. There's a guest room. He didn't have to sleep in our bed. Why did you let him?" It was there, in Brendan's face, the pulsating muscle that indicated severe tension, and Marie felt sorry for him.

"I didn't *let* him, Brendan. I wasn't *here*. I was sleeping on a sofa myself, next to my *baby*. And you weren't here, either, or you would have been sleeping in your own bed." She felt the need to transfer some of the culpability.

"You could have called someone else...my sister, or father...or someone. You didn't have to call him." His voice was rising.

And so was hers. "I called who I know. It was late at night. Grace couldn't breathe. I called the person who I knew would come. I called Claire too. I wasn't going to spend hours searching for people while Grace's breaths were coming 150 times a minute!" She was the one heaving now.

"Next time Grace can't breathe, I'll be sure to tell Manny where he can sleep when he comes rushing here to take care of *my* children because their father is always away on business trips."

How is it possible to be just with everyone, including taking one's own fair share of happiness? How could so many answers be right and still leave so many people hurt and dissatisfied? Marie thought that she had at least found some reconciliation with herself in loving Manny, but who would sympathize with the life she had chosen? No one, because she had not chosen at all. That was perhaps her biggest sin; the selfish keeping of everything. Later, that would be a verse in everyone's judgment of her: but why didn't you leave, Marie? If you loved one, why did you continue to hold onto life with another?

And why was she so good at maintaining every illusion? She still made love to Brendan regularly, refusing to cheat him of what was his, and she still admired him like some starstruck paparazzi, looking directly into his silky brown eyes and laughing at his funny stories like a groupie. On the weekends, she made Brendan tea, touched his hair when she placed it next to him, or sat beside him as he watched a Ranger game or played chess with one of the kids. She took out her homework and did it as she soaked in whatever scene was before her; the landscape she called "family," and never once did she feel the need to sneak off to call her lover from a pay phone on a empty street during some errand invented just for the purpose of getting away. Marie separated her lives precisely and evenly, and took from both the joys they provided, as if she were an estuary for two bountiful streams.

She convinced herself that Brendan didn't know; didn't see, because she was that good at her roles – and certainly, there were times he still encouraged her to go out with Manny, "enjoy herself" – but there were other times, too, days that he arrived home and saw the remains of two cups of tea on his kitchen table, and touched the side of one to see how warm it was.

"What does he do, rush out right before I get home?" he asked one day.

"Well, Brendan," Marie said playfully, "You always say you hate coming from a day at work to find company in your house. Even Claire leaves right before you get here." And he had no reply to that.

In July, they planned to return to Ireland, a trip that of course could not afford but one that once again Marie pushed for.

"Everyone is getting older over there, Brendan," she said, "Don't you want your kids to have met them? Don't you want to see them again before they're gone? And what about the ones who just had babies?" He resisted, as always, and then relented, as if again realizing that he at least would have another thing to hold against her later. That was how it was, and Marie accepted it. No matter how many poignant memories were made on the trip, Brendan would only see the cost; as if the credit card statements should be mounted in their photo albums alongside precious images of Achill Island and Auntie Bridget in the garden, cousins playing among the nettles, and cows coming home to be milked.

Manny, also, was distressed about the trip.

"Three weeks? You are going to be gone three weeks?" he moaned.

"Well, yeah," she replied with no remorse, "It's Europe. You don't go to Europe for the weekend. Well, you don't buy six tickets at $600 apiece for the weekend, anyway."

"Three weeks," Manny said again, "and you know I'm going to Puerto Rico to see my family after that. Shit. We'll be apart for a month."

Marie might have been distressed as well, but she was selfish, and she was greedily reaping the rewards of one of the lives she sought to maintain. She loved Ireland and the people who lived there, and Manny could not give her this. Only Brendan could show her the country in a native way; in kitchens with slate floors and stone walls built by hand, and pubs untainted by Americans, where men fell asleep upon their ales and then suddenly woke up singing drunken ballads while other patrons hushed to listen.

Marie recalled Auntie Bridget's words on her honeymoon, about the realities of life in Ireland, but the country remained magical to her in its simplicity.

They landed in County Clare in early July, missing Independence Day in their own country, and began the trip in a coastal town called Lahinch. They did not want to impose on anyone now that there were four children in tow, and so the first relatives came to their hotel, sometimes at the end of their workdays, and sometimes to spend a warm day on the beach.

Marie kept a daily journal of the trip, from the first jet-lagged day that carried that tiny tinge of unease one feels in a foreign country, no matter how familiar, to the day three weeks later full of tearful goodbyes.

They traveled from the farm outside Ennis to a home with 7 children in a place outside of Galway, then over to Dublin and down to Cork, and up to another seaside town called Kilkee, ending always back in Clare. Wherever they went, they tried to stay in a hotel room but the relations wouldn't hear of it, pushing their own children into rooms together to free up some beds. And Marie watched her children play with first cousins and tried to puzzle why she could tell the Irish youngsters from the American even though they were of the same blood but different sides of the Atlantic. It couldn't be her infusion of "Brooklyn-ese" that softened the bone structure of her offspring, could it? Or maybe it was just in her head?

In any case, Marie was painfully aware that this was who they were, descendents of a Celtic family, and it was the part of them she would not share if she ended her marriage. Not that she was planning on it; but she did begin to picture the possibility and was always stopped cold. It couldn't happen. There was no way.

At night in one of the farmhouse kitchens, after the children were in bed, Brendan and the cousins went through photo albums, looking at themselves when they were children.

"Who is this?" one would ask, "Is this Padraig? Or Seamus?" and Marie as surprised that she could help; she was that in tune with the family's background.

"Those are the cousins that live in Massachusetts," Marie said, "You can tell by the front door. 604. That's their address."

"Oh, that's right, you're the writer, aren't you," they all nodded. "Wouldn't we all be completely out of touch if it weren't for your letters?" And Marie beamed, and squelched the image of a letter telling them that she was no longer part of the family. It would never happen.

When they couldn't identify a person in the grainy Kodachrome, they immediately dismissed that person as an "outsider," meaning one that managed to be in their lives for a moment but was not family.

"Hmmm…must be an outsider, that one," and it became a game, until Marie asked, "Am I an outsider?" and they laughed all that much harder.

"You were after your first visit here, of course. But now you've been here more than the rest, so I suppose not." Marie remembered of course how they greeted her with arms far extended when she came on her honeymoon, and now they were up late in a dimly lit kitchen, laughing, and these people were finally hers. She would not give them up.

Kristin and even little Grace cried with every goodbye in every kitchen, and when they came upon their last stop before the airport, Auntie Bridget warned them against further tears.

"You will not tell these girls you're leaving here today. Tell them you are just going to Ennis to shop or to go buy some milk but do not tell them you are leaving for good now." She had her gnarly finger pointed at them and her face was stern, "I mean it now. I'll not have these children crying all over me."

After 21 days and at least six counties, they flew home, and Marie wondered if this was their final trip. The day after they returned, she brought eleven rolls of film to be developed at the local drugstore, but didn't have a cent to pick them up. A week later, Manny returned from Puerto Rico and got them for her.

She looked at his photos of Puerto Rico and he looked at hers, noting the stark differences in the people they visited. Manny's parents had only recently returned to their homeland, and Manny reported that his father loved it but his mother yearned for the states. They brought with them his youngest brother Petey, a change of life baby now in his teens. Manny's sister had joined the military, and he had only an older brother that lived nearby in Queens. All were featured in different poses in the glossy 4x6's that Marie flipped through, and so was his wife, and something else.

"Manny…could it be? Are you wearing a *wedding* ring?" Marie held the picture closer, examining the band of gold that glared upon his tan finger.

Manny smiled sheepishly, and answered, "Required attire for family visits, m'am. I can't believe you noticed that. You are a detective now?" He pulled his photos away, and picked up hers.

"What about your little images of connubial bliss going here, huh?" he jeered, then attempted to speak in an Irish accent that came out as tragic as the race itself, "Oh, here we are, me and the man sipping our tea by the fire. Don't you know I always make him a spot of tea in the evenin', like the good wife I am. Then we go upstairs to have good clean Catholic sex that bores me to tears, and…"

"Okay, okay, stop it, you still sound more spic than mic anyway," and they were laughing, but not without some sense of melancholy. The people in the pictures were the people they would hurt. They were the people that had no interest in being reorganized or reclassified into something they were not; people that would not welcome any new definitions of the word "family."

"So, remember, Marie, next year, we coordinate our vacations. You go away when I go away. This was too fucking long," he said, and took her hands, and left both their families and extended families right there on the checkered tablecloth and he led her upstairs.

"Why aren't you close with your older brother, again?" she asked him later.

"Dominic?" he mused, stroking her hair, unwilling to leave the momentous for the mundane, "Ummm…probably because…I think, well, he isn't my father's child?"

He explained, "See, I was born second, but I am the one named after my father, not him. So, I always wondered if maybe my mom had him before? I don't know."

"You didn't ask?" Marie wasn't all that interested, but something made her keep asking, as if she had been remiss on her homework and may be tested soon.

"Nahhh," he answered, "What's the point? We just weren't really close, even though he lives right around the block from me. Maybe cause he's so much older. You know, his son is the same age as my little brother. I was always closer to my sister."

"Do you still talk to your sister about me?" Marie asked, more interested now.

"Always," he replied quickly.

"What does she think?" Marie asked optimistically, but without real expectation.

"Well, she can't stand Madeline, that's for sure, but well...she doesn't understand *this,* either," he answered, gesturing over the two of them to define what he meant by "this."

"But I think, when all is said and done, she would be true to me, and accept whatever makes me happy. And she would like you, if she knew you," he finished.

"Do you understand *this*, Manny?" she asked, squirming out of his arms to turn and face him, her body scantily covered by partial redressing. "Does God understand it?"

"God understands that I love you," he answered with all the earnestness he could muster. "I have to believe that this counts for something." He nimbly unbuttoned the only two buttons she had fastened on her shirt, and reached in to caress her breast, his thumb brushing over her nipple in the simplest of all prevailing and persuasive gestures; sending a surge through her that would have her believe that all transparencies showing inside the human body in books were wrong. Surely they left out that chord or vessel that led from her breasts in a straight and direct route to her clitoris and all the folds around it, and whatever traveled through this mystery canal moved far more quickly than blood.

"Well, it's his own damn fault," Marie said, "God's, I mean. He had 16 years to fix this," she added and wondered if she was really talking about God at all.

"So," he said, "When are you coming to the 7-0? I want you to see me do roll call. It will make you wet for sure. I am a powerful guy, you don't realize that."

"Depends," Marie leaned back, covered herself again, "Did you tell them I was beautiful?"

"Yes," he answered, reaching, but she held back.

"And that I had a great body?"

"Of course."

"Then…I guess I'll come when I am actually beautiful and have a great body," Marie answered simply.

He pulled her close and gave her no escape, simultaneously yanking down her panties and separating her shirt, his fingers diving inside her and his free hand led a breast to his mouth. Now he was a man on a mission, and he knew how to complete it.

She swelled around his fingers and he continued to play until she reached the brink; the moment that delirium leads one to believe that they would do anything to keep this rhythm going: send a silent prayer to the gods, sell one's soul, give up all treasured possessions, or even threaten nothing short of murder should a lover misread the signs. And, then, right then, while she teetered between holding her breath and screaming, he stopped.

"Say it right now or I'm stopping. Say, 'I'm beautiful.' C'mon, let me hear. Say, 'I am so fucking beautiful, Manny.' Say it."

She was silent and he started to withdraw his fingers, his mouth, himself, and her muscles contracted hard to keep him there.

"Noo," she moaned, and he eased back in, and then started again to retreat.

"Say it."

"I'm beautiful, I'm beautiful, okay?" she breathed, and it didn't take long after that, and she was soaked.

"Good girl," he smiled, satisfied. "So, you will be at the 7-0 soon, then, right? To see me do roll call?"

She nodded, weakly. But she never made it to the 7-0 while Manny worked there. She meant to, but never seemed to have the time.

****

Summer ended, and everyone was caught up again in time that was no longer their own. September is a time filled with paper: course outlines, emergency cards, codes of conduct to sign, and letters to read; letters that always started with a line like, "I can't believe that summer is over already," even though it happened every year and was certainly believable. Colin was in 8th grade, and Daniel in 6th, Kristin in 3rd grade and Grace had just started kindergarten. Marie increased the amount of classes she was taking at community college and would be done in two semesters. Her classes this semester were difficult; one old bitter professor locked the door promptly at the start of class and would not let students even a minute late in, while the other kept giving tests in topics Marie swore had never been even mentioned in class.

There was a long hill that led down from the buildings of the campus, and a park across the street where Manny often waited for her, in his car. Marie always remembered that walk and it's accompaniment of sensations; the milieu of a misunderstood summer month that only turned to fall in its final week, the feeling of loss for unencumbered sapphire days and gentle nights, and the glowing awareness that at the bottom of that hill and across the street, Manny waited for her. His Toyota was at first hidden from view but she knew it was there, like a refuge, and she only had to get to it to be safe from the crossfire she imagined life to be.

He was sitting in his car, allowing her image to clear some trees and come into view before jumping up and opening the passenger side door, taking her books like a schoolboy, and then watching her as she settled in. He always waited for her first words to set their tone, like they were both on a game of Jeopardy and it was her right to pick the category.

Today she leaned back and shut her eyes, unwilling to taint the moment with grumblings of the mundane, and still filled with the wonder of anticipation that she experienced walking away from school and towards him. Now she was inside, enclosed by his scent and encircled by his faith that he could live a lifetime inside of those moments when he shut his car door and left the world outside.

She remembers when she was young, he gave her books about a place called Narnia, a land discovered through a wardrobe door. The stories were Christian allegories, but the thing that always struck Marie was that the characters could spend years away in this magical country and return to their own without any time going by at all. What if she could open his car door and be in a place where they could see it all through, end each day together and begin another after that, each one an amatory adventure surrounded by the ordinary things that it sustained? And then, after they experienced all the gradients from sorrow to supreme satisfaction, she would return and be at the school doors by 3, in time to take her children home?

All this went through her head while the September sun magnified through the windshield, and warmed her closed eyelids. She still hadn't spoken, so finally Manny did:

"What do you say, Marie," he asked intuitively, "Should we just drive until we've crossed six or seven state lines, and settle down wherever our gas runs out?"

"Definitely," she affirmed, with eyes still closed, "but will I be back in time to get my kids from school?

"Of course you would," he said simply.

"Manny," she opened her eyes and sat up, "if you married me, how long would it take before you got used to me?"

"I would never live long enough to get used to you, Marie," he said in that voice that he held steady and full of strength.

"No, really...what if for the first year you brought me roses every day and thanked me for being there, but in the next year, well, you only brought me roses once a week and gave me a little kiss on the cheek, and then after that..."

He was smiling, shaking his head.

"After that," she went on, "You started to come home empty-handed and said, 'oh, are you still here?' when you walked in. What if that happened?"

"I mean, Manny, isn't it better to just preserve the fantasy?" she finished.

"Marie, I am going to wait, and I am going to outlive your husband. I'm doing the treadmill every day at work now, and taking my vitamins and eating my Wheaties, and I'm going to be around, and I'm going to start saving for those roses now. Got it?"

"Brendan is pretty healthy, though," she said, "and his uncle is in his 90's".

"He's looking a little flabby," Manny said, and she shushed him, so he changed the subject.

"Right now, though, just in case there is a tsunami or earthquake or nuclear explosion," he rambled, "there is something that I want from you."

"And what is that?" she asked him, still thinking they were teasing but he was suddenly serious.

"A whole night, Marie. I have never spent a whole night in bed with you. Sleeping. Waking. Can we pull that off?"

"I really don't see how," she answered honestly, and thought again with the same negative result: "Nope. I can't imagine how. You're going to have to put that on our to-do list," she finished, but he had other ideas.

He called her late one night a week later, "Let me spend the night with you tonight," his voice came through the wires.

"Manny? Are you nuts? No way, I'm…it's late, and…why are you calling my house this late? Are you nuts?"

"I know Brendan is out of town," he said urgently, "I've been checking your little notebook every time I see you. You always make a little notation when he'll be away. I saw it. He'll be gone another three days. Let me come."

Marie's heart tapped out erratic and contradictory summations in fast words that echoed through her blood; words like violated, and coveted, and trapped, and prized, licentious and pure, afraid and relieved. She only had to choose which expression to defend and which would become the title of this evening.

She tried. "Manny, it's really late, and by the time you get here…"

"I'm here," he cut her off. "Right down the street. I know you put the kids to bed. I saw their lights go out. Marie, I'm coming over there."

"You *can't*," she nearly screamed and she added 'fearful' to the mix of verbs and adjectives, but how closely related is fear to excitement, and which was governing her pulse? Again she had that suspicion she often had with Manny; that they were living out the ongoing script of some love-deprived author, and that it was in fact his or her pen that Marie was trying to keep from flowing across the page. It was always Marie's job to put up the fight, and also her job to lose it, and let the ink spill how it would.

Weakly, she said, "My dogs will bark when you come in, and the kids will hear, and the neighbors…"

"Marie? Do you know that your dogs never bark when I come in?" Now she could hear the amusement in his tone, and it heightened every perception at once, like words throbbing in all the appropriate lobes and glands.

"My doors are locked," she said.

"Your doors are never locked."

"I can go downstairs and lock them right now," she threatened like one bluffing a kidnapper.

"Okay, have it your way. I'll go home," he said dejectedly, and Marie raced to her window and with a new list of ricocheting sentiments – disappointed, relieved, incredulous, unfulfilled, purified – she watched his car go away.

She was on the third floor of her home; a space still unoccupied by any family members and used only for guests. She wore a thin cotton dress, white embroidered with little flowers, a nightdress that would not be ashamed to walk along a beach on the right summer day, with the sun framing the body beneath with unreserved innocence.

She went back to doing what she had been doing before the usurping of her contentment, what she did whenever Brendan wasn't around to tell her to come to bed. She was organizing, and arranging, cleaning out closets and improving things; the kind of work one could do for hours without seeing any visible difference or evidence of the effort, yet a feeling of accomplishment prevailed nonetheless. When she ascertained that Manny's car was indeed gone, she looked around and her whole being juxtaposed the purposeful ennui before her. Items were scattered in anticipation of organization, but they would have to wait until she rejoined her prior sense of purpose, and that wouldn't happen until her hands stopped shaking.

Marie sat, on the edge of something, and idly picked up something else; and that's when she heard his footsteps on the stairs. She swore that she believed he had really left; was incensed that he hadn't believed she would keep him out, but now he was here. He had won, and she stood up to meet him on the landing, her heart no longer recognizable as an organ that had a steady, rhythmic job to do.

"We'll sleep in this room," she pointed, and he nodded.

"No matter what it takes, you will make sure that I'm out of this bed and down in my own before my kids wake up," she said, and he kept nodding, his eyes in so modest a face another contrast of excess and temperance. Some eyes may be windows to a soul; but Manny's were a window ledge where his soul stood ever threatening to jump.

"No matter what, Manny," she said again, "No one in this house will see me sleeping with you. No one waking in the night with a nightmare or wanting water…no one. Okay?"

"Okay," he answered and these are the scenes the burn into the banks of memory. Marie watched deliberately where his first touch landed: on her thigh, moving up under the white cotton and resting on her hip, just under the seam where the bodice of the dress met the skirt. The night, or what was left of night, carried all the wonders of skin on skin and breath on breath, but it was that first convergence of flesh that Marie trembled to remember. She kept the nightdress long after the seams unraveled and the white dulled to gray.

And she needn't have worried; because Manny never slept. Whether it was wonderment or fear; he stayed awake, stroking her hair, alternating between watching her sleep and waking her for more. At six in the morning, she left their bed and crept into hers to await the first sounds of life in her house, and he went to sleep then.

Still, an hour or so later, he managed to slip out her front door and re-enter through the side, where Marie was feeding her crew Cocoa Puffs and urging them to hurry for school.

"Want me to drive them?" he asked of everyone in the room, and all agreed.

"Manny is here early," Colin observed, and Marie looked over her son's head at Manny's face, with all the heat of the afterglow lighting her eyes.

"Yes, he is," Marie answered, "Yes he is."

****

Marie strained to recall something besides them as September became October but her recollections came in a blur of bridges and smiles, and touches and talks and Melissa Etheridge lyrics that were the new embodiment of their own feelings – "She's a lesbian, you know," Marie said, "that means all this passion is for a woman." "That's okay," Manny answered, "so is mine." – and errands shortened by sharing them, and police stories, and their lives in between.

Marie inevitably became overwhelmed maintaining life in such fullness, and made more to-do lists with due dates and asterisks signifying their level of importance. No one asked at the end of the day about her productivity versus her available time; her time was not an asset to anyone but herself.

"I have to attend a Race Reconciliation workshop this weekend," Marie announced at the dinner table.

"Which is?" Brendan asked, and Marie got a fleeting image of Jay Leno on his talk show, talking to some boring guest but maintaining a childlike look of total absorption. She deliberately delayed answering to see if Brendan would pursue it, but he was soaking up the gravy of his pot roast.

"It's for the church," she went on, "It's like this thing where black people try to get whites to see the world the way they see it, and to react more appropriately to their struggles, and..." Marie faded off.

"Well, anyway, I'll be gone all day Saturday, okay?" she said and Brendan acquiesced, turning his attention to the kids.

"Maybe I'll take you for a canoe ride that day," he said, "Do a little fishing." Marie knew Brendan liked having the kids to himself, although he still called it 'babysitting,' as if their mutual offspring really belonged solely to Marie. It was a perception typical of nearly all the fathers she knew, and Marie didn't mind it much, because she believed the children to be hers alone as well. Love, and the people that bring it, would always be just a part of the emblematic man's life; something he could leave if he had to.

The workshop was in Manhattan. Marie was taking the bus in, but had already arranged for Manny to bring her home, partly for the sake of nostalgia, and partly because he had asked her to baby-sit his Scottish terrier for a few days. They had not driven home from the city in years, and Marie relished the thought.

She was covering the seminar for the newsletter, but like Saul arriving in Damascus, Marie felt as if her eyes were opened. Black women stood and spoke from their hearts of the unspoken and subtle slurs that were part of their daily existence, and how even the best intentioned of white people often missed the point.

It got to be a bit much; charismatic Christians being fueled by drama. Black and white women were embracing and crying; the latter apologizing profusely for centuries of persecution, weeping so inconsolably that it appeared that they were the ones who had ultimately suffered. Still, Marie was touched by the experience and the light it shadowed on her own fallacies, and she excitedly told Manny about it as soon as she entered his car.

"It's like, white people, they always say things that they think aren't racist, but in a way, they are," she chattered, "and I thought I wasn't like that, but I do things. I was raised by racists, and I thought I was better than that, but there are just things you don't realize...hey, why are you so quiet?"

Manny usually jumped heartily into the theoretical, truth-seeking topics she introduced, but in this he seemed to have no opinion at all. He kept his eyes on the road, excessively interested in each and every traffic light.

"Hmmm...well, do you want to know what I think?" Manny asked her and she leaned in closer.

"I think, now that seems like a bunch of people who have absolutely nothing to do on a nice fall Saturday," he let go, and waited for the fallback.

She was startled, because Manny never disagreed with her in so head-on a fashion. They debated, surely, but he always presented a different side of the same coin. This answer was surely a whole other form of currency.

"What?" she asked; infuriated, since she of course was one of the people who wasted her Saturday. "How can you *say* that? I mean, you of all people."

"Marie," he said with patience, too much patience, and she suddenly knew that this was his 'cop' voice, used in domestic disputes and other situations where humoring was required, "I think someday you ought to come down to lock-up with me."

"What's *that* supposed to mean?" she asked, her anger heightening at his betrayal, of her ideals and of her trust, and of her expectations of him.

"It means, Marie, that most of the people down there are black or Hispanic," he said, "and yeah, these are my own 'kind,' I realize, and sometimes I sit down there just to talk to them, see what happened to put them on the 'dark' side, no pun intended. Sometimes there is a reasonable story, but never one really good enough. It's reality, Marie, so maybe you should just come and see."

"Well, maybe I will," she said, defeated.

"Good, while you're at it, come watch me do roll call," he added, and she almost smiled.

"Five more pounds," she said, referring to her midsection, but they drove the rest of the way in silence. She hated that Manny corrected her. That was Brendan's job.

Taking advantage of her freedom, they stopped at Kids R Us on the way home, where she spent 176.91 on clothes for her kids; items that Brendan never considered a necessity because Marie enjoyed buying them too much. Manny paid $50 of the amount to lower the figure that would appear on her charge card, and they spent the time dodging clothing racks and talking about safer subjects.

Afterwards, they drove behind the Cost Cutters, or Jembro, or one of those factory-like stores with a freight entrance, and there, she would allow him to kiss her, figuring anyone else parking in such a desolate place was probably practicing an indiscretion of their own. They kissed sorrow and they kissed forgiveness, and she took his face in his hands. He unbuttoned her shirt but could only maneuver to kiss her right breast, then buttoned her up and looked in her eyes, while the dog in the backseat had begun to whine.

"Oh Marie, what are we going to do?" he asked.

He didn't come in when he dropped her off, it being Saturday and family time.

"I'll be by to pick up the dog on Wednesday?" he said furtively, perhaps still surprised at himself for confronting her earlier.

"I'll be in Boston, by the way," he added when her foot was out the door, and she maneuvered her packages and the leash, "With Madeline. Her idea, of course. It's okay about the dog?"

"I don't know," she said, thinking. "He is *black*. I'll warn my white dogs." And got out of the car for the last time.

****

Marie used his absence to dive into her multi-streamed time, because that is what her life looked like to her now; a multitude of thin streams, each one barely making much of a blue line on her map, but still in need of maintenance. Some led to larger, more significant bodies, like the way volunteering for the PTA led to the well-being of her children, but too many of them led to the vanity pool that was her ego, which perhaps needed the most care of all.

Her objective was to write and call and study and clean and drive nonstop, so that she could make quality time; there was a new children's museum in Paramus and she wanted to bring Grace, and she had initiated a breakfast day for each child each Saturday with alternating parents to give each some one-on-one time. Their friends and neighbors to the left had invited them to dinner the coming Friday night, and there was a new family just moved from Los Angeles across the street that Marie was attempting to befriend.

And there was Brendan, the scorecard in her head. Whatever she took from him in undiscovered moments through thought or deed, she attempted to give back tenfold even though she never could. She resolutely planned dinner dates and movie dates, and the magazine she wrote for provided ideas for day trips and getaways designed to keep the fire burning in a marriage.

Manny actually returned Tuesday afternoon, as evidenced by a short email Marie received that day:

"I'm back and I hate Madeline. See you tomorrow." Marie still felt mild satisfaction at this lack of news; his complaints about his wife no longer carried the validating ability it once did. Love covered a multitude of sins, and she had finally acquired the wisdom to know that Madeline's transgressions would be readily forgiven if she had her husband's love.

Still she asked about it as soon as he arrived, and he readily explained.

"We were in Boston, Marie. Boston. There are things to see in Boston. Fenway. Quincy Market. That pub from Cheers. The friggin' Freedom Trail." As he talked he paced around the kitchen looking for things to do, and finally settled on taking the trash out of the can.

"It stinks under here, you know? I think it needs to be hosed outside," he said and brought the bag out and returned to finish his lament, "But you know what Madeline wants to do in Boston? She wants to go to Benetton. The Gap. The Disney store. She runs me ragged going to *franchises*. I mean, does she think that Mickey Mouse is different in Boston? That he squeaks with an accent?"

Now he brought the barrel to the driveway and she followed. She watched as he got detergent and filled the can with sudsy water.

"We barely saw Boston," he murmured. "Ariella didn't have a clue we were in another state, even. It was just another mall trip. What was the point of going?"

Marie nodded sympathetically, but she was really thinking about how touched she was that he was cleaning her trashcan, and wondered at how clearly love showed itself in details. Then she remembered the postcard she sent him early in the week, one free of erotica this time, containing instead a snippet she had found in a book:

> *In love you have loosed yourself to me like seawater;*
> *I can scarcely measure the sky's most spacious eyes*
> *And I lean down to your mouth to kiss the earth*

It was the kind of poetry she understood but could not explain; the kind that to her resisted all analysis and had to be received with one's gut. She knew he would feel its impact as she intended, and she hoped he would find the card waiting for him when he went to work tonight.

He finished the pail and asked if he could leave it out to dry in the sun. Then they were inside; and she made tea and Marie remained contemplative of him as he spoke.

"I'm leaving her for good, Marie," he said affirmatively, "in January. I figured one more Christmas. I still have stuff in your garage, right? Brendan didn't toss it? Well, I'm going. I can still be a good father to Ariella. I started to do lunch duty at her school, did I tell you that?"

Later, she would wonder if there were any clues in this reunion that made it different from other separations they had experienced. Marie knew that she was quieter and more watchful, appreciating him in a simpler, less dramatic way than usual. When there was a lull in their idle talk, he looked around the kitchen again.

"Need me to do anything?" he asked.

"Ummm..." she pondered, and then consulted her endless notes and notations.

"I need my trash can cleaned...oh, check." He appreciated the joke, knowing that she added things already completed to her list just to have another thing to check. She looked again, "I need to finish an article and I need a new shower curtain liner."

"Finish the article now," he said standing, his energy high, "I'll go get the liner. I need a few things myself. Anything else?"

"Yeah," she said, looking at him purposefully, "I need my left breast kissed. The last time I saw you, you only kissed the right one."

"Ten-four," he saluted, and left and she went to her computer and wrote well and fast, and freed up their last few hours together.

Lovemaking is indeed like wine, in that it comes in many forms to suit a myriad of needs, from the raw and cheap to the kind that you want to forever savor on your tongue, and everything in between. The only difference is that you choose wine to match a mood or a meal, but lovemaking; well, this always chooses you. It makes the mood for you or at least it finds it underneath the dispositions or inhibitions one strips away with one's clothing. With wine, you expect to get what you asked for, but lovemaking is always a surprise ordained by a force inside. You don't want to expect anything; you want to find out what you've got.

When Manny came back, they made love, not for hours and hours but perhaps for hours and hours in their moments. The clock on the night table ticked but ecstasy, at least, knows how to ignore time. They breathed, and laughed and looked into each other's eyes and made sure they understood each other, and fought off the sorrow.

"Do you believe we'll be damned for this?" Marie whispered; at which he pulled back and quoted a line from a song they both knew.

"You told me you loved me," he whispered back, "That's all I believe."

There were two emails waiting for her in the morning, one written in the wee hours that was half in Spanish, half in English:

"Got the postcard. That's Pablo Neruda, by the way.

Te quiero con todo mi corazón. Thanks for taking care of the dog. Keep that trash can clean. Te echo de menos."

And one composed in normal waking hours:

"Last night was BUSY. I was able to sneak in a quick, intense 45 min. treadmill run but after running up and down stairs all night, it seems like being on patrol was a bigger workout. I mean it was intense. I had the normal 11 patrol cars working but we were running from disaster to disaster the whole night. One thing that I was happy about, on one of the jobs where I had to race straight up four flights of stairs, my driver (28 years old, moderately overweight) was so winded that he could barely talk on the radio. I on the other hand really wasn't winded at all. Not bad for an OLD man, I told him. Well, gotta go. I do have my noontime lunchroom dad duties. Be well, and I will see you tomorrow?

And she wrote back:

"I'm getting to that children's museum tomorrow if it kills me. I'm bringing the new neighbor's kid, too. They both work and have an Egyptian nanny and she doesn't do anything cultural for the kid but cook Egyptian food. Who is Pablo Neruda and what did all those Spanish words mean?"

He never answered this one, but she went about her business on Thursday, stacking up her checkmarks in order to be free on Friday. On Friday morning, however, she couldn't find Manny; there was no call and no answer to her calls, and no emails either. She felt disappointed, anticipating a day of light banter veiling all intensity beneath; an easy day where the children played in their worlds and she and Manny supervised with watchful eyes and a sense of well-being. Plus, he always drove, leaving her to sort through her papers and books on the seat beside him.

'Where is he?' she thought to herself, but determination would not allow her to consider rescheduling the trip. Instead, she called up another kindergarten mom, and they went together, picking up their respective children and the neighbor's child and driving to northern New Jersey.

It was a nice day. They followed their offspring through hands-on experiments and dress-up rooms and displays, chattering together about the particulars of their unique child's development, and Marie thought perhaps it was good that Manny had not come. She had recently told him that he was making her far too anti-social, like some lovestruck teenager who becomes a "flat-leaver."

"No one likes a 'flat-leaver,' Manny," she joked, "That's an official Queens term for a girl who stops hanging out with her friends when she gets a boyfriend."

As pleasant as the day was, Marie's mind strayed from kindergarten anecdotes and playful "socks on the floor" husband-bashing to internal philosophical debates in her head about passion and where it could learn to live in such mundane days, and also noted how just having it somewhere – a day ago or a day to come – sustained her. Just the promise of passion provided the vivid backdrop that shone through all the clutter, and even if the disorder obscured the view completely, it still radiated warmth that would not be encumbered.

She also noted how utterly weird her life was, for after today's drill in suburban motherhood, she was going to a worship service at her charismatic church, and then for coffee – with Brendan and the kids – at her liberal neighbor's house.

'That's me,' she thought, 'My version of having it all. I just don't pick a side,' but she didn't hate herself for it for once, because behind the complete mess she had made of everything, her backdrop was still keeping her warm.

Marie was making spaghetti for just the children, smiling at the sounds of her house as usual, when Manny called.

"Hi," he said, "Sorry I missed you today."

"What happened?" she asked, maneuvering strands of pasta with the phone under her ear.

"There was a cop funeral today. I forgot to tell you. Although you would know if you ever read the papers." He sighed deeply.

"What's the matter?" she invited, because his voice was seldom sad.

"Nothing," he answered, and sighed again, "I just really need to see you."

"Yeah, the weekend is here already," she sympathized, "Monday?"

"I have to be at work early on Monday," he groaned, "for a meeting with the captain. Working a day tour on Tuesday. Damn."

"Okay, then, Wednesday," she finalized, but his breath again filled the phone with loud wet fog.

"Wednesday is so far away."

"Okay, then, Monday, Manny. Monday."

"I have only, like two hours on Monday…"

"Okay, then, Monday *and* Wednesday," she soothed, "How about that?"

"I thought you said I was coming out too much? Making you unsociable? Stopping you from your cookie swaps and book clubs?"

"Ha ha," she chuckled, then grew serious. "Forget about that," she said, "I can be unsociable for you."

And then she said something that came from nowhere but the culmination of her internal deliberations all day, but this, too, must surely have been ordained from within.

"Manny?" she asked softly.

"Hmmmm…" he mused.

"I want to tell you that all my best realities do not measure up to just one thought or memory of you."

"Wow," he breathed softly and did not sigh, "What brought that on?"

"Nothing. Everything," she rejoined. "It's just the truth."

"I gotta go back out now," he said, "I just stopped in for coffee. See you Monday?"

"Monday. And Wednesday," and she hung up, fed her children, and took them to church.

****

A charismatic church is a place of celebration, even though the participants are essentially rejoicing in deprivation. With hands waving and heads upturned, they praise God for allowing them to do nothing at all, seemingly unaware that there is no real pleasure in this. Like the final scene in The Emperor's New Clothes, church participants follow along, only there is no practical and innocent voice proclaiming that there is nothing here to be had; that it is all just an illusion perpetuated by group dynamics.

Marie wasn't the voice to call the bluff of the Friday night worshippers; she was merely the skeptic in the crowd that yearned to believe, and placed her faith in the possibility that these drunk-with-God folks were the ones who had it right. She yearned to believe that they were satisfied with the Lord as their provider of all; even the passion that led them to church on a Friday night instead of doing what all good sinners prefer.

The sermon, not surprisingly, was about sin. After thirty or so minutes of ecstatic singing, it was always time to deliver the blow. We, you, all of us: we haven't gotten it right with God. Never will, in fact. We don't have ability or sense or self-control, no! All we have are His good graces when we screw things up. Praise God, for his goodness, maybe but really, was this a healthy relationship? Wasn't it hard on a human's self-esteem to be forever required to apologize for ineptness? Didn't it give God the eternal upper hand in love?

Marie listened; she always listened to the words of wisdom that came in bursts like fireworks over treetops in the black night. We must come clean with God. We must come to him with a clear conscience and a redeemed heart. Nothing was impossible with Him. His love overpowered all evil. Marie listened, but always searched for something new, something she hadn't heard before, and not just advertising but instead something she could actually use. A bit of practical, hands-on advice for sin elimination, something that would start showing results immediately with regular use. She was beyond ideological. She wanted viable solutions.

And so, when she went up to the altar for prayer, she was no longer a weak child begging for divine forgiveness. She was a conscientious objector, demanding answers and demanding action. She knelt down under the hands laid upon her and made her request swift and clear:

"You are the one with the power, Lord. If you want this fixed, then you will have to be the one to fix it. I've tried, and I can't." These would be her final words with God, and as she spoke them, an image of "this" appeared in her vision: Manny's visage, and from the angle of his face, Marie knew it was on top of hers looking down, and from the gust of arousal that swept her, she knew that he was inside of her. Right there in church.

She stood, and felt some satisfaction, as if she had checked in with her probation officer and made an honest accounting of herself. The singing resumed in full throttle and the pews emptied, and Marie greeted some followers with the confident defiance of a genuine charlatan. She verified that she would lead Bible group at her house next week; she sympathized with someone whose child was sick, and even listened to a horrific story about the untimely death of someone's husband, told bravely and without tears by the widow. *I'll admit one thing about these people,"* she thought, *"Their faith certainly allows them to sustain things."*

Brendan was home when she arrived, and they headed across the street to their friends' house. Sonya and Larry were caring people, beautifully unburdened by the threat of hell and damnation, and mildly surprised that they liked Marie in spite of her misguided attachment to Christianity. Larry was Jewish but non-practicing, and Sonya converted to Judaism to practice for him and maintain the faith for her three sons. With them also was another couple she and Brendan had befriended through Sonya and Larry, and Marie felt the anticipation of an enjoyable evening before her.

"Anything exciting happen at church tonight?" Larry teased, and Marie played along.

"Yup. We all walked on water," she retorted.

"I did that once," Larry rejoined, "although I think I might have been high at the time."

Marie loved these people; they were friends that she could really laugh with, although they would not speak for a long time after this night. It made it easier that Brendan also was fond of them, feeling none of the discomfort he felt with Marie's church friends. They had real educations and real jobs, and a healthy amount of cynicism and real world views.

They were doing just that – laughing, talking, eating organic foods – when the phone rang. It was Colin, who had stayed home with Sonya's oldest son.

"Marie, it's your son," Sonya said, handing her the phone.

"Mom?" Colin said, a little impatiently, as if he had been interrupted. "Your dad called. He said it's very important. He said you have to call him back."

Marie relayed the message to the group, and said she would just go home to call her father.

"Although," she said, "I can hardly imagine what's so important if he was alive to make the call and not hysterical crying."

"You can call from here," Sonya offered, but Marie declined, assuring them she would be right back.

She would always remember the walk across the street, half-smiling and replaying her friends' conversations in her head, and only slightly wondering what her father wanted. The night was cool and fresh like October; the moon making a solid appearance and the grass scented with the last mow of the season. She walked slowly in the quiet, as if she knew that there was some significance to this short passage.

Up the driveway and through the side door, greeting the dog and heading for the phone on the desk, she would wonder later why she had only been curious and not apprehensive. Maybe she thought that she had suffered enough; having lost her mother to cancer and then survived cancer, she thought she had a free pass for a bit. And besides, Colin clearly said that her father made the call. So he was alright.

Fred Meyers answered on the first ring.

"Marie?" he said with caution in his voice, like he wanted her to hang up and run.

"Hi dad," she said, still with some buoyancy but tempered with required weightiness. It was obviously something important to *him*, and she should be ready to be sympathetic. Perhaps another spouse had left one of her siblings.

"Brace yourself," he said, and she stood straighter, as if getting ready to be pushed but not slaughtered.

"Okay," she said, and he breathed deeply.

"Your friend Manny is dead," he said, and thoughts burst into flame in her head but were quickly moistened by streams of hope that didn't have a prayer.

"No, he isn't," she said weakly, "I just talked to him an hour ago." Was it an hour ago? No, it was more like four. Still…

"Your brother's working tonight," her father explained. "He heard it on the radio. He called to tell me, to ask Manny's last name. Torres. He was shot, Marie."

Marie dropped the phone. And then she screamed. She kept on screaming until Brendan walked in the door.

Chapter Fourteen: A Kiss from a Rose

Grief unrestrained is the sound of an anguished voice bawling from the mountaintops, or the rooftops, released wildly and abandoned into the vastness, and falling into the valleys and backroads that painfully absorb and dilute its woeful sound. Although he or she may not realize it; it is the lucky one who gets to release misery so completely, because grief restrained is a cancer that inhabits from within and only has its own body in which to fiercely echo again and again.

Marie's children would later say that they had never seen their mother look like this or sound like this, alternating between wracking sobs and kicking feet, and intermittent screams, some of which formed words and others having no distinct form, just a discharge of air and wounded baying. It would be the last time she would be permitted to forsake reason so completely.

She spent the first moments trying to disprove the words her father laid upon her, turning on the news and hearing, *"Cop Shot,"* but not the name of the fallen officer, so maybe it was someone else. *It still could be someone else,* she whispered fervently and without care for the unknown heart that would shatter if it hers remained intact. She called the precinct but they would not confirm or deny, because Marie was not family, and icy fear chilled her being as this insight grasped her: she was not family. She was not anything, and no one would call her.

People around her began to offer comfort, coming dimly into focus and then retreating when Marie shook them off almost physically, violently shaking her head, and ranting, "You don't know, you don't know." Brendan was somewhere; she didn't know where because everything seemed on the periphery of the explosion in her head, blurry the way things look through heat. And then suddenly she remembered who did know, and she raced to the phone.

"Claire," she screamed into the receiver, "He's dead, Claire. I'm only 35 years old, and he's gone, and I have so much time left. He's dead, Claire."

As if she morphed through the phone wires, Claire was there, and Marie was in her car, and they drove for hours. Songs played on the radio, songs they knew but would never again sound the same, as Marie stared out the window and observed a world that no longer had Manny in it.

It was the same pain, lodged in her chest; exactly the same as the tumor that once lurked there, viciously squeezing aside any organ in its way. It hurt enough to scramble in a drawer with fingers begging for a knife to cut it out, this minute, at all costs, only this occupant was by far the crueler. The tumor was tangible but no knife would ever find the silent toxin that poisoned Marie now. She didn't sleep that night, or what was left of it, but only waited, and when it was light she turned to Brendan and told him she was driving to Queens.

"I'll go with you," he said.

"You don't have to," she said, hoping that this would be only a polite offer on his part, one in which he would be relieved to be excused, because she needed all the space around her to be vacant so she could fill it with her pain.

"C'mon, Marie, of course I'll go with you," he restated, adamant, and weariness overtook it because she knew that there was nothing inside her strong enough to argue with him.

"We have no babysitter," she said, but somehow, one was found. Marie would have no recollection of who took care of her children the day after Manny died, only that she left them to seek something that would not be found.

Brendan drove and Marie only stared, clutching herself as if stopping a wound from spilling blood. The only shift in her awareness came when she noted that they were passing through Brooklyn on the Belt, and she turned to see the water from the Narrows rise over the side of the road where the fishermen cast their lines and she and Manny used to sit. It was pouring, and windy, and later the local papers would show photos of floods in different areas, and cars half under water. But on page one today, of the Post, and the News, and maybe the Times, there was only Manny's face, staring back at her.

It was the classic cop picture, the one from his ID card, with his shirt buttoned to the top and his neck strangled by a tie, making his cheeks appear fuller than they really were; but his eyes, his eyes were true to memory. His hooded lids lazily contrasted with his deep and concentrated orbs below, and even swathed in black and grey newsprint, Marie felt his gaze, as always, to be for her alone. For a moment she felt aroused by the close-up of his face, recalling the last time they were together, but then her eyes traveled up to the boldface words above – COP SHOT – and with a jolt she understood that last time *was* the last time.

"Where are we going?" Brendan asked.

"To his house," she answered.

It did not seem like a wise place to go, but she knew what she was looking for: a friend. In the midst of blue appearances, she hoped to find a secret look that would acknowledge her and offer a place to relinquish her despair, and another thing that Manny had promised, months ago.

If anything happens to me, what would you want?

A letter. A letter that tells me how you feel.

Manny told her that there were things for her in his locker, and that it was where he kept everything that she had ever given him. In his locker lay their entire history in letters, cards and photos, and all the things that she would not allow to be in her house. Marie needed those things now.

There is a cop named Santiago. You remember him, you met him a few times. He knows our story. A cop will get to my locker before anyone, if something happens. Santiago will know what to do.

They drove on, past the 70 precinct, and the 63 and off the road a bit, the 84, and finally exiting at Woodhaven Boulevard in Queens and taking it past the gray and battered places of meaning leading to Manny's apartment. Marie found that she was terrified but she did not know of what; only that it was the only emotion that kept her heart beating above the deadly silence of pain that at last comprehends that screaming will not help.

Marie again studied the world through the pelting rain, seeing as she and Brendan exited the car people exiting a mini-mart with bags on each arm, balancing umbrellas and shielding impassive, weary faces. Like those before her whose lives have been shattered, she noted that the world keeps on going as if nothing has happened at all.

"They're not home," someone said, as Marie rang Manny's doorbell in the vestibule, "I think they went to a funeral home. I saw them all leave. Shame, what's happened," he continued, but Marie left the hallway as soon as she heard no one would be letting them in. She stood in the rain, trying to think. Should she sit in the car and wait? Sit in the vestibule and wait? And then she remembered Manny's older brother, who lived around the corner.

"Let's go," she said to Brendan, who surely must have disapproved of some of this but could not express it to Marie because she was not listening. She was a madwoman, riddled with repeated spasms of relentless agony, and she was searching for a cure.

The second vestibule had the same façade and the same name on the doorbell that doubled as a mailbox, only this time, a buzzing noise bid her entrance.

Apartments in Queens smell like the people who live there, like their sweat and their cooking and the products of their hygiene; individual cultures that come to mingle in a musky sickening scent in the hallways. Marie felt these odors encase her like mist as she traveled up the elevator and raced down the hall to the second door that said Torres.

"Dominic," Marie cried, and hoped that the man who answered truly was Dominic. She had only met him once. "I'm Manny's friend, and I…" and she was crying and he let her come in.

There were other visitors in the apartment, but they were not cops and they were not family members. They were reporters from the New York Times, there to interview

Dominic and paint a picture of the police officer the city had lost. Marie marveled at Dominic's composure; he seemed to almost enjoy the celebrity, and Marie remembered that he wasn't close to Manny, but still, they were *brothers*. Why wasn't he falling apart? She listened vaguely to the questions and answers tossed back and forth; standing still, like one who fears the slightest move will aggravate the already unbearable hurt.

And then she heard a question that only she could answer.

"Why," the journalist asked Dominic, "did your brother become a cop?"

Dominic floundered, saying, "Well, I guess he just wanted to help people, and..."

"No," Marie jumped in, "It wasn't that. It was you, Dominic. You hit him with a rock when he was little, 8 years old. He was bleeding and a police officer came and carried him home. The officer let Manny wear his hat."

The reporter turned his attention fully to her now.

"And you are?" he asked.

"Marie...Kavanagh...I'm just a friend," she said weakly, deflated at her own words, *just a friend, just a friend, just a friend.* She added, "A close friend."

"He told me that story. About his brother, and wearing that hat. He said he always thought it was a sign that he would a cop someday." She breathed in hard. "He loved that job. He loved the streets. He wasn't even sure he wanted to make captain because it would take him off the streets."

They turned back to Dominic, who was watching her, smiling. "Yeah," he said, "I remember that day. I remember it."

The next day, Marie's words would be headlines in the New York Times, and she would be quoted in the article that followed, and she would be grateful for that moment. It was the only validation that she would get.

Dominic walked with them around the block to the other apartment, having gotten a call that they had returned. Manny's home was filled with familiar faces, mostly milling about, struggling to be useful. In the center of the tumult sat Madeline, her pale chubby face ruddy and streaked with tears. Marie went to her first; hugged her, still believing that all her sins were unrevealed. Then she began to roam like everyone else, only she was far more focused. This was not her home, but it held her memories nonetheless, and she conjured up images in each of the five rooms. Manny in the kitchen, making her an omelet, in the bathroom the time he shaved her legs in the tub, in the living room, the dining room, Ariella's room, and of course, the bedroom.

It was in the bedroom she stopped, because she noticed the computer. Slowly she approached it, thinking herself unnoticed. She knew his password and thought that she could quickly sign on his AOL account to do...what? She didn't know, but suddenly she felt movement behind her, and heard Ariella's voice.

"My mom canceled his email account," she said, "She did last night...as soon as she heard."

Ariella. Marie had forgotten about her; this 9-year-old child who no longer had a father. Marie walked over to her, her thoughts still whirling – why would Madeline make canceling Manny's email account a priority? – and put her arms around her.

"Ariella, I am so sorry about your daddy," she said, and her body shook as she wept against the child's stoic frame.

Back in the living room, Madeline was still being soothed by a circle of policeman and Marie heard her ask, "Will I still be responsible for his credit card bills?" and seethed inside. What was wrong with her? She didn't have time to think long, however, because abruptly, she spotted Santiago, and bounded to his side.

"Santiago...Ricky? You remember me, right?" Marie begged, touching his arm.

Remember me, her mind screamed. *He told you he loved me. Remember that? He told you stories about me, and you knew when he was talking to me on the phone. Please remember.*

When the police officer turned to look at her, however, his gaze was cold and controlled, and he didn't say anything.

"Please," she pleaded, "I just want you to go to his locker, that's all. There are things in there that are mine, and…"

"The locker was shredded," Officer Santiago said officially.

"That can't be," Marie said, but he was moving away from her, "He told me that…"

"It was shredded," Santiago repeated. "It was done within an hour after he was killed, by the sergeant on duty. Now stop. You shouldn't be doing this."

Marie looked around again, at officers bringing Madeline drinks of water, and answering the phone for her, and she understood. Marie was the most important thing in Manny's life once, but that was his life. In death, he belonged to the NYPD, and he belonged to his wife.

****

The story in the paper told of a 17-time convicted felon who was once again out on probation. He was stalking a woman, when fortuitously a police car happened by, and the woman raced over to describe her plight. Manny told his driver to stay put; it seemed not to require much manpower. He walked straight up to the offender, an older man, putting on his usual smile and beginning his usual question, something like, "C'mon, man, what's going on?" but never getting past the first word. The man turned and fired into Manny's face, and he was down, and he was gone.

Manny and his slayer died the same night, moments apart. The latter did what every cop must have hoped he would do: he ran. Sparing all the theatrics of a trial; Jeremiah Richardson kept his gun in his hand and sealed his fate by trapping himself in a vestibule soon riddled with the bullets that took his life away. Justice served, only much too late.

It made Marie think a great deal about heaven and hell, and whether adulterers and murderers ended up in different rooms of the same place. When she first told her Christian friends why she could not lead Bible group that week, they clucked their tongues and widened their eyes and asked, "Was he saved?" To which Marie hardened her expression and stared them down, finally saying, "I don't know. And neither do you." After that there were only weak references to the prayers that would be said on her behalf, but Marie was done with rhetoric to God. It was too dangerous.

The Unitarian in Marie's life was far more practical. She didn't pray; she acted. Claire shopped, picking up food when Marie found herself walking aimlessly up grocery aisles, unable to remember what she needed. She hid bottles of aspirin and sharp knives, and she watched Marie closely. She listened. She also attempted to protect Marie from the reckless words that would indict her; after years of guarding her secret, Marie now paid no attention to what fell from her lips and who heard.

"What am I going to do now?" Marie wailed, "He was everything to me. Who will ever love me like that?" And as Claire nodded, she also closed the bedroom door to keep Brendan and the future intact.

Marie joined those milling about for another tortuous day in the apartment, and then for three days at the wake. Brendan insisted on coming with her; something she considered not kindness but manipulation. He would say that he wanted to prevent her from making a fool of herself, but he only kept her from finding someone who would acknowledge her. No one at all spoke to her, and her nightmare was complete. She thought, wryly, of the cruelty of fate: the precinct that killed Manny was the only one that Marie had never visited. She had never seen roll call. And she didn't know a soul from the 70.

Faces she recognized flitted past her, and sometimes she approached someone who quickly moved away. She saw a female police officer from the 84, one who "knew," and cornered her.

"I remember you," the officer sneered, "You're that woman that used to make him a wreck, driving to Jersey and back all the time."

Marie was too stunned to speak and fell away, but a few minutes later walked back to the woman's side.

"You should have seen him when I didn't let him drive to Jersey. He was much more of a wreck then."

Finally, Marie could only hold her breath, and approach the casket, where an officer slowly saluted every few minutes the entire day. She had been afraid to go up, not knowing what she would do – scream again? Sob uncontrollably? Touch him, attempt to climb in? – but found she couldn't just leave without looking at him, in full dress uniform, and gone.

She knelt down and experienced her only sustenance, because there was someone kneeling beside her, and a dark hand covered her own, and a voice whispered in her ear:

"My son, he love you. I know. And you love him." Marie turned, and looked into the tortured eyes of Manny's mother.

Mayor Giuliani came to the wake, of course, causing Madeline to look starstruck, and then he came to the funeral to confirm that Manny had indeed been a good cop, a devoted husband and father, and a Yankee fan. The priest would add that he was also a churchgoer, and Marie would later comment that these were the most lies that she had ever heard in a house of God since she was a child.

Only one other person approached her in those four days: Aileen O'Brien, the woman she once feared in their months apart. She was friendly, and offered condolences, and then chastisement.

"The guy was crazy for you, you know," she said in her Brooklyn accent, "Why the hell didn't you just marry him? I used to always tell him that, I said, if she loves you so much, what's she still doing married to someone else? And by the way, I also told him I think one of your kids looks just like him." She said it right there, in the middle of church.

And then they all went home, which is the only option people have after death's rituals. Go home and continue. Go home and endure. Go home to a life that will always, from this day forward, consist of "before" and "after." Purchases made and things accomplished and prints in photo albums will all be delegated to one of those two categories; whether they came into being when a loved one existed in life or only in memory. Everything that is will have that hue on it, golden or gray, the color speaking for itself.

Brendan took her to lunch before they returned home, and there in the diner, over a pasty sandwich and weak tea, he came out of the periphery of her misery and temporarily into focus.

She looked at him and said something he would find forever unforgivable.

"You have to love me more now, Brendan," she insisted, "If you love me at all, you have to love me more than that."

****

The year after is always the hardest. That's what the experts say. Professionals always want to formularize something as unacceptable as sorrow, so that all can pretend it has some definitive end. Marie read all about it in her psych class, the denial and the anger and some other things before one arrives at acceptance, but did this recipe work for those denied the right to rant and rage and cleanse their wounds with hysterical tears? Didn't she deserve a stronger sentence to atone for her sins?

Marie began her anger stage by writing. She wrote to the priest that gave last rites to Manny even though he was gone, and she wrote to the priest who allowed the hypocrisy at the funeral. She obtained a password protected computer diary and wrote pages and pages of her memories, beginning with the day she walked into Treachers to find Manny in the back. When the electronic journal was completed, she printed two copies, and deleted it from her computer. She mailed one to Manny's sister, Naomi. The other one, with a cover letter, went to the commanding officer at the 70 precinct.

Naomi granted Marie one lunch, for which Marie had to drive into Queens on a gray school day. After they ordered, Naomi quickly set things straight.

"Look," she said firmly, "My brother loved you. But you had your chance. We don't like divorce in our family, but we would have gotten over that."

Marie tried to interrupt, but Naomi was merciless.

"What I cannot get over is you playing both sides of the fence. Manny was always clear when he spoke to me. He wanted to marry you. He *would have* married you. You didn't want to leave your husband and that was your prerogative. Only you should have ended it with my brother, instead of dragging down Madeline and everyone else in this mess."

At this, Marie jumped in, enraged. "He was leaving her for good in January, did you know that?"

"So you say. So *he* said. But January never came for him, and Madeline is his widow now. You have to let it go."

"Naomi, please, will you get me something of his? I have nothing. Maybe one of his uniform shirts or his cologne or anything? Anything," Marie begged.

"I'll try," Naomi said, but of course she never did.

A week later, the phone rang and Marie picked it up wearily to a voice that said, "Hi, this is Sergeant Lester at the 70. My CO asked me to call you. We got your…er…document. When would you like to meet?"

He met her exactly where Manny used to, in the cutout under the Verrazano. She got in his car, and he brought her back to the precinct to see the wall that was dedicated to Lt. Torres. On the way, he described the last moments of his comrade's life.

"He stopped in for coffee," Sgt. Lester said, "but there wasn't any made. So he made some. I kind of wondered, if there had been coffee already made, would that have changed everything?"

"Anyway, after that he made a phone call right here, at the payphone. He was on for a bit."

"With me," Marie answered, "He called me." She had dressed carefully for this meeting, and spoke carefully. She wanted the sergeant to see why she was worth it.

"Then he grabbed the coffee, and went back out. It wasn't 10 minutes before the call came in, officer down."

So he was already dead when she began praying in church. Well, no matter. She would still never trust herself to pray again.

"Can I see where it happened?" she asked, and he took her. It was just an ordinary dim Brooklyn street, with nothing to signify that it was the last place Manny drew breath.

"Are there crime scene photos?" she asked, "Can I see them?"

"That would be against my professional advice," he said, and she shook her head violently. "Can I see them?"

He looked at her with his cop face, an expression she knew. "Listen," he said, "It's not a good idea. He was shot right in the eye," he explained, and Marie quickly clutched both sides of her body for stability. His eye. *Her* eyes.

"There's another thing," Sergeant Lester said, and she looked at his face.

"He kept your photo under his hat."

Marie met Sergeant Lester once a week for the rest of the year. In the beginning she met him hopefully, believing that somehow, some way, he would produce Manny for her. Her eyes scanned his person when she got in the car, as if Manny hid somewhere in his pockets, but there was not a trace. She also learned that he was the one that shredded the locker.

"How could you?" she bristled, "How could you just destroy a whole chapter of someone's life? I *needed* that stuff."

"Listen," he said, shushing her, "It's SOP, standard operating procedure. There were hundreds of papers in that locker. I never saw anything like it. Hundreds of photos, letters, napkins, papers. I don't have time to figure out what's what. I have to get rid of it. I never met his wife, I never met you, I didn't know who the photos were of. I just had to get rid of it. It wasn't until the wake that I knew."

Lester never once broke their appointment. He let her know what was happening with Madeleine and Ariella, and he kept her informed of memorial ceremonies and dedications and other events. Whenever Marie showed up at any of the ceremonies, however, it wasn't long before two officers approached her.

"We have to ask you to leave, m'am," they always said, and she readily acquiesced. But she always came to the next thing, whatever it was.

Come January and the new year, nearly three months after Manny's death, Marie made a decision. She had to fake it. She had forsaken interest in everything but her weekly visit to Brooklyn, and another weekly visit to Queens to put roses on the grave. She greeted everything else with dull and listless eyes, and obligatory action when it was required. Her friends noticed. Her children noticed. And Brendan noticed.

"You didn't send out Christmas cards this year," he accused, "One of my friends mentioned it. Said he always looks forward to your letter and the picture of the kids."

She prescribed a regimen for herself that consisted of whispering to herself each morning. Following nightmares full of broken bluebirds and bloody eyes, she woke and began her mantra: *"Remember what you did before, and do it again, the same way. Do what you always did. And no one will know."*

And just as if it was written on one of her holy lists, it was done. She dutifully registered for Spanish, a requirement for her undergrad, even though it pained her to take it and was the first time she received a grade of B. She learned who Pablo Neruda was and found a book of his poems, each written both in Spanish and English, and held her tears and shelved the book. And she frantically kept her trash can clean and scrubbed her shower curtain, because they represented the last two services Manny performed for her.

She rose and brought her children to school, and wrote again for the local paper and magazine, and even once attempted to attend Bible Group, but this would become the only thing in which she would make a permanent break. It happened when they discussed the story of Jesus in the temple with all the high priests, and to the holies' horror, allowed a "soiled" woman to come to his side.

"And so," the Bible group leader said, putting on a smile that surely was perfected by the happy ignorant, "the lesson here is that if *Jesus* can accept *these* people, then we should accept them, too, even the serious sinners, like homosexuals and adulterers. Jesus did not turn them away and we shouldn't, either."

At this, Marie stood, and started gathering her things to a room that watched her with curiosity, as if God or Satan had entered her being. Before reaching the door, with her jacket and bag and Bible all askew, Marie turned and spoke to the faces awaiting some prophesy:

"The lesson here is not to accept '*these*' people. It's that we *are* 'these' people. I know I am. And it's up to me to accept myself. Because there is no compassion in anything God has to say." With that, she left the room and all notions of religion.

She cooked and cleaned and wrote and buried herself in tasks, and made no mention of Manny at all; studiously ignoring any references to the NYPD in the news or some cop show, and brushing away comments made by the children. Because the children did comment. Manny had been part of their lives, and they talked about his absence, especially Daniel, who said over dinner one night that he missed Manny.

"Remember the night he took us for a ride over the Brooklyn Bridge, with the lights and sirens going, and then he let us shine that searchlight on NY?" he'd say, and the others, except for Grace, joined in.

Brendan interrupted harshly: "Did you know Manny wasn't *allowed* to do things like that, that he could have been in big trouble for that? He didn't care. He did whatever he wanted, and that's probably why he's dead now." All eyes turned to look at Brendan for this seemingly heartless statement, all except Marie who simply changed the subject.

Marie kept a record in the margins of her schoolbooks, of how long Manny was gone; in weeks, in days and in hours. Five months after his death, she told Brendan she needed "time away," and went to Puerto Rico, where her main intention was to see the only person who said kind words to her: Manny's mother. In her four days away, she swam in blue water and walked through the rain forest, ate fried plantains and listened to the "coquis," the little tree frogs whose whistling filled the night.

"Why didn't I come here with you, Manny?" Marie's thoughts dominated more than her speech. *"Why didn't I tell more lies, and see your homeland, and complete our list together?"* She was no longer ashamed of the lies she did tell; only the misplaced sense of honor that told her that some things would be crossing the line. Surely the line had been long crossed; and there was only one line. Once it was crossed, she might as well have run.

She returned once again ready to go on, to intensify her efforts to take care of her family, because she did feel guilty to have abandoned them so thoroughly. The contrast between her inner and outer self was stark; the latter being functional and efficient, while the former withdrew completely into pain. She was like a crisp, white hospital room that houses the mentally deranged.

Brendan, too, slipped into a type of schizophrenia; playing his part as husband and father, but slipping into a fearsome character that Dr. Jekyll might recognize. He began to bait her, taunt her, and insult her.

His derision no longer had power over Marie. She felt invisible. To be visible, you need someone to see you; to be tangible, you need someone to touch you. Walking the streets, sitting down in class, getting in and out of her car, she perceived herself as completely unnoticed. She had lost the weight that had irritated her in Manny's final days, and she was only 35 years old, but had no clue if her mechanic or the postman or anyone that crossed paths with her showed any approval. The person that really saw her was gone; and so she felt gone as well.

One day, she developed a roll of film that had been sitting in her camera for quite some time, and saw the day she had gone to the children's museum. The photos were time-stamped, and there in the corner, she saw the date, 10/18, and shuddered. Most were of Grace and the other little girls that came that day, but one had her in the background, taken carelessly when the camera had been set down. Marie studied her blurry face, and took in every aspect of her demeanor. Did she look happy? Didn't she always feel that, in spite of all the complications and self-reproach, that she had something no woman gets in a lifetime?

She jokingly told Manny once that if he was gone, she would just find herself another cop. Weren't they all the same, she asked, and Manny answered with his usual dose of humor and seriousness.

"Marie, there is one thing I do know. No one, I mean no cop, no man, will ever do for you what I do for you. I listen to these guys, I mean they complain if they meet a woman who lives in the next borough. Meanwhile I'm driving over two bridges to get an hour with you."

"Two toll bridges," she added with eyes wide, but she believed him.

After looking at the photo, she raced to her closet to find the clothes she had been wearing that day; gray pants and a white turtle neck and a V-neck sweater, and she stroked them as if they held some of the aura of her stolen perspective. She folded them neatly around a manila envelope of the only keepsakes she had of Manny – a few printed emails, things she herself had written, newspaper clippings – and tucked them in the back of her closet, and stealed herself once again for life right now.

It happened; the way everyone says it will but the wounded party says it won't. Marie's pain to her was as constant as the sound of the lawnmowers on a Saturday morning in summer, only noticeable when it experienced a brief reprieve. Just as a person looks up and says, "what was that?" when the last mower shuts off, Marie was startled by the tiniest ease to the ache in her body, having embraced and incorporated it as a given. But of course, the respites became more frequent, and the memories became blades with duller edges.

She was driving with her children one day when she accidentally ran a red light, causing the car in the oncoming lane to honk viciously. She immediately used it as a learning opportunity for the ones she cherished in the back seat.

"See that? There is no point to all that honking. It wasn't a warning. It was just to tell me that I'm a jerk. But what's the point in that? You think I meant to run that light? You think I meant to risk the lives of my children? Of course not." She went on to her captive audience.

"The thing is, there is no point in that honking because if I'm sorry for what I did, then I'm already sorry. And if I'm not sorry, then I'll never *be* sorry. No loud horn is going to change that."

She finished, and then saw her metaphor clearly. Was she sorry for this sin? Or would she never be sorry?

After all, everyone had gotten exactly what they wanted. She heard Madeline was living well on her survivor benefits, and the indisputable illusion of her husband's undying love. Manny got his dream of dying a hero, and Brendan got rid of Manny, while Marie had gotten the solution she begged for from God, who didn't work in mysterious ways after all.

Summer passed; and the year anniversary with all its' commemorations that Marie visited until the inevitable approach of two, never one, officers asking her to leave. Her meetings with Sergeant Lester became far and few between, and she couldn't make it to the grave quite as often with her school schedule.

Some nights, when the little ones fell asleep, she wrote, resurrecting her own private agony, and going outside to beg the skies to give him back to her. The only other breaks from the numbness were the jolts of pain, brought on by seemingly innocuous things, like the badges of her daughter's girl scout sash. Manny had sewn them on for her, because he was used to sewing patches on uniforms.

Now, a year later, she saw a chance to think of him freely; to unleash the whole lot of stifled reflection from her subconscious back to cognizance, and sort it all through once again, and try to make peace with it instead of stuffing it fearfully aside in the interest of self-preservation. Indeed, a year after Manny's death, Marie felt she had almost heroic. Like him, she had taken a bullet, but she remained standing and nobly carried the pain.

And then Brendan delivered a blow of his own.

"I spoke to a counselor today," he said, facing the assortment of coins and tattered pocket objects that aligned his dresser. "She recommended that we separate."

She was on her feet. "We can't," she said. "We won't. We will not do that to our children."

"The counselor said you needed time to grieve, and…"

"Time to grieve? I did grieve. I'm done grieving. I've had a year, I…I'm fine," she almost shouted, but was ever conscious of the children.

"He was your *lover*, Marie. Your closest friend, and…what did you say? 'The only man you ever believed loved you.' You can't possibly be over that."

"That's *my* business, not yours. It doesn't say anywhere that he was my lover, so don't add what wasn't there. And it's my job to decide how to grieve. I've spent all this time doing what I had to do. I have the goddamned Christmas cards all written out and ready to go this year, dammit. Don't you *dare* say I need more time to grieve."

He said nothing so she stood close to him and repeated her ruling: "We will not separate, Brendan. We will work on this. We have to. It's too late to separate. It's too late because…" she stopped, and finished the sentence as a thought, *"because I didn't leave when I should have. I didn't go to Manny when he begged me to, and I cannot bear to give him what he wanted when it's too late."*

"…because we made four children together, and our lives are no longer the ones that matter," Marie said, and that answer was the truth as well. Divorce was not something that could happen to her children.

She redoubled her efforts with Brendan, and yet another year went by, a year of fulfilled traditions and weeks again at the shore, regular lovemaking that Marie secretly named "calendaring," because she made sure it happened every three days without fail.

"Mommy, when you look at daddy, do you ever think, wow, I really love him?"

Kristin asked the question while they were sitting in the car, waiting to drive

Brendan home from the train station on any icy evening. He had just emerged from the station with all the other suited clones and their briefcases, but he was still a sight with his dark Irish looks. Marie noted the female kinship that she shared at that moment with her daughter: they both knew they had a claim to the attractive man approaching their car.

"Well, yes, of course," Marie answered, but the sadness that overwhelmed her was immediate, "Of course I think that."

"You should tell him that," Kristin offered up the wisdom of her ten years, and the car door opened and Brendan filled the car with his scent and the chill of his commute and the love reserved only for his children.

But what if I can't?, Marie thought.

****

And so, the next Sunday morning, Marie woke Brendan early to go out to breakfast.

"CCD was canceled, Brendan," she whispered, "So we don't have to wake the kids. Let's sneak out for a bit."

He rose to comply and the morning was brisk and sunny. They went to a little bagel place that had a wood floor and red and white plastic tablecloths, and old lace curtains. Marie took all this in as they chose a table near the window, where the light created patterns and brought to life the tawdry look of the place.

Brendan got up to order and Marie felt the growing warmth of morning, and realized that she felt good. She had nothing to do but think, because it bothered Brendan when she brought other diversions out with her and so she went sans the pens and notebooks that accompanied her everywhere. Still she had a sense of wellness, and if she believed in God's mercy in that moment, she would have surely thought he was giving her a sign that the worst was over.

She watched Brendan carrying the tray towards her, and took a breath. It was the innocent moment that came before the moment that changed everything; a snapshot of how things looked before they began a drastic change.

He sat down, and then stood up again quickly; he had forgotten the sugar or a napkin or something, and Marie grew impatient, waiting to immerse in what she considered a promising day; an arrival at a peaceful shoreline after days on tumultuous waters.

Brendan sat down again and began speaking as if they were already in mid-conversation.

"So," he said, sipping his coffee fastidiously, "Let me ask you something." He placed the coffee down and folded his hands.

"What do you ever do for me?"

Marie looked at her husband and felt the crack inside her; as if suddenly she was struck by lightening that split her down the middle. She looked around and the sun was still foolishly shining across through the imitation crystal vase and in and out of the red and white checks. But everything had changed.

"What do I do for you?" she asked him.

"Yes, for me. Only for me. Not for us. For me." He leaned forward.

"Okay, Brendan. For starters I am sitting in a bagel shop on a Sunday morning without a pen or paper even though I like having pen and paper near me, but well, you don't. I stop everything when you get home from work to stand and greet you because you told me that you want that, so I do it, even when I was adding numbers for a girl scout cookie order and had to start all over, I stopped to greet you."

"I wake up each morning but I don't take a shower because you like the bathroom free, and then I drive you to the train station, and if you miss your train or bus, I drive you to the next stop to try to beat it. I do this even in summer time when I could be sleeping late. Let's see, I plan weekend getaways even though I'm not really good about leaving the kids with anyone, and nights out as well, because you told me that we should have time for ourselves. No matter how tired I am, I make sure we have sex."

"I sit with you and have tea when my mind is spinning with a hundred different things, and I can barely sit still, and I make Scottish recipes and Irish recipes just to please you. Oh yeah, and I raise my children as Catholics even though you do nothing in church but fall asleep and I think it's all complete bullshit."

There was a pause as she thought of more to say, because she knew that there *was* more. All that had come from the top of her head, as if she had yearned to say it for weeks. In the gap, however, Brendan found his voice, and said resolutely:

"Well, if you don't want to have tea with me anymore, don't." And Marie knew at last that there was no magic cure and no amount of effort was going to save them.

It's okay, Brendan," she replied quietly, "I only brought you here this morning to tell you that it's okay for you to go."

"One Hand Waving Free"   Hofmann

Epilogue: Altocumulus Stratiformis

She was at the shore this year with only herself and the children. Brendan always said that life was a gift; that we should treasure every moment, but Marie never agreed. She said life was only something given so there was something, always, to take. She remembered how her sister-in-law used to bring hand-me-down clothes from her daughter for Kristin to wear; bagloads of colorful Osh Kosh overalls and Laura Ashley dresses that delighted Marie until Monica said, "Now take care of it all, because I'd like it back when you are done." Then Marie had to stress when Kristin wore the clothes and watch for every stain or torn knee or missing button, and it just wasn't worth it so she never bothered to take the clothes out of the bag. Life was like that. It was only a loan, and you had to watch it over obsessively, every day, and wait for the day when someone came to collect the part you loved the most.

It wasn't that she thought she had a more troublesome life than anyone else; it was that even the best life comes with it an abundance of things to lose, and after one thing goes, all that's left to do is worry about the rest. Maybe that's why the Tambourine Man kept one hand empty; not to try to grab at more appealing things, but only to stave off and defend the precious things he clasped in his other fist.

Still, Marie came home one day the week before and there was Grace, sitting on Brendan's side of their bed, doing her homework with the dog next to her and a lollipop in her mouth, and Marie instantly could see all the transgressions Brendan would see as he completely missed the charm of the scene. For all his preaching, it was Brendan who missed the most, and Marie who recognized the moments that were true gifts.

The sunset was mediocre tonight, lacking the cloud formation that captured and held the fading rays. *Altocumulus stratiformis*, that's what they were called, but no matter. She had tomorrow again to search the skies, and the day after that, and sooner or later, she would capture it, and she would not die afterwards. She would go on to capture it another day as well.

*****